D1138023

Daniel Pascoe was born and brought up in London, but has worked in the north-east of England these past twenty-seven years. He has never been in the Army and would never take up a rifle to kill anybody; he's a pacifist and a doctor: he looks after people, tries to make them better. He lives on Teesside with his wife, teenage daughters and cats, who all claim to be pacifists as well. This is his first novel.

EAST SUSSEX COUNTY COUNCIL
WITHDRAWN

0 1 JUL 2022

04447866

THE LONDON SNIPER
Daniel Pascoe

*A fictional tale of alternative history set in London
during the year of its Olympic Games, 2012*

Book Guild Publishing
Sussex, England

First published in Great Britain in 2015 by
The Book Guild Ltd
The Werks
45 Church Road
Hove, BN3 2BE

Copyright © Daniel Pascoe 2015

The right of Daniel Pascoe to be identified as the author of
this work has been asserted by him in accordance with the
Copyright, Designs and Patents Act 1988.

All rights reserved. No part of this publication may be reproduced, transmitted,
or stored in a retrieval system, in any form or by any means, without permission in
writing from the publisher, nor be otherwise circulated in any form of binding or
cover other than that in which it is published and without a similar condition being
imposed on the subsequent purchaser.

Typesetting in Caslon

Printed and bound in Great Britain by
CPI Group (UK) Ltd, Croydon, CR0 4YY

A catalogue record for this book is available from
The British Library.

ISBN 978 1 910298 94 7

Thanks to Colonel DB for his help with army matters.
To Sandra for her gentle guidance.
And to Anna for her patience.

Contents

Prologue

Seldom do teenagers know what they want to do for the rest of their lives. And when they do make up their minds, they often rue the day by the time they reach thirty. For Jarvis Collingwood it was easy. He had no trouble fixing his ambitions on what his father had done and, with a devoted mother to support him all the way, there were never any moments of uncertainty. If Jarvis had a problem, his mother turned it into a temporary nuisance and they overcame it together. If Jarvis was undecided, his mother would encourage him to make the decision that *she* wanted and they would stick with it. Gwendolyn had a knack of always finding the right solution that suited them both.

There was no question of clocking a regular nine-to-five job, of being a wage slave. That would not have been good enough. At sixteen, Jarvis knew he did not want to stay at school any longer and he did not want to end up stacking supermarket shelves or working on a building site. He wanted to be a soldier.

His father had been in the Household Cavalry and had seen action in the South Atlantic. His two older brothers had followed in his footsteps and had fought in Iraq and Afghanistan. With Jarvis, Gwendolyn had visions of further family glory, proud moments on parade, impressive reports of bravery in service to his country, Mentions in Despatches. She wanted to see her handsome boy in the distinctive dress uniform of the Horse Guards, in mounted line with helmet and breastplate glimmering in June sunshine, the red plume shimmering in the breeze at Her Majesty's Birthday Parade.

And although such dreams were never quite realised in that fashion, Jarvis did join the redoubtable Parachute Regiment at 18, in time to serve in Iraq. He thrived on the arduous routine and became an expert rifleman, admired by fellow soldiers. His nine years as a trooper made him physically strong and emotionally detached. He returned home at twenty-seven with a war story to indeed make his mother proud.

Military life with its neat order and clear lines of authority had suited Jarvis. He knew where he was and what was expected of him. Returning to civilian life had not been easy. There was enough material stored in his head to keep him awake at night. Like all tough Paras before him, he never readily talked about his experiences. Physically unscathed, his memory was sprinkled with unpleasant images that he shared with no one.

A succession of unsatisfactory jobs and an increasingly unrewarding marriage had left him feeling exposed and restless. The offer of a specialist job requiring some of his old skills tempted him to pick up a rifle again, a decision that, on turning thirty, with the plans for his future life in some disarray, he came to regret.

PART ONE
The Shooting

1

Mid-January, early evening, and every time the black doors of the Samuel Pepys swung open, as people came and went, noise, warm light and the smell of beer gushed out for a few attractive moments over the dimly lit cobbles of Stew Lane. The sky was darkening rapidly and the temperature was dropping. A light fall of snow that afternoon had turned the streets wet and slippery. Gloomy buildings encroached on either side of the narrow way down towards the River Thames, visible in the gap as streaks of moving silver. A stray dog sniffed among discarded rubbish along the pavement and dislodged a plastic bottle that rattled into the gutter.

Leaning in wait against old brickwork opposite the entrance, with a newspaper tucked under his arm, was the slight figure of Jimmy Bullock, trying to keep the cold from penetrating through his cheap clothes by hugging himself with his elbows and stamping his feet together. With a grey mackintosh belted tight and grubby cap pulled down hard over his birdlike head, he was trying not to be noticed. A shifty, rough-looking bloke in his fifties, with pockmarked face and filthy laugh, he wore dull clothes and dull expressions and kept himself to himself. He did jobs for other people, a bit of this and a bit of that, ever playing the optimist against all the odds. Destined to be one of life's countless also-rans, he would limp towards an unremarkable finale in an unknown side street leaving nothing for nobody – although he did have Rhoda, a Welsh wench with broad bosom and heart to match, at whose place in the Mile End Road he was known frequently to spend the night.

Jimmy sucked nervously on a pathetically thin roll-up cupped in his hand, inhaling deeply. When he spied Jarvis Collingwood emerging with his few companions, all male, in overcoats and winter boots, laughing, shaking hands and exchanging farewells, he discarded the butt and pushed himself off his wall to join the group, all of whom he knew vaguely, ex-Army lads of a younger generation than his. They were all moving towards Upper Thames Street, their heated breath condensing in the chill air like so many puffs of smoke. Nobody acknowledged him as he ambled up alongside without any fuss.

Jarvis Collingwood was easy to pick out in the crowd, taller and leaner than the others. Wearing a heavy leather coat with the collar turned up and muddied Timberland boots, he had his shoulders hunched against the bitter wind and his fists stuffed deep into the outer pockets.

He felt Jimmy's tug on his arm. 'Glad I caught yer, Jarvis, right.' There was a slight Irish lilt in the accent and alcohol on the breath. 'Got a message from Sid Price. Let's take a cab, you and me, right?'

Jimmy was short and had to tilt his head far backwards to catch the indifferent frown on Jarvis's good-looking face. He twisted one side of his mouth into what he would call a smile, displayed to the younger man, remembering so well the cropped blond hair, the pouting mouth, and those steely blue eyes that gave nothing away.

Everyone was dispersing in different directions, conferring best wishes on the birthday boy, leaving Jimmy and Jarvis standing on the street corner. 'So it's yer birthday, Jarvis, right? I forgot, congratulations. What are we now, must be 28 if a day, right?' And Jimmy cackled. Old enough to be Jarvis's father, he would never have admitted to envying another man's youth, convinced there was a shit load of juice still left in this old dog. 'I heard you was drinking at yer favourite watering hole. Just wanted to catch up, personal like. I recognise those lads, from the old days, old Army mates o' yours, right?'

'Yeah, guys I mucked out with, Iraq and the rest, you know.'

Jarvis had a rumbling voice, croaking a bit in the chill air. The usual city traffic was bumper to bumper, cars, buses and assorted vans squelching past on the wet road, their headlamps catching swirling flakes of snow. Taxis were aplenty.

In the darkness of a black cab as it jerked its way through the queues, Jimmy confirmed that Sidney Price had a special job, could be worth a bit. Wanted him to meet some friends to discuss details, tomorrow morning if possible, early at the club. 'Remember Sidney's Hut, a while since you showed round there, right?'

Close by Liverpool Street Station, Jimmy called to the driver to drop him off. 'Really good to see yer, Jarvis.' That Jimmy smile showed itself again as he reached across to the door and hopped out with unexpected agility. 'See yer, mate, tomorrow at eight, don't be late, ha, right'. He still had his cap on his head, his optimistic cackling disguised in the dark shadows. He left the day's paper across Jarvis's lap.

'Yeah right, thanks. And you, Jimmy,' Jarvis muttered, but Jimmy was gone, the cab door slammed shut, leaving an icy blast inside. 'I'll pay for the cab, shall I, Jimmy?' He caught the amused face of the cab driver in the rear-view mirror. *And actually, it's thirty.*

As the cab moved off again, Jarvis sank back wondering what all that was about. *If Sidney wanted to talk to me, he could have called, couldn't he?* Jimmy Bullock was a humble crook, a little man who did what he was told, but Jarvis knew he had been a friend of his father's many years ago, and so out of respect he tolerated him and gave up some of his time for him. Sidney Price, another of his father's old work friends, was a bigger fish, running a pawnbroking business and second-hand car sales and God knows what else down the Commercial Road, and did it pretty well by all accounts. And he had the boxing club, where boys could find something that took them off the streets. It gave Sidney, an ex-pro himself, access to the local gossip and he always seemed to know what was going down around his patch. Jarvis had trained there himself many times in years gone by. Sidney kept a tight ship, loyalty being a crucial element to his success. And Jimmy Bullock was loyalty personified. Jarvis knew that if Sidney had something for him he had better show. He paid well for services too, so maybe there would be a nice drink in it for him.

The paper was folded at the front page. Jarvis had to lift it up and angle it towards the passing street lamps. The big headline 'EX-PM RETURNS TO CHILCOT INQUIRY' shouted out above a close-up of a strained Gerry Morley, looking earnest with the usual hint of a smirk. 'Anger as Gerry Morley admits regrets over Iraq' read the subhead. Jarvis was just able to pick out the first paragraph in the semi-darkness: 'Damaged but undaunted, the ex-PM returned to the Chilcot Inquiry today at the Queen Elizabeth Conference Centre, Westminster, to face another grilling over Iraq. Earlier it was reported that in several bomb attacks in and around Baghdad today upward of 130 mostly civilians died.'

The close-up of Britain's former Prime Minister, taken at the inquiry earlier that day, stared up at him. The thinning hair at the front, the furrows on the tanned face, the chin dimpling all looked familiar. *Gerald Morley is not going to admit his mistakes,* Jarvis mused. *He is never going to apologise, not to the people of this country, not to the families of all the dead or injured soldiers, not to the people of Iraq.* He stuffed the paper under his arm and called the driver to pull over. Woollen beanie in place, he paid the man and walked the short distance from Shoreditch Park, over the canal, to Baring Street, which helped a little to freshen up his thoughts and clear away the effects of the beer from his head.

Wishing for a quiet evening ahead, but expecting confrontation from Pamela, he noticeably wilted as he approached his front door. He frequently walked the London streets, jogged the towpaths and worked out in a local gym. Keeping himself in good shape was a major motivator, although a time-consuming business. But after a hard week, all he wanted to do was crash out on the sofa with the day's papers and the remote control.

Jarvis missed the army life, he would readily admit; he missed the danger, the tough-guy routine, the shooting. He liked to be on the move. He had been thinking about going overseas, perhaps with the Foreign Legion, or doing mercenary work or private security duty in some dangerous place or other, like Pristina or Kabul, or Baghdad even. He had been tempted to join in the action in Libya. He would have made good money and life would have been a lot more interesting than living in boring old East End London, with boring old Pamela.

Somehow Pamela and Jarvis, with an outward appearance of normality, had turned their marriage into a convenient habit of coexistence, easier to leave in place than painfully disassemble. They shared a sense of mutual mistrust, neither knowing nor caring too much about what the other did all day long, or who they mixed with. They did not have the same friends and were seldom seen out together. After several years of growing indifference, they survived largely by deception.

He let himself quietly into the narrow hallway. Braced for a high-pitched voice calling from inside the house, he pocketed his keys, hung up his coat and kicked off his boots. Pamela was prone to spring unexpected guests on him out of the blue: *Tony and Linda are coming, I told you about them last week, they're really nice and we're working together on a project and it's really important for my work, so it would be really nice if you could be nice to them, really.* As expected, Pamela was clattering about in the kitchen, saucepans steaming, mixers buzzing and timers ringing, the dishwasher churning in unison, while a radio played pop music.

When it came, the sound still jarred his nerves. 'Did you

remember the bread and milk, Jarvis?' Oh God, he had forgotten her Italian focaccia or ciabatta or whatever the frigging stuff was. 'You know we've got Barbara and Evelyn coming round, really as a birthday treat. They'll be here soon.'

Jarvis glimpsed his bustling wife through the half-open kitchen door, all tarted up, with smells of cooking simmering around her. *Oh, sorry, not Linda and Tony, my mistake. Why do you always bring back such boring posh people you never mentioned?*

Prepared, Jarvis stood his ground in his socks at the bottom of the stairs. Pamela stood framed in the doorway, an apron about her waist. Neat and smart, with broad shoulders and a goodly bosom, she expected to get her way. Dressed confidently in a figure-hugging low-cut dress, flame coloured, she was brandishing a wooden spoon, nails flashing red. Her shimmering hair, cut retro-fifties style and dyed copper, was what made her so magnetic, she often joked, in ignorance of basic physics. With a velvety golden eye shadow over a fake tan, she had a seductive sun-kissed glow, in contrast to every other woman's pale complexion during a typical English winter. She had been chopping onions and her thick brows were squeezing the tears from her eyes, like wringing out sodden clothes, and irritated, she rubbed them with the back of her spare hand, conscious of her make-up.

'You need to hurry, Jarvis, and make yourself respectable before they get here.' A smile of sardonic pleasure at her husband's obvious discomfort passed over the glossed lips that she twisted imperceptibly, while remaining quite serious.

'And how is this *my* birthday treat, please?' Jarvis sounded irritated and retreated into the front room. His few birthday cards were still on the coffee table, some torn-open envelopes, a few things piled up around them: a chunky-knit sweater, his present from Pamela, a collection of trashy paperbacks from Jonathan, an O'Neill striped beanie in Dresden blue from a mate, some aftershave and a tie from his mother. He pretended to sulk on the sofa, and a few minutes later dropped onto the floor face down, forcing twenty press-ups out of his tired body, before darting upstairs for a shower.

Well after midnight, once her guests had gone and most of the tidying up was done, Pamela laboured up the stairs. Jarvis lay prone, heavily asleep, one foot protruding from his side of the double bed. She tiptoed clumsily from the chilly bedroom to the bathroom, her clothes tossed onto a chair for the morning. After dabbing a warm flannel over herself to cleanse away the odour of sweat and cigarettes, she felt revived. Out of habit, she swallowed her little pill. Teeth brushed, face rinsed and moisturised, she leant over the basin towards the mirror, as was another habit these days, to tease at the flesh around her eyes and neck. She searched with trepidation for early signs of bagging or the faintest wrinkling as she worked in more retinol cream. She ran a brush through her hair and sprayed herself with whatever *eau de toilette* came to hand. In black silk pyjamas, she slipped into her side of the bed.

But she did not sleep, not for a while. Her little feet were cold, the sheets icy on her side. She lay still in the darkness, imagining the chunky symmetry of her husband's face, conscious of his bulk and steady breathing close by. She felt an urge to warm her feet on his side, but dared not risk his waking.

One night this week, she had had the courage to go to Antonio's place after work. She easily recalled her post-coital glow, embraced by need and love in the warmth of his body that he draped against hers. But then her imagination conjured up some other beauty that he would have taken to his bed this night and she rolled away from Jarvis onto her side feeling cold and guilty for wanting another man's body; ignored and rejected.

There was no denying her pride in Jarvis's handsome appearance, smooth and lean as he was. His attraction was indisputable and she called him her Dolce & Gabbana man. What success could he have modelling his body, she often wondered? The ladies' magazines would love him! He would make a small fortune, she had always said so. She recalled the scraps she had with her school friends as a seventeen-year-old over Jarvis's athletic prowess, so noticeable even then, his muscles rounded, his bottom firm, his jaw chiselled, which made them all so jealous. And for a fleeting moment, a nostalgic wave drifted through her mind and a sense of unexpected affection passed through her, tempting a hand to touch his shoulder and rouse him for some much-needed intimacy. With remorse, she thought if only they could both make more of an effort to work together, to find something between them that might be rekindled, perhaps some love even, for Christ sakes. After he came back from Iraq a few years ago, he had talked about having children, but she had cruelly squashed that idea. But that was then. Maybe sometime soon she might want to reconsider; after all, she was in her thirties and time was not really on her side, as her wretched mother kept reminding her. Maybe having children would make the difference.

Maybe she would feel not so left out and unwanted. When was the last time Jarvis had bothered to find out what she was doing or thinking? Had he complimented her recently on a job well done, or said how good she looked? Although she would readily admit that Jarvis seldom featured on her own priority list, what with the office so busy and her desperate for more promotion. She would never trust him with details of her earnings or the savings she was tucking away at the moment, or much else for that matter. She had tried showing off once, to draw attention to her growing importance at work, by casually mentioning some well-known personality she had had a business lunch with at Wheeler's or wherever, but Jarvis was distinctly unimpressed and mocked her for her superficiality.

More jumbled images of her daily life, the bustle, the pressures, the relationships and the thrills, combined with avaricious thoughts of extra pay and bonus money, drifted through her mind. She should arrange a shopping trip with a girlfriend, she really deserved that; plan her next holiday in the sun this Spring, Ibiza perhaps. For an average dim-witted comprehensive school girl from south London she had done well; she should be proud. She would certainly not want Jarvis to know about her colourful extramarital trajectory. She played the faithful card vigorously whenever she could, indignant at any suggestion she was anything but the most dutiful ex-army wife. But the shiny face of Antonio loomed in her mind, his jaw smooth, his mouth soft. She felt his cool hand firmly in the small of her back, lacy artists' fingers spread out over her bare skin. In black polo-neck and ponytail, his dancing full of suggestive movement, he was whispering in his breezy Italian into her ear that they should slip away to his apartment, where they could luxuriate on his white Afghan rug in front of a fire, with champagne on ice.

Children, of course they would make a difference – her life would be condemned to the mundane; she would grey and wrinkle before her time and become bitter, really. Pamela ran a hand caressingly down her own body, over silky hip and thigh, as she drifted into a dream of endless carefree copulation in some forever sunny paradise with her secret Lothario.

Jarvis woke early the next morning to the bleeping of his mobile alarm. He was up, dressed, drinking tea and eating toast before Pamela noticed vaguely that his space in the bed was empty. She looked through bleary eyes across at the clock: not yet half six on a Saturday morning – whatever was Jarvis thinking? She rolled away with a groan, her head feeling muzzy, and dozed off for another couple of hours. She remembered she was meeting her sister later in the afternoon.

It was grey and chilly outside, a cloying dampness in the air. Moving with long strides, Jarvis emerged from Whitechapel Station with a spring in his step. Here the street trade was getting under way. Foods and spices, every conceivable household product, clothes, shoes and silks, books, toys and games were being laid out on boxes, on tables, on carpets on the pavement, with overhead covers of plastic sheets, rugs or umbrellas; and the languages were from the East and Asia, mostly Turkish and Bengali. Jarvis dodged through the thin crowd of dark bearded well-fed men, young thin Asians with cockney accents, calm women in black hijabs, nipping in between the stalls, with their wafts of exotic smells and music.

In leather coat and jeans and unshaven, Jarvis chewed a piece of gum. White earphone cables led down into his coat, pop music loud in his ears. Confident, in control, he crossed over the main road to Fieldgate Street and spotted the shabby-looking front of Sid's Hut in the gloom, halfway down on the left side. He remembered the old and peeling paintwork, the windows filthy with years of grime. The front doors onto the street were open and he stepped into the unlit lobby, where old Christophe the Greek recognised him instantly, greeting him with a big man hug. Inside, the atmosphere was serious and professional. Overhanging spotlights high above strained to provide much illumination through the murkiness. The air was stale and dusty. Around the open spaces, young black and Asian men, half stripped or in hooded tops, were warming up with floor routines, skipping or shadow boxing, preparing for the morning's workouts – kids and would-be athletes in earnest conversation with their trainers. There was no sign of Jimmy.

Jarvis picked his way around the edge of the main hall and sprang up an uncarpeted staircase in the far corner, facing the open doors of Sidney's office ahead of him at the top. Behind the big desk in the middle of a panelled room decorated with framed photographs of past sporting heroes, boxing champions and winning horses was Sidney Price himself. Short and rotund, his head was shrouded in smoke from a cheroot, which he gripped in chubby fingers, with the bleak morning light slanting across his face from above. He squinted to see who was standing in his doorway, blowing away the irritating smoke. Bernard, a big shaven-headed man in an ill-fitting black suit and oversized Doc Martens, was minding the room, his impassive gaze fixed straight ahead, ready to leap to his boss's protection. Nobody paid him any attention.

'Jarvis, my boy!' Sidney boomed from the shadows, standing awkwardly and leaning over the desk with an arm outstretched. He was bedecked in a trim grey three-piece suit with a bright yellow buttonhole. Jarvis received a flabby handshake, feeling all the rings on his fingers. He could smell the aftershave. 'Got a blasted wedding later, Joe's boy marrying some bint from Chepstow. Come and sit down. Tea, can we get yer?' Sitting, he reverted to the asthmatic breathing of before, still puffing on his smelly cheroot. Everything that Sidney was made of seemed to wobble uncontrollably.

Sidney Price was clean-shaven, with a large face and flattened grey hair much receded to reveal a sloping forehead covered with bumps and blips like a shoreline dotted with flotsam when the tide was out. At sixty-six, he would have described himself as a man in his prime, fit and healthy, powerful and well-off. Which was mostly true, putting aside his persistent breathlessness on climbing a few stairs, and the fact that his sphere of influence was limited to a small patch of urban London along the south of the Whitechapel Road and 'feeling well-off' was a relative term. He had all he ever wanted in life, more or less, and had achieved it with dignity and respect, although he would not admit that to anybody but Mavis, in moments of pillow talk. He was not planning any more adventures, take-overs or expansions into new businesses, preferring instead to milk the ones he had. He had his Rollo, his Rolex, his indoor pool. He had given employment over the years to all his children and many dozen other people, 'doin''is bit for the local econmy, eh Jarvis?' At home, Mavis did not want for anything either and would invariably have a big dinner and a hug waiting for him every night. He had had six children with Mavis, all healthy and large, although none quite as large as Sidney himself.

The sounds of human effort, grunting and panting, the pounding of leather, rubber soles squealing on lino drifted up the open stairs. With a nod from Sidney, Bernard closed the door and shut them off. Sitting back in the shadows was one of the daughters, a lump of a girl in black, with heavy mascara, painted lips and a bouffant. She barely looked up at Jarvis, grunted something in response to his greeting, and returned to chewing gum and filing her nails. Her skirt was too tight and too short and she was showing off newly minted tattoos over her shoulders and upper arms. She looked about sixteen. As far as his offspring were concerned, Sidney would tolerate anything.

Jarvis sat in a large armchair, keeping his coat on, comfortably fiddling with the discreet gold ring pierced through his left earlobe. Sidney sank back into his leather chair. 'Now then, we should do some catch-up. Off you go, Sandra love, leave Jarvis and me to talk grown-ups. We'll have some nosh in a little while, eh?' And he raised a flabby hand in dismissal. Sandra clomped on her five-inch platforms out the door, her thighs rasping as she passed. 'Thinks she's Amy bleedin' Winehouse, can't sing for toffee.' Sidney's face did some more wobbling, his jowls juddering as he set his jaw in a firm expression meant to indicate he wanted to get down to business.

Every tentative step of Sandra's clumping down the wooden stairs could be clearly heard as they settled around the rosewood desk. 'So what you been up to, Jarvis lad?' continued Sidney.

'I'm working with a forestry crew, Sid – about to start on a new site down Gravesend way. A lot of trees to cut down, and then clean up and cart away.' Jarvis generally said little, but he continued, as Sidney seemed to be interested, leaving a silent gap to be filled. 'It's a private estate, Lord Somebody or other. There's ten/eleven of us, we'll be clearing a massive area, felling, logging and then later there will be some planting.'

'Money in that, is there?' Sidney was fiddling with a pen and for a moment Jarvis thought he was about to take notes.

'It's hard work. We sleep down there quite often in caravans during the week, 'cos of the distance, but it keeps us fit.'

'You *look* fit, Jarvis, I like that,' Sidney observed with a nod and a wobble. 'And so they pay you good, do they?'

'Yeah, it's all right,' Jarvis replied half-smiling, reflecting on the extra cash for overtime he had been accumulating recently with no spare time to spend any of it. 'I also do odd security jobs for my brother, here and there, driving, protection stuff, deliveries, that kind of thing.'

'Yes, how is Jonathan these days? Doing well, I hear? Hard working, dedicated.'

'Yeah, that's Jonathan. He's very organised.' Sidney offered Jarvis a cheroot, which he declined, as another girl, this time a slim slip and obviously no relation, brought in two steaming mugs of tea.

'Thanks, Doreen. So how's your mother? It's a while since I've seen her,' oozed Sidney when the girl had shut the door. 'Dear Gwendolyn.'

'Oh, she's all right, not seen her for a while myself, actually, spent Christmas in Madeira.' *Where is this conversation going? Sidney must want something.* 'Not me, my mother.'

'Thing is, Jarvis, we could go on chattin' all mornin', which, yer know, would be luvvly but time's pressin' on; we need to get to the point, eh?' Sidney coughed on his smoke, blowing little clouds up into the ceiling. A length of fragile ash at the end of his cheroot dropped silently into a grey powdery pile on his blotter. 'Some people I know and some friends of mine are lookin' for a man to do a job for 'em.' The big man crumpled his face into a look of gravity, his voice going into a croaky whisper, and he was leaning as much as his large belly would allow into the desk to get nearer to Jarvis. The bald minder stood motionless only a couple of paces away, legs slightly apart, large hands held loosely in front of his crotch like a footballer defending a free kick, but Sidney carried on as if he did not exist. 'It's a very particular kind o' job. Not a strictly legal kind o' job – it needs a specialist, someone with your sort of skills, Jarvis.'

Sidney looked confidingly across at the younger man, admiring his looks, his strength and his youth. He pursed his lips and knitted his brows into a look of sympathy. 'It would probably involve the use of a firearm,' he casually dropped in, nodding like an artificial dog in the back of a car. He took a hot slurp from his mug of tea. 'And the pay should be good, naturally.'

Somewhat detached, Jarvis tried to look as if he was listening. He was curious to find out more, if a little cautious about his own involvement in whatever this turned out to be. He respected Sidney for what he had achieved. He remembered the big man and his own father being good friends years back, when Jarvis was a youngster, and he still remained in awe of him.

'I want you to meet these friends. Damian, my first boy – you remember? – knows the family well, the Chigwells. Their oldest son David was workin' in Iraq, in Baghdad, just around the time you went out there, I believe. He was killed, under funny circumstances. I'm sure you remember the publicity.'

Jarvis frowned to show he was at least trying to think back seven or eight years. He would have been on active service at the time, and would have missed any fuss on the television back home. But he remembered reading something about the events some time later. 'His father and family have been struggling to find satisfaction, if you know what I mean. It's a while I know, but father–son relationships are very strong, you know that, Jarvis, and you know how these things fester and work away at yer mind.' *Was Jarvis some kind of expert in father–son relationships all of a sudden?*

Sidney was gesturing with his free hand. 'They want revenge – and they're getting fairly desperate. They talked to me a few days ago and I think you might be the right man. The hero of Baghdad returning to wreak justified havoc on the authorities and all that.'

Jarvis applied a sceptical smile and waved away the false praise with a little shake of the head. *What am I letting myself in for here?* He glanced over his shoulder towards Bernard. 'I'm not a hired gun . . .' he whispered urgently, 'not an assassin.'

'I know, I know, you're a professional, we all are, Jarvis, but this will be special. They're willin' to pay a lot o' money. Some up front – I 'eard like 25k or somethink – and lots more on completion. Plus the necessary costs and support and so on. You wouldn't be alone.' He carefully picked some loose tobacco off his lower lip, using the tips of the thumb and little finger of the hand holding the dying cheroot as though they were pincers, and then stubbed the remains into an already overflowing ashtray.

Jarvis and Sidney looked at each other across the wooden expanse. Apart from the occasional dull clump from Sandra's shoes somewhere below them, a mysterious quiet seemed to have descended over the place. The light slanting in from high above Sidney's head was catching the dust and smoke in swirling patterns, and Jarvis visualised trillions of tiny specs settling all around them. Thoughts of thousands of pounds settling all around him prompted a tiny adrenalin rush, and he spluttered something about being out of practice but willing to find out more. His heart thumping a few warning notes was ignored.

'That's my boy. You won't regret this meeting, Jarvis, you won't.'

Jarvis coughed on the smoke. He liked money, the physical stuff, the feel of it, the possibilities, especially having a thick curled wad of notes in the palm of his hand. He visibly brightened at the thought of stacking thousands of pounds into piles at home, storing them away in his safe under the stairs. *There is nothing wrong with being paid a lot of cash for doing something you are good at, something you enjoy.*

'When Damian told me about this job, I immediately knew we needed the services of a professional shooter.' Sidney brushed loose ash off his trousers with a flourish and took more tea with a satisfying slurp. 'I put your name forward as first choice without hesitation. Don't let me down, Jarvis.'

Jarvis felt a rush of blood pulsing through his chest and shuddered. 'So who exactly is the target, Sid?'

2

The next day, in the front room of a neglected terraced house off Victoria Park Road, Jarvis found himself standing at a window, waiting and feeling uncertain. He had been shown in by a gaunt grey-haired woman who kept squeezing her bony hands together like she was wringing out a wet towel. She had sounded friendly, but Jarvis could feel the chill in the place and had kept his coat on.

Following instructions from Sidney, who said it was a 'dead' address, unoccupied, 'but don't be put off', he had found his way easily enough. He was expecting to meet the Chigwell family, who wanted to sponsor the right man for a dodgy job. Sidney needed his guarantee that he would consider the proposal seriously, and that he would not breathe a word of this or any other meeting they may have to another soul. Jarvis of course had agreed and had phoned the landline number he had been given to confirm his intention; he had spoken to someone, a young man, and there he was, having arrived more or less on time.

He surveyed the line of grim houses opposite. A few vehicles rumbled by, rattling the thin windows. There were no parked cars outside. He fingered the purple velvet curtains that matched the purple velour of the settee and armchairs. The carpet was thin and discoloured. There were marks on the camellia anaglypta wallpaper where frames had once hung, but there were no pictures or family photographs anywhere. A small television on a stand stood next to an imitation coal fireplace not in use in the middle of one wall. A lone plastic clock on the mantelshelf was stopped at five past three.

He could hear mumbled voices from somewhere at the back of the house. The door opened and two men walked in, white shirts, jeans, open leather jackets. Jarvis was taller by some way than both. Paul was first, stocky, dark haired, unshaven, with heavy brows, and Jarvis vaguely recognised him from somewhere. His younger brother, Ainsley, had the same colouring but was thinner, with floppy hair and a clean face, wearing a red cardigan with big ruby buttons under squeaky brown leather.

After friendly handshakes, Paul explained that their father was coming to join them in a little while, but that he had been ill recently and was resting for the moment. 'Sorry about the temperature, the heating hasn't come on properly. Actually, we met a few years ago, at John and Margaret's wedding in Harrow,' Paul was saying. 'Remember, at the Tudor Lodge? 2009, think it was.' Jarvis nodded. While Ainsley stood in attendance, Paul did all the talking, low pitched, rough voice, without much expression. He was obviously cockney by the accent but seemed to be trying to speak a bit more posh. For whose benefit? Jarvis wondered.

The three of them sat on the settees in an arc around the television. Jarvis settled back, wrapped in his coat, hugging himself with his hands rammed firmly in his pockets, his legs stretched out and crossed at the ankles. 'Mr Collingwood, we appreciate you coming today. My family, my whole family' – Paul was doing his best to represent his whole family – 'are still so cut up by this business, and have not been able to come to rest over all these years. We are desperate for some sort of justice for our brother's death.'

'Jarvis,' said Jarvis quietly to no one in particular, 'call me Jarvis.'

'Our father has been ill every day since it happened; he'll never recover, I don't think. We've never seen the body, you see, they never found it; we have not had a funeral or nothing.' Now Ainsley was nodding, with some agitation. Paul was wringing his hands a bit like his mother had been doing earlier. He stared ahead, light from the front window reflecting oddly on the surface of his brown eyes. Jarvis wondered where old Ma Chigwell was – probably seeing to the father out the back, from where he could still hear the sporadic mumbling of voices.

'Before our dad comes in we want you to see this video, of Dave's death, to set the meeting in perspective. You might remember it was all over the television and in the papers at the time – it was 2004. Dave was kidnapped in Iraq, in Baghdad, on September 16th we think, and pictures of him appeared again and again on the news and what have you, every night for a week, until they had had enough. They executed him, beheaded him in front of camera, on October 7th. It was shown via webcam, and posted on the internet. We were sent this' – he pointed to an old-fashioned black book-sized video tape that Ainsley was holding up – 'an unexpurgated version of the execution, about three weeks later. To this day I don't know how they knew the address, maybe Dave was forced to give it, I don't know.'

Feeling more uncertain, Jarvis wondered whether he should be getting involved with this story; he pictured it getting a whole lot more complicated. He appeared calm as he prepared to indulge these boys, for the sake of Sidney and his father's friendship, but he was already preparing his rejection speech for later when he backed out, no thank you very much.

'This was shown on Al-Jazeera TV. If we show it to you' – it was Ainsley unexpectedly talking – 'it will help you understand how we feel, yeah?' His eyebrows had arched high up his forehead.

Jarvis took a sharp intake of breath through his nose, which he held for a moment before slowly exhaling; a tiny retraction of one corner of the mouth, a flicker of the eyebrows and a vague shrug all indicated agreement. Ainsley pushed some knobs and prodded the videotape into the front of a black box below the television set. The screen came to life, black-and-white images flickered, and some numbers flashed from top to bottom; then it all went dull again for a few seconds. Poorly focused pictures in grey with some colouring flicked back on, and distant male voices, shouting, the language uncertain, could be heard in the background. Ainsley was using a remote control to adjust the sound. The scene settled on a dimly lit interior, part of a larger warehouse or garage, where figures in black hoods with holes crudely cut out, dirty fatigues and jerkins, were moving about. They were all men, it appeared, six or seven of them, rifles casually slung over their backs, knives in their waistbands. Behind them, hanging awkwardly on a brick wall, was a black banner daubed in yellow paint with the Arabic words *Tawhid* and *Jihad*. The images were poorly focused and tended to flicker, the sound incoherent and muffled.

Coming into centre stage was a dirty-faced white man, bruised and unkempt, and wearing an orange prison-like jumpsuit. He slumped onto a metal chair. His feet were bare and filthy. When a glimpse of his face came up, it was thin and unshaven and he looked terrified. He was prodded by several men and started to speak, saying his name. 'I'm David Chigwell, an Englishman, working in your country.' He was made to read something from a board that one of his captors held up in front of him. It was not clear what he was saying. David's captors, in a line behind him, kept raising their arms and shouting over everything, and they were calling in English for the evil bastard to be killed. One man in particular, in a black sleeveless jerkin and baggy trousers, seemed to shout the loudest and most often, in English. 'You have seventy-two hours to meet our demands,' he screamed at the camera.

'It's not easy to know what they are shouting about,' explained Paul, 'but the gist is pretty obvious. That's David seated, our brother. He'd been kidnapped by some fanatical group, the *Tawhid*, and was being held somewhere in Baghdad. They make him shout things into the video camera, denouncing the war, sending hate to the United States, hate to the United Kingdom and the imperialist West.' David was pleading again into the camera, this time to Mr

24

Gerry Morley directly, saying that they won't release him. He was kneeling and they were clubbing him with their rifles about the head and shoulders. He was crying and shouting, 'No, no, this is not fair; they will kill me if Mr Morley does not take the British troops out of Basrah and release women prisoners in Iraq.'

The video was an amateurish production, almost laughable, if it were not so threatening. *It would be jolly difficult to make out anybody there, even if you knew them*, Jarvis was thinking. David was crying for help and being battered around the head, and then the main man had him by the hair, holding his head back for the camera to catch his face. Then they pulled him up and took him away, stumbling.

'This sort of thing was shown every night for two weeks, it's all much the same,' Paul continued, 'but we'll jump to the last night.' Ainsley forwarded the video, juddering images with blackouts and numbers flitting across the screen, but after ten seconds, a new sequence began. The jerking pictures were the same poor quality, presumably a little time later, maybe the next day, or the next week, but with the same scenario. This time David was kneeling on the floor in the middle of the room, his arms pulled back behind him, still in his orange suit and looking thinner and older, and with seven hooded men behind, impossible to recognise, shouting incoherently. There was a bright spotlight from the side casting sharp angulated shadows across the scene. A sudden close up showed tears running over David's dirty face, an anguished, frightened man. 'Please, Mr Morley, I beg you, if you are listening, please, they will release me if you would take the British soldiers out of Basrah'. He had lost his front teeth, bloodied gaps appearing when he spoke through swollen lips. He was straining his neck to face the camera, sinews and veins coarsely standing out in the oblique light. He was again made to read from a big card. 'The British are not doing any good here, they are trespassing on sovereign land. They usurp the powers

25

of Allah. This is illegal war.'

Neither Paul nor Ainsley was able to look directly at the screen. Jarvis sensed what was about to happen, feeling inwardly uncomfortable yet gripped by a morbid fascination with the madness of the encounter. To be watching these horrid scenes on a flickering TV screen in a strange house in East London on a quiet Sunday morning, seven years after the event, seemed bizarre and unreal. Ainsley had moved away to the window and looked back into the room, silhouetted against the colourless outside light. Paul had taken himself to another seat and was more intent on watching Jarvis than on looking at the video, which Jarvis presumed the brothers had seen several times before. Jarvis adjusted his sitting position and noticed his bright red socks as if for the first time, feeling suddenly embarrassed that he had not worn a more sombre black.

The kidnapped David Chigwell was whimpering in a husky voice, 'I am a simple man, I want to live a simple life. I haven't done anything wrong.' One of the hooded men cuffed him across the back of his head with a fist. 'Here I am again, very close to the end of my life. Nobody has done anything for me to help me. Gerry Morley has not done enough for me'. He was crying, tears streaking across an anguished face close to the camera. And then a taller man in white baggy trousers and dark hood, someone Jarvis had not noticed before, emerged from one side, holding in his stiff right arm a curved scimitar. He commanded obvious authority, as the others backed away slightly to give him room, and now they made less noise. He kept raising the heavy sword up above his head with both arms, as if practising and testing its weight at full stretch.

Then the first jihadist with the bare arms came closer to the camera and spoke in muffled English, saying the time had come for retribution, they had waited long enough for cooperation. He pulled his hood, that had been covering his entire face, up above his bearded chin and mouth and shouted, 'Coalition authorities not met our demands to release our women prisoners. We have been reasonable but English not listening. Now is time to sacrifice this man as warning to the West.'

'Long life to Allah,' they all shouted, raising their arms and shaking their weapons in the air.

'Because UK not serious in releasing our sisters,' the same fanatic shouted into the camera, 'there is nothing further for this malicious Briton than the sword. Our patience is exhausted.'

'Long life to Allah,' they all screamed.

Suddenly the bare-armed man with the black hood drew a knife from his belt, while two of the others grabbed Chigwell. They shoved him to the floor, at the same time wrenching his head back by pulling at his hair. The man yelled as he hacked his knife across David's neck, as if the kidnapped man were a sheep being slaughtered in the street. Several more strokes followed and David's yell became an agonising gurgle. Fresh blood splashed across the floor. Jarvis looked away from the ghastly chaos for a moment. When his sight flicked back to the screen, the distinguished dark-hooded sword holder had stepped up, shouting at the others, who all retreated to give him more space, and had raised both his arms high above his head, the gleaming scimitar poised vertically in position. There were howls from David, who was kneeling and trying to lift his head up, mixed in with the chanting and stamping from the surrounding circle of men.

The tall swordsman stopped and fumbled with one hand to pull at his hood in front of his face, and then petulantly pulled it off his head altogether and hurled it to the ground, leaving his hair standing out in comic disarray. Again he raised the heavy curved scimitar aloft, like a medieval axeman, wild-eyed and bearded. There followed a moment of stillness, while nothing moved, not the swordsman, not the crowd behind, not the victim, a pause while everything in that filthy scene was frozen. And then, accompanied by a sudden screech from the executioner, the scimitar was brought down at an angle with swift and violent accuracy. In a single clean strike across the back of David's neck, the broad blade slashed through sinews, bone and cartilage with a grating crunch. Blood splattered across the camera lens and for a second longer, the hush remained.

The head of the lonely Englishman, with tangled hair and dirt-stained face, imprinted for ever with an agonising expression of astonishment, seemed to remain in position for an impossibly long time, before tumbling onto the mucky floor with a thud. There was a gush of blood and the headless torso was kicked forward. The executioner lifted the severed bundle off the floor by its hair and held it for the camera, for the viewers to see.

Paul and Ainsley had their hands over their faces, both looking away. Jarvis too closed his eyes, but opened them quickly when he realised that the face of the swordsman without his hood on for coverage was in full view as he cheered jubilantly into the camera and then at his fellow jihadist killers. Jarvis presumed the hood had obscured his line of vision and that he had been unable to see properly down towards the floor when he had his arms raised, and so had pulled it off. He had black curly hair in a wild tangle around a gaunt face with high cheekbones and a crooked smile; there was a gap at the front of his upper teeth and what looked like a gash at his outer right eyebrow. The group of wild men were jumping and shouting victory slogans and their religious mantra, with their arms about each other's shoulders.

Jarvis felt embarrassment. At first the grainy and jerky images had made the whole scenario seem like make-believe, but then he realised he had intruded on the personal grief of a family made to witness the gruesome death of their beloved brother from a front-row seat. Because of his own first-hand experiences of battle scenes, of violence and death, Jarvis understood the anguish felt by these two men. He averted his gaze to the safety of the carpet at his feet, a miserable purple like the curtains, to avoid appearing to relish any of the moment.

'They beheaded two other American prisoners as well at about the same time.' Paul had resumed the narrative, with a faltering, croaky voice. 'Dave was thirty-one. He had been working for an international engineering company in Baghdad. He lived in the Al-Mansour district, with a number of other guys in the same company. He had nothing to do with the Army or the war in any way, he was a civilian. He was there to help build and construct things; he was a friend of the people, trying to help them get back to a normal life, not a soldier. Why would he be kidnapped like that?' Paul's chest was heaving, his breathing sharp and jerky, and for a moment Jarvis thought he was going to lose control.

The video juddered to an end, with a clunk. There was quiet in the room, and but for the occasional passing car outside, there was nothing to disturb any private thoughts. 'His body was never found,' added Ainsley, whom Jarvis would have put at about twenty at the time of his older brother's death.

Jarvis could hear the soft murmuring of Mrs Chigwell's voice from the corridor outside, as she coaxed the old man into action after his rest and into the front room to join the others. Mr Chigwell, wearing a tatty-looking grey suit with a green polka-dot bow tie, used a stick and his wife to get safely from door to settee, and then settled onto the cushions next to Jarvis. A slight waft of aftershave mixed with cigarette smoke settled with him. His greying hair was rather unkempt, swept back from a good hairline, and he looked older, his body more bent and his face more wrinkled, than Jarvis had expected. Mrs Chigwell perched herself nearby on a hard chair, looking frail without make-up.

'I'm Arthur. You're Mr Collingwood, I understand. Good of you to come.'

'Call me Jarvis, Mr Chigwell,' said Jarvis.

Arthur Chigwell had tired eyes, and shallow pools of moisture filled the sagging lower eyelids. He had furrows slashed deep into his cheeks and a fine web of violet veins coursed over his bulbous nose. His mouth was pinched and mean. There appeared to be little strength in his voice and Jarvis could not imagine him shouting for his dinner, let alone managing the simplest domestic task. He had a neat row of upper teeth, too big for his mouth – dentures, Jarvis assumed. 'You've seen the video?' was a question. The images on the television had gone, Ainsley had switched the machines off. Jarvis nodded slowly, eyeing sideways the older man slouched at the other end of the settee.

'The horror of those final days will haunt us for ever, Mr Collingwood. We had to watch day after day as those events took place, and then all the newspapers and television stories; there was no peace, no end to it. We have not had a chance even to grieve properly.' Arthur was almost whispering, 'Dave's mother is heart-broken; we have not had a funeral – no body, you see.' A look of deep distaste contorted his battered features.

Another long pause followed. Arthur was staring across the room at the silent screen, his expression empty. The others were still. A hungry crow screeched somewhere outside; someone's stomach gave out a low rumble. Arthur wiped his wet eyes with shaky fingers.

'Do this thing for us, Mr Collingwood, and we will be able to see some closure of this open wound. We will be eternally grateful to you.' Mrs Chigwell handed her husband a small white handkerchief which he used to wipe the end of his nose. 'Our only consolation is that Dave is at peace, somewhere away from all those crazy people who were capable of such dreadful things.'

After a while, with Arthur still fiddling with his handkerchief, Paul found his voice again. 'Our father wants to exact revenge, Mr

Collingwood,' determined not to call Jarvis Jarvis. 'We will supply the money and all necessary support. We will pay, some in advance. We can provide you with whatever weapon you might wish for. We just want the job done.'

Jarvis could not think of anything to say just at that moment.

'You must have seen some things yourself in your time, Mr Collingwood, in the war in Iraq. You were there, first hand. You were a hero, I understand, a super shot – could hit a mouse at a mile, eh?' Arthur reached out with a thin clawed hand to grab Jarvis's leather sleeve and was tugging at it. Arthur and Jarvis leant towards each other, their shoulders almost touching, and the old man looked imploringly into Jarvis's pale blue eyes. 'I miss my eldest son, Mr Collingwood.'

'We cannot get him back, Mr Chigwell, whatever we do.'

Jarvis tried to sound sympathetic, not so matter of fact. Questions were racing through his mind, as he tried to believe what he had just heard. He was taken aback at the ideas coming from these men. *Do they really think that I would hunt down some mad terrorist, after all these years, in Iraq?* Arthur looked thunderous and serious and sad all at the same time. *Obviously he does. I suppose this will get me out of London for a while, away from Pamela, into those more interesting and dangerous places that I've been dreaming about . . .*

'I know that,' Arthur Chigwell enunciated emphatically, finding new strength from the depths, a speck of spittle flying from his lips to land on his trousers, 'I'm not senile; this is about exacting revenge.' And with that he sank back into his cushions, tired by his extra effort.

'So who exactly is the target you're after?'

Ainsley sprang into life again, grateful to have something definite to do. He had a laptop computer to hand, although Jarvis was unsure where he had been keeping it. He opened it up and leant over to put it on Jarvis's lap. 'May I?'

He hit a couple of keys and a picture popped up – a poor-quality snap of a man standing with others, his arms raised above his head, his mouth open; a still photo, no sound. But Jarvis easily pictured in his mind the raging scene they had just witnessed, the executioner with scimitar in both hands. He was looking full into camera, wild black hair, heavy beard, dark fervent eyes, with that gash across the end of the right eyebrow. Jarvis recognised the face that was exposed at the kill, the face of the tall swordsman.

'His name is Abu Masoud Zadeh,' Ainsley said smoothly, well practised in the unfamiliar sounds, 'and we refer to him as Abu.' Another image was brought up, this time a clear colour picture of Abu in open shirt, chest hairs exposed at his neck, casual jacket, not obviously the army fighter, more a man on holiday; but the same face looking at the camera. 'This was taken we think some time later, a couple of years later maybe, in the streets of Baghdad.'

Ainsley had the irritating habit of flicking away the long hair that flopped over his forehead at the end of every sentence, and Jarvis was distractedly wondering whether he was gay. With another click on the forward key, an enlargement of the last image appeared. And then another better photograph came up, a close-up of a respectable-looking clean, washed man, with neat trimmed beard this time, streaked with grey, in a jacket, the office-worker look. With brilliant blue skies behind and sunshine glancing across his face, there was no mistaking the executioner from the video, with those straight black eyebrows like two caterpillars that didn't quite meet in the middle.

'This man beheaded our brother,' intoned Ainsley, containing his anger with difficulty. 'He should be taken out.'

Jarvis looked with surprise at the brothers, first Ainsley, then Paul, and back to Arthur Chigwell. *If they are thinking that I am going to return to Iraq to find this monkey, to assassinate him, they must be joking.* They remained silent, wanting to let the ex-Army

32

man kick his own thoughts around in his head for a while. Paul looked calm again, as if he had simply asked Jarvis for directions somewhere, and started to nod slowly, with a frown developing around his eyes. Jarvis was beginning to think that he had missed something of the plot.

'Abu Masoud was the leader of *Tawhid* and *Jihad*, responsible for some atrocious bombings, assassinations and beheadings of foreign hostages. He worked with al-Qaeda in Iraq, we believe, but there were differences of opinion, some sort of internal power struggle, and then he's lost for a while, but reappeared a year later on the other side almost. So Abu the murderer not only survived the rest of the fighting with the armies of the coalition and the civil infighting,' Paul added, 'but he is alive and well and is working for the administration, working with the Allies; he is now a minister in the Iraqi government, for fuck's sake.' Paul looked disgusted and Arthur snorted at the sick irony.

'You *have* been doing your homework,' mused Jarvis quietly, impressed with the earnestness of the brothers. 'How can you be sure this man is the one who killed your brother?'

'We have had some help from a friend in Baghdad who works for the Al-Jazeera station – he's a journalist and has done some digging for us and obtained these photos. He's used the new face-recognition software.' Ainsley produced some more colour pictures on the small screen. 'Look at these blow-ups – compare those earlier ones with this more recent photo,' and he held a colour print in his hand. 'The shape of the face, the slant of the eyes: they are identical. We only discovered this man a few months ago.'

After a few moments' hesitation, aware of his quickening heartbeat and feeling puzzled, Jarvis said, 'Hang on a minute, Paul, Ainsley, Mr Chigwell. OK, so this guy is now an Iraqi official, respectable even, living in Baghdad under heavy protection presumably.' Jarvis was struggling to find the right words to convince these good people that their request was futile. 'And Abu is the target. I mean, you cannot imagine that I would return to Iraq, with the sole purpose of targeting this madman?' He looked at them one at a time, from one to the other, the furrows of astonishment between his eyes growing deeper.

Ainsley pushed the laptop lid closed and placed on it in front of Jarvis a colour print measuring twenty centimetres by fifteen, that he retrieved from inside a brown envelope that he had also been keeping concealed. The picture was of a man with neat black hair and trimmed beard, in a dark suit, looking every bit the respectable citizen, apparently walking along a city street with a briefcase under one arm, a smiling commuter on his way to work. Next to that picture, another, showing the same face, close up, with the same slightly older but recognisable features of Abu. 'The same face, that little scar in the outer right eyebrow, and this dark mole on his right temple that we've seen before, the gap in his front teeth.' Ainsley pointed with a biro at each feature of Abu's face as he enumerated them in the photograph.

Ainsley's hands were trembling slightly and his voice faltered as he fixed on Jarvis's indifferent eyes. 'Now *these* pictures were taken,' he whispered, gesturing with upturned open hands, 'in London.'

Ainsley paused for effect. Jarvis glanced across at him, watching his dry lips stretch wide in his moment of triumph. Ainsley, keeping his gaze firmly fixed on Jarvis, handed him another colour photo of Abu in a busy city street to look at more closely.

'Last week,' Ainsley added quietly, for maximum effect.

A falling pin would have sounded like a drum beat in the midst of such silence. 'Abu was here, in London, four days ago, with the Iraqi delegation, inspecting the security arrangements for this summer's London Olympic Games.'

3

Early one frosty morning in January, Jarvis Collingwood found himself standing with a dozen others on some scrubland at the edge of a massive forest with much on his mind. Just outside the M25 near Dartford, this five-thousand-acre neglected site of broadleaved woods and hornbeam coppice sat astride a gentle ridge, like a saddle across a pony's back, centuries old much of it and currently in the hands of a local gent, Danny told his boys on their first day. Separated by the Gravesend-to-Bromley railway line, which cut across the forest's eastern borders, was the village of Longfield, about a mile along a country road. Lord Stonebridge wanted a new access road, more a gravel path wide enough for tractors, to run through the woodland from the valley side on the south over the ridge and down to join Highcross Road, that meandered along the northern boundary. This would give easier access to the dense centre and the northern parts, where a lot of clearing of decades' worth of accumulated damaged trees and rubbish was required. Danny said there were even fallen trees from the famous 1987 storm that hit southern England that still had to be cleared. The job was going to be tough and would take several months.

Danny Darthwaite was showing a group of men, built like tanks every one of them, around the site, starting at the clearing of flat scrub and concreted ground the size of half a football pitch at the southern edge of the boundary, earmarked for their own working 'village'. It was overgrown with grass and weeds, hawthorn and wild blackberries, and the wind had whipped tons of fallen leaves into piles and drifts around the periphery. Wooden gates hung off their hinges, the remains of a stone wall ran alongside the road, and a little hut of some sort was reduced to a pile of bricks. There were split bags of unused cement, broken furniture, rusty exhaust pipes and assorted rubbish scattered around. Two smart caravans that could each sleep up to eight men had left muddy tyre marks across the frosty ground and were parked on some concrete standing either side of a substantial wooden shed that would act as a kitchen and canteen. Hired toilet cubicles were hidden behind the shed, as well as a pipe that represented the site's solitary mains running-water supply. Power would come from a portable generator that was being fired up as they spoke. Another large shed for storage and work, which would become a permanent fixture, had already been erected at the far corner, and earlier that day Danny had helped park a couple of red Massey Fergusons, each with a trailer-load of high-quality cutting machinery, under plastic tarpaulins.

'Now, there's even a pub down lane, not more 'an a mile, and serves good ale. Mind, don' be chasing them wenches there, or yer'll get more then yer bargained fer.' Danny was from Yorkshire, and by the time the main workforce arrived, Jarvis had learnt that he had already chased after the head wench at The Green Man and had set himself up at said hostelry, despite having a wife back in the Dales.

'So this is part of Beacon Forest, and when we're finished His Lordship plans to open up t' public for walks an' picnic spots an' the like.' Danny headed up the sloping ground into the woods, with all the big lads – rough-faced thugs in their thirties, most of them, and, like Jarvis, chosen for their muscle and experience – traipsing behind him. Danny had worked with some of them before at other sites or knew them from the Army. He was in green wellingtons and a Barbour, and still had his limp from an old shrapnel wound. He pointed out various landmarks that would become familiar to them as they worked there for the next six months or more.

'Them tall straight trees along the top ridge are ash and horse chestnut; in front, coming down them slopes, are oak like solid towers over this coppice here; and soon in spring this whole lower sloped area will be a mass of bluebells like an Axminster carpet, so keep off this area, none of yer clodhopping boots over that. Everything looks bare now with the leaves down, but come the summer everything will be thick and green. So into the woods on the east side are mature sweet chestnuts, ten feet diameter and three hundred years old some of 'em, with larch, ash and western red cedars, some of the finest trees you'll come across in England. Will take some culling too, I don't mind saying. There's a problem with some of the ash, some sort of fungus apparently brought over from Europe, and the spores carried on the winds. There are many dead and broken ash and planc up there, and we need to weed 'em out.'

Danny carried on for a while, explaining where the road was to go, and what the phases of the project were. Diggers were due on site later. With a meal of sausages, eggs and beans on the go in the kitchen hut, where Charlie and his mate were setting up tables in the dry, the gang quickly headed back to get some food inside them before preparing themselves for the work that lay ahead. Beacon Forest was the biggest job Jarvis had been on so far. There would be fifteen or sixteen blokes in all, mostly Irish, Poles and Lithuanians, all like-minded men seeking a physical outlet away from the daily hubbub and domestic strife. They would gather each day at first light over a cooked breakfast and a mug of tea, hale, hearty and friendly. And again at the end of their shifts, tired and grumpy, battered and sore, ready to sink a few beers and eat anything put in front of them. They did not ask awkward questions: they just wanted to get on with their tasks without hassle. The piecework system was popular, the men able to work as and when they wanted. And the money was cash in hand.

Jarvis had been freelancing with various gangs on and off for a couple of years, clearing wooded areas, felling trees with heavy cutting equipment, culling and logging. The jobs had paid well because of the risks and the long anti-social hours away from home, often on remote country sites for days at a time. The work was hard and had its dangers; strength, endurance and not a little skill with cutting tools, petrol-driven chainsaws and other machinery was required. Jarvis enjoyed the physical activity and the sense of camaraderie with his fellow lumberjacks, although sometimes he would spend a whole day working alone, secluded in his own peace. By the end of most days, he would have cut hands and bruises, and was sore and bloodied, but he would carry on, into the late afternoons, even as daylight began to fail.

Jarvis wore jeans and a thick red-and-blue-checked shirt just like any traditional forest worker, with a peaked Canadian-style cap that had fur-lined ear flaps against the cold, and steel-tipped leather boots. And he would often wear extra earmuffs for sound protection, so with all the grinding and cutting and machinery noise, he was then unable to hear anything else around him; someone could approach him easily from out of the shadowy woods and surprise him.

In his middle teenage years when he roamed the streets of South London with his mates looking for entertainment, Jarvis had got himself hooked on sniffing petrol fumes, glue and other solvents, his way of disconnecting from reality, an experience floating somewhere between confusion and elation. But he grew up and the Army cured him of the addiction. Later, when working in the forest, he had found certain wood-sap odours with their addictive power could be equally alluring. Some of the toughest woodsmen he had met only found peace when lost in the quiet of an impermeable forest, safe in their world apart. Those men were reluctant to leave the cutting areas at the end of the day, choosing to work long hours to near exhaustion, even when the darkness brought extra danger, drugged as they were by the mesmeric effects of the wood smells into a soporific rhythm, as if captured by something mind altering.

After a long, exhausting spell without a break, cutting fallen damaged trees into manageable sections, Jarvis stopped and rubbed his shoulders, which ached fiercely. The air was cold and still, the grey skies overcast, and not much light reached down to the floor where he had been working. His efforts had made him sweat and a film covered his torso, a flow of wet trickling down the middle of his back into his pants. Drops collected along his eyebrows and fell onto his gloved hands and hot machinery, or darkened the colour of the sawdust scattered at his feet over the peaty soil. He stopped to catch his breath and quickly came to feel the chill.

Sweet aromas from freshly cut ash and lime, together with the bitter scent of cedar, lingered heavily in the still air, the clinging dust sticking to his clothes. Over the past two weeks, he had been turning over and over in his mind the quirky scene at the Hackney house where he had been offered money to do a dirty job. He had slept fitfully in the upper bunk of his caravan, listening to the rhythms the light rain played on the metal roof above his head, and the heavier sounds of his slumbering mates, thinking of Arthur Chigwell seeking revenge and of David's anguished face during those last harrowing moments of his life. For long periods during the day, while engines ground and roared and sawdust flurried, he was lost in his own thoughts, endlessly mulling over the proposition. David Chigwell had died a horrific death, as he had witnessed on the video, which looked entirely authentic. Jarvis had little doubt that the bastards who had tormented him deserved to be punished. He sympathised with David's father: what he and his wife had had to live through at the time and since did not bear thinking about. The Chigwells now wanted him to take up a different sort of trade, to pick up a different sort of tool, and use it to fell another man.

Albeit a monster sort of a man. Who now worked for the Iraqi government with some semblance of respectability, no doubt under constant protection.

Ainsley Chigwell seemed to think that Abu Masoud would be making regular visits to London between now and the Olympic Games later in the summer. Jarvis would have to know his precise visiting dates and routines. He was certainly not contemplating getting a visa for Iraq and infiltrating himself into government circles there with a view to carrying out an assassination on foreign soil. If he took this job on (and he had not yet decided whether he would), he would have to be in sole and complete control, devising his own plan that no one else knew about. However popular it might turn out to be with the media or public once they realised who the target was and what Abu had done in the past, he was damned if he was going to be caught for it.

It had to be perfectly planned. Twenty-five thousand pounds up front sounded good as a start, with more to come, the amount as yet unspecified. Maybe he should demand a higher advance sum for the work; if they wanted him so badly, he should make them pay. Perhaps fifty thousand pounds – now that sounded like a tidy sum.

And would he have to go into hiding? If so, how? He would not be able to spend all that money without drawing attention to himself, and on daily living it would not last long anyway. And where was he to hide if he had to? He would need a bolt hole, with some old friend who could support him; he would want to be able to move about and use the money without suspicion. He would need a second identity to allow him freedom of movement, use of cash machines and the means of escape abroad if necessary. And then what about Pamela? He was always looking for a solution to his Pamela dilemma, his little marriage problem, and maybe this would provide the incentive and the means to solve it.

He would need to think carefully about the how and the when.

He could take his time, but he would have to be totally in charge, not pushed or rushed into some decision he was not happy with, just for the sake of the Chigwells. His first thoughts were of a shot in the open, from a long distance, a street perhaps, crowd activity for diversion and able to blend away afterwards. There must be no forensics, no weapon to incriminate him and no link with the Chigwells.

Suddenly he felt the touch of a hand on his outer arm.

He jumped, straightened his back and half turned, with the rotating saw still firing and swinging round at waist height. Jarvis saw that it was Randy. 'We've made some tea,' he was shouting, jumping backwards away from danger. 'We're 'aving a break; it'll be dark soon, it's nearly four o'clock. Come on.' Randy was the youngster in the party, with a naïve and honest face, thick unruly hair and an unshaven jaw, as he was trying to grow some beard to match the maturity of the older lumberjacks. Jarvis would watch him down a beer or two with the men after work, when he would tend towards the giggly and be seen frequently dashing out to the gents. It was Friday again, and no doubt Randy was hoping to impress the pretty young barmaid at The Green Man, where the gang would go tonight after work, before dispersing for the weekend.

'I'll just finish this, thanks,' shouted Jarvis above the sound of the motor, and he turned away unruffled to continue grinding over a long-fallen ash trunk. Randy shot off with a roar and a puff of diesel fumes on a three-wheel tractor, its massive tyres capable of running over any terrain and of pulling small trailers, to talk to the next woodsman somewhere out among the dense imposing trees.

Jarvis cut his motor, which died instantly, leaving him shrouded in a sudden eerie soundlessness, his ears still reverberating. He packed everything up, with the cut wood neatly piled and covered in tarpaulin, to be collected next week. He was covered in sticky sawdust and wood shavings, and he rubbed himself down as best he could, shaking it off his jacket, out of his headgear. He trudged his way back to the 'village', jacket slung over his shoulder, carrying his heavy saw equipment, up a winding path over the ridge and along a corridor of tall cedars down towards the caravan site. Most of the others had gathered in the evening gloom, stamping their feet, brushing down their clothes outside, grumbling and laughing, warming their hands together by a simmering fire.

Inside the canteen, Charlie had brewed tea for everyone and had an electric fire on; the windows were misted up. There was a pungent smell of sweat and damp and wood sap, and the floor was getting muddied. The men were quiet from the strains of the day's work; they stretched tired limbs and aching backs, examined their cuts and bruises, sipped at their mugs of tea or gulped beer and munched cake and biscuits. With the evening cold settling in, it was a case of big jumpers, coats, boots and beanies, and once they were all jacketed up and packed and ready to leave, Danny locked the caravans and led them to an old Transit van to take everyone back into town, via the pub. A couple of lads with their own cars were off for the weekend in different directions.

In The Green Man they all had a few pints and a pie. Randy sat forlorn at the far end of the bar on his own, trying to talk in private to Rosetta whenever she passed, but mostly just staring into his pint, looking worried. He told the others he was staying late, Rosetta would give him a lift to the station later. Jarvis imagined them shagging in the back of her Nissan Micra, and wondered how they would manage in such limited space.

At London Bridge Station, the usual meeting and dropping-off point, Jarvis jumped out of the van and waited around until exactly seven o'clock, as instructed, before making the call to the same number as before, from a phone box on the causeway, and it was Ainsley Chigwell who answered. 'My father rather liked you.

Admired what you had done and everything, actually. He wants to meet you again, has another proposition for you.' Jarvis grunted. 'Don't know the details, like, money most likely. He wants to pick you up in the car, anywhere you like.'

Jarvis listened. He had been preparing himself to reply to the original request, but wanted more time to think so that his answer, when ready, would be a well-thought-out reply, rather than the first thing that came into his head. After a further pause, Jarvis said OK.

'He suggested tomorrow morning, maybe near your place so you don't have to come too far, he thinks of these things.'

'I don't mind walking.'

It was Paul driving the next morning, an old Jaguar that drew up alongside Jarvis, who was standing close to the kerb on City Road at exactly nine o'clock. Pamela had made a fuss again about him being up so early and leaving on a Saturday without much of a goodbye, but sod it, he was not going to be explaining to her what he was up to or who he was meeting. He would think of a story for her later.

He slid onto the back seat next to the old man, immediately conscious of the heavy stink of cigarettes. From deep within the folds of his velvet-collared overcoat, Arthur Chigwell grunted a welcome. Paul drove down to London Wall and Holborn Viaduct without a word, before descending into the dingy depths of an underground multi-level car park. Once parked well away from other cars, he hopped out of the car, leaving Arthur and Jarvis alone in the dark interior. There was nobody about and no one to observe them. Paul stood some way off, merging with the pillars and the shadows, keeping watch.

'This business is important to me, you know, Mr Collingwood. The house we met in – it's not ours, you won't find us there, it's abandoned, we use it for business sometimes. In case you had your doubts, I am taking this seriously.' Arthur spoke quietly, with a smoker's gravel in his voice. He sounded brighter, more on the ball, more in control than when they had last met. The creases were still there in his face, but his hair was greased and combed flat more carefully, there was more colour in his face, though his mouth was still pinched and mean. He had kept his gloves on, but the way he still rubbed his hands together, rolling one fist within the other palm, he looked as if he was about to punch someone.

'I know you are, I know, Mr Chigwell, and I respect you, sir.' *Where the devil did that 'sir' come from? He had left the Army way behind!* 'I just wonder whether we've actually thought all this through.'

'Damn well right I have. I know what I want from you. And if we can keep this thing strictly between ourselves, then we can get it to work, and no one will be any the wiser. Let me tell you some more. Paul and Ainsley will work for you, but they don't need to know any details, or any of your plans.'

Arthur paused, the rush of speaking making him sound more short of breath. 'I grieve for my eldest son. David was my first born. He was everything I wanted in a son and he meant the world to me and Dorothy. Taking revenge for his killing seems silly to you perhaps, pointless and unnecessary.' He sniffed hard, with one leather-gloved hand rubbing his chin and nose, as if he wanted to smell the leather. 'But we have not been able to push our anger to one side and "move on", as everyone keeps saying. We cannot grieve for him, not properly. I wake most nights hearing his screaming for help, that last gurgling sound we heard on the video. Or I hear him coming home, turning the key in the front door; or on the phone, I think I'm going to hear his voice. I haven't let Dorothy see the video, I couldn't. And then this bastard turns up, out of the blue. I owe it to David to do something, even at this late stage.' His voice had become thick, his delivery intense. 'The pictures bring it all back again. We feel so angry.'

Arthur looked away out into the dim recesses of grey concrete without apparently seeing anything, his eyes misted over. He needed to compose himself or he would be blubbing in front of this young ex-soldier. He turned to Jarvis, pulling him a little closer, his gloved hand gripping his arm like it had done the other day. Jarvis could feel his strength, even through the thickness of his own leather coat. 'I want to say this with you alone, I don't want my sons to hear this. There is another target that I and some of my friends want dealt with too.'

There was a trembling tension in his voice as he spoke through clenched teeth. Jarvis winced at the close odour of his stale breath, as he waited to hear him out. 'There was really only one man that was responsible for the whole debacle,' Arthur continued, and Jarvis could almost taste the venom in his words, 'the whole *fucking* mess, the illegal war, and all those soldiers and innocent people killed and the shambles afterwards. Well, you were there. You lost your brother. Pointless and illegal. And Gerald Morley walks free, making himself rich with his company directorships and wafting around the Middle East like some big-shot. I don't know how the world stands for it. I have some Palestinian and Arab contacts who would seriously like to see a hit on this man. And they will pay big for it. Two hundred thousand for you, Jarvis, in cash, for the job done.'

Jarvis was trying to show no reaction, perhaps a little quizzical smile, a slight flutter of the eyelids, although inside he was incredulous and surprised, and then more than a little elated. *Is this man for real? Am I really hearing this?* Arthur was rushing on. 'You need to pick your spot carefully. You will need another face afterwards too, so that you can disappear, until all the fuss is over, and then return quietly later and pick up with your life as before, only richer.' *What an opportunity for doing something amazing that would blow into the news like an explosion. And for a lot of money!* 'And a lot of people will be more than satisfied,' Arthur finished. He sat back, sinking into his seat with a sigh.

Jarvis remained quiet, not quite sure what to say. *I don't know whether this man is off his trolley or seriously offering me two hundred grand to bump off an ex-UK Prime Minister and an Iraqi terrorist. Where's he getting the money from?*

'I want you on board with this, Jarvis. I need an answer soon.'

Jarvis realised with some pride that Arthur Chigwell had just called him Jarvis for the first time. 'You want me to assassinate Abu Masoud and Gerry Morley, all for two hundred thousand pounds cash, and to get away with it scot-free? Am I right?'

'I mean two hundred k on top of the Abu job – we're talking two hundred and twenty-five thousand pounds sterling – now that can't be bad. When was the last time you had the chance to win 225k, tax free, in cash, wherever you want it? It's real and legit – a lot of it comes from the Middle East. I know them there, I used to do a lot of business out there.'

Jarvis threw his head back in disbelief and studied the discoloured lining on the roof of the old car. He needed to pinch himself, but wanted to act cool. Two hundred and twenty-five thousand pounds in cash, he repeated to himself. It was a large sum of money. 'OK, but I, I need a little time to think this through. This is a whole new ball game, the stakes are much higher now. The risks are much higher as well.' Jarvis was not choosing his words easily. 'You know, what you're asking is, is mega, and pretty difficult, given the protection and who he is. I need to think whether it's possible.' *And whether I want to do it at all, you madman. Two hundred and twenty-five thousand pounds for the crime of the century, notoriety, the most wanted criminal in Britain; and how would I get away with it?*

'Of course. Let me know soon, give Ainsley a ring, just yes or no. There will be twenty-five thousand pounds in cash up front for you as soon as you decide. Two hundred and twenty-five thousand pounds in all and nobody the wiser, just think about it.' *And me banged up for life in Belmarsh.* Arthur buzzed his car window down and called across to Paul, who emerged from the shadows and walked slowly over to the car, looking uncomfortably cold from standing around. 'I really want a yes, Jarvis, I know you can do it. We'll give you a week, eh?'

On the ride back to Shoreditch, wild thoughts of the various possibilities were spinning around in his head like clothes in a washing machine: how he would do the job, what methods he might use, where he would go for safety afterwards with his store of money, how he would get by with daily living and generally survive, how he would access his funds without giving the game away. Success would all be down to not getting caught, obviously; with having a good alibi. Jarvis risked being put away for years, never to be heard of again, as he would for ever be considered a danger; he could lose everything, his friends, his life – it would just not be worth risking all that, would it?

As he watched straight-faced from the comfort of the car, the street crowds in the drizzly rain were going about their normal businesses, unaware. He felt detached. *I bet none of them is thinking about assassinating a famous politician.* He would need a bolt hole, a safe house where nobody could find him, that was for sure, some-where nobody knew about, especially not Pamela. Or his brother, or mother, absolutely no one. He would need a second identity.

4

Jarvis had finished early for the day on a tedious security job. Once home, he changed into his running gear, skipped down the carpeted stairs and left through the front door without a word, before daylight started to fade. He set off jogging, on a planned six-mile circuit out through Dalston that would take him fifty minutes at an easy pace, finishing along the canal. It was chilly and his body felt stiff and sore from his forestry work, but he soon loosened up and fell into his stride, consistent pace, consistent breathing. He fixed his thoughts entirely on the dilemma set him by Arthur Chigwell, almost without noticing his surroundings as he ran along familiar streets, semi-lit with a yellowish glow. Instinctively he knew he should turn his back on the whole thing and have nothing to do with the Chigwells. The risks were ridiculously high. But there was something about the whole sorry tale that made him sympathise with old Arthur – something that attracted him to the challenge, the promise of sheer exhilaration if he were to pull it off. He did not doubt his own abilities for one moment and imagined himself in the role of superhero. And of course the sweet vision of piles of cash stacked around him was never long out of his mind. This was once-in-a-lifetime territory.

Pamela had also been home early and was ironing in the front room when Jarvis thundered out of the house. She was surrounded by piles of clothes on seats and tables; shirts and blouses on hangers suspended from the edge of the door, the window, picture hooks, anywhere she could find. She was hot and fed up. She found herself questioning Jarvis's excuses for being away from home so much, his sleeping away in a caravan in some remote forest, days and some-times more nights away on security duties for Jonathan, late nights with friends up in town – there were periods when they did not see each other for days on end. She was determined to check out his story with Jonathan sometime. Mindful that Jarvis probably did not believe her story either, she knew she needed to tread carefully, as the more she criticised him and suggested he might be cheating on her, the more attention she would draw to her own extracurricular activities.

She tidied away, making frequent journeys up and down the stairs, and made herself a coffee, relaxing for a minute with a cig-arette in the front room. She and Jarvis had lost interest in each other, that was the problem, and neither of them could summon up the energy to explore the real situation. Their pretence enabled a semblance of normal life to be preserved. Sometimes she felt she barely knew Jarvis at all. Except that they had known each other for twelve years or more. Pamela had been Jarvis's first girlfriend back in 2000. He was so good looking and adventurous then, he was exciting to be with. He had a quirky smile and perfect skin, not like the other boys around at the time. He had a physical presence and was more mature, with a brooding coolness towards others, which she admired. The Army had meant everything to him, and she was proud of him, genuinely distressed during his absences. But he was a different man when he returned to her, quietly living inside his head, consumed by his own thoughts. The other day, he had started to talk about returning to Iraq; she was dumbstruck and unable to reply.

Pamela worried about his job prospects. He was working with a forestry gang led by Danny, whom she had met years ago when he was an army sergeant at their Colchester base. She could not quite remember his wife, but he was a popular outgoing sort. God knows what Jarvis got paid – she never seemed to see any of it. He secreted his cash away in his safe, she knew that, but she had no way of getting inside. Then there was the security stuff with Jonathan's firm, so hit and miss. Jarvis needed to get something stable, regular, with a weekly wage that she could see, and then they could plan towards their future with more mutual cooperation. At the moment their future was not ever considered, not together; it seemed that an endless series of arguments and misunderstandings stretched out before them.

Jarvis would come and go at odd hours without explanation, whereas Pamela worked a solid nine-to-five plus overtime. She was beginning to reap rewards, not that Jarvis seemed to care, promoted to second assistant just after Christmas as recognition for what she had done on the Olympics brief. She was in with a group of young, motivated go-getters and loved it all. Her firm, Merriweather & Dunn, was a leader in marketing and public relations and was taking up plenty of new and lucrative contracts as well as anticipating the coming London Games with nervous excitement.

She had been in Singapore at the time of the winning announcement in 2005, and how exhilarating was that! She had met personalities from politics, from sport and the media, and she had been present at occasional briefings in Downing Street. Her head had been turned, her heart too, by the magic of it all, the exotic and romantic lifestyles. She would not change it for anything or anybody. This career was her number one priority, Pamela reminded herself, an essential part of her own self-worth. From ignorant office girl in the copywriters' department, lucky enough to make the tea, she had worked her way up towards the sharp end of a highly competitive and bitchy industry, and was well able to stand up for herself; she had done well. Jarvis would never have succeeded in her world, he was so obvious, so lacking in imagination, unable to think laterally. She was earning good money, with much more to come if she played her cards well. And Jarvis was not going to spoil it all for her. She could give as good as she got. She just wished that he was not so secretive.

By the time Jarvis returned, Pamela had worked herself into a mood in the kitchen. The feeling of being left on her own, with no contribution from him, was irritating her. Last week, the dinner party had not been the triumph she had hoped for, Jarvis having forgotten the bread, so embarrassingly they had had to manage without. Jarvis had sat sullen at his end of the table most of the evening. He kept forgetting Barbara's name. Pamela had to keep initiating the conversation, mostly about her world of marketing, and then had to endure listening to endless tales of how wonderful it was for Evelyn and Barbara living in their new house in Fulham, so close to the King's Road in Chelsea and Stamford Bridge, where Evelyn worked on the staff as a personal trainer, mixing with all those famous wealthy footballers. Barbara announcing with hysterical giggling that she and Evelyn were expecting was the last straw. It was Evelyn's second, of course, but that was a long time ago, and they had already designed a little baby bedroom and that very morning had been in IKEA buying the finishing touches. Jarvis made some disparaging remarks about how their lives would be forever covered in baby sick and baby poo, and pitied them their loss of freedom – and about how Barbara's employment opportunities would be forever marred. Jarvis and Evelyn later talked about football, while Pamela, having imbibed rather too much wine, butted in with remarks about Jarvis's supposed role as the man of the house, how he did not know where the hoover was kept, or which was the on/off switch on the washing machine, really. And how they were looking forward to starting their own family when Jarvis could get around to being the proper man he professed to be.

'Jarvis, we have your mother next weekend, remember,' she called out on his return, hearing him sloping through the hall, 'it's her birthday lunch, so you had better get yourself together.'

'Look, I know how to behave with my mother.'

'That's not what I'm saying. We all know how you behave with your mother. There will be lots of other people there, uncles, aunts and neighbours, so you cannot go around like a zombie. And Stella, you need to be nice to her.'

'I am always nice to her.' Jarvis was tired, still catching his breath and aching in the legs. He felt ravenously hungry and devoured some bread and biscuits in the kitchen, drinking down a pint of water. 'And what's that about my mother?' Streams of sweat were running over his body, his big shoulders glistening in a singlet vest darkened by the wet. He carelessly splashed cold water over his face.

'I'm not going to argue, just keep your mother happy, and talk to these other people, not like last week.'

'Last week was *my* birthday,' Jarvis said, staring at Pamela through the open doorway, wiping his face with a towel, 'and yet I had to sit through *your* fatuous tarty friends talking rubbish.' In the moment it took Pamela to draw breath to offer a robust reply, Jarvis had turned away into the hall where, at the bottom of the stairs, he indulged in some cooling-down slow stretching of his calf muscles, before trudging upstairs for a shower.

It was a relief for Jarvis to leave the house on his own and head up to the Essex Road on foot. Although he lacked a formal plan as yet, his mind was buzzing with Chigwell's proposals and possibilities were pinging around inside his head like the silver ball in a pinball machine. He was aware he should have contacted Ainsley sooner with his answer, but every time he thought he had made a decision, a film of cold sweat broke out across his chest and the palms of his hands went sticky; niggly doubts made him hold back. A tiny voice of warning kept murmuring in the background; but it was only tiny.

In preparation for the following week's family gathering at his mother's to celebrate her sixtieth birthday that Pamela had kindly reminded him about, his hair needed a trim. He sat waiting in the familiar hairdresser's thinking that he also needed a new girlfriend. *Someone to look out for me, someone who doesn't know exactly who I am and doesn't ask questions, someone loyal. Someone safely tucked away who I can turn to when I want to disappear.* Pamela would be the last person to rely on for help. One sniff of the sort of activity Jarvis was contemplating becoming involved in and she would be yelling for him to stop, calling in reinforcements if she did not get her way. She would shop him, he was sure of that. He could not talk to anyone else in the family – they would react the same as her. His army friends would be amazed but might have more of a sympathetic view. Would any of them risk their own freedom and job to support him in pulling off a major criminal act? They would be loyal to Crown and State and all that, and although Abu Masoud would be an attractive target for who he was and what he had done, the rest would be unacceptable to any of the good guys he knew.

He watched the Saturday-morning trade in full swing, the colourful bustle and talk over on the women's side, with dryers blowing noisily, in contrast to the soberly dressed girls (all with neat styles of their own, dark bobs or pageboys) on the men's side, chatting quietly behind their customers, getting on with the simple short back and sides most of them wanted.

His turn came round and he sat on a black swivel armchair facing himself in a mirror. Maybe he could pick up someone new and start dating again – perhaps through the internet. He recognised the slim girl standing behind him with a black sheet in her hands and the 'come on' smile from previous visits, although usually he paid no particular attention. She was tallish and quiet, and looked shy and giggly. She wore black-rimmed glasses and her own hair was dark auburn, straight and short. She showed off a wide smile, displaying an upper row of giant white teeth that gave her a goofy-looking face. Jarvis glanced at the customer next to him and at his hairdresser, who was a mousy-haired girl, pleasant smile, nice chest.

'So what are we doing?' Goofy asked from behind, as she pulled the black nylon cover up to his neck, like a shroud, and Velcroed him in.

Jarvis blinked back to attention. 'Oh, just the usual, you know, we've done this before.' He managed a weak smile and tried to make some eye contact in the mirror.

'Yes,' she giggled and shrugged, looking the other way, 'I didn't notice it was you. What are you up to today, then?'

Jarvis left her to get on with it without watching her or saying anything. She combed and clipped efficiently and after a while the preening effects lulled him into sleepiness. His breathing became slower and deeper and all his thoughts began to drain away. The girl applied her touches with gentleness, her cold fingertips like transient snowdrops on his scalp. Imperceptibly a hip was pressed against his jutting arm as she took a better view across the top of his head. Without a flicker betraying what was going on inside his head, he fought hard not to turn his eyes towards that point of contact, desperate to focus all his attention to that one tiny feeling – he so wanted to press his elbow into her soft flesh. He waited with delicious expectation for the same electric touch on the other side when she moved round him, while his eyes were closed and his mind drifted. He hardly wanted her to stop. The hairdressers were obviously trained to make the male customers feel good so they would make regular returns for more grooming; a brilliant ploy, because Jarvis felt decidedly disappointed when she had finished.

He opened his eyes sharply, blinking. She had not noticed anything. He tried to read her name badge pinned to her T-shirt. She wore no ring on her left hand. He found the girl's shyness both innocent and suggestive. He paid his twelve pounds at the end and left, thoughtfully, without further words.

Despite the grey overcast day, he felt unaccountably buoyant. He decided to go for a long walk to give himself more thinking time, and headed south via the Angel and City Road towards the Barbican and then to the river.

In heavy leather coat and walking boots, he prowled the wet streets of the city, skirting along the north embankment from Blackfriars to Westminster and returning via the Strand. At Charing Cross Station he found a phone in the ticket hall and called Ainsley's mobile. They agreed to meet the next day to see if they could reach an agreement over Jarvis's major decision, and then they could talk business.

It was not raining for once, and Jarvis, arriving early in Bethnal Green, chose to sit on a park bench under bare plane trees with a bottle of water and an apple, watching the world go by for ten minutes. Outside The Misty Moon pub along the road, smokers collected in groups on the pavement, quietly stamping their feet. Inside the gloomy interior, there was little chatter among the few old men scattered around on leather benches and wooden chairs, concentrating on their pints. It was a stale-smelling place, not particularly welcoming, but it had an empty recess far at the back, and Jarvis moved there with his lager, hoping to warm his chilly feet in front of the feeble open fire. A couple of young men were playing darts nearby. Going over his early plans, layering on more detail with each run-through, Jarvis sat lost in thought when, soon after one o'clock, Ainsley Chigwell appeared round the end of the bar with his own pint jug in hand. Jarvis looked up with a slight nod of recognition.

Ainsley was wrapped in a thick coat and scarf and looked more confident than when Jarvis had first seen him. He dropped leather gloves and a newspaper onto Jarvis's table and flung his coat over a chair. In a dark cardigan and jeans, he sat carefully with his back to the rest of the room and launched jovially into business.

'OK, are we up for this, or are we having second thoughts?'

The two men were roughly the same age but Ainsley looked weedy by comparison, not as broad or heavy. With a clean-shaven face, quick flitting eyes and small features, and that habit of flicking his long fringe aside after he had spoken, Ainsley was naturally fidgety, never at rest.

'I have made my decision,' Jarvis said without expression. He leant forward, intently watching Ainsley's face, wondering what his reaction might be, and observed the flickering of his upper eyelids. 'I will do it. I will go ahead with it.' Jarvis sounded deadpan. *So there, you didn't think I would, did you?*

'Cool. Good.' Ainsley smiled and fixed Jarvis's stare with his own confident eyes for a moment. 'I'll talk to Dad later,' and he flicked his fringe aside. He reached his hand out to seal the deal, and Jarvis gripped it quickly. Ainsley had a briefcase with him that he had dropped on the floor between his feet, from which he pulled out some papers covered with his written notes in a thin neat hand. 'So,' he said in a serious tone, 'what do you think you might need? Apart from the first down payment.' He smiled ironically.

Jarvis leant forward again, ducking his head down within Ainsley's shadow so that no one who could lip-read what he was saying from a distance. 'I reckon I need a new identity. A new name and a false passport. And a new bank account.'

'No problem, we'll use one of our fictitious addresses; any mail sent to you can be picked up there. When you apply for a current account, you will need regular payments in, wages, earnings, then they'll issue you a credit card. We can transfer monies into it once the job is complete – perhaps a few payments over some months would be better than one big one. Get an internet bank, then we can make the payments straight in.' Ainsley scribbled on his pad and was thinking as he went along. 'You'll need a utility bill with your new name and address on. That can be done – should be no problem.' He flicked his hair away again and reached for his glass for a drink to fill in the pause, and now looked up at his companion, waiting for him to list further requirements.

'I don't want to leave a trail with the mobiles, Ainsley.'

'What you need to do is Pay As You Go, no contracts, no registration, buy your sim cards in the small corner shops, change them regularly – then we'll be fine, no trace. Remember to create a new PIN if you use voicemail – don't leave it as the default, which is 1234 and easily hacked into.' Ainsley was confident in his advice. Jarvis paid attention, nodding his understanding.

'The weapon I want is highly specific,' Jarvis continued. 'A British Army-issue sniper's rifle.'

'OK, cool, I'll get onto that. What are we talking about exactly? Does it have a descriptor, a code number?' Ainsley was pleased with himself – he seemed to be speaking the right language to gain Jarvis's trust. 'Can you write it down?' And he passed Jarvis his notepad and a biro.

'You write, Ainsley. Listen carefully. L115A3. Got it? With a Schmidt & Bender II night-sight telescope.'

Ainsley wrote with studied carefulness the exact letters and numbers and names that Jarvis dictated, and then read them back quietly to him to check that he had them exactly right.

'Correct,' agreed Jarvis and downed the rest of his beer.

'L115? This a rifle?'

'The best. Must be the exact one.' And then, 'I will need a lock-up.'

'Right. For a car, you mean?' Ainsley flicked his hair from his forehead.

'No, doesn't have to be, not as big as that, small, for storage, motorbike perhaps. I'll need to keep things there, clean, dry, with electricity, must be completely safe, lockable. Near here, not too far.'

'OK, done. Anything else? Enough to be getting on with, eh? I'll need two passport photos.' Ainsley slipped a brown envelope across the table. 'When you've got them, you can put them in this and give it to George over there. He looks after things for us sometimes.' Ainsley indicated a balding middle-aged man with excessive paunch and sideburns, pulling pints behind the bar. 'Contact me in two weeks.'

'I want more.' Jarvis, unblinking, looked straight into Ainsley's brown eyes. 'Tell your father the amount is not enough for what he wants. It needs to be doubled.'

And with that, Jarvis slipped the envelope carefully between the pages of the newspaper. With his coat still on, he stood up, the paper under his arm and his hands casually stuffed in the coat pockets. Without another word, he sloped off, leaving Ainsley alone, nursing the remains of his pint.

5

Jarvis knew how important it was for his mother to have her cherished family together for her sixtieth-birthday Sunday lunch. Her two boys and their families were everything to her. It had been three boys, but six years ago she had lost Edward, killed fighting for his country, although she would feel his presence just as much as if he was still there for all that. She would put in much effort for the occasion and it was only fair that her family responded in kind. Jarvis had not seen her since Christmas and was feeling suitably guilty. He had her present wrapped and ready in the hall. He did not need Pamela lecturing to him about how to behave.

Jarvis had started to let his beard grow and was sure to attract adverse comments. He was hardly in the mood to face a whole load of family and elderly relatives chit-chatting aimlessly about nothing in particular, or worse, about Pamela's stunning career prospects. His every waking moment was occupied with developing the details of the difficult challenges that lay ahead for him. His thought processes, that Pamela would have described as simple, were increasingly hooked on the fundamentals of his project, as he called it, and his motivation was hardening by the day.

Jonathan would be there with Brenda. At one time Jarvis had suspected his brother of taking liberties with Pamela when he had prolonged periods of duty away with the Army. Remembering Sidney Price's words, he knew not to share anything with anyone, certainly not Jonathan. Sid obviously did not trust Jonathan any more than Jarvis did. The two had history – Jarvis was aware of that, although he was uncertain about the details.

Jarvis had ironed a clean white shirt the previous night, was wearing a new pair of ankle boots and a dark jacket, and was ready to set off long before Pamela was ready. He paced the floor downstairs and had become irritated with her even before the journey began. When she finally descended the stairs, elegant in a two-tone purple knit dress, low-cut and tight, wearing high wedges and excessive make-up, expecting admiration, she and Jarvis simply exchanged ironic looks.

Icy conditions and unexpected traffic made the drive longer than anticipated. Pamela argued about the best route to take: she wanted to go round by the Blackwall Tunnel, he said straight south through the city over Tower Bridge would be best. She wanted to take her new car with its navigation system that she knew they would need, given Jarvis's previous record of getting lost driving through South London trying to find his mother's place. Jarvis told her to stop showing off.

Gwendolyn lived off Belmont Hill in Lewisham, in a respectable detached house that was only able to accommodate twenty or more guests due to the fact that her dearly departed with some foresight had invested in a glass conservatory at the back. That it was difficult to heat properly in winter and often leaked after a downpour did not detract from Gwendolyn's enjoyment of the space, with its parquet flooring and French windows out onto the patio and small garden beyond. From spring onwards the place was bursting with decorative pots of flowers, and she would likely spend afternoons dozing in a recliner, surrounded by colour and smells of geranium, lost in memories of her life with Derek before 'his attack'.

They parked the Nissan Juke in a distant side street, finding no spaces nearby, and the house seemed already crowded by the time they hurried through the front door to get warm, bumping into Jonathan with his two children in the hall.

'Hello, bruv, Pamela.' Loud and confident as always, Jonathan grappled with Pamela, cheek touching each cheek, hands holding her by the arms through her thin imitation fur coat. 'Glad we're not the last. Brenda's upstairs with Mother, powdering noses or something.'

He shook Jarvis's cold hand, clutched a forearm and hugged him like he had not seen him in years. 'Forgotten to shave, Jar?' Jarvis frowned in annoyance. They dumped their coats and Pamela bent down to give some attention and hugs to Jonathan's little ones, while Jonathan gave some attention to her not-so-little ones.

'My my, look at the pair of you – aren't we growing big, Amelia? You're nearly up to my waist. And look at little Barney.'

'Just look at the pair of you,' Jonathan said straight-faced, ogling unashamedly down the front of her dress. Jarvis was not amused and pulled his brother away. In the sitting room over-looking the winter garden through floor-to-ceiling windows, they started to mingle with the other guests. Jarvis was hoping for a quiet word, but Jonathan was already pitching in. 'Business is really looking up, bruv. I need you to join us full time, mate. Talk to you later.'

They became absorbed into the mêlée of subdued chatter and tinkling of glasses, the calls of welcome from relatives and neigh-bours who had not seen the brothers since, oh, since the last war, and how they both had 'grown into such fine young men'.

In the middle of the enlarged room, with the sliding doors between the lounge and conservatory folded right back, was a dining table groaning under generous heaps of food for everyone to serve themselves. Gwendolyn's brother Duncan had been over earlier in the day to help with the arrangements. Tom and Sylvia from next door pumped Jonathan's and Jarvis's hands like old friends. An avuncular Uncle Duncan with his short back and sides had taken centre stage, with his commanding sergeant-major voice.

'Million-pound bonuses for City bankers?' he was asking, trying to engage Jonathan in conversation. A likeable bloke, never married and quite capable of looking after himself, Duncan always found something to complain about and was capable of being quite witty at times. 'I'm confused by your old Labour Party. You remember them saying they were "intensely relaxed about people becoming filthy rich", whenever it was?' He was swigging at a pint of beer and warming his backside on an extra radiator brought in during the cold snap.

'Hah, *my* Labour Party, excuse me! Who voted for Gordon Brown last time?' retorted Jonathan, prodding Duncan gently about the shoulder.

'Well, the bankers are now hated for taking Peter Mandelson rather too literally, stealing our millions,' Duncan continued, ignoring Jonathan's riposte, 'whereas at one time the Labour leadership were holding their hands and throwing them honours and gongs and seats in the House of Lords willy-nilly.'

'Actually, nobody has ever voted for Gordon Brown,' muttered Jarvis, smiling and nodding at some people he did not recognise while fixing a drink for Pamela.

'Banker bashing is now official Labour Party policy,' cut in Uncle Ian, Gwen's brother-in-law, who was standing beside Duncan in a similarly truculent style, 'now that the voting public has realised who the villains are. While that bugger Gerry Morley sets a fine example of sacrifice in these austere times, with his mansions and company directorships and all that peace envoy stuff in the Middle East. Much good that will do him. It was Gerald Morley who took us to war in Iraq in the first place, don't forget, with no idea how to get us out.'

Jarvis picked up snippets of conversation, while his mind endlessly pored over his own thoughts. Pamela joined them, boldly commenting on the need for stripping company bosses of their bonuses and their knighthoods and making them work at the ground-floor level again to remind them what life was like for the workers. *While you plot your next move into the celebrity world,* Jarvis was thinking, *all superficial glitter and meaningless overspending; and you have sympathy with the overworked underpaid working class, you little hypocrite!*

'I'm seriously thinking of giving something more to charity, maybe Oxfam or one of those local shops.' Pamela popped an oversized sausage roll into her mouth and tiny flakes of pastry stuck to her glossy lips. 'At this time, we have to do our bit.' She munched quickly while her tongue kept flicking out to wipe her lips clean along the edges. She sneered and half closed her eyes, ungraciously snatching the napkin that Jarvis held up for her.

Jarvis moved away. Pamela pontificating was painful to his ears and he wandered off into the kitchen, where he found Stella alone, pale and quiet. After Edward was killed, Jarvis had come home to console his mother, but soon returned to duties after the funeral. At the time, he had hardly spoken to Stella, who constantly crumpled into tears and had not held up at all well. He did not really know her, she was simply his brother's wife. He disliked any show of emotion and wanted to return to his beloved routine, where he did not have to think about home life. On leaving the Army, safely returning to the civilian world and the new London home that Pamela had created for them, he had visited Stella at her Romford flat, where she lived alone in cold gloom, working for a local insurance company. While telling her how Ed had died, Jarvis had held her small body close to him, protectively. She had sobbed silently into his shirt for an hour and implored him to stay. They spoke in hushed tones and lay still together for some hours on a settee, Stella's petite form enveloped by his comforting bulk. At around midnight, their grief dissipated, he left, wishing her some light to brighten her life. Perhaps she was still waiting.

He had only seen Stella a couple of times since, a Christmas get-together and a family do, and had not thought about her at all. She and Ed had had no children and she still lived alone. So now he smiled shyly across to her, with a half greeting and little eye contact. She was looking sheepish, in a cream and green pastel outfit that suited her understated character; she gave him a fleeting smile, quickly looking away.

Brenda and Gwendolyn came into the kitchen together, with broad smiles and the children. Gwendolyn hugged and kissed everyone, said how wonderful they all looked and thanked them all for coming.

'Happy sixtieth, Mother,' Jarvis said with a bit more effusiveness.

'What's this, growing your whiskers?' she asked. She kissed Jarvis full on his lips and held him by his prickly cheeks, which especially irritated him in front of the others. Then she sat at a table, hugging her grandchildren. Brenda was asking Stella about some event they were planning to go to together and Pamela came in to join them. Jarvis again slipped out of the way of the womenfolk, and joined Jonathan in the hall.

'Listen, Jar. We've been approached by the big boys, GS Security, to work with them at Stratford Park for the Olympics. I'm gonna need some more admin help, some organisation. We will be hiring, I don't know how many at the moment, but it will be hundreds, so there is all the advertising, appointing, training; it will be massive. The contract's worth several million pounds, and we should be getting a slice of that. So there is plenty of money in this, mate. Great opportunity for the firm.' Jonathan was on to his second beer and looked flushed. 'I'm organising a workshop on a Friday morning in about three weeks, after my holiday, with a business management consultant talking to us about our future development and things. I want you there, brother, I've got great ideas for you.' *All these great opportunities I keep hearing about, and everybody wanting me,* Jarvis was thinking, with a wry smile.

Later on, as more food and alcohol was consumed by an increasingly merry crowd, Jarvis was trapped in a corner by Uncle Ian, who looked so like Jarvis's father, it was uncanny. Jarvis wanted to hug him for a moment, even though it was more than ten years since he had last seen his father. 'You look so like your daddy,' Uncle Ian was saying, having to look up at him from his five foot four, 'tall and straight backed. Eh, Gwen, fine lad, your Jarvis.' But Jarvis had slipped away, feeling uncomfortable.

Back in the conservatory, where the heaps of sausage rolls and vols-au-vent were subsiding at last, and where collections of empty beer cans and wine and champagne bottles had gathered on the floor under the table, a tipsy Duncan was still loudly chatting to anyone who happened to be nearby. 'Did I hear the word money?' he asked mischievously, with a twinkle in his glazed eyes. 'Are you boys plotting something brotherly and exciting – legal I hope?' Duncan gripped yet another can of lager in one hand while a sausage roll in the other hand was about to be stuffed down his gaping mouth.

Jonathan said 'It's a fucking big heist, Uncle Dunc, and it will make us all famous millionaires!' And everyone around laughed loudly as Duncan's laden hand stopped immediately on its journey, with his eyes and mouth wide open. He had to sit down suddenly on a chair, coughing.

Puddings were brought in on trays and more champagne corks popped. Everyone seemed merry and relaxed among the family warmth and the noise level of conversations had reached a high point. Pamela was smoking; she was being asked repeatedly about her job and children, and having to fend off the questions with some deft talk and the appearance of easy affability, but underneath, with growing irritation.

DANIEL PASCOE

At one point Jarvis caught Jonathan and Pamela in close conversation, she leaning into him holding his wrist at the foot of the stairs across the hall, their backs towards Jarvis. 'Forget it, Jon. That was ages ago, leave it alone,' he was sure he heard her say. They parted awkwardly on seeing Jarvis, Jonathan skipping upstairs to the bathroom and Pamela turning on her heel, heading past Jarvis with an overdone smile. Back among the main guests eating jelly and chocolate cake she was soon chatting about the wonderful world of marketing and the part she played, rattling off her answers automatically for all to hear, about knobbing with Lord this and Sir that, and rubbing shoulders with all those important names in Westminster. She included her last visit to Number 10 in the conversation and announced how she expected to be at both the opening and the closing ceremonies of the Olympic Games at Stratford Park that summer. There was a pink flush to her neck and chest.

'Oh, how exciting for you, my dear,' piped up Gwendolyn, with her hands in a clapping motion in front of her face, her eyes actually sparkling, ever the supporter. Jonathan made a short speech, toasting his mother, wishing her many more years, and everyone joined in with a cheer. Presents were given with much clapping and they all soon got back to drinking and smoking. Jarvis stuck to bottled water.

Helping himself to more sticky toffee on a long spoon, Tom from the local Bowls Club was sounding angry as he spoke with a full mouth. 'You know this man Zuckerberg is due to make himself twenty-three billion dollars from Facebook when it goes public later this year? I mean, that's obscene, isn't it?' He slurped some more beer down as a chaser. 'What's more, because they are paid in shares and dividends, they don't have to pay any corporation tax for ten years or more.'

'And meanwhile it's us,' Brenda chipped in, 'who do all the

work, tapping in all the details of our lives and our little secrets captured in jolly spontaneous pictures. But it's not us that will see any of this money.' She was comforting her sleepy children on the nearest couch.

'We are all in this together, as they say in the coalition,' Uncle Duncan pontificated again, ever quick with a quip. Not for the first time, Jarvis was wondering how much Pamela must be making on the Olympics project; she was probably due one of those fat bonuses that she claimed to be so set against.

'So what's it all about, Pam, can you explain that to me?' pleaded Ian, taking his turn at staring wistfully upon her flushed bosom.

'Well, they are just getting their cash out as fast as they can, before it all disappears. There is no social conscience among the social networkers, it's all about money.' She smiled broadly, pleased with herself for showing off her familiarity with these modern times.

'Yes, but twenty-three billion dollars . . . that's obscene,' repeated Tom from the other side of the room.

'It's only on paper, not actual cash,' was Jarvis's smart contribution, even if nobody was listening. 'Anyway, it will all turn pear-shaped; Facebook won't survive in the long term.'

'You think? When they own the wedding photographs of a seventh of the world's population?' That was Brenda again. 'That's powerful. They know everything about all of us – where we go, what we eat, who we sleep with, what we like, what we don't like – and they're gonna use clever advertising to squeeze even more money out of us.'

At the end of the afternoon, Pamela drove home with Jarvis in silence. Somewhere across the Thames, Jarvis heard the message ping on his mobile in his top pocket: 'Mr C agrees price demand.

Go ahead. AC.' Despite the warming sense of elation that flooded through his body, Jarvis kept his face expressionless and his eyes indifferent, completely ignoring his wife's enquiring sideways look.

6

Jarvis had the makings of a mission in his head and was up early. Unusually warm spring sunshine had been caressing the wet streets of London. Colour was returning to the city at last after an interminable winter that had been so tediously damp and dreary that even the hardiest had felt peeved and glum. But now, with so much cherry blossom covering the pavements like snowflakes, everybody felt better. Reticent people were out and about, more optimistic, less preoccupied, happy to smile and chat and call out to each other in the market.

Jarvis stopped by a stall in Church Street for an apple and then walked down to Old Street Roundabout. He had taken some time off work with Danny and the forest gang. Planning a gym session later in the afternoon, he had arranged to meet up with a flame from his Colchester training days, now in hotel management in Covent Garden, a woman a touch older than him, loyal and discreet, with no hang-ups, who invariably spoke her mind. They would have a few drinks, a bite to eat and a chat, but best of all Suzanna might be able to answer some of his quandaries, about finding a safe house, using a bolt hole, lying low. Pamela was far from his thoughts.

For now, he was on his way to SecureLife headquarters in Pitfield Street for a ten-thirty start. Jonathan had reminded him earlier in the week and a strongly worded note had arrived in the post that morning, from Jonathan Collingwood MD, on company headed paper, that made him chuckle. It was written as a rallying cry to meet the challenges ahead in the changing world of security.

On giving up his army career, Jonathan formed SecureLife using his pension and everything else he had, with some help from friends and family, including Gwendolyn. He threw himself fully into the new business, expanding in under five years from a handful of ex-servicemen fitting domestic alarms to installing complete security solutions and offering surveillance and protection, with over three hundred and fifty people in the company. SecureLife was Jonathan's pride and joy, and all much more above board and respectable than once thought. Ironically, as some of the bigger companies were looking at SecureLife, they needed their own protection from the security community.

The offices were a cramped collection of stuffy top-floor rooms in an old building that used to be a warehouse, where a few clerical people sweated through summer and shivered through winter. Jonathan had plans for a move to bigger premises in a new block being constructed nearer the roundabout, but that was nine months away. On the first floor was a conference room hired for the morning.

Jarvis took the stairs. There were already several men in casual dress milling around the room taking the coffee and biscuits on offer. The blinds were drawn and the room darkened, a screen pulled down from the ceiling at one end and chairs laid out in several rows.

Jonathan Collingwood, tanned from his ski break, suave and savvy in a shiny Italian suit, bounded in from another side door, with a striking lady in red close behind him. Solidly built was Jonathan, ex-rugby player, with thick neck and wide shoulders, just under six feet tall, his strong frame looking to burst out of his shirt. He oozed the two commodities essential to his business – brawn and balls. In a loud voice he thanked everyone for attending on time. He was confident that they were all going to have a fruitful session, listening to an industry expert, a lady who worked for an agency close to the government, with experience and know-how. *And balls to boot*, thought Jarvis, looking at the perfectly presented beauty standing next to him.

'These are very exciting times,' enthused Jonathan, 'as Georgina Stutterfeld will explain in a minute. So we need to settle down, get ourselves a coffee or whatever, and be prepared to listen and to rise to the challenge.' Jonathan was obviously prepared to rise to the challenge of Ms Stutterfeld. And then he noticed Jarvis at the back and bowled over to him, with much hand shaking and shoulder slapping.

'Bruv, hello, well done for making it!'

'Wouldn't want to miss this, especially with Georgina – you're kidding, right?'

Jonathan gave him a wink. 'Gorgeous, isn't she?' he murmured, and they both stared disbelievingly at the curvaceous woman in front of them setting up her presentation at the projector stand nearby. Auburn-haired, in a sharp business two-piece the colour of water melon, Ms Stutterfeld was preparing her session from the back of the room using an Apple tablet.

Jarvis took his place at the back where he could watch the presentation and the presenter at the same time. He was hoping to use the time to think over the last few weeks, the meetings with Sidney Price and Arthur Chigwell and the propositions that would either make him a small fortune or result in imprisonment and humiliation. But the lovely Ms Stutterfeld was standing only a few strides away, in profile, calling the room to order in a schoolmistress style with definite Scandinavian overtones, and he was hooked. All other thoughts were erased from his mind as erotic cartoon images leapt across his imagination from goodness knows where, of a buxom teacher with lolloping boobs whipping with a cane a line of boys' bare bottoms bent over school chairs.

Gorgeous Georgina, the only woman in the room, introduced herself as a management consultant, which made Jarvis blink and shake his mind back to the present. Georgina was definitely all woman, and from the moment she started speaking, Jarvis fell in love with her. She had an intoxicating voice. Her glossy lips colour-matched her outfit. The short jacket was open at the front, where a full bosom cleaved a lime green blouse. Her skirt gently rode the hump of her belly and stretched taut across an expansive and rounded backside. *Full house: bum, tum, tits.* With narrow ankles and strong calves, she pivoted on five-inch heels. She looked expensive and about thirty. She moved with assurance and spoke with authority. Olympics security was her number-one agenda item, apparently. Distracted from the beginning, Jarvis struggled to keep his mind on the job or on anything else but Georgina for all of the twenty minutes of her talk. The heels were lime green too, suede.

Ms Stutterfeld told the room packed with thirty to forty testosterone-imbued thirty-to-forty-year-olds that the London Olympics 2012 would be the most security-conscious public event ever. Already more than a hundred people had been arrested for security reasons in relation to the coming Games, she claimed, to some sniggers around the room. Jarvis barely heard the sales pitch about Jonathan's company, about its various sectors and operations, its supply workflow, its balance-sheet statistics and future trajectories. He looked at a summary slide about where the company saw itself at present and the slide about where Ms Stutterfeld expected the company would be in five and ten years' time, but failed to grasp how the one moved to the other.

Thoughts were whirling inside Jarvis's normally tidy mind, tripping over each other in a chaotic muddle. Identity change, safe houses, the uncertainties of his task; support money, weapons, sniper rifles, escape routes, survival prospects. His priorities were finding somewhere safe to hide and someone to hide with. He desperately needed someone to look out for him, someone for his new persona who was not involved with his real life, past or present.

But he was mesmerised by GG, her light movements, her hand signals, and by the way her buttocks tensed and relaxed in rhythm as she shifted her weight from one side to the other, while the free leg rocked on the point of its stiletto before swinging inwards and upwards behind the other ankle, the supporting leg bending at the knee with the artistry of a ballerina. He wondered whether she was part of Sweden's Olympic judo team, practising her pull-throw foot sweep or some other clever manoeuvre. Undressing her deliciously in his mind, he tossed her blouse across the room, tugging at her tight skirt, clawing at thin elastic, ripping her panties off her ankles.

'But the most exciting immediate development,' Georgina concluded with a lick of her pouting lips, 'is the need for extra security, and lots of it, at the Olympic events this coming summer in London. There will be over two hundred and fifty thousand people each day coming and going into the main park. The eyes of the world will be watching, with billions of viewers worldwide expected. So it's a potential logistical nightmare for the organisers, but that means masses of opportunities for a company like this to latch on to some well-paid work. The government has made big provisions for extra security officers – over twenty thousand of them – so SecureLife needs to get out there and grab a piece of it.'

Ms Stutterfeld smiled and paused. 'Any questions at this point?'

Jarvis just wanted to get out there and grab a piece of her.

The rest of the session was questions and answers, with time to refresh coffee cups, before Georgina went on to enumerate the opportunities for SecureLife, and the investment it needed to attract to ensure success. It was all about expansion and moving into the right territories, like internet security, surveillance, intelligence gathering – even counter-terrorism was now a wide-open field. All of this was far more lucrative than the heavy man-intensity of old; it was what the modern world was demanding and SecureLife needed to be in the right place to offer it. Further development meant taking on extra staff, despite the current talk of recession and gloom around the country.

Jarvis's attention had strayed again and he missed the details of setting up groups and coming up with a forward plan. Flip charts and laptops appeared, tables were moved about and everybody settled into smaller huddled groups to find the answers Georgina was looking for. By this time Jarvis had predictably concluded – as all the other alert males in the room would also have done by now – that Gorgeous Georgina would be a fantastic lay, but for somebody else. Underneath her power-dressed exterior, Ms Stutterfeld had a stunning figure, obviously, and Jarvis imagined that Jonathan, with his wandering hands all over her, had probably already had a taste of it. But he shook his mind awake at the finish, and almost spoke aloud what he was thinking: *she is not for me.* The complications would be too massive, the consequences unthinkable. He sensed that she was a man-eater of the first order. Unfortunately.

Jarvis had just experienced the shortest love affair of his life.

'I want you involved here, Jar. You heard the lady, so many opportunities. For all of us. We should be able to coin it with this lot. We must bid for all the security outsourcing that's planned at the Olympics; it will be massive. Don't you worry, I need you to be involved. Right?'

Jonathan thanked everybody and continued talking enthusiastically, with saliva bubbling at the corners of his mouth. His secretary would be collecting all the ideas together, and once he had worked on it with his finance man and other senior team members over the next week, there would be some written statements and plans for the teams to study. Jarvis left in a confused state of mind, disappointed that he had apparently not found the solutions to his immediate worries, and in desperate need of a woman.

One cold evening a few days later, Pamela was home on her own watching Sky News, including a phone-hacking story and the latest ups and downs at *News of the World*. On hearing the front door close, she dimmed the sound and tentatively called out, 'Jarvis, that you?'

Jarvis had walked up from Liverpool Street station and was in need of a rest. He inwardly groaned at the sound of her plaintive voice. *Who the hell do you think it is?* Finding no empty hooks in the hall, he dropped his rucksack on the floor and slung his leather coat over the banisters. He pulled his tight boots off and padded in his socks into the sitting room.

Pamela had been drinking alone for a while. She was reclining on her leather lounger, in skinny jeans and bare feet, magazines and papers strewn around her, wine glass, coffee cup and full ashtray within reach. The smell of cigarettes hung in the air. A gas fire was on and the room felt cosy. Harsh light from a table lamp slapped shadow lines uncharitably across her face. Jarvis remained cautious, determined to keep his comments neutral and not to end up in an argument.

'So where have you been these last few days? I don't know when was the last time I saw you, really.' She looked weary but the slight edge in her voice warned that she was ready for a fight.

Jarvis ignored her question. 'Do you want another drink, Pam?' He decided to placate her and moved to get himself a glass of water, which he took down in one long gulp. He poured her a white wine, and took the glass to her side.

'Really, now there's a nice thing. So, where *have* you been? You're not answering me.' Again there was an edge in the question and the poise of her body showed her to be wound up and waiting for release.

Jarvis dropped onto another sofa. 'Working – there has been a lot on.' Pamela was still looking at him for an explanation. 'Beacon Forest, I told you about it. Double time over weekends, and the boss wanted a push on to get the job moving; so we were all there, ten, twelve of us. We're working on the new road layout, but there's masses more clearing to do. And logging. The weather was foul and it was cold.' He would have rattled on about nothing in particular to distract Pamela but she quickly interrupted him.

'Yes, but what about some time off? Who else is mad enough to do this? You stayed away for four days non-stop, including Sunday night – how come? I don't believe it.'

Jarvis wandered back to the kitchen to look for some food. 'I left a message for you. Look, we work right through the daylight hours,' he called through the open door, 'and sleep in the caravans so we can start early – it's too far to be trooping back and forth from town every day. Just like in the past.' Jarvis found ham and cheese in the fridge, together with a sliced loaf, and put together a quick sandwich. He gulped down more water.

Pamela lit another cigarette and puffed heavily, blowing the smoke up towards the ceiling. 'And what do you do for entertainment, really, while you are down there?' she pondered, as if to herself, when he wandered back in the room. 'You must have slept with someone Sunday night, eh, Jarvis? You wouldn't stay on your own!'

'Pam, don't be ridiculous, these are twelve big sweaty men with bad breath and smelly armpits. There's nobody else to sleep with there, I can assure you. Nobody has showers in these temperatures. We play cards, there's a TV; last night we watched an old cowboy film, *How the West Was Won*. There's a pub a mile down the road, some of the guys go there, they do meals.'

'You're crazy. You have no break for four days, then straight back into the security job.'

'The money's good.'

'Yes, and do I ever see any of it?' What do you do with it?' Pamela seemed destined to work herself up into a tizzy fit, she could not seem to stop herself.

'Look after it. Like you do with your money. I pay my allowance. Do I ever ask to see what you're making? No, I leave you to get on with it. I'm not interfering.'

Pamela drank some wine and puffed more urgently on her ciga-rette. Her face was rounded and pale, for once her hair hung limp. The remains of bright red rouge on her lips and dark lines under her eyes added to her look of general disappointment. The slackness of her mouth gave her a guilty look too – maybe that was it, she was trying to focus on him when really she was the one who had been naughty.

Pamela reached disinterestedly for her magazines, flicking the pages over. Lonely and in need of distraction, she had looked for Antonio earlier in the day, hoping to spend some time with him, but had been fobbed off with excuses, and she felt hurt, that he was playing hard to get. Last week he had pressed her about her relationship with Jarvis, whom he had never met. And now she was feeling vulnerable, wanting Antonio to be closer and more under-standing, yet frightened that she may lose Jarvis if she were careless.

Jarvis continued, 'Look, I enjoy it, there's peace there, and then working with the lads, it's a tough job, it's good. And it keeps me in good shape; I can drink some beers and not put on any weight. Danny got me into it last summer and it suits me.'

'So, how is Danny? I've not seen him for ages,' she said, remem-bering the distant time when the lads were fun, spending lazy weekends outside in the country, mixing with friends; long-ago days, she lamented.

'He's fine. He's the leader of the gang, and deals with Lord Snooty, so he makes the deals and works out the schedules. He gets paid more than us, but he's at it seven days a week. I couldn't do that. He's a good bloke though. He left his wife just after Christmas, she's up in Yorkshire somewhere. He sleeps at the pub, with one of the girls at the bar – nice girl, Betty. Ten years younger than him. Her husband was a bit pissed off. But Danny's a big bloke and this fellow just accepted it and moved out.' Jarvis chuckled and finished his water and sandwich.

With nowhere else to go, the conversation petered out. Other thoughts crowded her mind but Pamela remained quiet. She leaned her aching head on the back cushions and closed her eyes. The television quietly dribbled on. Jarvis thought she might be dozing and was about to switch it off. 'Is that why he's a good bloke, because he left his wife at Christmas?' she taunted quietly, still with her eyes closed.

Jarvis did not rise to the bait. He preferred her to suspect him of having a bit on the side rather than to have any inkling of what it was that was occupying his mind. 'I need some sleep, I'm going up.'

'And who are you keeping in good shape for, really, Jarvis? That's what I would like to know.' Although actually she did not want to know. 'Not me, I know.' She stubbed out yet another cigarette into the already full ashtray, just before it started to burn her fingertips. If Pamela had any inkling of the killing plot or of its promised financial reward that now filled Jarvis's every waking moment, she might have shown a keener interest in her husband's activities.

Pamela wanted to speak of her frustration with their relationship and her despair at his attitude. She was sick of seeing the shallow picture he was painting of himself, the special star with the beautiful looks. He should be true to himself and not play-act like some caricature. She wanted to say all sorts of things, but his immobile expression and her inability to articulate without getting angry made her dry up and all she could manage was, 'I miss you, Jarvis,' unconvincingly. Jarvis gave her a sceptical look and muttered, 'Like I said, I'm going up to bed.'

He walked past her and out of the room casually. The fact that he had not spent Sunday night down in Kent on site at the forest, but had actually been with busty Penny up West showed in his demeanour not at all. He had showered well at her place afterwards, so there was no danger of any lingering body smell or perfume that might give him away. He took care that no lipstick or make-up had ended up on his clothes and he had checked in the full-length mirror upstairs that he had no fingernail scratches down his back. Penny tended to scream and screw her face up and claw with her fingers during moments of ecstasy, but they never lasted more than a few seconds before she flopped back in release with gasps of 'Oh God, that was wonderful, you brute, hold me, hold me!'

Jarvis felt stiff across his shoulders, and his legs were aching from his four-mile walk as he took the stairs two at a time. Dropping all his clothes behind the bathroom door, now locked, he stepped into the shower, washing away the grime and smells of another workday, knowing that in a little while they would both come together in bed, as so often they did after a heated exchange.

The bedroom lights were dim and Jarvis dozed against his pillows. Pamela crept her way around the bed to perch at her dressing table, her fragrant slipstream alerting his senses. His sharp hearing picked up all the tiny sounds of her close proximity, as she undressed deliberately, toying with his instinctive arousal. There was her musky breath with seductive sigh, delicate patter of bunched necklace on glass surface, wool peeled over shoulders, hair emitting electric crackles, arms strained and elastic stretched and unhooked with flip and click, thin cotton dropped into side drawer closed with a thud, denim cased over wriggling hips, tugged free of rounded rump with scrape and silky sashay, crumpled onto spongy pile and bare feet padding softly. To the sensitive ear, a star-turn striptease in harmony from a consummate artist.

Pamela's shadow cast across Jarvis's face as she drifted past him towards the bathroom. He glimpsed her tantalising flesh and pillow-white globular bottom within easy reach. She stole a critical look at her full-length mirror reflection, a pleasing boys' magazine impression of womanhood, soft and fulsome. Smacking her tummy with the flat of her hand, resigned to the way she was, she felt her skin tingle with anticipation. While she might be thinking of how much she wanted to find a man who would pay her more attention, she still craved Jarvis's physical being and domination.

Washed, sleekly oiled and trimmed, she glided naked to his side, guided by a narrow streak of light from the bathroom, which betrayed his dozing form, bare arm behind his head, armpit tuft bristling. She stooped to tickle her tresses lightly across his chest, stroking back and forth, while peeling the sheet away, relishing sight of his lean body. With her tongue, she trickled a wet trail along the dark line of hair that ran from the lower dip of his navel to feed like a tributary into the darker curly delta below. He tensed his abdomen and puffed out his chest.

His arousal was something beautiful, a rapid transformation from shapeless soft toy to garnished ornament. Hovering over his crotch, she teased and coaxed his newfound abundance to jump like a performing circus dog. With quickening breath, he sank his firm grip into her haunches, playfully squeezing and slapping her buttocks. Long fingers probed deeply, stroking her silky purse responding with warmed juices that seeped through her under-growth. He sat up, swinging his legs round to hang over the edge of the bed and Pamela, sinking to her knees between them, her breasts bouncing sideways against each other like an executive toy, descended on him with relish, her wet mouth working him expertly towards a state of ecstasy.

Her coffee eyes gazed upwardly on his; I'm totally yours, they said. She released him and slowly rose to present herself before him, her body his to command. He pressed a warmed cheek against her belly and licked the skin that tasted of mandarin. Exploring her from neck to groin with his eager fingertips, he followed all the natural and familiar dips and mounds of her rounded form. Using a moistened thumb, he stimulated her with small circular move-ments. Arms uplifted, she dragged her hair back with both hands and started to shake for a while, before sinking and crawling to the middle of the bed. He gripped her hips from behind and corked her with his circus dog without resistance. He was in control, pounding against her buttocks with loud slapping sounds: strong, capable, working alone in the silent woodlands, cutting effortlessly through flesh, bark, pulp and bone, chopping, chopping repeatedly. They bounced and gyrated in unison, bringing their passions to the boil.

Released by a sudden explosion, he gave off a dull diminishing scream and his piercing of her soon quelled. He fell away and sprawled across the bed, panting. Mildly disappointed but at the same time relieved that it was over, Pamela sank back, just short of full release, but with time to turn and lick him clean. Gradually his breathing subsided and, coiling away from her, he was soon asleep.

Pamela assumed an achingly still position, lying straight, holding herself tense for a while, afraid to move too soon. Her passions subsided, her juices dried, she rubbed the blotchy patches around her bottom. As the night air cooled, she pulled the sheet up to cover her discarded body and assumed her usual separate sleeping mode. Slowly she gave in to the inevitable, and fell asleep with the vague hope that another day might bring her something better.

7

Ainsley and Jarvis arranged to meet one evening in March in The Blind Beggar in Whitechapel. It had been five weeks since they had last seen each other.

They sat at a wooden table at the shadowy end of the public bar on battered leather chairs, surrounded by an aroma of stale beer and old socks. A smattering of regular drinkers, men mostly with nothing better to do, muttered about the unexpected early spring weather and the price of a drink these days, drifting out onto the street every now and then for a cigarette. Jarvis had a stubbly beard and moustache, darker in patches than his hair, and softening his chiselled features so much that Ainsley had to look twice at him when he arrived at the table to be sure he had the right man.

'I got your pictures.' Ainsley spoke quietly, under his breath. 'Very nice – a beard for added disguise – pretty obvious, but all right.' He produced another brown envelope. 'So, this is what we've got. False gas bill, false new passport and driving licence.' He flicked his hair away from his forehead as he withdrew his hand from the table, leaving the envelope there for Jarvis.

Jarvis opened the flap, fingering out a letter that was a gas bill for somebody called Joseph Cooper. 'Joseph Cooper? Where did that come from?' Headed with the purple British Gas logo, it was a monthly invoice for £280.00 for an address in Merton Park, South West London, and it looked authentic. Also in the envelope was a deep maroon UK passport, a touch battered, a few coloured stamps to be found among the stiff pages. On the photo identity page, he saw his own smooth-chinned face staring straight out at him, fresh and looking a little younger than thirty, he thought, with the name of

COOPER JOSEPH ROGER. BRITISH CITIZEN
Date of birth 23 JUNE/JUIN 82. M. LONDON
Date of issue 12 MAY/MAI 08
Date of expiry 12 FEB/FEV 19
It looked convincing. Inwardly impressed, he was determined not
to let Ainsley know.

Ainsley whispered, 'same initials, see, which we thought would
be helpful. You can apply for a credit card and a new bank account.
We've got five thousand pounds used here' – and an oblong padded
envelope was pulled out of Ainsley's inside jacket pocket and passed
across. It felt warm to Jarvis's hands as he rustled it between his
fingers before tucking it deep into one of his own pockets. 'When
you give me your new account number and so on, we'll pay in
the twenty thousand pounds remaining; and then the rest of the
fees can be paid in as and when. Access the account from any
cash machine anywhere, once set up.' Ainsley flicked his fringe
off his forehead and looked satisfied with himself. Jarvis dropped
everything back into the envelope, which he folded and slipped into
an inside pocket.

They both talked into their chests so that no one else would
hear them. 'As for the weapon, it can be done, but will take a little
time,' continued Ainsley, who had not yet touched his beer. His eyes
seemed to sparkle despite the dim light. 'You wanted an L115A3
long-range rifle, manual bolt action, with 8.59-millimetre-calibre
bullets; a five-round magazine. They're British made, but not easy
to obtain on any black market. We need to be careful, we don't want
to attract attention.'

'Must have the night sights I wanted, magnifier and suppressor,'
Jarvis insisted through gritted teeth.

Ainsley nodded. 'I know. Where do you want us to deliver?'

After a short pause, while in deep thought, Jarvis said, 'I work
sometimes out near Gravesend, off the A20, in a forest complex.

There's a small lay-by and parking place, away from the main road. I'll drive there one Sunday morning. You can send a delivery man; I'll link with him over a mobile. I can test it nearby. I'll want several rounds, two dozen perhaps.'

'OK, give us a few weeks.' Ainsley flicked his fringe aside and took up his pint glass. 'I think I've found you a lock-up as well.' Jarvis looked up, searching Ainsley's thin, expressive brows but saw no flicker. 'It's near Bethnal Green station, under the main line to Liverpool Street, Witan Street – this one is owned by us, rented to one of our blokes, but I can get him moved. It's small, in a little cul-de-sac on its own, well protected – you'll like it.'

'Sounds good, let me know when I can give it a look.' Jarvis leant forward to speak more closely into Ainsley's ear. 'I will need details of Abu's movements, his visit dates in England over the next six months. I want copies of all the pictures you showed me and any others you may have.'

Ainsley had a close-shaven face, smooth and soft around the eyes, without a hint of any of those little wrinkle lines Pamela persistently worried about. From the side, his lean hooked nose gave him an authoritative appearance. 'Where do you get all this from, Ainsley? You got insider help, I suppose?'

'Let's just say, we have contacts. Dad knows a few useful people. You don't need to know more.' Ainsley smiled crudely, expecting applause. Jarvis had a sudden desire to punch his smug face right on the nose, but contented himself with stretching his large hands into brown leather gloves, announcing his departure.

'I will get you copies of the papers and any photo information we have,' Ainsley continued. 'You need to keep them safe – we can't afford anyone else seeing them. I'll get the Abu information when I can.' He drank the rest of his beer, touching his wet lips afterwards with the back of his fingers. Jarvis stood up, meeting over.

'So, what are *your* plans and ideas, Mr Collingwood? I mean for the job,' continued Ainsley, looking up at the stonefaced ex-serviceman, genuinely expecting an answer.

Bending forward, Jarvis returned his look, barely disguised contempt on his static face. 'My plans and ideas, Mr Chigwell,' leaning into the other man's face and fixing on his dark eyes, 'are my own affair and private, know what I mean? Known only to me, and that's the way they'll stay. I want complete control of this operation, I want to choose the place and the timing, without anyone else interfering. That way I reduce the risk of a double-cross or a cock-up. I will deliver your target, and you will know when I've done it; but you will not know beforehand when or where. Understood?'

Despite his rudeness, or perhaps because of it, Ainsley was sure inside that they had chosen the right man, careful and ruthless, busy with detail. Jarvis downed the rest of his beer and was moving away when Ainsley caught his arm and looked up again. 'Okey dokey. But, Jarvis, where are the guarantees? Once you have the money, what's to stop you running away with it?'

Jarvis bent forward again briskly, breathing warm beery breath into Ainsley's flushed face. 'What? A lousy twenty-five thousand? You think that would tempt me to cheat on you? I wouldn't normally get out of bed for twenty-five lousy k. You want a guarantee, buy a toaster.' He moved closer so his lips brushed some of the loose hair over Ainsley's ear. He spoke through closed teeth. 'You have my word, Ainsley boy, and if that's not good enough for you, the deal's off.'

With that, he straightened to his full height and breezed out of the bar, out of the pub, into the chilly East End afternoon, where thin wintry sunshine was fast fading out of the sky behind the lights of the Gherkin skyscraper easily visible towards the City. Even though there was the risk of rain, he decided to walk home via the Vallance Road, which would take him around twenty minutes at a good pace. And there, with a bit of luck, he would have some respite from Pamela, who had said something about being late tonight, so that he should be able to inspect his second-identity passport and count his cash in peace, without fear of interruption.

Late the following Saturday afternoon, Jarvis returned to the hairdresser's in Essex Road, determined to make his move. He was in a small corner of the salon by the window, along with two other men waiting their turn, trying to manoeuvre himself to be Goofy's next customer. She was there, with her glasses and her hair bobbing up and down with jerky head movements, and she had only just started clipping away on a sandy-haired middle-aged man in a Harris Tweed. The next girl available was an older blonde woman he had not seen before, pretty enough, but not the one he wanted. Jarvis offered his place in the queue to the overweight man sitting next to him reading the *Sun*, who looked duly surprised. 'No, no, after you.'

'But you were before me, I think,' suggested Jarvis, under his breath.

'Nah, you were next.' He almost shouted it out as he sat stolidly, crossing his ankles and re-opening his paper.

'No, I really don't mind, I'm not in a hurry,' murmured Jarvis, out the side of his mouth, aware of some heads turning. There was a pause and the two looked sideways at each other. Jarvis shot him a friendly smile, his wide eyes indicating the empty customer chair.

'OK, if you don't mind?' And the heavy man heaved himself up, dumping the paper in a bundle on the seat behind him, and wandered over to the waiting blonde. Jarvis willed the fat man to get stuck in the chair and settled back, trying not to catch anybody's eye, listening to the soulful background music as a distraction.

And now another hairdresser was tidying up her customer's back, brushing the hairs off his shoulders and giving a final clip here and there. *Oh God, not another one.* He stared at the lad waiting opposite him, looking at a car magazine, and indicated with his hand that he could go up next.

'No, it's not me, mate. After you.'

'No, no, you go, I'm happy.'

'You were here before me, mate.' Jarvis, peeved at being called mate, spoke with some irritation in his voice. 'Look, I insist you go next.' *The things I do, for what? Goofy, you had better be worth it.*

And finally she was next. He leapt up before anyone else could step forward. 'Ooh, 'ello,' she said, with a smile, her head tilted to one side, slight recognition in her face. He sat down heavily with relief and she covered him with her black shroud. 'All right?'

'Yes, good, ta. How are you?'

'So what we doin', then?' Whether she noticed his beard or not, she said nothing.

'Same as last time, you remember?'

She gave his already short hair an all-over crop, which did not take long, with barely another word spoken. Jarvis watched her via the various mirrors with fascination. She caught his eye and giggled silently. Despite her awkward movements, her jerky head and shrugging shoulders, she was gentle and dexterous with her slim fingers. He studied her body, dressed in tight trousers, tight black T-shirt not tucked in, down-at-heel black leather booties. A line of white flesh flashed at her waist whenever she stretched up both arms to cut the top of his head; a neat shadowy curve of breast caught his keen eye in the mirror when she leant forward to the low shelving in front of them. He glimpsed a laced edge of turquoise silk at her waist which added something to her mystery. He noticed a small tattoo along the inner surface of her wrist. She had a tiny dark mole on her cheek just to the right of her mouth. Her make-up was understated, minimal eyeliner, earthy colours around her eyes. He would not normally have thought for a second about her, but the more he observed her, the more he took to her.

Jarvis paid her at the till, retrieved his jacket and left. Traffic was buzzing past in both directions. He skipped across the road between cars and waited around, pretending to look in estate agents' windows. It was getting dark with rain in the air, and he was expecting the salon to be closing soon. He looked back at the entrance, unsure whether the staff would leave that way or via a back door. He paced up the road a few times looking into other shops, hiding in doorways. After about twenty minutes, with daylight rapidly fading away and yellow street lights in full glare, Jarvis was cold and almost ready to give up for the night; but then he saw the last of the customers leave and the lights in the shop being dimmed. A couple of the girls came out the front door, going off together. He watched carefully from the other side of the road and saw her come out last, in winter coat and hat. She seemed to have the responsibility of closing the shutters, heavy worn metal slats that descended from high above to the ground and had to be padlocked with a key, a common sight for security along these roads.

Jarvis raced over to the shop front and stepped into the entrance, almost knocking into her. She had closed the door and was reaching up with both hands, her bag slung around her neck. 'Oh, sorry, it's me again. Hello.'

'Sorry? Who?' She was not sure, in the semi-darkness of the shop entrance and without her glasses on, who the tall blond man was, surprising her with his sudden appearance. 'Yes, oh yes.'

'Sorry. I'm glad I've caught you – just before you close. Do you need some help?' She was obviously having some trouble with the heavy mechanism and was still hanging on to the lower edge with both hands, which almost took her feet off the ground. 'Actually, I left my scarf here earlier – it's hanging, I think, on a hook. Stupid of me – do you mind? Wanted to get it back before you closed.'

While she was pulling with all her might to bring the sliding shutter down, Jarvis was standing with an arm holding the shutter up. She stopped her effort and giggled. 'Gosh, these shutters get stiffer and stiffer! OK – a scarf, you say?'

'Yes, it's green.'

She sighed, ducking her head, turned back into the shop and walked through to the back office, soon to emerge with the green scarf that Jarvis had left on purpose on the coat hooks.

'Good, we was wondering whose it was.'

'Thank you so much.' Jarvis put on his most amicable face.

'No problem.' She smiled her quick smile and handed it to Jarvis, who took it slowly from her, catching her fingers for an instant, and made a big thing of gratefully winding it around his neck. He stamped his feet in mock attempts to keep warm, while he looked up at the forlorn sky to see if it was raining. Goofy was reversing backwards out of the shop to pull the door closed and backed into Jarvis's side. 'Oops, sorry.'

'It's OK. I thought it was going to rain.'

Once again she reached for the shutter, and this time Jarvis lent his considerable strength to the task and it scraped down with a horrible grating noise, crashing onto the concrete floor. Goofy had the keys in her hand and bent down to see to the padlock.

'Thanks.'

'Oh, my pleasure,' said Jarvis. 'Look, erm, are you busy now, dashing off somewhere, I expect?'

He half looked at her, but his eyes cast around on the pavement as he feigned diffidence. 'I mean, would er . . . would you like to go for a drink or something, somewhere, a coffee perhaps or something?' Jarvis was speaking haltingly like a shy schoolboy. 'You know, before you go home?'

'I must get home soon, actually, erm, but . . .' She hesitated now, rather taken aback at the proposal from this complete stranger. She stepped back, pulling her bag across her chest and up in front of her, probably feeling more awkward than Jarvis at that moment, but at the same time not wanting to be abruptly dismissive or anything.

'Erm, we could, yes.'

She stood quite tall, in a tight black jacket and a funny hat shaped like an upturned flower pot. But he was still more than half a head taller than her. She looked about twenty-five, the street lights playing across her fresh face, her eyes squinting in the confusing light.

'There's Brown's up at the Green.' Jarvis was indicating with his arm and she nodded.

'They have good chocolate cakes and things, and the best cappuccinos,' she said enthusiastically, which emboldened him in his fiction.

'Come on, I'm paying.'

She didn't put up any further resistance and they walked slowly up Essex Road. She was not used to men making approaches and was both flattered and flustered, wondering why the hell she had said yes – although she had to admit this chap seemed nice and was quite good-looking, a bit of a hunk really, with his blond crop (that she remembered she had cut a few times before without really noticing him). But she knew her awkwardness would put him off – it always did, and explained her ultimate singleness in the romance stakes. Going out with boys was an unusual event for her, except in groups of friends when there was a celebration or something.

She retrieved her glasses from her bag. The coffee shop was crowded but warm, and having been on her feet all day, she was well relieved to be sitting down. A coffee would be welcome and she felt grateful, even happy. A goofy smile sprang across her face as she saw the hunky stranger bringing over a tray with two large white cups of froth covered with powdery cocoa dust, and a dark chocolate brownie to share, although she told herself she shouldn't.

'I'm Naomi, by the way.' She pronounced her name with three distinct syllables and gave him a large smile, showing off her teeth, while holding out her hand across the table. Jarvis placed the tray on the table and took her cold hand in his large one, gently squeezing and shaking it.

'I'm Josh. And you're cold.' He was amused. He had chosen Josh (actually short for Joshua) as he preferred it to Joe.

'Your hands are warm.' Which was odd, Naomi thought, as she had worn gloves and he hadn't. He was watching her amused and the hand contact lasted longer than she had intended; blushing slightly, she pulled hers back. She concentrated on moving the cups and plates around the small round table between them and then on stirring her coffee. Accidentally they kicked feet and knocked knees, while adjusting positions to find space for their legs. They laughed, awkwardly.

'You girls should have name badges.'

'Yes, we do, but I've lost mine.'

'So, do you work every day at the salon?'

Close up, he decided he liked her wide smile, her active lips always on the move, revealing her complete set of strong pearly white uppers, like tombstones, with a bright pink contrasting and undulating border.

'Five days, sometimes six days a week.'

'Long hours. Hope they pay you well – I don't think hairdressers get much, do they?'

'We rely on tips. It's pretty mean, actually.' Naomi sipped at her big cup and left a thin line of milky froth on her upper lip. Fascinated, Jarvis watched her darting tongue pop out and curl over the upper edge a few times to wipe it clean, and then she tucked her upper lip inside the lower one for a final clearance. 'Are you having some of this chocolate cake?' he asked.

She dabbed her mouth with a napkin. 'Yes, I'll have a little bite.'

Jarvis liked the name Naomi and wanted to tell her. 'I like the name Naomi, it's unusual.'

'Thank you. That was my mum and dad. I just have one name.

They chose Naomi.'

'Yes, I imagine they did. Don't tell me, but I expect you've been Naomi all your life.'

'Yes, sorry, I'm silly.'

They both laughed hesitantly and cast quick glances at each other. Jarvis didn't want to rush, but needed to know more. He studied her face with quick glances when she wasn't looking. She had amber eyes that seemed warm and honest and a lovely creamy complexion. Her neck was strikingly long and with her thin face and narrow nose, especially when she wore her glasses, made her look quite serious, but she constantly broke that up with nervous giggling, so he would have labelled her as fun.

He did not at first hear her question. 'I said, what do you do, Josh?'

He started awake, toying with the gold ring in his left earlobe, tilting his head away and, as if not particularly relevant, said something about cutting down trees. 'Like a surgeon. And we help clear rubbish, the dead wood. We're clearing a forest at the moment down in Kent, where this Lord bloke wants us to do a new road through the woods. I think he wants to open up a playground for adventures, day trips.'

'That sounds unusual. Tough, I expect.'

'It's hard work, especially in this cold weather, but it's going well. Keeps me fit.'

It was dawning on Naomi just how good looking this man really was, and he wore it so casually, appearing to be so natural. Which she liked – no pretence or showing off. He just talked openly, with a pleasant voice. She liked his dress sense, the leather and the boots. She admired the extra-large face of his wristwatch with its big numbers and the mixed leather and coloured bands he wore on his other wrist.

They talked on for a while until their coffees were finished. Jarvis, as casual as he could be, said, 'Do you live round here, Naomi?'

'Not far, down that way,' she replied, pointing vaguely, 'in Northchurch Road. I take the bus sometimes, it's not far, I usually walk actually.'

'Good area, down there, isn't it? Sounds nice.'

'Yeah, it's all right, not quite Islington, but you know, it's quiet. A few posh people. We have a ground-floor flat, a bit damp. With a patch of garden at the back.' She shrugged, smiled, showed her teeth, giggled a little.

'Oh, right. Is that with your mum and dad, then?'

'No, no, I have a flatmate, a girl I share with. We have our own rooms and that, but she's not often there. She has a boyfriend now,' she wrinkled her nose, 'so she's always out with him.' She shook her head a bit and was picking her bag and gloves up. Jarvis was relieved at the luck that she was not living with a bloke and smiled. 'Well, thank you ever so much, thanks for the coffee.'

And do you have a boyfriend, Naomi? They parted, but agreed that it would be nice to meet again sometime.

'When you need another haircut,' Naomi giggled.

'I'll have no hair left at this rate,' he joked, seriously.

A few days later, early morning, Jarvis was hovering on the pavement close to the hair salon, trying to spot Naomi walking to work. He did not have to wait long. He stepped up beside her, with a little mumbled hello, fed a folded piece of paper inside her hand and gave her a wink. 'Must dash, may see you later.' He darted away in the opposite direction, with a quick glance backwards. She waved half-heartedly. She unfolded the note once she was in the back changing room, when there was nobody looking. It was written in a bold hand with large lettering on a scrap of paper from a school notebook.

Naomi, it was lovely talking with you the other day. I would like to do that again. Can I call you? At the shop, sometime? Josh. To which he had added a mobile number.

And he did call her, the next day, at the salon in the lunch hour. He had found the number in the directory and used the phone at his local pub. And so later he found himself waiting on a bench under bare trees on the Green, where they had agreed to meet after work, with the evening darkness closing in and traffic trundling noisily past in all directions. The place was not well lit and a few wasters sat around in the shadows with their bottles and cans, staring into the chilly air, smoking and drinking freely, clutching plastic supermarket bags of old clothes and more beer cans. On the bench next to him the bundle of a man in wretched clothes and covered in a coat, was lying full length, his mucky worn boots sticking out at one end.

The pavements were crowded with people milling about rather aimlessly, and lights from passing traffic were reflected distractingly off the wet uneven surfaces. Jarvis saw Naomi headed towards him and waited for her at the gate. 'Hi, sorry, you haven't been waiting long, I hope?' She seemed genuinely pleased to see him.

'No, I only just got here,' he lied. She was in black again, tights and boots, a black coat with belt and her funny hat.

'Where shall we go?' he asked. 'There are a few pubs here, along Upper Street, and some posher restaurants. Just a little way, there's a Weatherspoon with food and a lounge. Would you like that?'

She nodded, gave him a smile and they started to walk together. Nothing was said for a while. Naomi was tired and he was tongue-tied; they would both benefit from a drink. He needed to develop a rapport with her and create the Josh façade, but he must not rush it or she would be frightened off. He recognised her shyness, quite liked it, not a bad thing: he was prepared to take the lead. He needed to find out what her likes and dislikes were, offer to take her on trips, Regents Park canal, the Zoo or something. And at the same time avoid the risk of bumping into Pamela.

He was becoming nervous as she was so quiet, and the longer it went on the harder it was to start a conversation. But on reaching the noisy and crowded pub, they settled at a table and then he ordered drinks from the bar. He watched her face as she studied her stiff menu card, admiring her soft look, the cool foundation over her cheeks, a copper tone around the eyes and salmon-coloured lips, with minimal mascara.

They ate their way through a pile of chips and burgers, with a couple of beers, and chatted about nothing in particular. Naomi droned on about her day, telling him about the salon routine and the other people she had to work with. 'One of the girls is moving out to set up her own hair salon on the canal. She's rented a barge with her boyfriend and he cuts hair and stuff, so they're going to work together. I think that's really good. Must be nice to work together like that, at something they like, you know.' And other such stories began to spill out, without Jarvis having to add much at all. Naomi's boss apparently was a married man in his forties who owned more shops around North London. Played the field a bit with the other girls, she added.

'He tried it on with me once in the changing rooms, one lunch-time. I wasn't havin' any of it. Told him I had a fiancé who was six foot and a wrestling champion. Haven't been bothered since,' she giggled, shrugging her shoulders. She did that a lot, nervous bouncy shrugging of her shoulders along with all her smiling activities.

'And *do* you have a big wrestling boyfriend, then?' asked Jarvis jovially, with a lift of the eyebrows.

'God, no, I was only, like, putting him off. Not since last year, I thought I had a boyfriend but that didn't last long.' She looked shy again and filled her mouth with the last of the chips, tomato sauce squeezing out at the corners. She giggled and shrugged and wiped her mouth with paper tissue all at the same time.

Later she talked a little about her family. 'My mum's no longer alive and me dad, he's an electricity inspector working in Kilburn, lives on his own with my two younger brothers. They've both left school, one is going into the Army, the other works for the electricity board like Dad. He sometimes has to help me with the rent on the flat. It's quite expensive. I'm doing a Health & Beauty Studies course at college, two evenings a week at the moment up Holloway. And on three nights a week I work in a pub in Dalston, just to earn a bit more, and sometimes at weekends as well.'

'You sound so busy, no time for anything else, eh?'

'Well, no, we go clubbing sometimes, that's Celia and me, she's my best friend; that's not Maureen who shares with me, 'cos as I said, she's always out with Mickey, her boyfriend.'

'They planning to get married or anything?'

'Not that I've heard, not yet, she's only twenty-six, quite young. And we like the pictures.'

'Do you like music?'

'Oh yes.'

'Right, what are you into at the moment?'

'I love Coldplay, the Script and Beyoncé and Rihanna, of course.' She kept raising her eyes to heaven in some sort of embarrassment. Just what Jarvis had expected and he nodded his encouragement. He was thinking that music might be a good way they could get to know each other better.

'I saw there's a good looking concert coming up next month at the Roundhouse,' Jarvis persisted, 'with Florence and her Mechanics and Mike and his Machine.'

Naomi laughed at his muddle. 'Sounds a good combination,' she said.

'It's live and that. I thought I might try and get hold of some tickets – would you like to come?' Jarvis looked eager.

Later he walked her to her bus stop and waited with her for the number 38 to Hackney. They agreed to meet Saturday afternoon and if the weather was all right, they might take a walk up Primrose Hill.

Another week, another pub meeting with Ainsley, and Jarvis waited for him with a small beer at his side, this time in the shadowy back bar of The White Hart, a tatty old establishment in Whitechapel. It was early evening and it had been another surprisingly warm day. Inside, it felt especially stuffy and stale while trade was building up, the usual gathering of disgruntled male workers with dirty hands and dirty overalls.

What exactly was Ainsley – an associate? An assistant, a dogsbody? An accessory to a crime, a crime not yet committed? How reliable would Ainsley be in difficult circumstances? Would he squeal under interrogation? And if it all went pear-shaped, would the Chigwells take responsibility? Jarvis might need to be able to point a finger of suspicion at Ainsley's father. Even as he explained his innocence to the Metropolitan Police, he would plead that he had been used as a pawn in the bigger game, that his head had been turned by the offer of riches. Although that would not cut much ice, he suspected.

Ainsley was dressed smartly in a suit and looked a little out of place as he arrived late and in a flutter, complaining about the traffic and the crowds on the Tube, but he settled with his bottle of Stella on a stool at the bar, like any other business partner, getting out papers from his case to discuss. They huddled close, talking quietly, nobody taking any notice of them.

'The money is ready to go. I hope you won't spend it all at once,' Ainsley purred; Jarvis did not move a muscle. 'What else? Yes, I have some more details about Abu and his whereabouts. Our friends in Baghdad have been keeping a check; one of them now has a clerical post in his office. Abu will be in London again, but not until May. He is expected to travel with the small Iraqi team to London for the Games in July – don't know yet where they will be staying. Expect him to be part of the official delegation and to make use of all the perks available, the special status, with hotels, travel and so on. He will have tickets, probably free passes to everything, knowing us lot.' He flicked his fringe away and downed a goodly mouthful of lager with a noisy swallow. Jarvis watched his pointy Adam's apple flick up and down the front of his scrawny neck. 'You are still adamant about not going to Iraq yourself, are you? You could get there with a security firm, there are lots of them there.'

'All right, I'm considering it. But I would prefer London. Now, what about the weapon?'

'Can we deliver it this weekend?'

'You have it?' Jarvis sounded surprised, suddenly animated. Noticing the crude reaction of the ex-serviceman, Ainsley nodded with a broad smile, like a father explaining to his son that the repeatedly asked-for birthday present would be arriving in the post later in the week. 'Yeah? Sunday, then, and I'll be at the rendezvous like I said, off the A20, near Longfield. Nine a.m. Make sure it's folded and packed in a case. I want no traces on it.'

'This one is brand new, not even registered, not been fired. There was no problem. The driver will be one of ours, but he knows absolutely nothing of all this, he'll just deliver. I'll give him your mobile number so he can find you on the day, yeah?'

'OK. Use my second number: the 07659 number, don't use the first number again, delete all record of that.' Ainsley nodded his agreement. 'Fine. Tell the driver that when he gets to the destination, he needs to park and wait. He needs to be on his own, no tails, no backup.'

They both sat back to drink their beers. Ainsley raised his bottle in quiet salute and Jarvis, to his credit, stretched forward and touched Ainsley's bottle against his own. 'Salaam,' whispered Jarvis.

'OK, just let me know the bank details when you have them, so we can make the payments.'

'I have them.' Jarvis fished a piece of paper from his pocket and slid it across the bar towards the other man. 'Copy the numbers down,' he commanded, leaving his long fingers pinning the paper flat on the counter. Ainsley retrieved a biro and his notebook and busied himself with copying accurately the numbers Jarvis had written down. Jarvis screwed up the scrap of paper, walked over to the fire and tossed it in, watching it give off a little flare.

He wandered back to stand beside Ainsley and leaned into him, much as he had done the last time they met, enunciating his words carefully to impress upon his companion the seriousness of them. 'I want no pressure from you people. I am planning the job; it will be done, to my way of things, when I'm ready, and not before. OK? No pressure.' Jarvis was nervous, he wanted to end the meeting. 'We're done. If I want anything else I'll call you.'

'OK – and when I get some more info, I'll call you. Cheers, mate.'

Jarvis was on his way out. Ainsley stayed awhile to finish his drink, although the grim atmosphere in the pub felt unsavoury and he soon took himself off.

'We seem to be going through a bit of a heatwave,' puffed Naomi as they climbed to higher ground on Primrose Hill, a trip delayed a week because of spitting rain. That and Jarvis being exceptionally busy. The weather though had turned quite balmy and many people were outside to take advantage of it. With only a few wispy clouds to puff across a clear blue sky, there would be some sunburn on pale English skins this weekend. The grass remained damp from over-night, but it smelled fresh and thick yellow bundles of daffodils in full bloom were still being blown around in their thousands. Jarvis and Naomi were hot and regretted bringing their coats, trailing them along the grass. They sat on a bench near the summit to get their breath back, and Naomi produced two small bottles of juice that they drank gratefully, while warming their faces in the sun and taking in the views of a familiar grey London skyline, hazy in the distance.

'I never get bored with this view.' Naomi was in a loose skirt and a pink top, while Jarvis was in jeans and his new red Converse trainers. He had a pair of shades on, but she had forgotten hers. 'Cool,' she had said at the bottom of the hill, endeavouring to look straight into Jarvis's eyes, but only seeing her own distorted reflection.

A couple of super-fit troopers with shaven heads and army fatigues were running in synchrony at a brisk pace up the steep path, grunting past them in heavy black boots, heaving backpacks. They disappeared over the top.

'I used to be in the Army,' Jarvis mentioned casually some while after they were out of sight. A group of teenagers were playing Frisbee down the hillside on the slippery grass, screeching when someone caught it, moaning when they didn't.

'Were you? When was that?' Naomi squinted against the sunlight to look at Jarvis's face, with its faraway expression, as he continued to survey the London distance.

'Oh, seems like ages ago now. I joined at sixteen. I went to Iraq twice, first was 2003 and again in '05. Afghanistan 2006. Cyprus. Germany. I left June 2009.' He went through the list slowly, thoughtfully, with hidden pride. His approach was modest, but Naomi sensed that at the same time he wanted to talk more about it.

'Was it, like, awful – I mean, was there a lot of violence and that?'

'Some. Yeah, it had its moments. Actually I quite enjoyed it most of the time. You know, you learn skills, you get to know some lads, you make friends, I still see a few of them, those that are still alive.

I lost a few.'

'That must have been terrible.' Naomi had her hand over her mouth and was watching his face sympathetically, but he showed little emotion. 'Did you have to kill anybody?' Naomi tried to sound innocent, offhand, as if she was asking him if he would like sugar in his tea.

'Yeah, one or two.' He looked a little bashful. 'But I came away without any scars, I never was injured or anything, I was lucky really.' He turned and smiled at Naomi and she confirmed to herself that at that very moment she was quite definitely looking at just about the most good-looking man she had ever been with. Ever. She had to swallow some excess saliva in her excitement. Jarvis carried on with some tales of life in barracks in Baghdad and Basrah, the dry heat and constant dust, the unexciting food, the boredom waiting, the card games they played, the different habits of the US troops; how they all smoked but Jarvis had managed to resist it. 'Actually I've never smoked, which is good.'

'Me neither,' smiled Naomi coyly.

Jarvis offered her some gum. 'My brother was killed out there.' Naomi twisted her face into an expression of repulsion, but she was fascinated and wanted Jarvis to continue. He looked bleakly at his hands, chewing vigorously. 'We were patrolling together in the streets, in Basrah. There was this surprise gun attack, a group of Sunnis on foot suddenly appearing around a corner, close range. They sprayed us with automatic fire. Ed was front man, hit several times. I was at the back and . . . protected. I dashed up some steps onto a terrace overlooking the square and took out three of them as they scampered across to the other side, three shots, back of the heads.' Jarvis mimicked shooting a rifle from the shoulder, first finger on the trigger, phut, phut, phut, with pinched mouth and a slight sneer on his lips. He looked away from Naomi self-consciously, grimacing with the recalled pain of the day and a shake of his head. The sun caught the side of his face, sprinkling its glare over his beard, glinting on his earring.

'When I got down, the injured lads were fallen into a side street. Ed was crumpled up, blood spilling from his neck – I thought he was dead. I unclipped his helmet, he had wounds in the side of his face and head. I shouted to the other guys for a medic – I shouted into my radio. I tried to stop the bleeding with my hands, I ripped off my shirt and pressed it into Ed's neck, but I knew by then he was dead.' He clenched his hands, for a moment his eyes closed. 'The light had gone out of his eyes, you can tell. I sat with him, his head in my lap. He drenched through my fatigues, could feel it warm, soaked through to my skin. He had this tiny picture in a silver frame of Stella, his wife, in his palm, gripped tightly. He must have been holding it all the time.' Jarvis turned his left fist over and looked intently into his empty palm, remembering vividly the photograph in his brother's hand.

He sat quite still, his head down, reliving some formative moments in his past he thought were long gone: the noisy chaos of Arab street life, the stifling humidity, dust in everything, in the spiced food, in the bedclothes at night, in underpants; and the flies constantly irritating, big black buggers, some of them would bite like horse-flies.

A long moment of quietness passed between them, and Naomi could sense the powerful emotions that had been struggling to find daylight within the solid frame of the man beside her. She reached across to comfort him. 'Oh gosh, poor you.' She pulled his hand across to the softness of her welcome lap. 'That must have been so awful for you.'

It was all he could do to restrain himself from caressing her bare thighs, where she had placed his hand for comfort, where her skirt had ridden up and creased. He was scared to move his limp fingers in case she misunderstood and thought he was taking advantage of the moment. They sat still, lost in their own conflicting thoughts.

Jarvis turned towards Naomi and she smiled as sympathetically as she knew how. He stood up suddenly and said, 'Come on, we mustn't live in the gloomy past. Let's go get an ice cream or something.' Naomi followed after him at a trot and slipped a hand through his arm, pulling herself up against his bulk. For his part, he looked down on her gratefully and showed his feelings by slightly squeezing her hand with the inside of his arm.

'Josh, do you want to come back to my place for a drink or something?'

Thought you'd never ask, darling. Jarvis felt a little skip of triumph. He had made progress and had won her interest. And he had simply used the truth, he hadn't had to fabricate anything. So far. He needed to draw her further in. He would have to tell her sometime about being married to Pamela. He also needed to think of a plan for her afterwards. Maybe he would just disappear as quickly as he had appeared.

They reached his car and drove quietly back to Northchurch Road, with its straight rows of bulky white-fronted villas. Some of them looked up-market and prosperous, newly whitened stucco, preserved crenellated architraves, large sash windows with painted wooden shutters. But quite a few had missed out on the gentrification plan and looked dilapidated. Naomi's flat, number 106a, was in the basement of a not-so-well-looked-after house where the lack of proper curtains in the windows was the giveaway. The front door was below street level, hidden from view and tucked away underneath wide stone steps that led up like a bridge from the pavement to the main entrance of the solid villa above. What had once been a grand residence for a single prosperous family was now converted into eight flats for poor families, penniless students and short-term lets, crammed in over four floors and grateful for a London address near all the amenities, paying high rents to an anonymous grateful landlord. Prams and bicycles were crammed inside the glass porch at the front.

Crinkly old leaves had been blown in around the entrance; inside was dingy. Naomi darted around the small spaces of her life, putting things away, trying to make it look a little more respectable, pulling drying clothes off hanging lines, grabbing at underwear, gowns and other things off her bed, sweeping a collection of make-up stuff off her dressing table into the drawers, as they walked around the rooms, which did not take long, while explaining where mostly an explanation was not required. Standing at the French windows at the back, Jarvis was able to look out over a small wall-enclosed area with a tea-cloth-sized piece of grass and decrepit shrubs, and a mouldy brick patio, bare and unkempt.

She made instant coffee and they sat in the front room, with the light fading through the front window, listening to Adele. 'I find her a bit boring now, I prefer Sade,' he confessed.

'So where exactly do you live then, Josh?' Naomi piped up between songs in a quaint voice.

'Not far actually, down Hoxton way. We're close to the canal.' Naomi's head came up, her eyes a little wider, but she said nothing and went back to sipping from her mug. 'Not been there long, about two years,' Jarvis continued. 'Place was nicely done over before we moved in, so not much was needed. Some paint work, new light fittings. Nowhere to put the car though, just park outside when there's room.'

'We?' A little taste of anxiety filled her throat.

'Well, she's going, more or less, we're kinda separated. Pamela – it didn't work out. After the Army and all that. So she's moving out.'

'You're married?' She needed to suppress the urge for hysteria to bubble up into her voice.

'Yes,' he said regretfully, 'but not for much longer.'

'So she's living with you? Pamela?' Naomi felt a knot forming deep in her middle and held herself tense. Her eyes were now much wider, but she studied the awful pattern in the orange carpet at her feet. 'She's not actually left you – yet? I mean, you and her, you're still sleeping together?' She found herself standing up, now looking up at the fine strands of spider's web hanging from the central light fitting. Just not able to look straight at Jarvis. And her breathing stopped for a horribly long moment. She wanted to scream.

'This is getting personal all of a sudden,' snorted Jarvis, who detested personal. He looked uncomfortable, his brows knitted. Many times he had gone over in his mind the inevitable questions and how he was to reply. He needed to rescue the situation quickly. Standing beside her, he shrugged, arms apart, hands turned up. 'Look. I don't know where this is going. Pamela is moving out, we're separating. It's a process. Takes time. We haven't, you know, done it for ages; we don't any more.'

'Josh, I'm sorry, I didn't mean to pry, I mean, you don't have to explain . . . I have no right . . .' Naomi felt lost, she wanted to rush out of the room and wipe her face, recompose herself. She told herself there was no problem, the poor man was entitled to be married and it was none of her business.

'Naomi, I'm sorry, I should have said something earlier, but you know, it's not the first thing a man talks to a new girl about, is it, like when they first meet? I like you, and I will be honest with you. Pamela and I will separate and go different ways. I really would like to go on seeing you. If you would let me?'

They were facing each other, their coffees cooling on the side table. 'Do you?'

'What?'

'Like me?' This time there was no nervous smile or giggle. Unable to make direct eye contact, she settled her gaze on his generous mouth, her teeth well hidden.

'I do, very much.' He leant towards her, a big, handsome, relaxed man reaching for a plain, gangly, awkward girl, the explanation for the juxtaposition of two such opposites unclear. He held her by the upper arms and slowly pulled her towards him. A cheek came to rest on the top of her head, then pressed against silky dark hair imbued with odours of lemon and marigold mixed with the freshness of the spring day. She tilted her head back after a while, lifting her face, her eyes filmed over. He turned his mouth down toward hers, long lashes tickling her brow, and their dry lips experienced the merest of contact. She tried to shape hers into a kiss, but they were stiff. Her heart thumped wildly inside her chest. He prized his own lips apart from the inside with a slide of his tongue, creating a moisture trail, and was able to pout and press firmly on hers, a tactile sensation that had Naomi feeling weak at the knees. Her eyes were closed, her breathing had stopped, definitely, and everything else was in slow motion. A man's hot body was pressed against her soft breasts. Her mind seemed otherwise blank. His solid grip on her arms was hurting, but without it she would certainly have crumpled to the floor.

Jarvis's mind was as active as ever. Temptation nagged. He sensed her soft rounded shape against his chest, a limp body unprotected in his grasp. He recalled silky strips of exposed underwear in turquoise, the flash of flesh around her middle. But with an effort he backed off, relaxing his grip. They both regained their ability to breathe.

Jarvis broke the silence. 'I do want to see you again, we've got a concert lined up next week, remember?' He tried to sound cheerful.

'Yes, that will be good.' She sounded doubtful.

'You still want to come?'

'Yes, I do.' She snivelled and wiped her nose. 'Please.'

'Don't worry, it will all work out, Naomi. I am working it through, and *will* be shot of Pamela soon. Promise.'

'Yes, Josh, OK.' She shrugged and gave a silent giggle, showing him all her now familiar white front teeth again.

'And then I will show you where I live.'

And soon after that, with a promise that he would phone her later, Jarvis left to return by car to his wife at home.

The concert at the Roundhouse was the following week, on Good Friday, and it was crowded, sweaty and noisy. The rhythms pounded in their ears and the excited crowd throbbed and gyrated in participation. Naomi and Jarvis were carried along and enjoyed the experience. They stood close together in the crammed spaces, in the dark with flashing lights and the crush of hot young people all around, perspiring heavily and unable to hear each other speak. When the crowd became more boisterous towards the end of the evening, Jarvis put his arm around Naomi's shoulders to protect her, so they were pressed closer together, face to face. She came up to his chest, where she placed a hand against his toned muscles, her bendy fingers providing a cushion between them. The throb and bass thump of the music reverberated through them and she was excited to feel him through their thin T-shirts and jeans. He stroked his fingers around bare flesh of her waist and then risked a kiss, but with all the jostling it landed awkwardly on the end of her nose. She jerked away but realised that he was only being friendly and gave him a quick peck on his cheek.

The heat exaggerated her body smell, with its enticing perfume. He did not mind her gangly legs, her glasses or her repeated giggling. On Naomi he found these attractive. She had bony hips and a round bottom that gave her the looks of a young girl, with no untidy fat rolls. She wore simple soft make-up, in pastels, which suited her unpretentious nature. She often wore loose tops that concealed her true shape, and he was not sure whether that was out of modesty and not wanting to be too provocative or whether in fact she did not have anything worth speaking of and did not want to make that deficiency too obvious, lest it put him off. Most girls believed that blokes were only interested in a good pair of boobs, suitably displayed.

After the concert, two weeks went by without Naomi hearing a word from Josh, apart from a message on the flat phone saying he had to be away in Kent for a whole week to complete a big job at Beacon Forest. She was hoping that when the next Saturday came by, after a slow fortnight without his company, he might pop into the shop and surprise her, but he didn't and she was cross with herself during the afternoon for letting herself even half believe that he would do that, which made her feel sullen as a result. Although she did not think Josh was necessarily the type to be drawn in by a woman's appearance, she decided that next time they went out, if there was a next time, she might show something of herself – a bit of cleavage perhaps would not go amiss. She shopped aimlessly after lunch for a couple of hours and then decided to visit some friends in Dalston for the afternoon, ahead of an evening working at The George.

8

It took Jarvis a while to find the right place. He followed the railway lines on their long curving viaduct out of Liverpool Street Station over Spitalfields and beyond, walking along less familiar pavements, and eventually east along Three Colts Lane, passing Bethnal Green station, all the while noting where the arches underneath the line had been bricked up, the space used for garages or storage. All of these had numbers painted large in white on the brickwork. They had standard hinged doors or up-and-over rollers, most with a neglected appearance. Some were opened up, with signs of activity within, the sounds of hammering and radios playing, engines revving, men in overalls wandering around, smoking, sneering and possibly thinking about doing some work. Some of the units did not open on a Saturday, and some were not in use, business closed.

He found number 208 at last, tucked out of the way as Ainsley had said, along Witan Street, at the point the viaduct split into a northerly branch alongside Cambridge Heath Road while the main line continued out east. The line of arches ended there; there was no number 209 next door. And the road that ran alongside the railway turned abruptly under the overhead lines at the V-shaped junction, through where 207 might have been, so 208 existed as a solitary unit, in a narrow cul-de-sac formed by its own high brick walls, with no street lighting anywhere near and nothing to attract the interest of any passers-by, unless they were specifically looking. It had no name boarding on the outside and no advertising signs like so many of the others, just the big white numbers stencilled on the brickwork beside the door.

A narrow branch road turned around on itself fifty yards further up, fronted by more nondescript businesses in stand-alone buildings with broken windows, mostly shut up at nights and weekends. Piles of old rubber tyres and discarded exhaust pipes were stacked outside and oily patches marked the concrete approach. There was a metal fence across the end holding back a mass of wild nettles, and weeds and thick grass sprouted in every crevice. Bulging black plastic bags had been thrown up against a wall, domestic rubbish tipping out, and there was the smell of dog, making the area thoroughly unattractive; all of which made it perfect for Jarvis's needs.

Ainsley was waiting to show him the place, the man who usually worked there having been sent on his way. Jarvis had made it clear that he did not want to be seen by anybody who might remember him later, so Ainsley should come alone, and if any work needed to be done, then Ainsley himself would arrange it and supervise it, using workmen of his own choosing.

There were two doors, a standard metal one on hinges with a brace and a padlock, and a wide motor-driven shuttered roller for vehicles. Ainsley had the keys and let them into the dark and damp interior. He switched on a single neon strip light that hung high above them from the curved brick ceiling to reveal an oily concrete floor and brickwork streaked white with damp and mould on three sides, recessing into darker crevices at the back. There were no windows and no escape route. It was about the size of a big garage, enough room for two cars at a pinch. There was an electric supply for the roller door, with a switch on the wall and an electric meter, read and paid for once a month on a Friday. Surprisingly, an old BT phone sat on a wooden sideboard, with a workable landline. Cold water, apparently safe, dripped from a tap which they found in the shadows at the back. There was a wooden table and a flimsy swivel plastic chair. The previous occupant had cleared out most of his stuff, but a workbench on one side was covered with stacks of tools and car manuals and there were two large under-car jacks leaning against one wall, with more tyres and oily cloths scattered about.

Jarvis was satisfied with the place, but as they walked around he told Ainsley what work he wanted doing: heavy-duty hinges and a sturdy replacement lock operated only by a memorised digital security code on the door; better lighting and more power sockets – he indicated exactly where; all rubbish cleared out. Ainsley noted all of it down and promised to have someone onto it within the week. As they left to go their separate ways, Ainsley clutched his notebook and mumbled something about still having time to get a bet on the Grand National later that afternoon, but Jarvis was not listening.

By the time Jarvis took ownership of his railway-arch hideaway about ten days later, an expert locksmith had come by with new door fittings and the security lock, a plumber had put in a basin and cured the drip on the tap, an electrician had set up better lighting and power sockets and a local builder had knocked a hole in the back wall, fitting a four-foot solid wood three-quarter frame and door, heavily bolted, that opened inwards. Ainsley had phoned him before he arrived with the security PIN, which Jarvis altered immediately. Inside he crouched to exit through his new back door, which gave out onto a wasted area between high brick walls beside the road that curved through the railway cutting, and which was strewn with rubbish bags and broken masonry, and wildly overgrown, like the area out front, and thus completely obscured from prying eyes. It had a high metal fence running beside the pavement topped with spikes and a single strand of barbed wire, to deter vagrants and drug addicts from seeking a place of refuge, and on it was a rusted Network Rail notice that warned 'Keep Out: Railway Property'. He found some discarded crates that could be propped up close to the fence, allowing him to climb to the top, place a booted foot carefully onto the barbed wire, and step over, jumping down the six feet to the pavement on the other side.

Intending to make the lock-up his own private sanctuary for a while at least, with no one to know about it, he gradually transformed the cold and ugly space into something more pleasant, with lighting and, for warmth, an oil-fired radiator. He bought old carpeting to soften the floor and cover the oil stains, and obtained a sturdy chair and a small fridge, both second-hand, and a fold-away camp bed. He planned to store stuff here for another life – an assortment of clothes, shoes, a case or two, some boxes and books. Papers, pens, Sellotape, and a large roll of wide cling film covered the table top, and in the sideboard behind were various tools – screwdrivers, wrenches, a power drill, a small torch, a pair of binoculars.

He bought a second-hand scooter from a trader off the Whitechapel Road, a three-year-old 49cc Vespa that was easy to drive, nippy around the streets, doing a maximum of 35 mph but only needing twenty litres of diesel every two hundred miles or so. Noisy maybe, but cheap to run and perfect for Jarvis to make quick forays across town incognito, as no one would recognise him behind the tinted visor of his new shiny black helmet.

When arriving and leaving, Jarvis perfected ways of shaking off any potential followers that involved taking a twisty route around the side streets, pausing, doubling back, or slipping into a narrow side alley between the brick pillars supporting the railway structures overhead, often used as the local convenience, with a resulting pungent smell. Even in broad daylight this was a dingy, wet place, water dripping from above, streaming down the bricks and across the pavement, leaving it slippery and dangerous for the unwary. By flattening himself into a shadowy brick recess, Jarvis could observe unnoticed anyone who might be coming along behind. As an added precaution, he mostly used the lock-up only at night, when it was eerily dark and nobody ever seemed to be about, and if he stayed over, he would leave at first light in the mornings.

During April, Jarvis was working particularly hard, with Jonathan's security jobs and heavy sessions at Beacon Forest with Danny, and of course with his own busy activities. He had the house in Baring Street to himself one morning, when Pamela was out at work. He emptied his safe under the stairs of most of his accumulated cash, running into several thousands of pounds, and collected a few other items round the house, a sheet, some old kitchen utensils Pamela would not miss, some boxes and books. He needed another blanket and was rummaging in a storage shelf high up in a wardrobe in the spare bedroom, when he came upon a ladies' shoebox pushed right to the back and out of view, filled with folded letters and photos, personal mementoes, some in packets with elastic bands round them. Jarvis sat on the edge of the bed and sifted through them without much interest. He found an early love letter he had written Pamela in 2000, a ticket to a millennium party at the Palladium, some early family pictures, holiday snaps from Tenerife he remembered, in swimming costumes on beaches, some pictures of him as a soldier on parade, the brothers in uniform, an invitation to a summer ball, pictures of Pamela with some male friends, with female friends, at functions, of Gwendolyn and Pamela's mother and brother, mostly all long forgotten images, of teenage years and typical family life.

Among these things, he came across a thin unmarked white envelope that simply contained three colour prints, unfamiliar pictures of a younger, slimmer Pamela, that he was sure he had never seen before, when she had straight shoulder-length brown hair. She was smiling easily at the camera, wearing only an unbuttoned man's white shirt and nothing else, by what Jarvis could make out. Standing in a doorway running her hands through dishevelled hair in one, draped over a settee with a come-hither expression in another, and sitting at a dressing table with her partially exposed pert breasts proudly reflecting her young beauty in the third, she seemed more than happy, with an 'I've just been fucked' look of rosy satisfaction about her flushed cheeks. Jarvis recognised their bedroom, their bed and their clothes on the shelves from their Army house in Colchester, where they had lived at a time when he was often away on active service, but he definitely had never seen these pictures before. He turned one over: on the back in pencil was writing that he recognised. 'July 6 2004. Terrific day. Terrific girl. Love.'

A nasty taste welled up uncontrollably in his mouth. His normally steady heartbeat stuttered for a moment as he struggled to absorb the meaning of the information in front of him, while the sound of his older brother's burly voice shouting commands to squaddies on a parade ground filled his mind.

Jarvis said nothing. He was meeting some Army friends on the Embankment later to watch the London Marathon and he would see Pamela afterwards, sometime in the afternoon. He left the house early and walked across to Finsbury Park, where he picked up a hire car for the day, to take him the ninety minutes driving time, through the Blackwall Tunnel and down the A2, to get to their agreed rendezvous. It was on the fringes of Beacon Forest, a place he had come to know well and to love over the last few months, and was no more than a flattened clearing the size of a tennis court and surrounded by heavily overgrown borders, hidden from view half a mile along a track that looked as though it was hardly used, where local walkers and picnickers would occasionally park their cars, if they knew how to find it. Heavy overnight rain had left puddles in the many potholes and sunshine, piercing the overcast sky, reflected brilliantly off their still surfaces.

The driver Ainsley had arranged to do the drop arrived on time and alone. He parked a dirty white Transit, its plate partly obscured, opposite Jarvis's hired Renault. Jarvis remained hidden at a distance in the undergrowth, watching, with his hood up. The man looked around, could not see anyone and reached for a soft brown case from the back of the van, closed the door and carried it over to the Renault. He opened the boot, dropped the case in, easy enough and closed the lid with a clunk. He looked around again and then returned to his van and promptly drove out.

Jarvis stayed hidden for a while, watching, feeling a fluttering of excitement in his belly. He walked slowly over to the car, climbed in with the keys in hand and drove out of the lay-by, back to the feed road, with his hood still up, cautiously looking out for the van. But it had gone. Heading south along the quiet Whitfield Road for a couple of miles, he followed the edge of the forest land on his right, going over a humpback bridge before turning right into Main Street and moving along the southern perimeter, which led past Danny's 'village'. He had keys to the gates, spares stolen unnoticed from Danny's caravan last week. He had checked that there would be no active work on site over the weekend and that all would be quiet. He let himself into the fenced compound and parked out of sight of the road, behind the barn-like workshop of corrugated aluminium and plywood. He sat for a while, watching and listening. The caravans, mess hut and toilet box were sitting neglected, a skip half filled with black plastic bags nearby. Nothing moved.

Signs of the recent work were everywhere, with felled trees dragged down from the higher forest areas for cutting, stacks of newly cut trunks, logs and rubbish, sawdust in trails and piles, some of it blown across the concrete enclosure, piles of sand and gravel stones for the road construction. Fifty yards away was the start of the new road, the crushed brick and concrete foundation clearly laid out, cutting its path through the open spaces and then rising through the woods and disappearing deep into the forest. A lone orange JCB digger stood forlornly to one side.

Jarvis inhaled the sweet smell of sap and pungent aromas of

cut wood that he had missed over the last week and smiled with the pleasure. He opened the boot and unzipped the case, in which he found exactly what he had asked for. Ainsley had certainly not let him down. Wrapped in layers of cellophane and Ministry of Defence packaging, he unwrapped a brand new L115A3 sniper's rifle, a formidable beast. Developed for the sole use of the British Army, it was especially lightweight with a detachable titanium and steel barrel. Distinguished by its light brown wooden folding stock, it had a separate grip hole for the thumb and was nicely curved for a large man's hand. It had a neat bipod at the front of the stock that folded forwards and a heavy sound suppressor screwed into the front of the barrel. Included in the bag was the latest in tele-scopic-sight technology with night vision, an S&B 5 with powerful magnification, a spotting scope and a laser range finder. Lying separate and flat in the bottom were two empty grey aluminium magazines taped together and two cardboard boxes each containing two dozen copper-tipped bullets, 8.59mm and uniquely capable of travelling without deflection over at least 1000 metres at 936 metres per second, little grey torpedoes packed in rows like sardines.

Jarvis cradled the beautiful weapon in his lap, sitting in the back of the car, familiarising himself with its details, its easy feel and fine balance. The whole piece could be folded into a tight package and stowed in an ordinary rucksack. And it took Jarvis less than 8 seconds to clunk it all together.

He left the car clutching the packed case and walked away from the compound along an obscure path through woodland, winding through thick foliage, wild with bramble and thorn, across the eastern part of the forest where the gang had not yet worked. It took him into higher and denser parts of the forest, further away from the road, involving a scramble in some places, up steep-sided paths, over rock and through thick undergrowth. He was quite scratched when he emerged into the open daylight on the eastern edge, marked by a few wobbly posts and an occasional length of wire fence. He was now looking out over a wide area of scrubland spread out beyond him, four hundred metres across and a thousand metres long, running beside the edge of the forest from south to north and rolling away from him, with the approach road that he had driven along earlier easily visible through a distant row of bushes. From there he could see the Gravesend railway line running across the bottom corner of this scrub area, and a little brick-built bridge that the road popped over. This scrubland had probably been forest many years ago, semi-cleared with plans perhaps to convert it into grazing fields or building plots – plans that never materialised. Instead, it was now craggy and undulating, covered with mixed grasses, thorn bushes and weed, as well as rocky outcrops and cut-down tree trunks. About halfway across it was cut through by a deep dyke where the edges of the ground dropped suddenly into dark crevices which, after a downpour, ran with clear water. Through binoculars Jarvis could see a makeshift bridge of fallen trees and some fencing over the dyke in the distance. From there the ground rose up on the other side to a line of plane trees and another wooded area about a thousand metres away. A public footpath, which began at the lay-by where he had parked and picked up his delivery earlier, ran along in front of this tree line, gently rising from right to left.

As he emerged from the darkness of the thick woods, shafts of spring sunshine glanced across the quiet landscape, the peace disturbed only by occasional birdsong. There were no trains or cars, no people out in the fields. He could make out the rooftops of the village of Longfield about a mile away over the railway line.

He looked around for his best position. Up on a slope to one side he found a flat-topped promontory of soft earth and rock covered in long grasses and winter fern which came up to his waist as he waded through it. He dropped the case and placed a waterproof plastic sheet down, flattening the soft greenery. Lying face down and with the surrounding overgrowth acting as a natural screen, he was effectively hidden from all sides. He edged forward until he could see through the grassy screen in front of him and across the scrub spread out ahead. He breathed in the pungent earthy smells mixed with thyme and wild garlic and relaxed in the thin warmth of the sun.

Pamela had denied Jarvis his pleasure last night, to punish him. He had been avoiding her these past few weeks. Love-making had become an occasional event, with Jarvis more urgent and less relaxed than usual, afterwards promptly falling asleep and paying her no further attention. But he expected her to be available and willing whenever, and she was damned if she was going to be at his beck and call. But maybe his grooming sessions in the bathroom were taking longer recently, maybe he was dressing with more attention to detail, new shirts, natty jackets, brushed shoes; and maybe he was listening more often to the pop music radio stations. Although unable to read any signs of guilt in his expressionless face, his less frequent demands on her and the fact that he had taken to creeping out of the house without explanation made Pamela increasingly suspicious that he was seeing someone else.

But at the same time as she was annoyed by his selfishness, she was basking in the pleasure of her secret liaison with Antonio, having been with him several times recently. She was feeling loved again and was loath to disturb that inner warmth of contentment, so hard to achieve, so easy to lose. With Antonio, their late evenings of passion involved operatic music, play-acting, dressing up and undressing, love-making with slow build-up and dramatic release, repeated again and again through the night – at times he was insatiable. Even at seven o'clock one morning when he was stirred by the bright daylight seeping around the velvet curtains of his bedroom, he had coiled himself up behind her and found a gentle rear approach to her soggy sanctuary. Despite his own weariness he had completed his act with a triumphant flourish. She had been horribly late for work that day.

All week she had been tired and had taken to going to bed earlier than usual, too sleepy to respond to Jarvis when he slipped into their bed. She rolled away from him, murmuring something about periods, headaches or exhaustion, taking an inner pleasure at his frustration, while still feeling the Italian's passion deep within her. The last thing she wanted really was Jarvis poking around with his oversized kingpin on one of his overhyped power trips.

Sitting up, he retrieved the folded rifle from the case, along with a box of rounds and an empty magazine that he tossed onto the groundsheet. He reassembled the rifle in a few moments, unfolding, clipping, slide-and-clunk, and laid it down propped on its bipod beside him. He lay face down, legs slightly apart, his boots jabbed into the soft ground beneath, holding himself up on his left elbow, slowly screwing the front suppressor in place. It had been a long time since he was last in this position, lying on the ground while gripping a snipers' rifle, and strange feelings of déjà vu were bubbling up in his head. He watched himself settling in for the long haul, flicking away a fly from his face.

He had become adept at lying hidden for hours, sometimes for days, blended into his background, unmoving and patient, waiting for his target to appear. That was what snipers did – lie still in enemy territory waiting patiently for that one moment, for that one shot to take out a person of interest. It could make all the difference to the success of a military operation, so a successful hit would be greeted with delight and hero worship by the lads on return to base camp.

He nestled his chin on the cool adjustable piece, lining up his line of sight. He squinted along the length of the barrel and went through the motions of sighting a faraway target. He practised on the trigger, that could be squeezed with the slightest pressure without any stray movement of the barrel sight. Perfectly shaped for his large hands, the butt fitted smoothly into his shoulder. Its lightness of touch and sweet balance gave it a hidden power, like sitting with your foot hovering on the accelerator of a turbo-charged sports car, anticipating its rush, its kick. He caressed the weapon with satisfaction, he knew they were going to be friends. He just had to think of a good name for him: the rifle was quite definitely male. Martyn perhaps, after the late John Martyn, the enigmatic anti-establishment folk singer whom Jarvis had adored.

It all began to feel quite natural again. There was no one about, this quiet Sunday morning in April on the edge of a remote forest in rural England. He confidently left his new friend half-covered by the long grasses and set off at a brisk rate across the scrubland, crossing the dyke at the makeshift bridge and feeling hot by the time he arrived at the other side. He had two cans of drink with him, and after taking a gulp from one of them, he placed them on the top of two fence posts, twenty feet apart.

Looking back to where he had set up his shooting position about half a mile away, he had difficulty making out exactly where it was, camouflaged as it was among the natural forest and wild landscape. He walked back following the route he had just taken, confirming the distance to his two little targets of about 1100 metres.

He repositioned himself on the groundsheet with Martyn and looked out towards the line of woods but could not make out the fence posts, let alone the cans that he had placed on them. He lay quietly, waiting for his breathing to return completely to rest. Through the telescopic sights, magnified details of the trees and the posts were clearer. With some focusing he found the cans and was even able to make out the familiar red lettering.

Jarvis had the ability to keep his mind entirely focused on a task when necessary, but today his memory recall kept playing tricks on him. His mouth was dry and his lips felt cracked and for a moment he was lying face down in an open street drain in the humidity of Zubayr on the southern outskirts of Basrah in the dead of a hot sticky night. The sky around him was a clear midnight blue and thousands of stars twinkled in clusters. With a slight shake of his head, he opened his eyes and he was studying once again the English landscape ahead of him. He loaded a magazine with five rounds and slotted it upwards into the underbelly of the stock, and the rifle felt subtly heavier and more powerful for that. With his thumb he switched forward the small safety catch on the side and worked the simple bolt action, filling the firing chamber. Patiently searching again for his two targets, he concentrated on the first drinks can, on his left, shutting everything else out of his mind. It almost filled his circular viewfinder as he slowly applied pressure on the stiff trigger suspended behind its protected guard, keeping the whole weapon in line, as if it were an extension of his own arm. He ignored the pressure he was beginning to feel on the point of his left elbow. There was a muted crack in his ear and a sudden jolt hammered into the front of his right shoulder. The metal can in the distance remained perfectly upright on its post.

A small flock of birds fluttered chaotically above and dispersed somewhere else among the treetops, although he was sure no sound would have been heard over the scrubland. Nothing else had moved. Too high, he concluded, and twiddled with the sighting adjustment screws. In single-shot mode, Jarvis retracted the bolt and a casing flew out past his head into the long grass. He shot the bolt once more and his friend Martyn was ready with the next shot. He settled himself to try again, with the same relaxed posture, holding the butt more firmly into his shoulder. This time the drinks can spun away dramatically off its post, squirting out liquid in all directions, never to be seen again. Aware of thumping pulsations in both sides of his neck, Jarvis felt thrilled.

He edged the weapon a hair's breadth to the right, aiming for the second can with an identical routine. With the same satisfaction, as he squeezed the trigger the can disintegrated silently off the post almost simultaneously, with a crack in his ear and another jolt into his shoulder.

Stimulated more by the smell of cordite that was fresh in his nostrils than by the sound of gunfire, further flashes from the past returned, unwanted. Having crawled through sloppy drains, tunnels and trenches somewhere in the godawful slums of Zubayr, he had settled in position overnight to be ready long before handover at first light, and lay face down in that open drain, the smell of wastepipes and excrement so foul he wanted to vomit.

The skin of his face and the back of his hands were blackened for the overnight operation and he blended so perfectly into the background of desiccated scrub and shit that a dog had come in the early hours of the morning and cocked his leg over him, unaware of the still soldier underneath. The wetness over the back of his legs was still warm. There was plenty of water in his CamelBak and he sucked frequently on the feeder to keep hydrated, while craving those cold beers he had promised himself when he got back to base. His bent arms were aching, taking his weight on the elbows. His combat uniform was stiff and stained along the front where it had been in contact with stagnant water. His scalp was sticky and itchy, and he desperately wanted to take his helmet off to scratch at the irritation. The air was still; there was no breeze to blow away the smell or to cool the skin. His eyes were sore from the arid and dusty air, his lips dry and cracked. Already an army of flies was buzzing around his face, crawling over his skin, tickling his eyelids. He blinked and blew them off his lips. He could not risk a single untoward movement, not even a swat at the little buggers.

Soon after five, he was alerted by the rumbling sounds of military trucks and jeeps in the far distance, raising dust behind them. Below him was the theatre of this particular piece of war, ostensibly a simple exchange between the British Army and one of the many Muslim infidel groups that operated independently round there, who had kidnapped an English journalist and was demanding through some pretty unreliable local intermediaries the release of six Iraqi Muslim 'freedom fighters' in return for her freedom. The whole scene had a number of ramifications that in Jarvis's opinion had a high bungle potential.

Over on the far side along the distant desert perimeter four hundred yards away, in the red, white and blue corner, the British had parked their several vehicles; while down to Jarvis's right at the opposite edge of the bowl, in the black corner was the infidel group, emerging between ramshackle buildings in breeze block and corrugated roofs.

Jarvis's hiding place was well chosen, the drain emerging between broken huts that were home to thousands of poor and elderly Iraqis halfway up the side of a shingly slope, its effluent openly directed down the sides below, flowing to nowhere in particular. With the sun coming up behind him, he would remain in the shadows, with sprouting scrub weeds and grasses protecting him from view. He would not be squinting into a glare or running the risk of light glinting off the front lens of his telescopic sights.

In his grubby hands, Trooper Collingwood clenched an AK12 sniper's rifle, perfectly adequate for the job, good sights for a distance of 600 yards, balanced neatly on a small bipod at the front of the barrel. A magazine of twelve rounds in place should have been more than enough.

The agreement had stipulated no advanced spotters or outriders. The first three prisoners were to walk slowly across the space towards their Muslim brothers; then the Englishwoman would walk slowly the other way, towards the Brits. When they had passed, the next three would start out from the British lines and do the same slow walk. Jarvis had been told that the Muslim commander Hakim al-Wajaka ('Ali-Wak') was also being persuaded with a caseload of cash (five thousand US dollars, apparently), and the second to last prisoner doing the walk would be carrying the money in a shoulder bag, as an extra personal thank you from British command. Jarvis was to take out the infidel commander before the man with the money reached him, providing the woman was safely in British hands by then, and not before.

The disorganised rebel group emerged shambling through a shadowy gap between the buildings down to Jarvis's right, on a side road that led from the centre of town. There were about a dozen of them spaced out, in black robes, with red scarves wrapped around their heads and bullet belts slung over their shoulders, wielding an assortment of Russian automatic machine guns and rifles. There were a couple of young guys at the back lugging a rocket launcher along with them to set up a position behind a low wall, but exactly what the idiots were supposed to achieve, Jarvis could not imagine. Their noise must have disturbed the local wildlife, as there was a sudden fluttering around a mangy tree nearby as hundreds of sparrows took to the early-morning skies. A dog barked somewhere, setting off a brief sequence of barking, as though messages were being passed from one to another across the outskirts.

In the middle of this ragged group, arriving in an open jeep with a blonde woman in his grasp, was big, muscular Ali-Wak, with bare head and bare arms and a drooping moustache. He wore a black sleeveless jerkin over long white robes open at the front to reveal his stomach and an array of weapons around his waist. He dragged the stumbling woman to the front of the group, one strong arm holding the back of her neck, while he toyed with a heavy pistol by his side in his other hand. She was in jeans and a dirty white shirt with a loose scarf around her head and neck that obscured her face. She was moaning, a high pitched incongruous sound, and a white bandage was wrapped neatly around one arm from the elbow downwards. She was trying to hold it into her body for support and appeared to be in pain. She whined and grimaced with each yank from Mister Muscleman as he walked out in the midst of his little army.

The early sunrise emerging low behind Jarvis was beginning to throw sharp shards of yellow light, casting long shadows of the players across the dusty plane below. As Jarvis watched intently through his telescopic sights, he realised that something was obviously wrong. The woman was not as blond or as tall as he expected, her skin was darker, her voice too accented for an educated Anglo-Saxon, especially a politician's daughter; a detail of information Jarvis had quietly been informed of at the last moment and hence the vital importance of this exchange, 'laddie. And that's why we need you in position just now, to check if anything goes wrong,' Captain Sandy Ashcroft, his commander, had urged in his infuriating soft Scottish accent, complete with lisp, just before Jarvis had set out more than twelve long hours ago. Their information was that the Englishwoman had been in captivity for more than three weeks, that she was injured, even that her left hand had been cut off as a way of putting pressure on the negotiators, and that it was unlikely the wound would have been attended to properly. She would be shocked, dehydrated through weight loss, she would be weak. Whereas the woman in Jarvis's sights did not seem to be suffering in that way: she looked sturdy, she looked Arab, she looked all wrong.

Both groups had edged in and the gap between them was only about seventy-five yards, three of the exchange prisoners clearly lined up on the British side. Ali-Wak held the woman roughly by her hair, and she was on her knees at his feet, still moaning. The big man shouted towards the Brits in a thick accent, something like,

'Hey, come on then, let's see what you got.' Prompted by a British soldier, three unshaven Iraqis started to shuffle forward in a single file, binding around their ankles preventing long strides, their feet unshod, their hands tied behind them, all bare headed, in flimsy western clothes. When they were more than halfway across, the big man started to pull the woman up onto her feet, shouting obscenities at her, pushing her from behind to walk forward. She acted frightened and seemed reluctant to move, as though foreseeing her fate. She turned and implored Ali-Wak hysterically in Arabic, revealing some of her face. Although she was stumbling backwards in the general direction the man wanted her to go, this was no performance of a defiant English woman close to freedom. The man slapped her face and shoved her again. He shouted to the shuffling prisoners ahead, the one with the money bag over his shoulder, in Arabic: 'The money, huh?' Jarvis was able to see in the distance his British commander standing to his full height in his jeep with a pair of binoculars to his eyes, apparently calm.

The first Arab, still shuffling across the open space, was only ten yards from reaching his Muslim brothers. The woman turned and shouted again angrily in Arabic. Ali-Wak, whose patience and ability to keep up this pretence were clearly wearing thin, raised his pistol towards the stumbling woman; and Jarvis knew what was to come.

He had already made up his mind. The dishevelled woman was a fraud, not the English captive they were making this deal for, and she was about to be sacrificed. Focusing on the easy target of big Ali-Wak, with his shiny bare arms and comic face in profile catching the sun, was easy. He applied one firm squeeze on the trigger, his weapon perfectly balanced and delivering only a small kick-back. With a fountain of blood spurting vertically, the man's head was ripped apart silently, the bullet erupting the other side of his skull. Ali fired a shot harmlessly from his pistol into the ground, as his body tumbled away to land face down with a thump. The pretend English woman stopped running and whipped round, bringing her hands up to either side of her horrified expression, rigid and unsure.

Jarvis took out the first prisoner with a bullet that exploded through his chest, tossing his body backwards, somersaulting into a heap. He was counting on the other two prisoners turning to head back the way they had come, which, surprisingly, they began to do, wisely thinking that they were safer returning to the British than embracing their brothers on this side and getting caught in the crossfire. Jarvis immediately turned his attention to the straggly group of fighters standing close together like idiots, taken by surprise at the sight of their bloodied commander in a motionless heap on the ground, a thick dark puddle spreading through the dirt around his head.

Three shots in quick succession took out the two front men with head hits, but missed the third, who darted away quickly in a crouch. The rest of the British soldiers started to engage the group with fire from the far side, resulting in more casualties. The remaining rebels were jolted into panic, and turned as one and ran, dropping down into safer positions while trying to fathom where the first shots had come from. Jarvis dramatically broke cover. He sprang up out of the wet filthy drain, over the concrete edge, dragging his stiff body into an uncomfortable crouch and scrambling for more cover up against the earthy side of the nearest shack, out of sight. From this higher position he began to track the retreating movements of the bedraggled Arabs, as they ran back through rows of dilapidated shacks to their own hideout, a two-storey concrete building about half a mile along the same road.

The fake kidnapped prisoner had sprinted over to the far side of the compound, putting as much distance as she could between herself and the flying bullets, and Jarvis last saw her jumping clean over a wall with remarkable agility, her bandages unravelling comically in her flight.

Some unexpected movement in the distance on the edge of the woods close to the fence posts caught Jarvis's eye.

He looked up across the scrub and picked out a tiny figure in a dark coat holding a stick and with a brown dog bounding around. It was standing a few feet from one of the posts where the can had just spun off, as if by magic. The person had probably heard two loud pings and saw the cans burst away one after the other, dropping with a clatter among the stones. Purely as an exercise, Jarvis squinted through his sights at the now magnified figure standing still, clearly identifying the features of a man with trimmed moustache in a Barbour and brown trilby rooted to the ground in surprise. He was looking towards Jarvis's position and back again at the nearest fence post. Placing his index finger in the trigger guard, holding steady the tension, Jarvis imagined pulling firmly and watching the face of the anonymous man splitting apart, his features disintegrating in a splurge of colour and the body dropping to the ground, no one the wiser. Except for the dog.

Careful, Jarvis boy, do not get carried away.

Spread-eagled, prone, elated and frustrated, his hands casually draped over the rifle stock, his eyes closed, his erection hard under his weight, he thrust his pelvis against the ground with clenched buttocks, massaging rhythmically for a few seconds. Fresh grass and garlic smells calmed his mood and the flood of old memories gradually subsided. He ceased moving and dropped his wet forehead to the cool groundsheet. With a heavy sigh, his whole body limp, he felt release pouring inside Naomi's tight and fragile body, her innocent nakedness breached at last. After a short moment of dream-like contentedness, his self-confidence reasserted itself and reality returned. He felt overwhelmingly certain of what he had to do.

Lifting his head up, he peered out across the wasteland ahead: the unknown stranger and his dog were gone.

It had just started to drizzle.

At the British Army airport base camp later that day, Jarvis Collingwood had become the local hero when news of his exploits reached the expectant squaddies. Much to his surprise, he had been able to easily track the half dozen retreating Arabs back to a battle-damaged house only a few streets away from the location of the aborted exchange. From an adjacent rooftop he had watched the disorganised group, young men, inexperienced and leaderless, who seemed to be debating whether to kill the prisoner in the basement and run or stay and fight for the ransom money. Jarvis could not afford to wait and went in through the roof, disarming and knifing one Arab, before taking his automatic to shoot the five others one at a time as he moved rapidly down a back staircase. Below ground level he kicked in a locked door to a filthy prison room that smelt of excrement, where a young blond woman was gagged and half unconscious on a rotting pile of blankets. She smelt unpleasant and unwashed, even worse than he did. She was weakened by her wounds, that included a severed wrist wrapped in strips of blood-soaked muslin. Her face was bruised, her lips cut and swollen. Jarvis activated his radio that had been silent for the exchange and called his platoon, who rode through the ramshackle district in three jeeps, clearing the roads of any possible hostiles as they went. Jarvis carried the poor woman out and they were rushed safely back to camp, where Jarvis had the best shower of his Army career, cheered on by his mates. The woman, Jennifer Tomkins, he never saw again.

Captain Ashcroft was angry and delighted at the same time: he had been tricked, but the Second Battalion Parachute had secured the release of a valuable British asset (immediately operated on with the hope of a full recovery from her ordeal, she was returned to the Honourable Sir Richard Tomkins, MP), had retained five of their six captives as well as the five thousand US dollars, and had disposed of one notorious local bastard, one fewer to deal with later. He made absolutely sure high command became aware of the unit's success, and of course of the vital role played by one brilliant sniper, Corporal Jarvis Collingwood.

9

On May Day, a British government-sponsored meeting for top security people was in full swing at the Millennium Edgware Hotel, and Jonathan Collingwood's team was out in force to seek a firm foothold in the business and beat off the competition. Suits from all the well-known firms were gathered. A junior minister nobody had heard of was on hand to give the opening address, and the deputy head of the Organising Committee for the London Olympic Games gave the standard pep talk, reminding the predominantly male audience of hardened ex-servicemen and assorted blockheads about the importance of working in the spirit of cooperation, with security at London 2012 being the ultimate priority. Papers had been laid out around the tables in the main meeting room, providing a full description of the scope of the challenge, details about the various venues and sites of activity, as well as the personnel and the tasks involved, with illustrations flashed up on the surrounding multi-screens. Making sure everyone understood the responsibility they would have, allocation and scheduling were the main tasks of the day, along with ultimate matching of specifications to project applications. Performance would be target driven and closely monitored, with Home Office scrutiny and close overview. The challenge was there for all. It was generally agreed, however, that although the rewards would probably be plentiful, there were no easy options.

Jonathan was fraught with nervous energy, hopping from one presentation to another, wanting to negotiate his way around every possibility. He had brought the delectable Ms Stutterfeld with him to advise – oh yes, Jonathan was always full of the spirit of cooperation. The moment Jarvis arrived, he spotted her now familiar backside across the crowded lounge, in stretched apple green, her auburn hair shimmering with every shake or nod of her pretty head. Fawning young men, and some not so young, gripping smart phones and tablets, were surrounding her, hanging on her every word, thrilled to be basking so close to such glamour, in such a typically unglamorous world. Drinks were flowing aplenty and those that could not get close to GG contented themselves with arguing about last night's Manchester derby.

Jarvis was listening out for details of security jobs and recruitment. Jonathan was there to ensure his SecureLife bid successfully for the most prestigious venue, the main Olympic Stadium at Stratford Park. 'The potential capacity we need is for more than double our present staff,' Jonathan was saying, 'and we need to start recruiting in now, before the others get to the market, or we'll fail.' Jarvis was supposed to be there to calm his older brother, but all he did was pass comment on the beauty of womankind and complain about how unfair it was that he was not going to get to shag Georgina any time soon.

During the afternoon the bidding became more competitive. There were plenty of reputations and lucrative contracts at stake. As Jarvis learnt later, Jonathan's SecureLife won a number of concessions on the day through behind-the-scenes nods and handshakes, complementing its already established outsourcing agreement with GS Security, the largest private security firm. These included a share of Stratford Park, involving patrolling the sites and arranging the transportation of athletes and VIPs around the Olympic venues and central London. Jarvis studied some of the schedules that were being drafted, and was interested to identify the arrangements being made for the small Iraqi team of eight athletes to be housed at the Sports Village in Hatfield, part of the University of Hertfordshire, apparently with the British Virgin Islands team, before moving them later to the new Olympic Village. He half expected to see Abu Masoud himself there negotiating for his Iraqi friends and checking the arrangements, but much to Jarvis's relief, he was not there.

Jarvis wandered over to the reception bar to join some other company men for a drink and spotted Jonathan and Georgina close together, laughing. In fact Jonathan could hardly keep his hands off her, guiding her here and there with his fingers in the small of her back. He bought drinks for everyone, delighted with the day's work and dreaming of his margins and company profits. Over the next few weeks he was going to set in motion a series of special meetings for all the staff, to tackle the workload that they were now faced with.

'Eighty-seven days to go,' he beamed, and sank another vodka and tonic, slimline.

'I will draw up implementation plans for you, Jonathan, yes,' Georgina gushed in her juddering Scandinavian English, 'but after that it will be over to you. I will be back with my team, but you must give feedback when it is over, obviously.' She had a way of moistening her vowel sounds inside her mouth before popping them out through pouted lips, like a fish producing bubbles in its tank. 'It will be wery useful to hear experiences and what you have learnt. And of course how effective the planning was with your consultant team,' she beamed with a special pout. 'Wery useful.' The surrounding circle of adoring fans had their own mouths open and their eyes fixed on the glistening moisture that spangled along the edge of her deep red smile, snow white teeth intermittently gleaming within. As she spoke, her shoulders fluttered, her bosoms juddered.

Jarvis observed Georgina and his brother, as transfixed as everybody else. Jonathan looked eager to kiss those lips full on, licking all that red gloss off, no doubt calculating the odds of getting her upstairs to one of the hotel rooms before she returned to her accountant husband in the Home Counties. He must have wished all the others would now simply bugger off and leave them alone together. Jarvis slipped away, leaving Jonathan in his state of suspended frustration.

A week later, Jarvis had a further meeting in The White Hart. Ainsley was clearly excited. He had some new information about Abu Masoud's travel plans, obtained from his source in Baghdad apparently who worked in Abu's office, and Ainsley guaranteed absolutely its authenticity.

'These plans cover the next three months, including London, as you can see here,' he said, putting some sheets of paper on the table between them. 'Two more photos, one blown up for identification purposes.' Jarvis inspected the paperwork, careful to keep the pages close to his chest. 'So, it's going to be at the Olympics, yes?' Ainsley probed.

'It's mind-your-own-business time again, Ainsley.' Jarvis sounded techy. 'You freak me out, you know that?'

'No need to be techy, Jarvis. I'm not going to spill any beans.'

'No, you're not.' Jarvis wagged a finger and stared at him intensely for a moment, trying to read him. They both drank some beer, taking the opportunity to think their thoughts, but nothing was said for a while.

'Money come through, Jarvis? No problem?' Ainsley was staring across with eyebrows raised, and he flicked his hair off his forehead.

'No problem.'

On returning from a day's security work one evening, Jarvis found Pamela at home, after her weekly facial and eyebrow session, in the kitchen unloading shopping. 'Right, I must go up and wash my hair,' she announced, with a pleased look that reminded him of her smiling flushed appearance in the hidden photographs he had found. 'I must preen myself for the evening,' she added with a pouting twist of her lips and a swagger, planting a cheeky kiss on his mouth as she passed.

'So where is it this time, Pam?' Jarvis, leaning on the door post, sounded disapproving.

She looked back at him with well-practised innocence. 'We have a reception in town, Covent Garden, for some of the IOC members and their partners. A pep talk from the boss, meeting and greeting, just playing host really.'

'And who's going to be there?'

'I've just said – the high and mighty . . .'

'No. Among you lot, who are you going with?'

'Oh, nobody special, nobody that you would know, Jarvis.' She sprinted up the stairs like a teenager, escaping for a nice long period of preparation in peace, away from his annoying questions.

Whilst he could hear distant tinkling sounds of running water from upstairs, a dull-sounding mobile buzzed downstairs and it took Jarvis a while to locate it. Deep within Pamela's handbag that she had left in the lounge, he found it after rummaging for a while, but the caller had rung off. He checked in the missed-calls log and saw the caller, 'Antonio'. He watched the screen for a while and sure enough, thirty seconds later a message was received with a ping. He opened it: *Feeling lucky tonight, hope you are too – see you in hall, back to mine after? Ant.*

He dropped the Blackberry back into her bag.

Although it seemed a long wait until August, when London would host the Olympics, Jarvis was a painstakingly careful planner and was determined to see that everything was in place before he made his move, as the logistics, involving two wildly different but prominent targets, would be complicated. But in fact the weeks of late spring and early summer passed quickly, for both Jarvis and Pamela. They were kept so busy in their own worlds that they had little spare time to get in each other's way. Ironically they were both working on the same major event, Jarvis in preparation for his security duties at the newly built Stratford Park, and Pamela with Merriweather's team preparing the marketing and design material for their greatest-ever public relations challenge. In between, Jarvis was beavering away at his personal project, fitting out his hideaway and practising his shooting skills whenever he could. He also pitched up with the forest gang every second or third week, although Danny had confided in him one evening in the caravan over beans and a meat pie that the work at Beacon Forest would be closed down sooner rather than later as Lord Muck was running out of cash. Jarvis reminded Danny of the hardship that that would cause to many of the men from the gang he had come to know, who would find it difficult to get work elsewhere.

Jarvis returned from a supermarket trip late one afternoon and was carrying the load from the boot of his car through to the kitchen. Pamela was relaxed in tight jeans and a Banksie print T-shirt, having a cigarette and coffee in the lounge while watching a TV chef cooking something exotic with fennel and turmeric. She had been looking through cookery books and recipes for ideas in preparation for her dinner party at the house the following evening, which she correctly predicted Jarvis had forgotten about.

'What bloody dinner party? No, I can't be here, I'm going out with a couple of the lads.' Jarvis pushed the front door closed with the last of the heavy bags, kicked his boots off and walked into the kitchen. 'And no, you didn't warn me.'

'I want you to be here – a couple of Italian guys are coming who I've been working with, and their friends, and I wanted to show you off.' She tried to sound light hearted and encouraging about the whole thing, when her real purpose was not so much to show Jarvis off, as to have an opportunity to show him up, as a useless, unsupportive husband. Once Antonio had seen what an asshole

Jarvis really could be, he might be provoked into making a more direct bid for her, out of friendship, jealousy – or love, maybe. The trouble with Antonio was that basically he was a coward and he would not stand up to Jarvis, who was far bigger and fiercer than the smooth-talking smooth-skinned little Italian. Even if he did bring his friend Pietro with him. Or at least this was how her thought processes had been working lately.

'So who are these people?' Jarvis asked, with barely disguised curiosity.

'Antonio and Pietro, with two girlfriends – they all work for a design consortium, interiors mostly, and they have been working with the British teams. That's how I met them. I wanted to have them round – they're amusing, you'd like them, Jarvis, I'm sure.'

So she intended bringing her lover-boy into his home, tempting fate. Actually he was tempted to meet Antonio just to see what sort of weedy lover-boy he was. 'Not if they are anything like the usual toffee-nosed prigs you bring round,' Jarvis muttered under his breath as he unloaded his shopping and packed things away. He did not really intend for Pamela to hear his comment, but of course she did and that started her off, telling him to clear off, she could manage without him. 'You can bloody well cook your own meals today.'

She insisted on having the kitchen to herself, so she could start some food preparation, and Jarvis sloped off to the lounge out of immediate range, with a beer. He watched the TV aimlessly, thinking what an impossible tart she could be.

'So, this Italian, Antonio, you met him the other night, right?' Jarvis called through the doorway. 'Is he getting fresh or what?'

Pamela came to the doorway, holding a jar of tomato sauce. 'What do you mean?'

'I saw a message for you, on your phone, it was very personal. Are you seeing him or something?' Jarvis narrowed his eyes from across the room, as he tried to read her guilt.

'What are you doing with my phone?' she asked coldly. She stomped into the room feeling indignant and searched around for her discarded mobile, as if protecting it now would somehow reverse the fact that Jarvis had already come across something he shouldn't have.

'It was lying on the table; a message beeped, so I read it. You were in the shower. I kept quiet, none of my business, but it seems you have something going with this Italian bloke.' Jarvis, as provocative as he might be, knew that he was asking for more, and knew that he should stop asking. Pamela was weighing the heavy glass jar in her hand and had a mind to hurl it at her sodding husband.

'OK, and what about you and these other girls I know you see? I know about Penny. She's an old slag who's been round the block a few times, Jarvis – surely you can do better than that? And I know you've been round to her place, you were spotted in Soho last week.'

'You've got a bloody nerve. So you've been spying on me?' Jarvis felt the blood in his temples buzzing. He was well aware that he should cool it, walk away if anything, before he said something he would regret. Except that maybe now was the time to confront the truth with Pamela anyway and be done with it.

But Pamela beat him to it and flew at him. 'You make absolutely no effort,' she fumed, trying to control her temper and rising voice, but speaking with such unexpected force that she took the wind out of Jarvis's sails, 'to understand me or find out what I'm doing or anything. I like meeting people, I like Antonio, he's very amusing and fun to be with. They're working colleagues and good friends, they both have their own girlfriends.'

'So what makes you think I would want to meet them, talking posh about stuff, talking money and privilege and crap like that?'

'Oh you are such an idiot. They are go-getters, Jarvis, these people, they work hard and do things. They play hard and they are good to be with. And they care about me, which is a damn sight more than you do,' and of course Pamela could not stop the tears from welling up, or her face from turning pink, with stamping of feet and the need for tissues. She wiped along her eyelids with a stubby forefinger, her nails of purple varnish looking out of place. A teardrop or two darkened her woolly top, but Jarvis took no notice.

Pamela's mouth was taut and her lips narrowed, trembling with anger, at her own perceived weakness. 'If you think I'm going to idly sit here all day waiting for you to come home to share a part of your life with me, to live a part of your life with me, to take any interest even ... then ... you are much mistaken. I've got my life to get on with,' she stated firmly, 'my career and my friends to worry about ... and if you can't see yourself being involved, then, then that is *your* loss.'

She headed back to the kitchen with a hand over her face, sniffing, still trembling. Jarvis followed her because he hated to be shouted out and then not to have the last word. From behind, he grabbed her by the arms, shook and squeezed her to calm her down and stop her hitting out at him. He called her a tramp and a hypocrite. He wanted to strike her, but she had her back to him. Suddenly he felt a sharp pain on his shins as she kicked backwards with her heel. He was infuriated and threw her away, across the room, wanting to bend down to rub the painful spot. Pamela hit her hip against the edge of the sink and stumbled painfully to her knees, trying to hold on to the side. Jarvis thought again about hitting her and came close but sensibly restrained himself.

'I know about you,' he was speaking emphatically, slowly and under control, 'and Jonathan, years ago, when I was away – fighting for my country – do you think I don't hate you for such a thing, with my own brother?' He paused, but had said enough. 'I'm going out.' With a look of thunder across his face, he stomped out, pulled his boots on in the hall, gave his sore shin a rub and headed over the road to The Baring, where he bought a pie and a pint.

Pamela recovered but flopped onto a high stool in the kitchen, leaning over the breakfast bar with head in hands, and cried rather soundlessly. *Shit.* She was hurt and wondered why she had not hit Jarvis with the jar still in her hand, when she had had the chance. *That Jonathan business is so old, why raise that now? Had Jonathan said anything to him?* Her pride was what was hurt most, and losing her temper never helped. She had been screwing Antonio and Jarvis had been screwing Penny, so what was the difference? She had to blow her nose several times.

Sometimes she felt her head was in an empty space, a sort of void, that should have been filled with the joys of living, two ambitious people striving in their lives, trying to better themselves, to achieve better things. But instead, they were competing, confronting each other without affection, one always trying to gain the upper hand over the other. This was no partnership, just a frustrating battle, and it would soon turn to violence unless she did something about it. But her mind felt tired, and her head empty, as if its contents had been stolen by someone sweeping around the inside of her skull with a sharp blade. To Jarvis, she was a flimsy mindless tart, whereas really she was simply searching for her way of expressing her personality and feeling desperate for recognition, for appreciation.

In the middle of the afternoon, Pamela curled up in bed to hide her tears and hurt. When she awoke, bruised about the arms and hip, a sour taste lingered around her mouth. Dishevelled hair, pasty face, dark shadowing under the eyes, sagging breasts, these were what she saw in the mirror. She pulled back the curtains to reveal the misery of the day outside and sank back onto the bed thinking of Antonio. Did she dare phone him? They had vowed never to contact each other at home, although she wondered whether that suited him more than her. *Who would he be with right now, who would she be disturbing? Who would he be dazzling with his funny accent and Mediterranean charm?* Pamela conjured him up in her mind's eye, in black silk in his cosy Mayfair apartment, watching the drizzling rain from inside his private retreat. He should be hugging a soft toy, longing for Pamela to be beside him, surrounded by his plush accessories, like the white Afghan rug, the silk cushions, the pretty abstracts and carvings, the blow-up photos of himself lining the hallway, while his beloved opera blasted out in surround sound. It would be Pavarotti at full volume, or maybe something a little seductive from Julio. He would be humming along as he rearranged the knick-knacks of his life, on shelves or table tops or on the white piano, joining in the choruses enthusiastically, wafting from steaming bathroom to perfumed bedroom to sumptuous lounge in his tight trousers and body-hugging polo. The Italians knew how to deal with sorrow and upset: they called upon their beloved musical heritage and sang their troubles away, just like their heroes, whereas the English just wallowed in self-pity.

Pamela felt gingerly for the bruises on her upper arms and in the bathroom studied the blue smudge over her hip. Any residual hope of finding something attractive within her relationship with Jarvis, that might be salvageable, was in tatters. The flimsy fabric of her inner feelings was weakened and with each battle it seemed ready to tear apart. Where would that leave her? *Antonio to the rescue?* She doubted that. In truth he rather used her for his convenience, in the absence of some other suitable woman; she had no delusions about Antonio's true feelings. So without Jarvis and her brittle marriage, she would be left with nothing, and no children to comfort her. She implored her image to find a way out of the mess.

She had a mind to cancel the dinner party for her Italian friends; the trouble it might cause was not worth it. She descended the stairs with ladylike care, not risking that phone call.

Jarvis had spent the rest of the afternoon pacing around the Hoxton streets in the wet, the light rainwater pleasantly cooling his cheeks. He needed a shower to wash away his feelings, which had boiled over with pent-up anger. He regretted his reaction, knowing he could have done better; he did not want to cause Pamela harm; at this stage of his project that was not a good idea. After some hours, beginning to feel weary as he returned home, he came to much the same conclusion as Pamela had, although from a different direction – his emotions were flat, structureless and without texture, he felt sometimes there was a vacuum inside his head, that something important was missing. He was just as much in need of emotional contact and physical touch as she was.

Later that evening, when their simmering tempers had abated and the light of the gloomy day had faded away, after a grimly wet afternoon, they met each other in the kitchen. Pamela prepared a supper for them both, which they consumed in silence, sitting apart.

10

The centrepiece of the London Olympics at Stratford Park lay like an abandoned shipwreck, with its side pieces missing, steelwork and concrete exposed, its innards open for all to see. The future stadium, which from the air resembled a huge Polo mint, towered over its surroundings, massive white pillars criss-crossing around the outside, while its distinctive pitched roof of canvas gave it the majestic appearance of a giant crown. Within its framework could be seen escalators, unfinished stairways, causeways, walkways and gangways. At ground level at its four corners, dark featureless tunnels, wide enough and tall enough for articulated lorries, burrowed under concrete tiers of seating into the arena, with the wide skies open above. Here a flat green rectangle of grass lay tranquil in the middle, surrounded by an oblong of pink running track, and massed all around in concentric circles were grey and white plastic seats, row upon row of them, raked steeply up to the top outer rim, one hundred and fifty feet above the concourse.

Despite the persistent drizzle, Jarvis thrilled at every bit of the preliminary tour of the site, arranged to familiarise senior security and management staff with the park facilities. He took in all the details that he could and tried to imagine how the stadium would feel filled with 80,000 enthusiastic spectators. Much of the inner fit-up work was still in progress and plenty of activity continued on the surrounding roads, buildings and security areas. The group of thirty were shown around the concourse areas, the entry and exit pathways, the perimeter fencing and the security areas at the Stratford and Greenway Gates. A middle-ranking Metropolitan police officer was on hand to update them on crowd-control issues.

Within a few days of working at the Park, Jarvis was used to the routine. Transport from their Shoreditch warehouse for the SecureLife staff was arranged in company vans, early morning arrival at eight o'clock, return journeys after six every day. Some of the lads were already allocated to perimeter duties and security control, others were on intensive training courses. They would join the queue of site workers filing through a crude scanner at the south entrance before heading for the changing rooms. Most of the sophisticated scanning equipment had not yet arrived, but vehicles were being randomly inspected on Warton Road, just ahead of the railway bridge, with spaniel sniffer dogs and security men using under-vehicle mirrors, before being allowed to enter the secure areas within the Park.

Naomi and Jarvis continued to see each other regularly, once a week or so, and Naomi in particular gained in confidence. Celia, her best friend, would have described the pair as close, were it not that she suspected Jarvis of having a darker hidden side. They chose crowded cafés or pubs to go to, or music gigs, when they could be together without having to talk too much to each other, which particularly suited Jarvis. Neither liked dancing or the mindless thumping beat of night clubs. They preferred sitting at the side at live events or music nights in pubs, in the shadows, holding hands, when Jarvis might steal a kiss or two, if he was feeling adventurous. Towards the end of an evening, if Maureen was out, he might walk Naomi back to her flat, where they would listen to music or watch television, with cups of coffee.

That they had not progressed much beyond hand holding, hugging or kissing was down to Naomi, who rejected the idea of going any further because of her uncertainty since hearing about his marriage. Jarvis struggled to restrain his natural instincts but was juggling his two relationships rather well, he thought, needing as he did to keep both parties happy at the same time.

Sometimes Naomi wondered about trying to find out where he lived and perhaps meeting with Pamela. She would never be able to follow him through the streets though, he would out-walk her, spot her and humiliate her into the bargain. And she probably could not cope with meeting the wife – it was unlikely to be a friendly moment. She had tried to find him in the phone book, but there was no Josh Cooper listed. She really did not know what to do. He evaded her questions about his past life and about Pamela, and so she had stopped asking, but she was still disappointed when he told her that his Army friends were too rough and rowdy for her, so she would not like to meet them; it seemed he did not have any friends that she could meet.

He was being secretive about so much, and seemed especially afraid of Pamela finding him out. Maybe Celia was right about him hiding something, but Naomi's kindly instinct was to be at Jarvis's side and rescue him, not catch him out. If he was in trouble for some reason, she would prefer that he confided in her so she could help. If he had another secret life, apart from his wife being hidden away in some mystery home, Naomi wanted to be part of it so she could understand him better and they could share their lives better. These days she was certainly contemplating being with Josh on a more permanent basis, and had even thought about inviting him to live with her, maybe asking Maureen to find somewhere else, which would give them more privacy.

On the other hand, it suited Naomi to take things slowly. Again Celia was on hand to remind her how young she was, how she should be having bundles of fun. At least Josh was providing some fun, but she should wait a bit longer for anything deeper, until she was absolutely certain and until he had divorced the mysterious Pamela. Celia grudgingly admitted how hot and handsome he was and how attractive he was to probably every living woman in the whole of East London, but then annoyingly repeated her theory about his darker side, and how Naomi needed to get to the bottom of that, in a manner of speaking, before really committing herself.

Union Jack bunting and flags were out everywhere throughout Britain, it seemed. It was late May, and coincidentally Naomi's birthday. She was twenty-seven, and Jarvis took her up to the West End to see the show *Billy Elliot*. Even though neither of them were born at the time of the miners' strike and the confrontation with Margaret Thatcher, they both loved the show, and Naomi clapped and giggled all the way through and thought she was having the best time of her life. And spoke non-stop about it afterwards on their way back to Upper Street, where they were meeting some of her friends. Jarvis tried to come up with a good excuse for not being with her at this juncture, as he was worried about the possibility of later recognition by these new faces, but in the end it was only a small risk that any of them would remember him sufficiently, and better that he should not upset Naomi. So they called in at O'Neill's, where there was a small crowd at the bar, lots of Naomi's friends it appeared. She introduced a few by name – Bert and Dusty, Frizz and Aimie – all of which Jarvis promptly forgot. And she introduced him to them with a shy smile and a shrug of her bony shoulders as her friend 'Josh'. He listened to them chatting and laughing, teasing Naomi and reminding her of funny incidents from the past, that meant absolutely nothing to him. He was not remotely interested in any of them but acted the cool dude, the tough boyfriend who said little. He watched Naomi, seeing a funny goof, fond of pulling faces, giggly and girlish. Celia arrived late. She was a chirpy cropped blonde with boyish hair and a flat chest, café-au-lait brows and blueberry lips. Clothed all in white, with noisy bangles around her wrists, she simulated kissing Jarvis on both cheeks and then promptly sank half a lager with some choice words of pleasure. 'Fuck me, that was good!'

Naomi opened presents and everyone sat at a long table, eating burgers and chips. In the toilets later the girls told Naomi how impressed they were. 'What a great-looking guy!' 'He's hot for you, Naomi!' 'Blimey, what a catch!' and so on until Naomi was sick of hearing it all.

The boys were impressed too, and told Jarvis later in the gents, 'Wow, Naomi's a lucky girl, you serious or what?' 'You goin' with her?' 'What do you do, I suppose you're loaded as well, drive a BMW, do yer?' 'Fancy a snort, mate?'

Naomi, having drunk far more than she was used to, including some unidentified cocktails, was feeling warmly amorous. Jarvis sensed her relaxation, her heady look, an inner happiness in her smiling face. She had a way of leaning against him with a look of pride when people remarked about them, as if there was some own-ership involved. She adjusted his shirt collar when it was twisted, moved his wristbands around to align them, pulled his sleeve up occasionally to read his watch.

She was sitting at the crowded bar in coloured print trousers, legs awkwardly crossed, when he leant over purposely to kiss her on the lips in front of her friends, not caring what anyone thought. She felt the warm closeness of his body. She knew she would fail to resist Josh tonight, and the anticipation of walking back to her flat together to explore their feelings was electric. She started gig-gling under his kisses. She would reward his patience; she knew how much he had restrained his natural temptations for her sake. He had reassured her that his marriage was breaking up, that he wanted to part amicably from Pamela, and that that would take some time. And Naomi, in her easy-going way, not wanting any conflict, accepted what he said, but was ready to express her own feelings with honesty like anybody else. For his part, Jarvis wanted to move ahead to the next phase, to allow his plan to develop further, to embroil her deeper into his life, which meant that he needed to coax her passions from out of their hiding place.

They both sensed a crucial moment approaching. There was tactile excitement between them. A shiver passed through her body as she hugged him seriously around the neck, rubbing her cheek against his thick beard. The others were saying it was time these lovers were allowed home, it was getting near their bedtime. 'Come on,' he whispered into her ear through her hair, 'let's go find some peace and quiet, and I will make beautiful love to you.' And she swooned, her eyes opening wider, that broad smile showing her front white teeth. She turned to her friends one at a time, thanking them for coming and for her presents, and hugged them all, agreeing that they should all meet up again soon.

Naomi and Jarvis made their exit with all the parcels and packages, putting most of them into Jarvis's rucksack. They crossed Upper Street arm in arm, leaning against each other, and headed through the quieter back ways. It was drizzling hard, and by the time they reached Naomi's place, they were wet through.

The trees lining Northchurch Road were still bare, the road was quiet and rain-swept. The front of Naomi's building was shadowy, the steps down to her door wet and slippery. Inside it felt barely warm. In the hallway they dropped their belongings and kicked off their shoes and did not switch on any lights, but slowly stripped off each other's wet clothes as they stumbled round to Naomi's bedroom. Leather jacket, denim top, trainers, patterned trousers, jeans and T-shirts, all dropped in a line on the wooden flooring. Naomi grabbed towels for them to rub themselves down with. Dim light glanced through the windows from the street, feebly illuminating their pale flesh, so white against the internal darkness as they stuttered around, like in an old black-and-white movie.

Naomi perched herself on the edge of her bed, pulling him nervously towards her, and he stood between her thighs. She buried her face into his warm hairy tummy, tasting salty skin. He fiddled with her bra clip, tossing it aside. And then she flopped backwards with both arms aloft onto the bed cover, shockingly cold. Diffuse shadows played across the contours of her smooth body, producing rounded patterns on the silky eiderdown and Jarvis saw that she had pleasing globular breasts that splayed luxuriously outwards across her ribbed chest.

He was eager and tense, his pants were down. She gripped his legs within her thighs like pincers and waited, terrified of what was to come. Any doubts she might have had about the strength of his desire or the means at his disposal disappeared as soon as she saw him. The only time she could remember seeing such an impressive specimen was on a horse at a riding stables years ago as a shy schoolgirl, when her mother had advised her to look the other way, but she had looked anyway, astonished.

Naomi was trapped, there was no going back. Her inner emotions had brought her here and it was her choice. She told herself that she had the situation under control, but feared the unknown nevertheless. She remembered the pack of condoms in the bedside drawer, a brilliant reminder from Celia one day when they had mused what Jarvis might be like in bed.

Jarvis knew to be sensitive, this their first time. He peeled her cotton panties down with care, tossing the warm bundle away across the floor. Naked and exposed, they scrambled up the bed and crouched together, excited by the feel of each other's skin. His muscular arms pulled her still for a while and he hugged her close, aware of the heartbeat bounding along within her bony frame. In the bleak light her cold pea-sized nipples looked like Smarties embedded in soft pink marshmallow, which hardened in response to his tongue teasing. He squeezed her white skin, kissed her lips and then her breasts again. Exploring her, tracing light fingertips around her armpit, around her breasts, over her ribs and up and down the rising slopes of her stomach, he felt goose pimples and tiny hairs rising. He admired the metal stud and dangling jewel in her tummy button, and combed her thin bristle with his fingers, cupping the hairy mound with a firm hold. Her hands began to feel him in the same way, and he hardened at the thrill of it.

Increasingly drawn into the moment, Naomi felt her innate inhibitions draining away and she surrendered to an unquenchable desire for him to penetrate her. Jarvis was heavy and she so fragile beneath, that what was at first a new and exciting sensation as he applied pressure became a sore and deeply painful moment. She flinched with each thrust, her legs stiffening against him, and he struggled to achieve any sort of rhythm. This angered him and slowed him down when he needed to rush, but he contained his frustration with her, and they spluttered to a halt. Naomi was whimpering, wiping her hands across her face; she had tears welling up in her eyes. He withdrew, fell back to reassess the situation, but was quick to reach for her, to comfort her when he saw her distress. He hugged her, genuinely upset at the pain he had caused, wanting desperately to make her better.

'I'm so sorry, Naomi, I didn't mean to hurt you, I'm really sorry. Are you all right?' He was almost weeping himself. They hugged tightly, to be close, and after a while, their passions entirely vanished, they covered themselves over with the duvet and rocked themselves into a sort of slumber.

On the TV news one night he watched with fascination the ex-UK Prime Minister Gerry Morley once again taking centre stage for a day, facing questions at the Leveson Inquiry. Jarvis marvelled at his ability to answer a question without answering it, or to turn the question into an opportunity to answer a different question. *What a fantastic performer in public!* he laughed quietly to himself. Live on camera in the courthouse, someone burst into the chamber during the questioning and shouted insults at him, accusing him of war crimes. Jarvis raised an ironic smile at the nightmarish scene. *That would have kept the security services on their toes.*

'Look, Pam, I'm sorry about the other day. I was out of order.'

Jarvis looked convincingly contrite even though it was a pragmatic decision on his part that a truce was for the best, for now. Pamela was ready to go to work, elegant in a navy blue trouser suit, white shirt, looking every part the middle-manager commuter that she was. Make-up, including heavy mascara, disguised the swellings around her eyes and the heavy lines on her face. She looked tragic in many ways, with her pale face and rouge lips set in a surly expression as she tried to protect what self-respect she had left. He dared not ask her about Antonio (or any other friend) she might be seeing tonight.

She stopped at the front door, car keys in hand, and turned to look at him, casual in his white singlet vest, his handsome features all too familiar to her. She walked back to him with clipped heels and stretched up on tiptoes to kiss his mouth, still holding on to her bag. He made no attempt to respond to her, but the mildest flicker of a smile passed across his lips for a moment.

She half-smiled as well without conviction. 'OK. If you say so. We'll talk tonight, shall we?' And she turned to leave.

'Yes, I was just wondering about the Games.'

'Were you?' She stopped and cocked a quizzical eyebrow.

'You'll be busy, I know, but you'll be getting some tickets, I presume?'

'You mean, was I going to have any spare for you? You'll be there most of the time anyway, won't you, working?' Pamela reached the front door.

'Yes, but even the working security staff will have some time off. I wanted to watch the closing ceremony from the stands.'

Pamela hung on to a slight pause, rather longer than Jarvis would have liked. And without turning to him, she said, 'I'll see what I can do. See you later.' She glided elegantly through the front door before Jarvis could make any other comment.

Jarvis was so preoccupied with planning his project and everything that he had rather neglected his mother. He had not visited her for several weeks. He was expecting to be duly admonished, knowing that she would be fretting that her favourite son was mixing with the wrong company or being wrongly influenced. She would question him about what Pamela was doing too, as her daughter-in-law's commitments were almost as important as her son's should be, yet she had not heard from either of them for weeks.

Not unexpectedly for a man of thirty, Jarvis's thoughts of late were less on his mother's well-being and more on the shape that his own life was taking. The pressures of his increasingly angry relationship with Pamela, the alternative life he was planning, the job he had taken on with its many questionable motives and uncertain outcomes – all were playing heavily on his mind. At times he felt terrified. He needed to keep his focus. He knew that he could bring the whole project to an end at any time if he wished – although loss of face and an ugly reaction from an angry Arthur Chigwell, to say nothing of the large sum of money involved, were strong incentives to see it through successfully. But even when he was in the middle of one of his less confident spells, Jarvis realised how intense his determination to succeed was, how strong his will to come through, another hero from another war. It made him feel alive and with a sense of purpose.

Driving his Astra into the gravel entrance at the front of his mother's house, he admired the colour of the garden, the climbing hydrangea and clematis. In honey-brown cashmere cardigan and skirt, and wearing a simple pearl necklace, Gwendolyn stepped out the front door to greet him. He was wearing clean jeans with a white and navy blue gingham shirt under a leather jacket. They hugged, Gwendolyn coming up to Jarvis's chin, and kissed cheeks.

'Mother, you look well, as always.'

She reached up to his shoulders and brushed his beard with her spidery fingers. 'Still got the beard – you're not serious?'

Irritated, Jarvis tried to dodge any more attention and pulled away round the side of the house to go and inspect her garden, which was something she always expected from her visitors. The house was too large for a woman living alone, but Gwendolyn remained loyal to her roots and was devoted to her garden. It had come alive after so many weeks of rain, the grass neatly cut and trimmed within its stone edging, and she was pleased with its colourful appearance. The camellias and yellow forsythia had recently faded, but there were rows of pink and yellow foxgloves and sweat pea running along the side, just starting to bloom, and purple clematis climbing everywhere; soon mature rhododendrons and roses would follow. There were tubs and hanging baskets bursting with blooms and the brown ageing brickwork of the house was being covered in Virginia creeper, which gave it an older, cosier look.

Gwendolyn had married a good Englishman, who had been commissioned into the British Army as a General Fitter in the Royal Engineers and later made a successful life dealing in second-hand cars; when he died unexpectedly of a heart attack one snowy winter in his early fifties, Gwendolyn was left in a slightly precarious position. Their three sons were Londoners, all of whom went off to fight for their country after modest educations at the hands of the state. Jonathan had his father's dark looks and natural way with business. Jarvis was tall and fair like his mother with strong features and pale eyes, and his only experience abroad was with the Army. And Edward, the one in the middle, was a mix of average height and mousy colouring, tough with a gentle side, the one who was least suited to the rigours of the Army, in the end paying for it with his own life.

'Come in. You're on your own, I see. How is Pamela?'

Gwendolyn spoke in brisk sentences, in quick succession, as if she had lined up a series of questions but had forgotten how to listen to the answers. 'I never seem to see my daughter-in-law any more. Too busy, I suppose, working, is she, in the city?'

'I'm sure she's fine. I don't see much of her either,' Jarvis confessed. 'She's working on the Olympics, public relations you know, very important. She's at some all-day conference today, so she couldn't make it. Sorry.'

'And no developments on the home front, I suppose, with settling down, the two of you?'

'Mother, please, I've only just got here, don't start with insulting me so soon.'

Jarvis followed his mother into the house through the conservatory and then took his jacket off, settling onto a sun lounger. While Gwendolyn checked the lunch, Jarvis helped himself to a glass of wine from a cool bottle already laid out on a side table. He would have preferred a beer.

'I'll have one in a moment, Jarvis, you help yourself.' Gwendolyn returned with a small bowl of nuts and continued chatting. Jarvis remained silent, pretending to listen, while he was actually thinking of other people, including moody Pamela and sad Naomi.

Soon they were working their way through a hot lunch with home-made pudding, an opportunity to indulge that Gwendolyn would never miss. And afterwards, enjoying the sloth that comes with alcohol and full stomachs, they relaxed on separate settees, enjoying the scene over the garden now drenched in warm sunshine.

'You are looking fit, Jarvis, I see. Still doing all that gym stuff, I suppose? What is happening between you and Pamela? You are seldom together now, is that right?' She had a habit of assuming that her family was still in her clutches, still there to be organised; she was slow to accept that they had become adults, with their own lives to lead and decisions to make, without necessarily consulting her any more.

'Pamela is fine, Mother, don't worry about her.'

'I'm not worried about her – I'm worried about you.' She looked concerned. She reached for the remote control, as a habit, tempted to watch the racing, but then thought better of it. 'You two don't seem to be getting along. Is there something wrong? Is she not satisfying you well enough?' Gwendolyn was not looking at him directly, but appeared distracted by a magazine on the sofa, while she straightened her skirt, smoothed the little doilies on the side table. She was watching carefully, though, for any signs of reaction on Jarvis's face, emotion, feelings of some sort, unhappiness maybe.

She rose up and moved behind him, resting her hands either side on his shoulders. 'Remember the old days when I used to massage your neck and shoulders,' she spoke in her velvety voice, 'when you used to tell me everything?' She was coaxing him into talking more freely. 'We used to work everything out together, didn't we?' and her hands rubbed and gripped his tense neck muscles, soothing the tension away.

'Yes, of course I do, but that was a long time ago, Mother,' Jarvis protested gently.

'Not that long; but you have not been here in recent times much, and we forget these things. Your father was a supporter of Pamela, from good family stock, he said, and we thought you and she should work well together, be good for each other. She's loyal, Jarvis, but she needs a purpose, all women do. You have to make an effort, marriages do not just tick along nicely on their own, unless you work at them. Have you seriously not thought about starting a family yet? It would make such a difference – look at Jonathan and Brenda.'

Usually, when her conversation turned to the subject of children, he smiled and forced his mind onto other things, avoiding a reply.

This time he was much closer to expressing what he truly felt. He sat forward abruptly and twisted in the chair to face her. 'But that's the thing, Mother, I want out, I've had enough. We both have. We argue and quarrel all the time, we don't talk to each other, we should be happy, but we're not, we're both miserable.'

'Oh Jarvis, please . . .'

'We fight over everything. It's just not worth trying to find a way through; it's just not going to work much longer. And Dad isn't here to see us, or to advise any more, I'm sorry to say.'

'Jarvis, dear, stop this talk. Does she know you are saying these things, does she agree with you, or is this you with your anger?' And she reached around for him, held his hands in hers and crouched in front of him, almost kneeling.

'She makes me angry. And she is less loyal than you think. We have tried to find a way but it's hopeless. No, she doesn't know that I am here to talk to you about our marriage.' Jarvis felt like a schoolboy again and, unable to look his mother in the face, stood up and walked towards the windows to look out at the garden.

'You didn't come here specifically to talk about your marriage, I know. We need you to remain calm.'

'Mother, I am perfectly calm.' Images of Pamela's angry face from the other night filled his mind and he felt he had come close to a decision. He sat back in his chair, and Gwendolyn resumed her massaging of his neck.

'Ooh, you have some tight spots here, in the neck.' Gwendolyn was so immensely proud of her son, always impressed with his appearance. He was a splendid athlete, perfectly proportioned, tuned and alert with unblemished skin and not an ounce of flesh out of place. 'You could be a real success in advertising or the film industry, or something like that, Jarvis,' she murmured, 'instead of doing all that dirty work for Jonathan.'

Jarvis had stopped listening and was ready to nod off to sleep.

But Gwendolyn seemed determined to remind him of his marriage duties. 'Pamela is a good woman, Jarvis, I feel sure you can work things out together.'

By the end of the afternoon, Jarvis was restless to leave. He was faced with a heavy week ahead, with dozens of recruitment interviews at the Park to get through, and he had promised Danny to put in an appearance at the forest, so he had an early pick-up at Liverpool Street station tomorrow. He gathered his things together. He needed to get home, have a brisk walk followed by a quiet evening and a good night's sleep.

Hesitating just for a moment, Jarvis spoke in his quiet rumbling voice. 'I'm taking on a special job in a few weeks' time, for Sidney Price. I saw him not so long ago, he asked after you.'

Gwendolyn was stacking away some plates and cutlery in the kitchen. 'Oh yes?' She sounded suspicious.

'It will be a big job for me, pays well. But it will cause a bit of a stink, I'm afraid, so I will be disappearing for a while afterwards. I don't want you to worry, I'll be safe. But don't try and contact me.' He stood casually in the doorway, hands in pockets.

Gwendolyn stopped and stared at her son with a slightly worried look on her face. 'Oh Lord, it all sounds very mysterious. It's not unlawful I hope, I never did trust Sidney, you know. I always thought he was a petty crook.'

'Actually not so petty. Well, it's not something to shout about, but it's an operation, sort of security thing, I can't say any more.'

'Not dangerous, is it?' She screwed her eyes up a bit, the lines deepening, and she sounded genuinely worried.

Jarvis was wishing he had not said anything; it was only in case something went wrong, he felt he ought to have warned her. 'No, no. I need you to be patient and loyal, Mother,' he smiled, 'and to say nothing. Don't worry, it will take care of a number of things.' He kissed her on both cheeks and then on her dry mouth, briefly.

'Drive carefully, Jarvis, and remember what I said. It may be that you need some help, professional help? Think about that. And give my love to Pamela. Tell her I would be happy to see her here at any time, even on her own, if she would like.'

'Thanks, Mother, I'll tell her.'

Thursday night, late on in May, just ahead of the Jubilee weekend, and a few weeks after his first tour of Stratford Park, Jarvis returned to the Shoreditch offices of SecureLife with his heavy black rucksack over his shoulder, well after dark, when there was nobody about. With his own keys, he entered the office block from the street. By the light of a small torch from his pocket, he disabled the alarm system with the code number punched into the front of the box situated behind the receptionist's desk. He moved stealthily through to the back stairs and down to the driver's office, took keys to one of the company vehicles off the wall and went out to the back yard. A security wall light helped him find the right Vauxhall in the dim shadows out of a long line of white vans of various sizes. They all had the firm's logo painted in green on the side ('SecureLife – your answer to all your security worries'), and were kitted out with all manner of electrical gadgets and devices, with tools, wiring, sensors, cameras, alarms and the rest. He checked the number on the key tab with the number plate of the Combo. In the back, he lifted up the floor panel by its chrome handle and unscrewed the fixings on the spare wheel, which he then lifted out and rolled away to a side wall, leaving it propped up and hidden by the refuse bins. Into the empty floor space in the van he laid the rucksack flat and replaced the floor panel, which he then covered over with tarpaulin sheets and various scattered boxes and a few coils of flex. He closed and locked the back doors, returned the keys to their hook inside the office and, with the alarm reset, left the building without trace.

The next day, Jarvis travelled in one of the other company people carriers, with his security tag swinging on its chain round his neck, chatting to the other men as they made their way to the Park. Ahead was the Vauxhall with his hidden package. And in Warton Road it was waved off into the covered inspection area by a big black man in a Dayglo raincoat and cap who looked soaked in the heavy rain. Although he was sure it had been chosen at random, he watched anxiously from the side windows as he rode past. Dogs on leads and men with mirrors on stalks wandered around the chosen Vauxhall and peered in. SecureLife had been through these security arrangements plenty of times and was working closely with all the other teams, so Jarvis was not expecting any difficulty, it all being fairly low-key and friendly. He waited nonchalantly inside Stratford Park at the staff huts for the inspected Vauxhall to arrive, and when it did the driver smiled, said no problem, nothing to worry about, cool. Jarvis took the keys off him, saying he needed the van later.

During the lunch period, with the rain abated, Jarvis nipped round the back of their temporary accommodation close to the press office and went over to his unattended Vauxhall. There was nobody watching as far as he could see and he climbed into the back, easily retrieving the bag from under the floor panel. The staff quarters consisted of a long, low prefabricated rectangular building, with a massive canteen area, offices and workspaces upstairs and, downstairs, the changing rooms where he headed, finding the men's area with its perpetual smell of sweaty feet. None of the staff had proper lockers, although there were a few lockable boxes for safe-keeping of wallets, wristwatches, money and the like. The rest of the hundreds of male staff who used these facilities, where they could shower and change, were lucky to be able to find a peg; personal items like towels and soap would be brought along and taken away in holdalls as needed. Jarvis's recently handed-out Olympics uni-form, as yet unworn, was hanging along with hundreds of others on a long railing to one side. He hung the rucksack on a peg, casually covered it with a dark raincoat, and left quickly, reminding himself that he had to return to the Shoreditch offices again that night after dark to put the spare wheel back into the floor space of the Vauxhall before anyone asked questions.

11

The atrocious weather of that London summer continued over the four days of the Queen's Jubilee weekend celebrations. Despite high winds and constant drizzle the crowds still came and the traffic congestion was monumental. Jarvis took Pamela along the Thames towpath from Wapping to watch the end of the river pageant at St Katharine Docks on the Sunday. To make her feel better. Everywhere along the river, locals and tourists were waving flags and Union Jack umbrellas and were crammed into every conceivable space, on every possible viewing ledge.

Pamela was not a pageant person herself really, she kept reminding him, but appreciated his gesture, and as it happened, enjoyed the unusual event. She was humming the national anthem with the best of them, even as she elbowed her way through the crowd lining the waterways around the docks. Jarvis enjoyed it too, rather liking public ritual, colourful parades, officers in uniform, royalty on hand, that kind of thing. Pamela hung on to his arm and chatted more freely with him than she had in ages, pointing out the Red Arrows overhead and the pictures on the big screens, where they saw Tower Bridge opening its jaws and an endless stream of colourful boats filled with eccentric people bobbing along the river. Everyone jostled for the best views, national colours painted on their faces, sharing drinks and jokes. Despite the drenching rain, cheers went up at regular intervals and flags were waved enthusiastically by everyone to the very end.

Taking advantage of four consecutive days off work over the holidays, away from the organised chaos of selling the Olympic story and preparing for the events of the coming Games, Pamela was determined to be more relaxed and accommodating. She seemed to be happier in her mind, her thoughts taken off affairs and arguments and what the hell they had in mind for their future.

Jarvis had told Naomi that he would not be able to see her over this period, as he was going to concentrate on sorting things out with Pamela. He needed the time off to work through some of the issues with her. There were also some security planning jobs to be done at the Olympic sites. She would have to be patient. Naomi had decided to spend the time at home with her brothers and her father, who had not been well recently.

The British weather was always a popular talking point, but that year it had certainly been bizarre by any standards. Following a drought over the south of England with a hosepipe ban, London had been blanketed by snow in February, simmered in a heatwave in March and was drenched by a monsoon in April. And rain had continued through the summer to create the wettest since records had begun.

For his next task, Jarvis needed a dry calm night.

He took a chance on the Wednesday after the holidays, a late evening in early June that seemed set to be dry, and stayed late at the Stratford Park security offices, after a day of frantic interviewing and a study of rotas for the duration of the Games, identifying who was in which team, with first, second and third reserves. A company van was parked outside for him to use when he was ready. The offices, looking one way over the great concourse towards the stadium and the other side overlooking a canal-cut tributary of the small river Lea that meandered through the Olympic Park from north to south, began to clear soon after five o'clock, and by seven he was alone. He had some sandwiches and a drink as he waited for darkness to gently descend around the Park.

Leaving the office lights on, he retrieved the weighty rucksack from his peg in the empty changing rooms. Wearing all black – trousers, T-shirt, trainers and gloves – and with his identity tag hung around his neck, he left the building, making sure the glass-panelled swing door closed without a bang. The night was pleasantly warm, and a mild breeze was blowing from the west. In the darkness, his casual long strides took him across the tarmac that surrounded the massive black shape of the stadium, jutting skywards like an abandoned ship on the seabed. Skirting around its outer pillars at the north end and then along its eastern flank, he moved quietly, darting in and out of the deeper shadows, a tiny figure swamped by the monster building. It was awkward to move at any pace in such darkness, impossible to judge the exact position of the ground, and he advanced with his arms outstretched in front of him. Only a few arc lights operated on site and these were flooding the entry-exit gates, where guards in pairs would be settling in their huts for another boring night on duty when absolutely nothing would happen. He stopped suddenly, crouching and listening, unsure if he had come too far, but then turned into the pitch-black tunnel he was looking for. At its far end the central arena opened up, and he stepped onto a tiered seating area. Here, out of the shadows, a touch of light from the night sky helped, and he started to climb steadily upwards, up hundreds of steps in the columns between the seats. He crossed and climbed in a zigzag fashion to the very top of the stadium under the outer rim of its roof, at Gate 4 (the number clearly emblazoned on the back wall). There, a metal ladder was aimed steeply up through an opening in the canvas onto a narrow platform above.

Ascending with caution, he stopped at the top, with his head protruding through the canvas roof. He tried to take in his weird surroundings. He was giddily high above ground, crouched on the windy edge of an eerie concrete construction, a vast grey vista around him. The city gave off a glow at ground level, with its twinkling street lights and passing vehicles far below, while over the canvas curves and steel structures of the stadium roof, way over to the west, there were still the remains of daylight streaking bright orange that speckled the reflective surfaces of the familiar skyline – Canary Wharf, the Eye, St Paul's, even the old Post Office Tower. An occasional aeroplane soundlessly passed across the sky to the south of him, a few disconnected lights moving towards Heathrow Airport. The magnificent size of the construction made him feel infinitesimally small and, not for the first time, he wondered what the hell he was doing.

The wind created a howl as it surged over the roof and down through the open structure into the bowl at its centre. It whipped into his face, cooling the sweat on his forehead but making him shiver in his thin T-shirt, while he listened intently. He held his breath at the sudden sight of a guard with a torchlight in a yellow cape far below strolling around the concourse. Motionless on the top step, aware of his thumping heartbeat, he was bent low and nobody could possibly see him at this height, even if there was anybody about who was looking. He was in almost total darkness, and when the man below moved out of his sight, he slowly rose into a crouch, stepping fully onto the metal grille platform, soundless in his soft rubber shoes. He drew a small torch of his own from the rucksack and used it to show him the way, not wanting to put a foot wrong on those narrow high ledges.

Black-painted steel companionways with single-bar handrails connected inwards over the canvas onto the inner rim of the stadium roof, like single-file pedestrian bridges over a river, fourteen of them in all at about twenty-metre intervals, giving technicians access to the lights and screen positions. He stepped up onto the one he had chosen as being in the middle of the east side of the stadium, directly opposite the important spectator enclosures on the other side. With some trepidation, he advanced up three steps and paced slowly towards the inner rim of the roof, imagining how easy it would be to topple over the low railing; and that would be that. The rows and rows of eerily empty seats that caught a flake of moonlight below him in the bowl were like faces looking up at him. He imagined the place buzzing with thousands of people.

He retraced his steps back to the outer platform where he had ascended. With the small torch gripped between his teeth, he bent low to feel with his gloved hand for the big plastic drainpipe that ran along under the steel meshwork of the walkway, carrying excess rainwater from the gutters around the canvas roof, and which connected to the downpipes every twenty metres or so that dropped to the ground alongside the white steel pillars. In his rucksack he found the battery-operated power drill with a 15-mm bit attached. Lying flat on his stomach now, he strained his head around the edge of the walkway so he could see directly; the dusty pipe was twenty-four centimetres diameter and was angled slightly to the horizontal. He started to drill through the plastic, four holes, one at each corner of an imaginary long rectangle measuring 40 by 12 cm, along the side of the pipe. The whining noise sounded harsh to him at first, but up on the top of the stadium with the wind howling there was no possibility of anything being heard on the ground. Changing to the jigsaw bit, with an even more jagged noise, he connected his four holes with neat cut lines, in effect creating a rectangular window. Careful not to drop it, he removed the curved panel of black plastic and laid it on the platform beside him. Now with a small drill bit, he created four 5-mm holes in the pipe in two pairs, opposite each other and at about 6 cm along the pipe away from his cut-out window on the down slope. He used a short length of coat-hanger wire, bent double at its middle like a giant hairpin, and threaded the two ends through one pair of holes, passing across the middle of the pipe, bringing them out through the holes opposite. With wire cutters he trimmed off the excess lengths, bending the two exposed short ends into little hooks so they would not retract through the pipe, even under pressure.

He returned to his bag and almost ceremoniously lifted out his friend Martyn, his top notch sniper rifle that he so treasured, wrapped tightly in several layers of waterproof cling film that had helped evade its detection by the sniffer dogs at security. Disassembled, folded and wrapped together with two boxes of rounds and the night sights, it formed an oblong package that fitted perfectly inside the cut-out drain pipe, one end resting against the internal hairpin wires that prevented it being flushed away with the next downpour. He made sure that it was secure and would not break loose. Repositioning the curved piece of plastic piping into its original window, he wiped the surfaces clean and dry. Then he fixed it in place using strips of matt black adhesive tape, carefully placed along the four cut lines, and he also covered the two shiny wire ends that protruded with more black tape. Rubbing some dust over the reassembled pipe, he convinced himself that unless someone was particularly looking for it, it could not be spotted easily, if at all, from a distance, tucked away as it was under the metal-meshed walkway.

He carefully checked that he had all his equipment with him and then went onto the companionway, walking forwards, approaching the inner edge of the roof above the open arena below. There he crouched down, giving himself a perfect if dizzying view over all the empty seats opposite, a couple of hundred yards away across the dark void. He looked at his wristwatch, illuminated and set as a timer, and after a few moments of careful thought, pressed the little red button on the side to start the count down. He withdrew in a backwards crouch to the outer walkway close to his hiding place in the drainpipe, grabbed his backpack that felt so much lighter and descended the ladder backwards, through the roof to the concrete flooring of the upper seating tier. Crouching by the folded seats in the darkness, he watched for any movement around the arena, for the guard he had seen earlier on patrol. He glanced at the watch and then descended the one hundred and fifty steps to return to ground level. He walked out through the same tunnel he had used before, all the time alert to any possible signs of movement, and then skirted round the north side of the stadium keeping close within its shadows and darted across the open causeway back to the staff huts. His shirt was wet with sweat, his breathing rapid. One hundred and sixty seconds had passed on his watch, from being high up on the stadium roof overlooking the arena to being back at the door to the office block. His heart was thumping with pleasure and excitement.

When it came to his escape, every second would count.

He left the stadium, casually driving a company van through the barrier at the Westway entrance, waving to the unfamiliar guards, and returned to the Shoreditch SecureLife car park, leaving the vehicle in its usual place. He walked to his Witan Street lock-up, not far from the offices, where he drank a whole bottle of water and chewed an apple while putting his gear back neatly in place, rehearsing in his mind for the umpteenth time every detail of the planned action.

At the weekend Jarvis decided to take Naomi out into the countryside in the Astra, as the weather was reasonable and he said he wanted to show her Beacon Forest, where he had been working. The journey took well over an hour, and they ended up south of Bluewater Park, stopping in an out-of-the-way lay-by down an unused track, where they walked through impressive wooded areas, across open scrub and down to a brook that meandered through the undergrowth. Among the ferns they found a grassy patch to lie on in the sun and eat the supermarket food Naomi had picked up on their way. Then they followed a rising pathway up the edge of a thickly wooded area and walked for some while into the dense part of the forest, where it was cooler and shaded, picking up a newly laid track that Jarvis said he and his mates had started, which went uphill all the way over a ridge for about half a mile and then down the other side to their camp, where the forest gang lived when working. There was nobody there this weekend, and Jarvis showed her around the caravans and work shed and they looked at some of the cutting equipment and the tractors lying idle.

Everywhere was so quiet, the creaking and rustling of trees in the breeze and occasional birdsong providing the only background sounds. Naomi felt elated and was full of questions, excited by what she saw. Her life was good. In one of the caravans she came over all amorous, pushing Jarvis back onto a bunk, scrabbling at his belt and zip and hefting down his jeans. She sat astride him, giggling and pumping him up with her cold hands, and then bravely went down on him, all open mouthed and wet tongue, trying something herself for the first time. She pulled her top off and dropped her bra so that he could ogle at her breasts squashed against his thighs while she bounced and sucked and eyed him at the same time from under her thick brows. He lay back with hands behind his head, watching and dreaming, and climaxed and she swallowed it all with a look of mixed pleasure and horror on her face. She immediately felt sick and quickly brought a hand up to her mouth, retching. She darted outside, to bring it all up over a wheel of the caravan.

On their return to the car, they kept to the sunnier places, walking arm in arm. On their way back to London, Jarvis bought ice creams from a stall outside the train station in Gravesend. They arrived home tired and late, both feeling that in their own way they had had a good day.

Two weeks later a large white envelope bearing the familiar logo, 'London 2012', containing two tickets for the closing ceremony of the Olympic Games, two Travelcards for August 12 and full travel instructions, arrived in the morning post. Pamela dropped it onto the breakfast table for Jarvis to see when he came downstairs.

All the pieces of Jarvis's planned project were in place. There were five more weeks before the start of the greatest show on earth. And Jarvis now just had to wait.

One evening in July, Jarvis discovered Naomi showering in the bath. He stood at the open doorway and watched her through the glass panel, a slim, awkward girl, a girl he was getting to know better, dousing herself in the water deluge. Soapy suds cascaded down her shiny marble-like back, bubbling over the bumps of her shoulders and spine and rounded buttocks that glistened like Scottish boulders in a flowing stream. She had a way of wiping her hands over her sides and stomach like there was someone caressing her. He noticed a tattoo normally hidden by her hair on the nape of her neck, three small solid black hearts lined up in a column. Aroused by the bobbing of her peardrop breasts and the peeking through soapy bubbles of her pink nipples, he dropped his clothes onto the floor where he stood and stepped into the bath behind her.

Naomi watched him, giggled a little and stretched out for him. She knew him better, not to be frightened by his nakedness. Conscious of her appearance, she pulled him into her steamy wet world too close for him to watch her. Their bare bodies squashed together and she began to lather him over his back with long sweeping movements, rising over the mounds and falling into the dips. She tugged at him with soapy fingers, pulling him between her thighs, enticing him to reach up into her.

She was more confident than she had been before, slowly transformed by his assured presence. His body had become an object of desire and beauty to her and she relished his touch, his cradling of her breasts, his grip of her pussy with his gentle fingers.

He turned her round, bending her forwards, sliding himself between her slippery buttocks from behind. She braced herself with outstretched arms against the tiled wall, hands flat. The force of his powerful thrusts pounded her bottom, which wobbled and splayed, reverberating through her frame, but he hung on to her, controlling the force, building to satisfaction.

After rinsing off, laughing and tumbling onto the big bed next door, only half dry, they wrestled in gentle play. They rutted like teenagers, rapidly and urgently. She gave a stifled scream and held her breath in surrender. He quickly exploded inside her. They were panting and smiling and holding each other. 'I love you,' she murmured. 'I know, I know,' he replied and rolled off, face down on the bed. She pushed herself up against him for closeness, wrapped her arms around him, her dear, her rock. They lay still in silence for a while, bright late evening light for once filling the small bedroom.

Soon afterwards Jarvis quietly dressed and left, to return to the strife-torn domestic life that awaited him, while Naomi remained alone and bereft.

Jarvis was watching a service to commemorate Armed Forces Day, shown on television, while there were reports of flooding from all over the country, with pictures of swollen rivers bursting their banks and old people being rescued in boats rowing down high streets. Leaving Pamela to herself, he went over to The Baring to watch football and have a pint on his own.

There was a bigger gathering than usual watching a big screen on the far wall. Jerome was there, showing off his sporting knowledge as usual at the bar. He was often hanging around The Baring in the evenings. He was a West Indian cab driver, a Londoner and a sports fanatic. 'Spain tonight!' he called out. Behind the bar, Joe was running a book on the match, 4 to 1 Italy straight win. Jarvis sat apart, wanting to watch quietly, to relax his mind and to stop thinking about Olympic Games and gangways in the sky and long drops to the concrete causeway below. But he joined in with the banter from time to time.

Cricket was Jerome's special subject, and there was not a Wisden missing from his collection, nor a single cricket fact, however trivial, from his quick brain. He knew his football too. And took pleasure in testing the regulars in the pub, whoever was in. 'Spain won four years ago – I reckon they gonna retain de title – it's never been done before in de European.'

'We'll go for Italy!' called out someone, willing to put down a fiver. *Don't bet against Jerome,* Jarvis felt.

'In de World Cup, it been done twice – so a fiver for anyone who knows which teams won two consecutive World Cups?'

There was a dumb silence from the men and couple of women, all sitting at the bar around the screen, automatically downing their pints and occasionally oohing and aahing at the action.

'No one?' Jerome, standing up and looking around him, had a huge grin across his shiny black face, the gaps in his front teeth exposed unashamedly, clearly thrilled that no one knew the answer to his question.

'Tell us, Jerome, put us out of our misery,' Jarvis called.

'Come on, for a fiver?' Jerome had his mouth wide open, his eyes sparkly and his hands turned upwards ready to catch the right answer from someone. Nobody obliged; Jarvis had not a clue.

'All right den. De first team was Italy in 1934 and 1938. Then Braaazil in 1958 and 1962. Yeah!' Jerome cheered. 'And Spain can do it tonight, in de European!' Everyone groaned. With Spain now one-nil ahead, the odds on Italy had lengthened to 5 to 1.

In due course, Spain proved Jerome correct in his prediction, winning in some style. Joe came off best though. Jarvis returned home after the match wondering whether he should take more interest in betting or in sport, or in both. Who would give him odds on success for the night of August 12th?

12

For the thousands of staff who worked at the Olympic Park, there had been no let-up in the past frantic week, with preparations, run-throughs and rehearsals all day every day, right up to the opening day of the Games. And that included the tens of thousands of volunteers who helped with crowd directions and control, ticketing and refreshments. Not forgetting the thousands involved in the opening ceremony itself, who had practised arduously off-site every day until the Wednesday before, when they had all come together inside the arena for their first dress rehearsal. There was no leave and the days were long, from almost first light to dusk and beyond for the security people. Jarvis was fully occupied with his duties, including supervising the security teams on duty. Despite controversy over the number of personnel available for the three weeks, and the supposed shortfall, Jarvis found himself overseeing the training of hundreds of new recruits every week. The Army was drafted in a week before everything was due to begin, with much sympathy expressed for the young troopers who would be missing their holidays after returning from the dangers of Afghanistan, and for some who were facing redundancy afterwards, in what a *Guardian* journalist described as a wickedly-timed government initiative to reduce the costs of running the Armed Forces. Senior security were in a state of constant high alert following the claim that an Iranian terror squad was out to kill the Israeli team and with numerous other threats and non-threats that kept surfacing daily, there was talk of Scotland Yard elite snipers being posted on the roof; Jarvis noted the details with concern.

The Olympic Park had become increasingly crowded during the final week; it seemed the whole world was watching. Press officers and journalists, photographers, radio and camera crews from all corners of the Earth were falling over themselves to get the best positions, to get the interviews, the previews, the exclusives. The place had come alive and was like a living thing. There was a real sense of nervous excitement among the support staff everywhere, just as much as everyone else, as if they themselves were going to be competing in the arena. In a way, of course, they all were.

Jarvis had developed a clear understanding of the set-up and like the back of his hand, he knew the best routes to and fro, the venues, the entrances and exits, the security issues and the rotas of the stadium staff. He had also come to know most of the snipers posted around various vantage points and their routines. He strutted around the stadium, feeling quite at home with all the squaddies on site, their presence turning the Park almost into a British Army outpost. He observed every detail he needed, sometimes with a heavy heart, acutely aware of the enormity of the task he had set himself. He kept trying to imagine the arena filled with spectators, the sea of faces spreading in a continuous circle like a massive ocean wave, constantly moving and changing. He had concentrated on extra night-time practice using the night vision apparatus on the rifle, but he well knew how difficult recognising tiny faces in the central VIP areas lost in a maelstrom of movement from over a hundred yards away in almost total darkness would be.

Compared with all the build-up, the actual three weeks of the Games were a pleasure because everything had been planned and rehearsed so well and everything worked so smoothly. Delivered like clockwork. Even the wet weather was ignored and there were some bright sunny days as well. Staff were on their feet all day, pacing the sites, constantly watching the crowds, instructing the teams, talking to the public – often quite a tedious and exhausting experience. And all the time they were in uniforms that had to be kept smart and clean, changing in the staff area, eating in shifts in their canteen, often missing meals. Most of the staff, including Jarvis, arrived at the site and left it on the transport coaches or company vans provided, with various pick-up and drop-off points around town. On several occasions Jarvis drove the VIP cars himself for SecureLife from hotels in Mayfair to venues along the protected fast lanes, dressed in his Oxford blue uniform with matching cap and green logo.

Pamela seemed to spend her time split between her offices in Vauxhall and the hospitality tents at the Park, and most evenings attended London venues for receptions and client entertaining. One night it was a creative industries do at the Royal Academy in Piccadilly hosted by the Deputy Prime Minister. On another she found herself at a fundraising event at the Arts Club in Mayfair, where leading lights of the fashion world strutted their stuff. It was all a mammoth networking opportunity, nirvana to the natural people people, having to decide between the glossy Bulgari Hotel in Knightsbridge to hear from some film industry bigwigs, or a more sedate walk around the White Cube Gallery in Bermondsey with prospective clients or maybe a visit to Lancaster House with UK plc, the trade investment agency. One afternoon she was offered a trip to a polo match with an emir from Dubai with the chance to meet the team afterwards. Everyone was seeking a taste of the Olympics experience, hoping that it would sprinkle some magic dust over their lives.

Pamela was in seventh heaven, drinking too much and eating too much, and doing what she wanted, among the celebrities and well-knowns and flash hangers-on, with all the attention that went with it. She hardly noticed whether Jarvis was around or not. They occasionally stumbled over each other late in the evening looking for something to eat or drink, or ridiculously early over a quick breakfast. Sometimes Jarvis slept away, at the Olympic site or with Naomi when her flatmate was out, sometimes he was at home.

Naomi, not particularly fussed about sport, stayed at home most nights watching the Games on television. She did not have tickets for anything, and just because he worked there did not mean Jarvis got any either. Anyway, it was nearly exam time for her Beauty & Health degree, and she carried on working in the hair salon, although it was noticeably quieter than usual at this time of the year, an unwanted effect of the Games. Jarvis promised that he would get some time off in the afternoons towards the end, although the security nightmare of the last event, the men's marathon, run around the streets of Westminster, was still to be faced.

By the time the last Saturday afternoon of the Games arrived, after three weeks of public celebration and emotional outpouring, Jarvis was suffering from demonic thoughts, plunging him into a state of nervous self-doubt. His sleep had recently been disrupted by wicked images of ogres and monsters, chasing him, cajoling him, laughing at him. At three o'clock that morning he had sat up to wipe the sweat from his face and chest, feeling the presence of a heavy body breathing next to him. Pamela's puffy face was turned away, pressed into her palm at an angle on the pillow, her cheeks loosely vibrating with each alcoholic-infused exhalation. Half-covered breasts tumbled atop each other against her chubby arms. She mumbled something with a fractional turn of her head, and the waft of hot cigarette breath repulsed him. And for the umpteenth time he asked himself what was really behind his planning – and would he really go through with it? Was it about money or some other deeper urging? He had crawled out of bed to pace around the house and then went out into the warm street, not finding anywhere to settle, anything to settle on.

Back early from the Park, he snacked on bread and fruit and then took himself to the gym, where he worked distractedly with skipping ropes and boxing bags. Images of old training sessions with his brother Ed gatecrashed his mind, of him clinging on to the hanging leather punchbag for Ed to smash, only for Ed to be smashed in the ring regularly by Army opponents who were invariably heavier than him. Frequent boxing contests in makeshift rings under low camouflaged awning, in sticky humidity and scorching Arab heat, were commonly organised to deal with soldiers' boredom, to provide a bit of excitement, a fitness workout and a flutter all at the same time, and everyone had to take their turn.

He heard Ed calling 'Enough' as the sadistic staff sergeant, always partial to a bloody fight, encouraged him to last out another round of brutality. Ed's eyes were cut from head contact with his thick-set opponent from Bolton, who lacked the long reach of Ed but knew how to rough it and carried a sledgehammer punch. It was a relief for Jarvis as much as it was for Ed to hear the bell at the end of each two-minute round so the torture could stop, at least temporarily.

And then Ed was in his arms in that Basrah doorway with bullet wounds across his chest and a vicious gash in the back of his head, lying across him, heavy and warm, his twisted helmet flung twenty feet away, upside down, still rolling from side to side in the dusty alley. He was moaning, not seeing through swollen eyes and blood, and the hot red stuff would not stop welling up from his head, despite Jarvis pressing hard on his skull with his own shirt and hugging him bodily against his chest, and screaming to get the medics, some morphine, where was the bloody backup?

After showering at the gym he headed by foot to his archway hide-out to prepare for the final day. D-day. Tomorrow. The day he had chosen, it seemed a long time ago, for his hero to step forward once again. The evening closing ceremony of London 2012, billed as a wonderful extravaganza, was not to be missed. The moment of truth was near and he was prepared to rise to the challenge.

He gathered his various props together and neatly laid them out in order on his table top, left to right. He checked the clothes, the belt, the metal-tipped boots; he folded an old grey raincoat and a flat cap beside them. Black balaclava in wool; two blue plastic surgical gloves, extra large; small pocket torch (he checked the batteries); pair of binoculars; small screwdriver; pair of cheap sunglasses; two pieces of white towelling the size of face-cloths, all placed in a row. And at the end, two small round tin dog-tags, like the old silver milk-bottle tops, on a cheap chain: his original Army IDs from when he was first commissioned, and on them, in crude punched-out lettering, blood group, eight-digit service number, surname, first name and religion in upper case: 'O Pos 28644119 COLLINGWOOD JARVIS CE'.

Two of them, one for the body, one for the coffin.

Next to them was the old Samsung mobile that he had been using with Ainsley, and its charger, plugged in; two Olympic ticket printouts for tomorrow's closing ceremony (with shiny silver security squares in silver and 'corporate' in the name section); his Olympics security identity card, with its dark swipeable data strip on the back, and his bearded image off centre, with its bright yellow lanyard. And lastly at the end of the table top was the silver Vespa scooter key. On the floor, his black rucksack.

He took yet another look at the colour print of Abu Masoud taped on the brick wall by the table, his evil face so familiar. He stepped back satisfied. Everything in order, tidy, well-organised. He rang Jimmy and arranged for them to meet tomorrow evening at seven.

Jarvis had a few hours' duty on the Sunday morning but afterwards was able to change out of his uniform and spend the afternoon with Naomi. They passed the time together aimlessly mooching around her small flat, looking at papers, watching some TV, eating distractedly. Naomi didn't notice Jarvis take her mobile phone from the kitchen table, switch the power off and slip it deep into a pocket of his leather coat. When she realised it was missing they spent time fruitlessly searching the flat for it, which made her more exasperated and convinced she must have left it at the salon, so she returned there with the keys to look. She was to go on from there to her father's place in Kilburn, as she had promised to spend some time with him before he went into hospital for a prostate operation the following week.

Once on his own, Jarvis felt the need to vomit in the toilet, anxiety creeping through his guts. He stripped off his sweaty clothes and plunged into a cold shower, forcing himself to stay under the spray, turning his face up straight into the cascade for half a minute, screaming with the shock.

He had been infatuated with his plans for so long that he was beginning to wonder whether he was suffering from a loss of reason. Was this a bout of mental instability, an emotional disturbance, or was he sick? After drying himself off, he took a single tablet of propranolol to calm his excitement. He lay for a while naked on the bed, eyes closed, waiting for stillness and calm to return to his heart and mind. Now was the time for a cool head and clear thinking. He needed confidence to make a stand for what should be recognised, for what was morally right. He needed all his courage. He would avenge the wrongdoing of an evil monster, for the sake of the dedicated thousands who made sacrifices every day for their country. The retribution would be just. There was nobody else brave enough to do it.

It was absolutely natural that at this, the eleventh hour, he should be experiencing a little fear and trepidation. He was about to step forward to make his indelible mark on history. This was not the time for second thoughts. The monetary rewards were too enticing for that anyway. A once-in-a-lifetime opportunity, he kept hearing. He felt spooked, that was all. If he was caught, trapped, he would be called heretic, non-conformist, and burnt at the stake.

With a shudder, he climbed off the bed and readied himself for what was to be his greatest night. He cleaned off his beard with scissors and a wet shave, three blades blunted before his face was nicely smooth. He relieved himself fully in the toilet. He dressed simply in jeans, white shirt, leather jacket, big wristwatch well covered. He admired his new less-familiar look in the mirror and a crafty smile drifted across his blond features. Now was the time to reap some reward for all the hard work. He knew he could do it. With his confidence high, he set off from Naomi's place for his hidden lock-up at a casual pace, taking all his belongings with him, including Naomi's phone, in a brown nondescript holdall.

Josh's story for Naomi was simple: he was staying in all night to watch the final Olympics show and she need not hurry back. He would probably go down the local to share some of the excitement, he might meet up with one or two of his friends for a pint or two. He would spend the night at home, expecting Pamela to return late, and he would see Naomi later in the week. Once the Games were over, Pamela and he would come to an agreement, he had promised. And Naomi was happy with that, totally believing in the Josh persona. Before she left he gave her words of encouragement, telling her to be brave and patient.

He was a good person, he reminded himself – his mother had told him often enough, a shining light she used to say. He would be recognised as such once his accomplishment was understood. He was sure that by the time he was out in the field, he would be fear-less, he just needed to get to the start. After so much preparation and waiting, he needed the action to begin.

He sneaked into his dank hideout, after the usual dance along the side streets, using the PIN for the security door. Under low lamp light he surveyed the equipment and props laid out the day before on the table. He stripped carefully down to his underpants. He first hung the cheap chain with his Army dog-tags round his neck, clasping them affectionately for a moment. He pulled on the tight pair of black cords with heavy belt, then the T-shirt and knit pullover with a zip at the neck and breast pockets, both in black. And then black socks and the black boots with their soft artificial soles. Into the rucksack he dropped the binoculars, the screwdriver, the balaclava, the gloves, his ID card, sunglasses, the two pieces of towelling, plus a packet of sandwiches. The tickets he slipped into a zip pocket. He put on the old grey raincoat, slightly too big for him, and belted it tight at the waist. The cap was folded in an inside pocket. Some money was folded in a pocket of his trousers.

The brisk rattling overhead of a passing train signalled that it was time to leave. Outside he opened the back of Naomi's phone and took out its battery and sim card, which he hurled into the mass of overgrown nettles and weeds beyond the adjacent fenced area, never to be found again, and the rest of the handset followed in bits. Back inside, he placed the Samsung on its charger, and made sure he had his iPhone in a pocket. He pulled his motorcycle helmet on, and with the scooter key in hand, wheeled the Vespa out through the side door. He returned to switch the light off and closed the door with its automatic lock. He mounted and fired up the Vespa with switch and throttle, its high-pitched engine sounding awfully loud in the confined space, even through his helmet. He set off towards Stratford Park, via Mare Street and Hackney, towards his destiny, his making of history.

Pamela had spent that same hot afternoon alone at home, relaxing at last after the busiest two weeks of her life, weeks of excitement and hard graft. She felt she had done a great job for the firm and had won over a number of potential clients. She was looking forward to her just rewards. She needed to prepare her outfit for the evening show. She was to be in a corporate seat with many of the Italian people she had worked with on design projects, although Antonio was not coming, being busy in town with some potential big business partners, allegedly.

She stood full-length in front of the mirror in fuchsia-coloured scanties, wondering where her impressive elevation of yesterday had gone and whether it was time to consider some enhancement procedure, as every other woman she knew advised without reservation, just enough to reverse some of the gravitational sag that had become a touch more noticeable these days, really. She puffed out her chest, inspecting her lovelies from different angles by swivelling her upper body left and right, scowling at her nipples that turned disappointedly downwards. Perhaps giving them a little lift would bring Jarvis back into her arms, now that she was resigned to Antonio having found himself alternative company.

She was still sleepy in bed when Jarvis had left first thing that morning. He mumbled something about being at the Olympic Park all day and said he would stay on for the evening's events, when, as she understood it, that little crook Jimmy Bullock would join him to watch from the stands. 'Enjoy your moment of glory tonight,' he had said, and he had sounded sincere, but at the same time his eyes were cold and she felt unnerved as if he knew something she did not. He said he would be thinking of her. 'You damn well deserve a good time after all the hard work,' he told her. And he kissed her good luck on her warm cheek, avoiding any direct eye contact, but lingering a little longer than usual. As he walked out through the bedroom door, she suggested that perhaps they should talk about things, tomorrow or the next day. 'For now, forget all your troubles and enjoy the moment,' he had said. This was more than Pamela was used to and it left her happy for a while, before some lingering doubts started to play on her mind. Although by the time she was dolled up, her face painted, gripping her corporate Olympic tickets and car keys and ready to go, she had forgotten all her concerns about Jarvis. She had selected pink, a silky sleeveless frock, elegant, tight fitting, just above the knee. She had a white loose blazer slung over her shoulders to wear for the evening chill, and with scarlet clasp bag and shoes to match she felt good – *and nobody would know it was all TK Maxx, really.*

The heavy sun was not yet ready to lower itself below the western London skyline but preferred to glow full into the early evening, highlighting with golden flecks the skyscrapers of Canary Wharf and the City, and bathing Stratford Park in orange warmth.

Jarvis parked his Vespa in the transport hub off the High Street in bright sunlight along with crowds of other cyclists. He was hot. He stowed away the helmet and covered over the scooter with its grey plastic coat. He folded his raincoat and cap and stripped off his black top, all of them going into the rucksack. The crowds around were building up and he fell in with the general movement towards the Greenway Gate approach. 'You need to be in your seating inside the Olympic Stadium by 7.30 p.m. at the latest, in time for the pre-show,' it said clearly in the official guide. The ride had lifted Jarvis's mood and his confidence was up; he strolled along almost jauntily, feeling just like any ordinary person enjoying the balmy warmth and the close feeling of excitement generated by the buzzing crowd. He watched the backs of people's heads bobbing in front of him, skipped forward into little spaces that formed between them, and continued towards the huge arched entrances with their purple-coloured decoration and 'London 2012' logos.

Jimmy was waiting for him. They nodded a welcome at one another and Jimmy, as dull-looking and craggy-faced as ever, smiled at Jarvis's clean-cut look. They moved forward with the flow, Jimmy having to skip along to keep up with Jarvis's long strides, with the stadium looming up ahead and the ridiculous red metal sculptured

'Orbit' tower to their left. Volunteers, easy to spot in their purple and red tops, were everywhere, encouraging everyone to have their tickets ready, to be prepared for the scanning and security checks, and to keep moving steadily, please. Jimmy and Jarvis chatted about the events of the day. They moved through into the Park perimeter and then easily through the canvas tents with their airport-like scanning and X-ray machines, putting their money and watches into plastic trays, no fluids. Some squaddies were standing around, occasionally patting down punters, but there was no sign of the big security boys, no armed police officers in yellow reflectives. The scanners and bag inspection slowed down the movement through the gates and short, good-humoured queues formed.

'This should be good, eh Jarvis? Never been to an Olympics before.' Jimmy had his twisted smile about him and gave off a filthy laugh.

'This *will* be good, Jimmy, you will not forget this one in a hurry.' He looked at Jimmy deadpan.

The noise of tens of thousands of feet moving over the concrete walkways was like an army haphazardly on the march. Through the entrances they poured in their thousands, chattering cheerful types from all over the world mixing comfortably in a remarkable spirit of camaraderie. They shuffled into the Park in light summer clothes, showing off their national colours and waving their flags. They were jostling eagerly around the concourses, queuing for food, drinks and the toilets before climbing the stairs and escalators into the arena to find their seats. Jarvis could feel a sense of friendliness among these effervescent spectators, as they basked in the evening warmth, with anticipation in the air of something special to come as the Games reached their final climax, even something that would match the bravado of the much-admired opening ceremony three weeks earlier.

Jimmy was in a light jacket with his usual cap, but he looked hot as they queued for drinks, standing in direct sunshine. They downed their beers quickly, then hurried across Bridge A for block 230 in the south-eastern corner. No one seemed to recognise the smooth-faced Jarvis, although a few stewards nodded uncertainly to him on passing.

Jimmy had one of the day's papers with him, with its headline plaudits for the brilliant way London had dealt with the Games, the sheer size and complexity of it all. It was good that everyone had held faith with London as the original choice, Jarvis read, and London had shown the world in return what it could do with such a big event.

But that was not what it shall be remembered for, Jarvis told himself: *I am about to give London something really big to remember.*

Jarvis needed Jimmy for his alibi and he buttered him up with more beer and a pie before explaining to him what he would expect from the older man. Jimmy popped downstairs for a cigarette and the toilet every now and again, and Jarvis wandered off around the stadium, pushing against the excited crowds and checking that everything looked as it should. Back in his seat halfway up on the south side, he was watching the VIP stands using his binoculars, checking his bearings and recognising some faces, even if not the names. He picked out the Prime Minister and his wife in the front and some other political faces and statesmen as they arrived, together with the officials and their entourages, and were shown to their special seats in purple, orange or turquoise, partitioned off in the mid-tier on the west side. Later there was applause among the crowd when the young prince and his brother's wife arrived; no Queen tonight, regrettably too tired after such a busy year.

Jarvis noted the various stewards and security staff in place, directing spectators along the routes, patrolling crowded areas, guarding some of the protected gates, some with walkie-talkies attached to their tunics.

With the sunlight finally fading away to the west, the sky over the stadium turned a dull grey. The packed stadium had already been entertained for a couple of hours with live music, practising choruses and Mexican waves, each block of the crowd led by their own cheerleader in silly orange hats and white coats, before the recorded chimes of Big Ben at nine o'clock initiated the full proceedings. The excitable crowds shouted and swayed and laughed at anything and everything. Every tannoy announcement that echoed around the bowl was greeted with cheers. Jimmy and Jarvis were in their seats by then, 68 and 69 at the end of their row, one third up from the front of the upper tier. A nice view, with the lingering Olympic torch flame flickering in front of them, one of the main tunnel entrances for the trucks and cars just below them and the smart seats over to the left, which seemed like a mile away.

Once the skies had properly darkened, the lightshow started in earnest. Positioned at the shoulder of every spectator around the arena at every level were cluster pads of LED lights on short poles designed to produce a unique colourful and moving pattern appropriate to the action in the arena. So as 'Freedom' was sung on the arena stage, the word was spelled out in the spectator lights and revolved around the inner stadium. One after another, musical and dance sets were accompanied by individual light shows showing flare and originality never seen quite like that before.

As the showtime spectacle of dancing and amplified music continued around the clock, Jarvis became increasingly nervous, his right leg bouncing repetitively. It was nearly eleven o'clock when he made his move. There was nothing more he could do, his planning was complete; if it turned out not to be good enough, he would have to face the consequences. Up to a certain point, he could have aborted and nobody would have been any the wiser; beyond that point, he was fully committed.

That point had arrived.

The sun had been down two hours and it felt cold. He had his black knit top back on, his security badge round his neck. He patted Jimmy on the thigh, rose and left his seat, with his rucksack over his shoulder. He moved away in a forward crouch, down to the nearest steps to a corridor, slipped along on the same row to the next block and then the next, before starting the long ascent at a steady pace. Sometimes in almost complete darkness, aware of the seething masses of swaying spectators on either side of him, their eager faces smiling and shining back at him, and sometimes picked out by the light of sharp reflections and explosions, up the one hundred and fifty steps he climbed to the top of the upper tier, a casual unremarkable figure. Other people were wandering around too, looking for toilets or more drinks or heading for the exit. A huge Union Jack made up of lights sparkled bright blue and pink far away below him in the central arena, while the light show and music extravaganza continued unabated, attracting all the attention.

Since he had last been up there, each of the nine sets of steps at intervals around the stadium that pierced the canvas and led up onto the roof had been enclosed in painted metal barriers with secure doors, and stewards were in attendance on all-day duty in yellow DayGlo jackets. In front of Gate 4, Jarvis was confronted by a young man standing wearily, footsore in heavy boots. His Collingwood security badge clearly around his neck, Jarvis tilted his head towards a hand cupped over his ear, indicating that he was getting a message through an imaginary earpiece.

'They want us up on the roof for a minute, seems something is occurring there,' Jarvis shouted close into the young man's ear, trying to be heard above the noise in the stadium. He jerked a long finger skywards. The steward, a certain Anthony Butt, looked a little bemused but unconcerned, as he had seen Collingwood around the Park before and had faith in the bigger man. He turned and swiped his security card through the grooved box, reached for the handle and opened the door inwards. Jarvis hustled him through into a bare enclosure, where the noise was no less, even with the door closed, but there was a dull light at the back to make some things visible – including the near-vertical shiny ladder that Jarvis was familiar with, rising up through a black hole in the canvas roof above their heads. In the semi-darkness, in the enclosed space filled with stadium noise, they could have screamed and no one would have heard a thing.

Anthony Butt peered innocently up at the dark skies above, his head tilted backwards, reaching for the metal bar on one side, a foot poised over the bottom rung. Jarvis smiled pleasantly in the semi-darkness. The ex-serviceman then stabbed his left elbow full force into the front of the steward's exposed neck, crushing the cartilage of his voice-box against the vertebral bodies and putting him into instant laryngeal spasm, with acute breathing difficulty. His peaked cap flew off, his astonished eyes widened and he raised both hands to his throat, but he was unable to make any discernible sound. Jarvis wriggled his right hand into a surgical glove from his pocket, ripped the walkie-talkie off Butt's lapel and switched it off. Stepping back to give himself more room, he swivelled neatly on one foot and kicked the young man between his legs hard with his other foot in an upward thrust, crushing his testicles agonisingly. Already gasping soundlessly, the poor man almost exploded with nausea, dropping forward onto his knees at Jarvis's feet, not knowing which part of himself to hold and wanting to retch. Again with another swivel on one foot, Jarvis hit the side of Butt's head with a crunching kick of his metal-tipped boot. Anthony Butt crashed sideways across the dark floor and mercifully lost consciousness.

Jarvis pulled another glove onto his left hand. He completed the job by standing on the fallen guard's bare neck with his full weight for a minute. Until he was sure he was dead. He dragged the lifeless body by the ankles, stacking it in a heap in a darkened corner under the ladder, and pulled off the reflective jacket, rolling it up into a ball and stuffing it behind the body, along with the radio.

There is no going back now, Jarvis.

He wedged the small screwdriver under the door; he pulled on the balaclava and left his raincoat by the body. With flashing explosions and a cacophony of unbelievable noise, amplified electric sounds of singing and screaming band music, as his backdrop, Jarvis climbed the narrow ladder carefully into the night, onto the stadium rooftop. He felt the sudden force of wind, cooling and evaporating the thin film of sweat across his face, as soon as his head appeared through the opening. On the outer edge of the roof, with just a wire for a rail, he sensed the long dark drop to the ground below. Behind him he had a bird's-eye view of the Park, with lights along the causeways and colourful reflections off winding waterways. Through the criss-cross of white steel struts around the roof, he had open views across a featureless sky, with cityscape and endless suburbs beyond. A giant helium balloon floated above him over the stadium, with its remote television camera positioned on a suspended platform beneath, delivering no doubt wonderful aerial pictures to viewers around the world. Erupting from the open space of the arena, explosive lights were illuminating his route in a flashing, epileptic way.

Jarvis checked, but he was not expecting anybody nearby. He knew the snipers had been taken off the roof hours ago, following his rota arrangements. He held his torch between his teeth and crawled forward to the right position, lying flat on the steel-mesh walkway, identifying in the light and by feel the stretch of piping where he had created his hiding place six weeks before. His gloved fingers felt the edges of the tape, which had not been tampered with. Peeling them back from three sides, leaving one long side in place to act as a hinge, he folded the cut piece of piping like a door.

Inside, the heavy object wrapped in cling film was jammed in place as he had left it. It came free with a yank. The film covering was wet and slimy. He dried his hands on the towelling and eagerly dug into the wrapping, pulling it off with his fingers, then carefully laying out the pieces of his military rifle on the metal walkway in front of him. He crunched the cling film into a ball and pushed it into the pipe opening. He unfolded the rifle stock, attached the barrel, the chin rest and the night sights and screwed in the suppressor. He inserted into the bottom of the stock a compact magazine with five rounds of ammunition, a procedure that he had practised many times in the darkness of his lock-up, so that it had become something he was able to do with his eyes closed. The rifle felt reassuringly heavy and powerful. *Martyn, welcome, I have missed you.* He needed only four shots, but squeezed a spare magazine of five into his trousers anyway. He pushed the sunglasses into place to protect his eyes from the blinding lights that were so close, and looked faintly ridiculous as he climbed the steps, crouching, onto the companionway bridge.

Moving forward virtually on his stomach and inwards along the metal bridge, the noises of the stadium welling up like regurgitation through the open roof, his view of the arena below was slowly revealed. He settled himself in a flat lying position, some four feet back from the inner edge, face down feeling vaguely dizzy, with the bipod of the L115A3 supporting the stock of his rifle, and his chin rested on the cool metal plate. He peered forwards into the void, into a burning hell of intense flashing lights and mesmerising chaotic human movement, and was nearly blinded despite the dark glasses. He blinked several times and then closed his eyes tight. For a second a scary feeling came over him of sliding irretrievably forward on the inclined metalwork head first over the edge of the roof and free-falling into the void below without being able to stop himself. Removing the glasses after a few seconds, he grabbed firmly onto the solid metal edges of the walkway and hooked his tough boots around the edges on either side, reassuring himself that he was secure. He took a view along his rifle sights, set for night vision, and started to scan the rows of faces in the crowd opposite. The lower tier was probably about one hundred and fifty yards away and below him; that was not a challenging distance in itself, but in those conditions the necessary shots would be particularly difficult.

Jarvis had always been worried about his ability to find the targets in the mass of faces, at such a distance in the dark and at one point had contemplated bringing a spotter with him, someone to act as his target finder, which was how most snipers operated in reality; but the complications and risks in that situation were too great. He was most unlikely to find a fellow traveller whom he could trust with the same feelings and motivation as him – someone whom he would have to pay, while doubling the risk, and then worry about being stitched up after the event. No, he was on his own, which was how Jarvis preferred it.

To his satisfaction, he found the twenty-times magnification setting provided fabulous images, the faces appearing clear in the viewfinder, like targets in a coconut shy – as if, when the lights were bright, they were merely ten yards in front of him. With night vision, the available light was digitally enhanced, so the technique was to time each shot to coincide with each flash of light as it brightened up the target image. He still needed time to adjust, and to know where he was looking among that wave of faces. He had had a good look earlier in daylight with his binoculars. He saw some faces of political leaders, some minor heads of state, diplomats and other public figures as he scanned along the front of the middle tier of the VIP boxes. There were the familiar smiles of the British Prime Minister and his wife, easy to pick out, next to the Duchess of Cambridge and Prince Harry. *My God, what devastation I could cause, what power in my hands!*

In the fourth row back, behind those VIPs, was Gerry Morley

himself, with his wife to his left. Jarvis searched for Pamela, finding his way back to the more shadowy depths, over to the right; there she was with a host of unknown fresh faces around her, twinkling, smiling and cheering with pleasure. He moved left, towards the south-west corner, catching site of other well-dressed besuited movers and shakers, hundreds of pleased and self-satisfied officials, special invitees and honoured guests, from all parts of the world.

But where was Abu Masoud Zadeh, the man for whom this party was planned? Ainsley had phoned Jarvis yesterday: his information was that the Iraqi group would be in row 29 – one from the back – in M13 of the middle tier. Jarvis saw numerous Arabs in their robes and other Middle Eastern gentlemen in suits scattered among the spectators, but no sign of Abu. He had the image of the man imprinted on his memory, having stared at his photo and studied it a thousand times; and he *had* spotted him earlier in the evening. But he was beginning to think that he might have left early. *Fuck, bloody fuck, where are you, you bastard?*

He desperately scanned again along the dense rows of moving people, back and forth several times, along the lines of faces, stopping sometimes when he thought he saw a likeness, but then moving on; and just as he was about to really panic, he finally spotted him. There he was, actually in the back row, middle tier, in front of glass panelling, in a light suit, with neatly trimmed black hair and beard. The face was so familiar, as if Jarvis had met the man in person, with the telltale twist to his mouth and the gappy upper front teeth when he smiled, the familiar cruel expression. He was leaning forward, gazing around at the spectacle of lights and dancers in the arena, trying to catch the eye of one of his countrymen among the revellers in the middle, waving and calling.

Jarvis increased the magnification to twenty-five times. The faces enlarged, clear and recognisable in a ghostly green, but then when he moved the sights, everything seemed to go out of focus and became blurred. He reduced the magnification one notch.

More fireworks erupted in unison, remotely-controlled, around the stadium roof. Rockets fired off from the apex of the lighting gantries above him and from the track running around the inner rim of the roof, just in front of where he was calmly lying in wait, the trail of lights arcing over the arena forming for short moments a bright roof, as if they were in a massive cathedral. There was a powerful whiff of cordite, and as the crashes and ear-splitting bangs went off all around him, Jarvis had to fight hard not to be taken back to the maelstrom of an Iraqi battle he had been caught up in, a lifetime ago. He lay flat, face down, looking onto the taut canvas roofing a few feet below him. He sensed a climax being reached as a popular girl band on the ground at the centre of the arena was reunited to play again in front of an adoring British audience.

The time had arrived.

Jarvis Collingwood, ex-paratrooper and British Army sniper, lone hero, acting grim reaper was ready to carry out his appointed task, and the sooner he did the deed the sooner he would be back at ground level and heading for the exit.

The surgical gloves Jarvis wore gave him perfect feel for the trigger, although his fingers and palms were wet inside them; he was also conscious of sweat collecting along his brow, inside the woollen balaclava. He returned the telescopic sights, already calibrated for a distance range of one hundred and seventy to one hundred and ninety yards, to Abu Masoud. He moved the cross hairs and focused precisely on a point on Abu's forehead. The face became clear with each burst of light in the arena. He pushed the magazine hard up into the stock and easily worked the bolt, taking the first round into the chamber. The catch was off: he had five rounds at his disposal. He knew what he had to do – he had done it many times before. He placed a piece of towelling over the stock to catch the casings and prevent contamination by the cordite spray.

Taking slow deep breaths, he filled his lungs with air that tasted bitter, while ice-cold waves flooded through his chest. His face froze with concentration, his left eye squinted, his right focusing through the sights. Timing his breathing calmly to coincide with the best lighting, he took his time, waiting for the moment when Abu Masoud was still. *This is the bastard who decapitated David Chigwell in cold blood. You do not deserve to live one moment longer. For revenge, for retribution, for the benefit of all.*

The rifle remained rock steady in his large hands and he took comfort in the close fit of the stock under his chin. He applied even pressure on the trigger. There was a cracking sound in his right ear. A shock thudded into his shoulder, a mere flick of recoil. In the viewfinder, a puff of dust silently erupted from the strengthened glass surface behind his target. A dark spot the size of a pinpoint disrupted the smooth line of Abu's forehead between his eyes. He worked the bolt again with ease and the empty shell case tinkled onto the metal causeway; without taking his eye from the rifle scope, he trapped it, still hot, with a finger, so it would not roll away.

For a moment Abu Masoud sat upright, wide-eyed and staring, while everything around him, the crescendo of sound, the clapping and cheering, continued unabated as if nothing had happened. All of a sudden, and Jarvis was surprised by the length of time it seemed to take, Abu's tongue appeared at his mouth, flopping wide open, and his head lolled heavily to one side. His body slumped against the person next to him, who tried to prop him up, pushing him away as if it was a joke, while someone else leant over him from behind. As Jarvis watched with fascination, his upper lip curled in a victorious twist, reflecting relief and satisfaction.

He lingered no longer to watch but moved the angle of his barrel trajectory a few fractions of a degree to the right, bringing his aim slightly forward to the fourth row from the front of the VIP boxes, almost directly opposite, for his second paid target, Gerry Morley. Adjusting the focus and magnification, he saw the face that was all too familiar, a face Jarvis had come to hate, for the lies, the trickery and the false claims. *For all the people, the civilians and servicemen who lost their lives, the wounded and displaced, both here and in Iraq, this is for you.*

Jarvis brought the cross hairs of his sights onto Morley's head and again started counting to the rhythm of the overhead bursts of light. He had a clear view. He applied firm even pressure on the trigger, one, two, three ... resulting in a sharp crack in his ear and a thud into his shoulder. Morley's head sprang back instantly with a violent jerk and the exit bullet hit the man behind, making him jump.

Jarvis re-cocked the rifle, moving his aim immediately a fraction to his right and fired a single shot into Amanda Morley's chest, ripping through its contents, lungs and vessels. The exit bullet at her back penetrated a man's groin sitting behind. Without hesitation Jarvis swivelled away a little to the right and backwards into the upper tier, not lingering to watch the after-effects, knowing he had made the hits.

It was time for his final target.

Jarvis lined up the last shot that he wanted, without hesitation. Lashed with desire for cruel vengeance, his treacherous spirit allowed no room for sentiment or moral judgement. Latent violence blended with his neurotic sense of romance and welled up inside to drive his ambitions. With stinging eyeballs, he pushed aside for another day the unbearable guilt that would torment him: *sorry for everything, but really this is best.*

He screwed up his eyes, his face puckered; he squinted along his sights at a black-haired slick young man in blazer and white shirt, as animated as all his surrounding Italian friends, unaware of the mayhem Jarvis had caused so far. Their revelry continued unblemished. Jarvis placed his cross hairs on the man's head, following its movement as it leant forward, craning its neck for a better view. Calculating the trajectory of the exit bullet with care, he fired with precision, without tremor, without rush, the rifle remaining steady as if part of him. He heard the 'phut' in his ear, somewhat obscured among all the other noises, and felt again the thump into his bruised shoulder. The bullet pierced his target's forehead high up, blowing a mess out of the back of the skull, and the young Italian remained upright and wide-eyed for a second or two, before slumping backwards against his seat, his face staring up at the roof, gelled black hair still in place, arms carelessly thrown out. Behind him, the semi-obscured figure in a white jacket and pink dress was jerking backwards with a gush at her neck, arms akimbo; people either side were springing up in surprise, wiping at the warm splashes on themselves and thinking for a split second that that was all part of the show. Then their mouths were opening and screaming soundlessly. There was a flooding and dark staining of the woman's clothes, and around those two mutilated bodies nobody moved, transfixed by the horror.

Elsewhere in the stadium everything seemed to continue without a hiccup. The ceremony carried on, the fireworks were still cracking and whizzing above the audience, the stars performing as planned, the dancers still working their lives away, the crowds cheering and singing along for all they were worth. Jarvis stole a quick glance down to the opposite side of the arena, looking for signs of the devastation he had caused, but nothing untoward could be picked out, the vast crowd continuing to enjoy the final moments of London 2012.

The time taken from the first shot to the last was 28 seconds, on Jarvis's watch. Four shots, four targets hit. Three collateral casualties: *unfortunate*. Jarvis felt as if he had just successfully felled an ancient oak, suspended high on lifting crane with saws blazing, and watched the mighty trunk fall with ripping, screeching sounds in an elegant arc, landing with a ground-juddering thump amid clouds of rising wood dust, like a skyscraper falling after an explosion. Not even the sniper shoots he had run in Baghdad on his second term working with the US boys had given him as much satisfaction as he felt now.

But this was not the time for gloating. His left elbow where he hit the young steward in the throat was hurting and his right shoulder felt sore. He took the towelling, carefully wrapped up the four empty casings from the metal walkway beside him, and slid himself backwards along the companionway. He was breathing excitedly, panting almost, his heart thumping and sweat running cold down his back. Around his face globules of sweat suddenly poured along his brow and started to leave a wet trail of drops along the metal walkway.

Crouched in the dark on the outer gangway, close to the ladder top, he disassembled the rifle quickly, removing the magazine with its fifth unused bullet, unscrewing the suppressor, sliding off the telescope, removing the barrel and chin piece, folding the stock, and placed all the parts on the metal grating at his feet. He took the four still-warm metal casings and tossed them through the cut window in the drainpipe below him; lying flat he stuffed the towel into the pipe as well along with the cling-film bundle. He brought the cut window piece back into place, pressing down the still-sticky tapes along the edges as before, wiping over the dust, confident that it would not be easily found tucked under the walkway.

He wrapped the folded rifle butt and stock and its accessories into the other piece of towelling and stuffed it into the rucksack, together with the binoculars, sunglasses and balaclava. He climbed back down the ladder to the enclosed lobby and hitched the bag over his shoulder, fitting it under his armpit, and then pulled his raincoat on to cover it. He took a quick look at the crumpled figure of his first victim behind the ladder. Removing the screwdriver from under the door, his flat cap on, he casually slipped out, closing the self-locking door behind him, and only then removed his plastic gloves stuffing them into his pockets as he moved from the top of the arena, viewing the show far below as if nothing had happened. He descended steadily the hundred and fifty steps to the nearest stairwell and walked down to the outside concourse without anyone particularly taking any notice. Jimmy would make his own way home.

He took the identification badge from around his neck. Lots of people were meandering in and out of the stadium, blissfully unaware of what had happened over on the other side. He imagined the chaos that must be erupting over there, with spectators scrambling to rush out, trying to avoid the possible line of fire of a deranged killer on the roof. Officials would be turning around in circles, uncertain of what had happened, trying to prevent panic and keeping the cameras off the spectacle, without the coordination to assess what had happened or the leadership and courage to close down the stadium and the Olympic Park. They would adopt a 'search and contain' procedure, pretending nothing had happened, while the show carried on, watched by millions of still-oblivious spectators all over the world. There would be panic among the senior ranks when they realised who the victims were. He dared not glance back, but joined the thickening crowds slowly making their way over the bridge across the wide concourse to the two main exits. Forcing himself to walk at a normal pace, when he was desperate to sprint, he stuffed the plastic gloves deep into an overflowing rubbish bin. His heart was pounding painfully and his right shoulder was seriously hurting.

He headed south to the Greenway exit, where the gates were wide open and spectators were being encouraged to keep walking, mind the busy road ahead, safe journey, hope you enjoyed the

Games and good night. He mingled in the semi-darkness and was lost in the crowds, in his grey raincoat and flat cap pulled down to obscure much of his face. Up ahead at the security area there was a hold-up and the crowds were jammed closer together, everybody edging slowly forward, trying not to trip against the people in front. Guards and soldiers were out in numbers, some with looks of shock on their faces, some were shouting at each other, some listening on headphones, but there was no coordinated action or any attempt to stop the crowd moving through the open barriers. Jarvis kept walking steadily, looking ahead. He arrived with a dense crowd of people over at the bicycle park, almost unaware of how he got there, and unfolded the plastic sheeting from his Vespa.

The time elapsed from the moment Jarvis squeezed the trigger for his first victim to the moment he reached his means of escape was a mere nine minutes. He spotted at least three helicopters droning in the skies above the stadium with powerful light beams raking over the roof and around the edges. He heard police sirens loudly screeching through the night towards the stadium along Stratford High Street and down Warton Road. He put on his helmet from the locked scooter box. He tightened the heavy rucksack over his shoulder, wrapped the raincoat around him tighter with its belt, and inserted his key into the ignition with a twist of the throttle. An ambulance with siren blaring was struggling through the congested traffic nearby. Jarvis set off, calm and elated at the same time, away from the devastation at the Olympic Park towards Bow, the Mile End Road and his secret lock-up.

Midlogue

Jarvis was back in his lair in Witan Street well before midnight. He was relieved to be able to shut himself away and take stock. He stowed the Vespa scooter and helmet and emptied all the contents of the box seat, his rucksack and his pockets onto the table. He placed the folded stock, the suppressor, its telescope and magazines in the cupboard underneath, with the towelling and binoculars; the sunglasses and screwdriver he put on the worktop. His old mobile was where he had left it, plugged into the charger. The balaclava he had separately disposed of in a bin he found in a front garden on his way back through Hackney. He stripped off all the clothes he had been wearing, damp with sweat, and draped them onto a coat hanger that he hooked up on a nail, the boots placed neatly beneath. He made a mental note to get rid of the security guard's DNA from the toe of the left boot.

He changed into his original clothes and reached in the fridge for the bottle of beer he had saved for himself as a reward for all his hard work. He sank onto a chair, suddenly feeling exhausted. He allowed himself a deep sigh, of relief that it was all over, of satisfaction that he had done everything he had set out to do, to the letter, to perfection. And of triumph that he had walked away unscathed.

He felt an urge to laugh. He had just shot dead four, maybe five, people, killed a security guard with his bare hands and walked out of the Stratford Olympic Stadium unnoticed carrying the offending weapon, at a time of the tightest security exercise ever held on these shores. *You cannot legislate for an inside job, that is what they will say. It does not matter how many fucking ground-to-air missiles you have on your side!*

He nursed his warm dog-tags for a few moments, then placed them in the desk drawer. He ripped the picture of Abu Masoud off

201

the wall and tore it into shreds, dropping the pieces in the bin. He kept his security badge in his leather coat. Picking up his house keys and leaving everything else behind, he set off on foot for Hoxton along the back roads and was home in less than twenty minutes. There was a deathly hush inside. Forlorn darkness filled the kitchen as he sat at the table with head in hands without putting any lights on. Somewhere between walking out of the stadium and reaching his house via the lock-up, he had decided to sit this out and play the innocent. He was not going to run, to become a fugitive, or to leave the country, not yet at least. That would have implicated him and confirmed his guilt. The option of using his second identity might have worked, for a while perhaps, but hiding as Josh Cooper, taking sanctuary with Naomi, he would not have been able to venture out, he would have been trapped, and the absence of Jarvis Collingwood would once again have pointed to his guilt. The police and security agencies would have been intensively searching for him and eventually would have caught up with Cooper/Collingwood, which would have been difficult to explain. The second identity might come in useful, but later.

Better to ride out the storm, knowing he had left nothing for the police to find. He checked around the house many times and knew there was nothing there to associate him with the shooting. His archway lock-up with all the incriminating stuff was only known to Ainsley. The only people who knew about the job were the Chigwells, and it would not be in their best interests to stitch him up because he would readily betray them. His alibi had some gaps, but he would claim to have been all evening with Jimmy, who would support his story. *If I stay as Jarvis Collingwood, I am most likely to get away with this.*

He drank a full glass of tap water. His initial elation at his personal success and pleasure, at how skilful he had been in foiling powerful organisations and in taking down Abu Masoud, the butcher, was turning into detached disappointment. He began to feel empty. It was as if he was in shock himself, an odd sort of after-effect. He thought he would want to shout to the world and share with people what he had done, what he had achieved, all alone.

He wanted to be their hero again.

But his mind for the moment was numbed. He desperately wanted to sleep. He moved into the sitting room and turned on the twenty-four-hour news channel. An announcer was shouting in near-hysterical tones and the ticker headlines moving across from right to left at the bottom in a red strip read: 'VICTIMS OF SHOOTING AT THE OLYMPICS, FIVE DEAD. EX-PM GERRY MORLEY AND WIFE AMANDA SHOT DEAD IN FRONT OF THOUSANDS IN STADIUM AT CLOSING CEREMONY.'

The pictures were night-time scenes of yellowy ambulances glittering under bright search lights, shell-shocked police officers being interviewed, reporters trying to say sensible things over background images of the Games, always in the shadow of the massive stadium, then quickly returning to earlier scenes of the ceremony and the fireworks, with close-ups of colourful costumes, dancers, celebrity singers and a few happy athletes biting their medals, competitors marching and waving flags. Then more voice-overs trying to describe the chaos and slaughter in the VIP boxes, without any pictures to support them. Some images focused on the moments long after the victims went down, but attempts at showing close-ups were diverted to the action in the arena. Emergency vehicles were shown arriving and leaving in numbers, sirens blaring, ambulances and fire engines parked up randomly around the concourse and police cars speeding in every direction, lights flashing. The commentators struggled to make any sense of the events, to understand any of the detail, or to say anything interesting.

He sat closer to the screen, nursing his sore shoulder, persuading himself that he was not involved in the tragedy, that the events in the stadium that occurred over an hour ago were nothing to do with him: he and Jimmy had been spectators and saw nothing untoward from where they were sitting. He had returned home by foot after the ceremony, innocently having a drink, watching some television in amazement, while awaiting Pamela's return.

There were more TV pictures from Stratford Park taken from the air and Jarvis could see stretchers being passed into the back of emergency ambulances, a rush of people, top people, moving in a disordered way out of the central exit of the stadium to waiting cars, big black limousines transporting the important ones away from high risk areas, leaving the masses to fend for themselves, and cars and ambulances speeding out through gates to the main roads and safety. There was the front of a bleak Royal London Hospital in Whitechapel Road and a tired-looking reporter outside in a spotlight saying she had seen some of the victims brought there on stretchers, and that the casualty department had been closed to the public, possibly expecting more. There were some casualties, she said, fighting for their lives in the theatres as surgeons battled with gunshot wounds and severe blood loss.

Jarvis mooched around for a while, his head increasingly besieged with sounds of crowds cheering and fireworks crackling in the night sky, and with images flooding his consciousness of faces in a circular window, of blood spots splattering on the glass, faint knocking sounds like a distant hammer in his right ear, looks of surprise on faces in the crowd soundlessly screaming. He went upstairs for a shower to revive himself. In the bathroom mirror in his underpants, he inspected the bruise on the front of his right shoulder, which was tender to touch (but should fade over the next three or four days, he reassured himself).

He looked at the TV news again for more information, but there was nothing further, just repeats of the same old images and sound bites. One news programme confirmed that five people had been shot dead and others wounded, although no one was saying exactly who they all were. When asked if any current member of the British government or royal family were injured, an Olympics spokesperson gave a categorical denial. No one was speculating at this stage who was responsible; the killer or killers had not been found.

He checked that everything in the house looked natural, untidy, as it had been left in the morning, such a long time ago. Pamela's clothes over the bed, unmade, smalls hanging over the bath, make-up stuff around the bathroom and over her dressing table, drawers half open. There were cigarette butts in ashtrays and coffee cups unwashed on tables, some newspapers scattered, and in the sink, plates and unwashed cutlery. A pile of ironing was waiting on the dining table to be put away.

He thought about Naomi for the first time that night. She was going to get the shock of her life when she found out, and heaven knew how she would cope with it. He would have liked to talk to her, but decided not to take the risk, not yet, and not at that time of the morning. He was feeling so tired, suddenly needing to rest his head.

Water was cascading over the stadium roof into its deep central arena from all around, turning red as fountains of blood as thick as strawberry jam sprang up around the track. Desperate spectators were scrambling over each other to stay above the blood line. Pamela was reaching for him, gripping his arms so he could not move them properly, screaming into his face. He was holding his rifle in both hands and floating away from her above the flow, but she kept grabbing at his ankles and pulling him back. He was struggling to kick her away, and then her face erupted into deep craters of exposed and brutalised tissue, oozing forth sticky rubescent material.

Suddenly Jarvis woke from heavy sleep. There was tapping out-side and somewhere a bell was ringing. His dreams disintegrated into fragments, but he was still searching for Pamela's face. He rolled over, face down in the pillows, but the knocking persisted. He sat up with a start, sweating in the cold room, eyes blinking and adjusting to the dimness. The clock by the bed said ten past five. He realised the noise was coming from the front door of his house. He heard more knocking and again the bell sounded, chiming downstairs. Seen through a gap in the bedroom curtains, the two uniformed policemen in black caps and DayGlo reflective flak jackets looking around under shadowy street lighting, gave him an uncanny feeling. At that very moment, one of them glanced up and looked straight into his eyes. He splashed his face with water in the bathroom, pulled on a T-shirt and a pair of Levi's and tumbled downstairs.

Mumbling okay, okay, pulling back the bolts, twisting on the Yale, he opened the front door a little. A faded yellow halo shone across the doorstep, but there was no one visible outside at first. Then he heard a stern voice: 'Jarvis Collingwood? Police, from Bow Road Station. Would you step out this way for a moment please, sir? So we can see you in the light.' And the figure of a large policeman emerged from one side of the porch, while the voice came from another even larger policeman on the other side; both had been holding themselves flat against the brickwork waiting for Jarvis's appearance. Jarvis stepped forward, eyes screwed up with sleep, and placed a bare foot on the cold tiles outside. They could see even in this gloomy light that he was not armed or dangerous, so they moved in to crowd around him. He noticed a blue-and-yellow-checked Volvo police car parked a couple of doors down, and standing on the pavement opposite, beside a police motorbike, its blue light switched off, were two further solidly built officers, their faces obscured, one in a white helmet, goggles and white gloves, the other dark and bulky in reflective jerkin and cap.

'Jarvis Collingwood?' Again it was the same gruff voice.

'Yeah, what's going on? What time is it?' He looked confused and sleepy in the poor light and he felt the cold air encircling him.

'This is Police Constable Abbot. I am Police Sergeant Thompson, from Bow Road Police Station, Mile End.' They were both holding up little plastic folders with white cards behind cellophane that Jarvis could neither see nor read properly, but he took their word for it. 'We would like to come inside,' continued Thompson, who was doing all the introductions, poking his card back inside his tunic, 'and have a word, if you don't mind, sir. I'm afraid there's been an incident and we need to talk to you in private. If we may, sir?' Both men, bulky and menacing, were pushing against Jarvis, so he had to retreat backwards into his narrow hallway. They stepped in one at a time after him in their oversized black boots and pushed the front door closed. Jarvis reached for a light. 'Okay, come in here,' and led them into the lounge, where there were sofas to sit on.

They all remained standing. The big men in their all-weather black jackets and yellow reflectors, bulging pockets, belts with tools attached, handcuffs dangling, stood side by side, almost filling the entire room. Jarvis, still blinking awkwardly in the light, rubbing his eyes, suppressing a yawn, caught a whiff of their body smell. Abbot spoke into the walkie-talkie hooked to his lapel. 'OK, Jock, we have the interested party secure inside. Remain alert.'

'Please, sit,' suggested Thompson. Jarvis perched on the arm of a settee.

'You are Mr Jarvis Collingwood, of 15 Baring Street, Hoxton?'

'Yes, again.'

'You have a wife? Name of Pamela Collingwood?' Thompson kept glancing at a notebook folded back at the relevant page.

'Yes, yes, but she's not here, she was at the Olympics, the ceremony at the stadium . . .' and a note of anxiety had managed to squeeze into his voice, rising to a slightly higher pitch as it faded.

'I'm afraid there has been a terrible incident, sir. You may have seen the television news earlier. We need you to accompany us to Bow Road Station, to help with an identification.'

'What! What are you saying?' Jarvis stuttered.

'We have a body to identify that we have reason to believe is Pamela Collingwood, sir. We need her nearest to definitively identify her for us.' Thompson at least had the good grace to appear upset at having to impart this news to Pamela's nearest and dearest, and Jarvis had taken on a suitably stunned expression.

'This can't be right. Pamela? Involved in all that . . . ?' His voice had risen again. Looking back sometime later, Jarvis thought he had done pretty well at this point, but both Thompson and Abbot would claim that he was as cool as anything, and that hardly a flicker of emotion crossed his face – 'as if he already knew what we was telling 'im'.

Outside, the early morning streets were empty, draped with eerie light and vacuous shadows as if nothing untoward in the world had happened. The two officers in the squad car explained to Jarvis that a number of people had been shot last night at the Olympics by an unidentified gunman or gunmen from some distance, probably from the roof of the stadium during the closing ceremony, and that they thought his wife for some reason was among that number. Jarvis, properly dressed, at least with some shoes on, sat tightly squashed and placid in the back seat between two hefty shoulders, feigning disbelief. By the time they reached Bow Road, it was getting on for six o'clock.

Jarvis Collingwood sat morosely at a bare table in an interview room on the ground floor of the old building. He was hungry, not having eaten anything since yesterday with Jimmy. His shoulder felt sore, but he remembered not to rub it. He looked around a few times, checking the CCTV above the door. The room had bare corn-coloured walls, a high ceiling and a tall white-framed window with a stone sill and frosted glass. The decor was dull and tatty, the chairs hard and plastic, the lino floor cracked.

Intermittently the sound of voices seeped into the room from the corridor outside, mumbling, sometimes raised. Somewhere doors were banged and footsteps ran up and down stairs. At one point a young WPC brought in a cup of tea, pouring the spillage in the saucer back into the cup before placing it in front of him. Sometime after that, he was collected by an unshaven man in a green jumper and worn-looking shoes, who led him along cream-painted corridors, apologising for the delay. They went down a few stairs, around a corner, along another dull corridor, and then down a metal staircase to the basement, to what looked like a part-time mortuary, decidedly cooler. Through battered swing doors they shuffled into a bright neon-lit room with white benches down either side, ancient air-conditioning chugging in the background. Technicians and porters in blue overalls milled about in floppy white boots. There was a sharp smell that Jarvis could not instantly place, pungent surgical spirit and ammonia perhaps, but sweet and cloying in his nostrils. He had an urge to sneeze.

Despite himself, Jarvis was nervous. The brightly lit room was chilly and a coarse trembling worked its way sporadically over his shoulders, down his arms. Three trolleys side by side, each with a white drape over a body-shaped bundle, were centre stage, although everyone else seemed busy avoiding paying them any attention. Hanging at the ends of each were buff name tags tied through a loop, and Sergeant Thompson, in blue plastic overshoes, was checking these before he signalled Jarvis over, with the diminutive police woman behind him. *Abu Masoud must be on one of these and the Italian man on the other. The Morleys won't be here, they would have gone to somewhere special.* Standing close by, a man with a few strands of hair plastered over his rounded pate and a grey moustache that barely concealed his distain was ready with clipboard and pen. A professor, one might have thought, except for the rubber gloves and a plastic gown that covered him from neck to blood-stained boots. He clomped forward and looked Jarvis in the face with a curious lift of dishevelled eyebrows, which peaked unexpectedly over the rim of his thick framed glasses. Reaching for the middle trolley, the man carefully peeled the edge of the sheet back to reveal only the head beneath, with nothing exposed below the chin.

Scrubbed clean for identification purposes, unfamiliarly plain without make-up, eyes closed, colourless lank hair swept back off a high forehead, the face was puffy but calm in repose, ashen grey in colour, and it took a moment for Jarvis to recognise her. He half expected her to open an eye and squeal at him with a twist of her mouth, as if she was playing a trick on him. He stared at her plucked brows, her prominent nose and the stark voids of her static nostrils.

A little moisture had gathered around his eyes. He clenched his teeth, bit into his lower lip and blinked. Holding a hand over his mouth, he pinched the bridge of his nose and a few drops spilt over, landing on the dusty tiles at his feet, which was what WPC Carter remembered most, because she had been looking resolutely at the floor rather than risking being upset by the appearance of the dead woman's face.

After a few shudders had passed over Collingwood's back, she placed a kindly hand on his shoulder. The beefy sergeant was now looming at his elbow. 'Are you able to identify Pamela Collingwood as the person here before you?'

Jarvis stepped forward and nodded a couple of times. 'Yes,' he was heard to croak. He reached out to touch Pamela's cheek with the backs of his fingers. She resembled a cold stone carving on a tomb. He wanted to see her eyes, they were always the best thing about Pam's face, those clear coffee eyes. 'Pamela,' WPC Carter swore later that she heard him whisper, 'I'm so sorry.'

Before turning back towards the door, he found a handkerchief in his tight jeans pocket. The sting in his tears surprised him.

And then Sergeant Thompson dictated: 'Mr Jarvis Collingwood of 15 Baring Street, Hoxton identified the body labelled OSS-2F as that of Pamela Collingwood also of 15 Baring Street, at Bow Road Police Station on August 13, 2012 at 06.46 hours.'

At about the same time, a call for the night duty officer came through from a senior policeman at Stratford Park. 'Have you got a Jarvis Collingwood with you? We need him here. This is urgent. He is a possible suspect, do you understand?' There was petulance in the voice. 'He might be armed and dangerous. He is a suspect, repeat, Jarvis Collingwood is a suspect. In the shootings at the Stratford Park Stadium last night. You will keep him safe, under lock and key. Do not interrogate him. We are sending a team of senior police officers to question him and pick him up right now. Acknowledge.'

'And you are?'

After a pause bursting with explosive indignation that could be felt down the telephone line, 'Her Majesty's Security Services, you dickhead.'

'Acknowledged, sir, thank you, sir.'

The middle-aged male duty officer, rotund and slow-witted, of some years' seniority, removed his headpiece, rose from his stool and ambled out of the communications room to find Sergeant Thompson and impart the good news.

'Some senior Met officers from the Incident Response Unit are on their way,' Thompson told Jarvis, 'and want to ask you some questions. I have been requested to detain you here in the station until such time as the said officers arrive.'

'That will be today, will it?' Jarvis asked without humour.

'That should be within the next . . .' and Thompson looked at his watch '. . . half an hour, I would say, if they can get through the traffic, sir. Now, if you wouldn't mind . . .' And with that, Thompson led Jarvis back into the original interview room, where he had first emptied his pockets, taken off his watch and been hand-searched, before signing a book which listed his meagre possessions. Jarvis was left alone once again. On testing the door, he found it was locked. He sat down, trying not to rub his sore shoulder while being watched on the CCTV.

Streaky daylight had crept over the grubby East End and angled in low through the windows of the interview room at Bow Road Police Station, where Jarvis was slumped in semi-sleep over the table, his bottom sore on the hard plastic chair. The inevitable single neon strip was shining its monotonous light from the ceiling. Thompson stepped inside the room unannounced and held the door open. Three men followed one after the other with noisy footsteps and Jarvis sat up with a jerk. In the lead was a uniformed inspector, his chest puffed out with shining badges and piping and black shoes, his cap wedged under his arm. He had an expression of concern and looked military in standing, with thin hair and thin moustache. Stomping in behind him came a stockier younger man in rumpled grey suit, poor choice of tie, with short hair and jutting jaw that was nothing if not determined, who stared at Jarvis, unimpressed. The last man was lean and tall, in a good-quality charcoal grey suit, Jarvis could see that, white shirt like the rest, and a tight-lipped puckered expression as if a hot chilli pepper was stuffed up his backside. All three looked sleep-deprived and irritable, for being there at that early hour, for having to talk to dross like Jarvis; and whatever discomfort Jarvis was feeling, theirs was much worse, having been bollocked all through the night from above for their incompetence and gross failure of their security responsibilities and their disloyalty to queen and country. They none of them looked friendly, and Jarvis sensed straight away their hostility towards him. Solid, uniformed Thompson closed the door and remained standing in front of it, armed and protective.

'Collingwood, Jarvis? Yes?' started the inspector, the most senior of the three. He carried no notes, only a leather stick, leather gloves and his cap, all three of which he placed on the table in front of him.

Jarvis braced himself. He stood and looked suitably distraught and bemused. 'Yes.'

'Chief Inspector McIntosh is my name. Scotland Yard.' All his emphasis in the surname was on the upper case I. 'This is Inspector Stephen Broderick, Inspector Robert Barnes. Both of the Serious Crime Squad and Incident Response Unit. Please sit.' Chairs were lifted and scraped towards the table in the centre, with Jarvis sitting on one side, and the three heavy-duty officers lined up along the opposite side, all looking far too bulky for the size of the plastic chairs. 'Broderick?'

Inspector Broderick laboriously offered Jarvis the right to remain silent but reminded him that anything he did say might be taken down and used in evidence. Inspector Barnes had a folder and was holding a pen, ready to take notes.

'Like to ask you a few questions, under caution. About tonight. Sorry about your loss.' For all the hostile expressions and pursing of lips, McIntosh managed to sound a little sorry, although why he was apologising, Jarvis could not imagine. He spoke in fast clipped tones in a diluted Edinburgh lilt as thin as his clipped moustache. 'Need to start with some basics. Broderick?'

And Broderick, pink in the face, looking cross, jumped in again, asking for date of birth, nationality, place of birth, parents' names and nationalities, address, marital status, for how long, children, these were the basics. Jarvis answered them all. 'You are ex-Army, yes?' Jarvis nodded. 'Parachute Regiment, correct? Served twice in Iraq, Afghanistan, time in Cyprus and Germany?' Jarvis nodded again. 'Not Special Forces then, but a marksman, a sniper, discharged with honours.'

Jarvis continued to nod his agreement to all this preamble, then sat up straighter and looked directly into Broderick's face. He noticed a small scar close to one corner of his mouth that gave him a slightly lopsided look. 'So, good with a rifle?' Broderick finished with some sarcasm. There being no verbal reply, he went on, with his lopsided smile, 'That was a question, by the way.'

'I served in the British Army as a regular in 2000, I joined the Parachute Regiment Second Battalion 2003, went to Iraq twice, discharged 2009, yes, sir. Not Special Forces, no, sir.'

'And recently, what have you been doing?'

'Security, sir.'

'Working with whom?'

'A private firm called SecureLife, sir,'

'Which is owned by one Mr Jonathan Collingwood, your brother, I understand, correct?'

'Yes, sir.'

'Working where?'

'At Stratford, the Olympic Park.'

'The Olympic Stadium?'

'Yes, throughout the Games. I'm due back for the Paralympics in two weeks. Involved all the venues, but mostly in the stadium.'

'Your own security pass? How does that work?'

'Yes, sir.' Jarvis seemed to fumble around his empty neck. 'It's at home. All the staff have them, some have more access than others.'

'And yours, access to everywhere around the Park?'

'More or less – a swipe card with its security code.'

'How long? When did you join this firm?'

'I've worked for my brother on and off for three years. I

joined the Olympic security team in March and worked with the Organising Committee through the months leading up to the Games. All Olympics employees were security- and police-checked. I was on duty earlier today, yesterday, but I was off duty from two o'clock in the afternoon. Sir.'

There was a slight pause before Broderick asked: 'So where were you last night?'

Jarvis looked into Broderick's face and studied the folds of his mouth. 'I watched the closing ceremony from the stands, block 230. Then I came home after midnight, watched some TV, went to bed.'

'You were in the stadium at the time of the shooting, around 11 p.m.?' fired McIntosh with astonishment.

'I must have been,' said Jarvis, sounding unsure.

'What did you see?'

'Everything carried on as normal, I didn't see nothing, I was with Jimmy, we left at about 11.20, came home. I only knew something had happened from the TV news, but I had no idea Pamela was involved until . . .'

'Who's this Jimmy – able to vouch for you?'

'Jimmy Bullock, a friend, you can ask him, we were sitting together. There was nobody at home when I got there, Pamela was at the Games.'

'And that was after midnight, you say?'

'Yes, just after.'

'How did you get home – means of transport?'

'We walked, Jimmy went to West Ham station, took the Tube, I walked home to Hoxton.' Easy and casual.

'Walked, on foot?' McIntosh again. 'How long did that take you?'

'About thirty-five, forty minutes.'

'So you arrived home when?'

'About five after midnight.'

'Anybody see you at that time?'

'No, don't think so. Sir.'

Inspector Barnes, speaking for the first time, with slow deliberation, while fixing his gaze on the pad of paper on the table in front of him, with his hand poised with pen to start writing, asked smoothly: 'And you know that five people, including a British ex-Prime Minister and his wife, were shot dead and two others were injured?'

'So it seems.'

'The other dead were an Iraqi official, an Italian design consultant . . . and your wife, who I understand worked for Meredith's, a public relations firm that had the Olympics account? She had corporate complimentary tickets, I think.'

'Merriweather,' corrected Jarvis flatly. 'Merriweather & Dunn, it was.'

'Merriweather, stand corrected, thank you. Were you invited to be with her in the corporate stands, or was that just for her alone?'

'Yes, no, I mean no, I did not get invited.' Jarvis was again showing distress, looking at his hands, with his legs crossed, one elbow on his knee.

Broderick continued: 'The two injured were English officials of the government. And you identified your wife earlier as one of the victims?' Jarvis again nodded, but he was wiping his face and trying to compose himself. Broderick paused as earnest expressions flashed across all three police officers' faces. 'I'm sorry, Mr Collingwood. Do you know how these people, including your wife, died tonight?'

Jarvis was shaking his head this time, eyes frowning, and he said, 'Shot?'

'They were all shot, yes. Single shots to each one it seems, deadly. Carried out with a long-distance rifle, someone on the stadium roof, it would seem. Looks like a ruthless killing. Like an execution, wouldn't you say? Now who would want to do that? Who would pay someone to do that?'

Jarvis looked blank. 'Why are you asking me? *I* don't know.'

'Someone with exceptional skills with a rifle,' Broderick persisted with a steady voice. 'He would have to have a pretty sophisticated weapon, wouldn't you say? To pick out those people among the thousands of faces? A trained marksman, police or army, I'd say, wouldn't you, Mr Barnes?'

And Barnes looked up, fixing his eyes on Jarvis's pouting mouth. 'Definitely a well-trained marksman. Looks like an inside job to me,' and he lifted his gaze a fraction to stare directly into those misty blue eyes that gave nothing away.

'Any ideas on these questions, Mister Expert Rifleman, ex-Army, ex-Paratrooper?' And Broderick punched with emphasis on the last two words, showing some degree of resentment. 'How does someone get on the roof?' he continued.

Jarvis realised he was being provoked. *They have absolutely no evidence.* 'For God's sake, there were security staff posted everywhere! I don't know. Why would I know about that? Why would anyone want to kill Pamela? Haven't you guys caught anybody – how did he get off the roof?'

Broderick and McIntosh spoke at the same time: 'Quite, that's what *we* are asking you.' And they both glanced at each other and, with frustrated frowns, stared back at Jarvis. 'Um?' they sounded in unison.

And so on, for over an hour, but the three police officers achieved nothing further, except to confirm what their earlier briefing had concluded: that Jarvis Collingwood was a cool customer, not easily ruffled, with no obvious motive, not obviously guilty; and although not altogether convincing in his mock distress, he provided enough naïve shock and surprise to persuade the senior policemen that it was safe, at least for now, to allow him to go home. He would be accompanied by a number of officers, they explained, who would want to search the house and remove certain items, computer, mobile phone, that sort of thing, and to withdraw his passport – and to that effect they produced a piece of paper, which they said was a warrant. 'Am I under arrest?' Jarvis asked vaguely.

'No, just we need to search your house. Couple of our men will stay with you afterwards,' McIntosh explained, 'sort of house arrest, for a day or two, until we clear this whole thing up.' And with that he was up, gathering his things and marching out with a straight back and a disappointed look.

Nobody thought to examine Jarvis in any way; had they done, they might have found the faint beginnings of a bruise spreading over the front of his right shoulder, which he would have had some difficulty explaining away. He was told a family liaison officer would be assigned to him and he would meet her later. He was asked to sign the warrant and Barnes proffered his biro, informing Jarvis that he, Mr Collingwood, would be required to make an official statement tomorrow (or later today, actually), which he would also need to sign off in due course.

Elsewhere during that long Sunday night of August 12th, emergency services had been hectically working without a break. The casualties were taken to the medical assessment room deep in the underground part of the stadium, where on-duty volunteer doctors and assistant nurses had assessed with X-rays that two of the men wounded in the shooting needed operations to remove embedded bullets, to stop bleeding and repair wounds. Although a tourniquet around his upper arm had mostly stemmed the flow, John Faulkner was still losing blood and a brachial artery rupture was suspected. The other wounded was Peter Cheshire, bleeding badly from the groin, probably from a femoral artery disruption with a fracture at the neck of the femur, was in a lot of pain and there was a messy wound that needed expert handling. With wailing sirens and flashing blue lights, and intravenous lines safely running, they were transferred rapidly to the Royal London Hospital three and a half miles away in ambulances that made good use of the designated official lanes through heavy traffic. Both victims were in shock and in need of stabilising before their general anaesthetics, but by one-thirty in the morning they were both on operating tables in adjacent theatres on the fourth floor of the new central tower, and all was finished by half-past five, both transferred to Critical Care for further blood replacement, antibiotic administration, observation and recovery. Cheshire was to have a second elective orthopaedic procedure for repair of his femur, or even a full hip replacement later. The two surgical teams debriefed afterwards in the crowded staff room, where they drank cups of insipid tea and considered the extraordinary events of the evening, with a TV news channel on in the background, blurting out hard-to-believe sound bites about the earlier mayhem at the stadium.

There were two other male victims, both stretchered down to the basement in agonising sequence, but with a lesser degree of urgency, being beyond help. They each had massive head injuries, apparently from single bullets and the overworked doctor had had to pronounce them both dead. The bodies were lying side by side on trolleys in an adjacent room, where friends and associates were crying and wailing and wringing their hands. One group being Arab and the other Italian made for a bizarre spectacle of emotional outpourings. Little could the poor doctor, whose main area of specialist interest was sport and exercise medicine, where the most potent prescription for his patients might be Algipan, have predicted, when he set off from home the day before to cover the closing ceremony of the Olympic Games, what sort of challenges the night would throw at him.

The former Prime Minister and his wife, both well-known and familiar public figures, were clearly dead before security officers had clambered frantically over the seats and fellow spectators immediately around them to reach their slumped bodies. Gerry Morley, flung back against his seat, had a thin line of blood trailing over his temple from a small, perfectly circular hole in the side of his forehead by his right eye. The trail ran down into the shell of his ear, where blood had pooled and spilled over to drop onto the purple seat behind him, where there was a further coagulated pool. His eyes were open, his face still and smiling. There was a crater blown out of the back of his head and cascades of blood and contents had spilled out onto the concrete floor below. His wife had crashed to the floor between the rows, a growing ruby stain emblazoned across her turquoise outfit in the middle of her chest. The force of the blow had first knocked her violently sideways into the lap of the lady next to her, who had blood spattered over the side of her face and remained silent and frozen for a long time before she resorted to low-pitched screaming. Which did not stop even after she had been bundled away. Amanda Morley had tumbled to the floor, pale faced and lifeless on her back with mouth gaping, a rich red-coloured puddle spreading out over the concrete under her.

The bodyguards and security officers were frantically pulling people down into crouched positions or dragging them away along their rows to clear the area, a degree of orderly panic confusing the authorities into thinking that this commotion was perhaps a medical emergency, a stroke or heart attack, before closer inspection had revealed the gruesome truth. First-aid workers were pulled to the different scenes, rugs ripped from their grasp to cover the disturbing sight of bloodied corpses and wounded victims, before other Red Cross volunteers and stewards were recruited to quickly remove them to the emergency room downstairs on stretchers. Meanwhile, security swiftly extracted the two well-known victims, their identities hidden, wheeling them on trolleys to a waiting ambulance that rushed off forlornly with a single siren wail to a private mortuary in Westminster.

The first casualty to hit the A&E department at the Royal London had been Pamela Collingwood. Her name had been obtained by the lanky young police officer in shirt sleeves who had been the first to reach her and had attached himself to her, trying ineffectively to stem the bleeding from the gunshot wound at her neck with pressure, at first with his bare hands, then with a handkerchief he had in his pocket, and then with a London 2012 Olympics souvenir T-shirt that someone had handed him. It was like trying to plug the spray from a high-pressure hosepipe. 'Hold on, lady, I'll help you, hold on,' he was shouting desperately, amid the cacophony of noise and screaming, trying to avoid looking directly into her wild fearful eyes.

Shocked spectators were standing around in the semi-darkness staring hopelessly, not knowing what to do. Others were scrambling away, terrified of becoming victims themselves, if there were to be more shots. 'My name is Ron, lady, hang on, we'll get help.' He could not help sounding desperate. She was slumped across several seats, trying in vain to lift her head up. Two stewards were dragging her onto a St John Ambulance stretcher. With bright warm blood gushing around his fingers and soaking through the cloth, PC Ron, knocking his shins painfully and repeatedly as they moved between rows of seats, was still clinging on to her neck. They tramped up concrete steps and along walkways, shouting at the aimless crowds obstructing their route, to the lifts that descended to the lower depths of the stadium.

Pamela had stopped trying to scream and was no longer struggling. Unable to move her numbed limbs, nothing felt real as her world spun around in meaningless clouds of distant chaotic sound that echoed inside her head. Half-congealed blood caked her face and hair like smears of mud on a playing field. Her face bloated as she struggled to get her breath. When they reached the medical room, Ron's sticky hands were glistening and aching with the relentless pressure he had been applying. He had never seen so much blood before in his life, but it was the smell that startled him, sweet and nauseating.

Orderlies and assistants swarmed around the trolley like worker bees, trying to get an oxygen mask in place, inserting a Venflon catheter into a brachial vein, cutting her clothes from her to expose the wounded area for doctors to assess the damage, and applying sticky cardiac monitor leads across her chest and wrists and ankle. The clothes were caked with deep crimson coagulant, leaving smears on everyone, their gloved hands, aprons and faces. Ron had to release his cramped grip. Blood pulsed up from the gaping neck, but the flow had slowed. He glanced at her chest to check for the rise and fall of respiration and felt embarrassed to notice how perfectly rounded her breasts appeared.

The volunteer doctor, hopelessly out of his depth, was aimlessly applying wads of surgical bandage. 'She needs to be at the London to deal with this. Let's move her quick. Let's go.' They were on the move again, wheeling the trolley back along the corridor to the lift, the beeping monitor slung on, an oxygen cylinder rattling in its cradle underneath, up one flight, with two nurses holding on to her and the drip, a helper at one end, a porter at the back pushing. As they retraced their steps through the bloody trail, further messing up the corridors, Ron remained behind to be sick into a sink. An orderly was left in the examination room with a bucket and mop.

Out into the warm night air, they piled into the back of an ambulance, manhandling the trolley, everyone grabbing hold of something for safety as the doors were slammed shut and the vehicle lurched away with a squeal, its blue lights whirling and its siren playing a sad last post.

Pamela was dead on arrival.

No one said anything, but bustled efficiently through automatic glass doors, through a deserted reception area bright with vending machines and harsh neon lights, to an examination area at the back. The doors were closed. A senior surgeon, unshaven in scrubs, roused from his sleep by an urgent call just half an hour ago, had to listen to the story and clinical detail flashed at him from all sides, as he felt futilely for a pulse, looked at the neck which had ceased its oozing, listened for a heartbeat and studied the monitor, which was beeping monotonously, showing a flat green line. He stood up grim faced, shaking his head, and pulled the stethoscope off his ears. After a short pause while everyone around the trolley stood back and adjusted uncomfortably to the reality of the cruel world they inhabited, catheter and monitor leads were removed and the wound wet-wiped clean. A nurse in dark blue uniform dejectedly drew a white sheet over the body, slumped and bare, with its ugly clotted rip in the neck.

It was Chief Inspector Andrew McIntosh who began to put the Jarvis Collingwood file together, although he was not wholly convinced by it, feeling certain that they were dealing with terrorist activity. He occupied the makeshift incident room set up within an hour of the shooting in a below-ground room in the stadium designed for athletes, and filled with training mats, equipment and soiled tracksuits. The Armed Response Unit was mobilised even as Jarvis Collingwood walked out of the Greenway Gate, and dozens of men in bulky flak jackets and hard helmets were seen crouching around corners, guarding and searching the stadium and concourse areas, adopting aggressive poses and wielding semi-automatic rifles. Soldiers from the Royal Logistics Corps were trampling all over the stadium well before the last spectator had departed, searching and making good areas guaranteed free from harmful ordnance.

It was several minutes after the mayhem had been discovered

that police helicopters got airborne, to beam their search lights over the Park, to scan the roof area of the stadium and check along the walkways, the bridges and the approach roads, all too late. It was not long before the body of the dead security steward was found, cold and stiffening in a roof access area. By first light a small army of men had been sent on to the roof where, on hands and knees, they carefully searched for any signs of the previous evening's deadly activity.

Over the following twenty-four hours, forensic pathologists and their teams studied the relevant areas of the stadium, obtained specimens and exhibits and carried out post-mortem examinations of the victims. Police were waiting to interview the two injured men, recovering after their operations at the Royal London Hospital, and under armed guard. All information was being fed back to McIntosh, now in charge of the Major Incident Response Unit and his small team at the stadium. Photographs, drawings and written details, including names and times, were beginning to appear on the activity wall. Engineers had been sent out promptly to set up direct links from the stadium to Metropolitan Police Headquarters at Scotland Yard, MI5, MI6 and the Prime Minister's office. Off-duty security and police officers were being recalled to build up a larger working team, tasked with trying to find eye witnesses and obtain statements in order to create a more complete picture of events, and with painstakingly examining every inch of the stadium, every nook on every level, from the roof down to every seat in the arena, paying special attention to the scenes of the victims' last moments, for any forensic clues that might prove useful.

McIntosh quickly recruited Inspector Broderick from Serious Crime, as he knew him well from the past. Inspector Barnes was placed in the team from Scotland Yard, although McIntosh suspected he was with MI5. Two senior field officers from MI6 (calling themselves Mopp and Bishop, and demanding an explanation from

McIntosh as to why the stadium didn't go into lockdown at first alert) had been around and were given the freedom to look at any material they needed. A string of raids on known terrorist cells and criminal types under observation in London and other cities in England had started during the morning and continued for several days, resulting reports awaited. Downing Street was constantly in touch and McIntosh was personally instructed that the Prime Minister expected to be updated every twelve hours with all the details, at seven in the morning and seven at night in the Cabinet Office. The Prime Minister's Office was to deal with the Iraqi embassy, to McIntosh's relief, and a special officer was allocated to work with the Iraqi security people on site. The Italian officials and embassy were to be kept informed, with a special liaison officer deployed.

Once Pamela Collingwood's identity had been ascertained from statements and the contents of her handbag which had been handed in by one of her companions – although, surprisingly, no mobile phone was found within it – it came to light that her husband worked as a security guard in the stadium, although he was off duty at the time and was thought to be at home. A team would need to visit him with the news, and he would be wanted at the mortuary in Bow (once the body was transferred) for formal identification purposes.

A model of the stadium was obtained from the design offices of the Games' organising committee and was set up on a display table in the new ops room, which was to be McIntosh's workspace for the next few weeks. Coloured stickers and pins marking the tragic events were placed at the various sites, to aid in understanding the sequence of events. Motivation for the killings had yet to be determined – at the moment it all seemed random and vengeful. There was no obvious pattern to the slaughter, no connection between the various victims that McIntosh could see, and why the ex-Prime Minister's wife was included, that seemed ludicrous. He was convinced the shootings were the act of a madman with terrorist links, perhaps through Middle Eastern connections. The protocol for a terrorist threat was in place, security was tight, and the whole country, particularly in London and at the airports and waterports, was on high alert.

PC Mark Green, a young policeman who found himself unexpectedly allocated to McIntosh's office in the early hours of the morning, when he had anticipated sharing a bed with his loved one, had been getting stuck in with some enthusiasm. He came off the phone announcing: 'Just been onto Army HQ, Aldershot: Jarvis Collingwood, born 13/01/1982, 30 years old, Parachute Regiment Second Battalion 2003 to 2009. Iraq, Afghanistan, Cyprus, Germany. Leading sniper, commended for bravery, honourable discharge 2009.' He looked up for compliments, still fresh faced despite the early hour.

'So he would have all the skills necessary,' mused McIntosh, ignoring the young whippersnapper. 'We will want a wee bit more personal information on this Mr Collingwood. Workmates and who's his boss? Where are the links between him and these victims (apart from his wife)? We will need to relive the events using the model. We need firearms and ballistics experts from the Army and the Home Office – and then we can reconstruct events, study trajectories and impact sites.' McIntosh needed a team to go and pick up Collingwood, for formal identification of his wife and for some early questioning. He might be armed and dangerous. Perhaps he would lead the questioning himself. Suddenly he was feeling tired and desperately in need of a few hours' sleep.

PART TWO
Hunting

1

Leon Deshpande emerged slowly from his thirty-minute swim in the Indian Ocean. A dark, stocky man of forty, he found his feet among the crashing waves that pound the hot shores of Kenya. Wading through the shallower waters, the midday sun splashing reflective light across his wet shoulders, he plodded up the deserted beach through soft sand that burnt the soles of his feet, watched from some distance by the pregnant Ramona. She nursed her swollen belly with both hands, standing under the shadows of the juniper trees on a grassy edge, admiring her man and his physique. He looked rugged and muscular, well-endowed and deeply tanned. Leon was her type of bloke, hot blooded and physical, quick and passionate, who worked hard and played hard. The fact that sometimes he had loved loose was a minor blip on his emotional landscape that she readily glossed over.

Two small children were playing with their French nanny in the glaring light on the grass nearby with plastic dolls and a bucket of water. They were bare skinned in swimming costumes and floppy hats, their backs and shoulders smeared with as much protective cream as they would allow. A motherly smile played across Ramona's sun-tanned freckled face.

Leon's male ambition and sexual desire were unashamedly mixed into a winning formula. He had a sixteen-year-old daughter from his only marriage, living in West London with her mother. Ramona well understood that Leon was a winner. She was not interested in how many other women he had serviced or how wide his seed had been flung. She had him now and was plotting a way to keep him. She thought that having his children might do the trick, but he remained as carefree as ever, travelling widely, always working on

229

important projects in different countries. She would sometimes go with him on trips to Africa or South America, while other times she found herself left behind at home or in a hotel, where she would crave his presence. But her strength of character allowed her to sensibly balance without bitterness his professional demands and her personal desires. If there were painful gaps in that arrangement from time to time, well, she was compensated by his charisma and generosity. With her own experience of working in the civil service to guide her, she was able to act as his foil and sounding board, and so they remained in many ways perfectly matched.

Ramona was a self-consciously luscious beauty, perfectly browned by the sun, and Leon was besotted. She adored being pregnant and had decided, even without Leon's agreement, that she would have at least another child after this one. She had been religiously creaming her legs, arms and chest, so the bright sunlight reflected exotically off her silky skin like metal. Her black hair flowed like a waterfall down her back.

Leon strolled across the rough grass, admiring Ramona's pumped-up breasts courageously tucked into their pink bikini top, and caught the towel she chucked across to him. He had cropped dark hair, stubble on his chin and lots of soft hair on his chest. Embellishing the curving wave of his shoulder and upper arm muscles was a bold tattoo, a warrior with vertical sword poised above a snake winding around the lower part of his torso, the magnificent male hero single-handedly slaying evil.

He called to his children and they squinted into the sun, making faces at him. Ramona helped to dry him off, and as she wiped his face and chest she told him in her seductive cross-European accent that there had been several phone calls and messages on his mobile. 'It sounded urgent, London wanting you back, I think.'

Leon had quick penetrating eyes and a sharp wit. His intelligence was instinctive, of the masculine kind, where actions were explained by context. Although currently involved with the maturing governments of East Africa on their security issues, particularly the Somali refugee problems in the North, he knew that this could not be what London was contacting him about.

'What? We've got three more days here – nothing could be that urgent.'

'The last one was Sir Hubert Lansbury from Five; you know how persuasive he can be.' The fact that MI5 had been in touch might have been cause for concern for anyone else, but he simply leant across Ramona's bulging abdomen and kissed her sweetly on the lips. They turned to gather up the children and, together with Françoise, they all headed along the beach to the café under the palms for lunch, keeping as best they could to the shade. The gentle wobbling cheeks of Ramona's bottom peeping below a floaty lace top in front of him drew Leon's undivided attention as they made their way in single file.

At Jethro's rundown shack under a few sparse palms, where the waves rippled over craggy rocks at their feet, the torn cloth shades fluttered sadly in the wind and barely kept the hot rays off their heads. After a frugal lunch of local giant crustaceans in garlic washed down with an ice-cool rosé, Leon and Ramona returned to their first-floor hotel room for a rest. Their shaded balcony gave views over a deep turquoise ocean beyond, the crashing noise of distant waves drifting through open windows. The air was still and oppressive. Leon approached Ramona on the balcony in lusty mood, cuddling up to her from behind and pressing his hard torso up against her bottom, his hands enjoying the feel of her swollen body with its warm oiled skin.

She leered over her shoulder at him and kissed his lips as they sidled back towards the cooler space within. On the bed they pressed their nakedness together. He probed from behind with gentle firmness, she yielded with moist assurance and their slow rhythmic motions engaged in synchrony, sensitive, intense and gratifying. They moaned and sighed together, reaching the heights in tight embrace. Leon, quite satisfied by all his day's exertions, and thinking not at all about the calls from London, promptly curled up into contented sleep, with Ramona drifting into a state of romantic bliss between kicks from her unborn baby.

Later in the afternoon, as slightly cooler breezes rustled around the room, Leon woke Ramona, flushed and radiant, with teasing kisses on the nape of her neck. Looking fondly upon her swollen bosom, he observed in his slightly Dutch accent how Sir Hubert was not half as persuasive as she could be. His smell was garlic and Givenchy.

Looking the epitome of the respectable international traveller in casual jacket, chinos and brown slip-on leathers, Leon set off to the lounge with its open veranda overlooking the sea. His white shirt open at the neck exposed tufts of curly hair. He lit a Marlboro and started making his mobile calls with a bottle of Keroro beer to hand. 'Hubert, you rascal, what are you up to?'

'Oh, Leon, so glad you called back. Are you on a safe line?'

'I came through Five's network; we should be fine for a few minutes. I'm in Nyali Beach, Mombasa, actually, just now, so make it quick.'

'OK. Listen, we have a problem here. You must have seen the news, the shootings we had here the weekend before last, at the Olympics. Inside the stadium, five people shot dead, including Gerry Morley, our ex. And his good lady. Dreadful business – embarrassing to say the least.'

'Yes, even the Africans have been reporting it front page. I watched Al Jazeera, they've carried updates for the last week. I've been following events. The details still seem rather unclear. But extraordinary.'

'Precisely. Well, we've got nowhere with the investigation. Forensics are unhelpful, there are no leads, and the Met, Special Branch, our own security boys, the Army, they are all at a loss. They're at each other's throats, blaming each service for its failings. The PM is tearing his hair out. The country is being made to look silly, incompetent. One of the dead was an Iraqi official, so the fuss they are making, you wouldn't believe. GCHQ have nothing. I'm now in charge of a special Number 10 incident committee – a COBR with a single purpose. I need your help, Leon.'

Leon was stunned for a moment. But he could hear the pleading in Hubert's voice, despite the poor reception, recognising its sincerity, and he was well aware that Cabinet Office Briefing Rooms were only set up in times of national crisis. He paced along the veranda in the dying light of another glorious African day, while pressing the small phone to his ear. The heat still played on his sun-tanned face, and with the high humidity he was sweating easily. Up until then, he had been feeling relaxed. A small lilac-breasted roller landed on a thistle branch, bouncing just out of reach. He cupped his spare hand over his mouth. 'Hue, the last time we worked together you nearly chucked me out; in fact you *did* chuck me out, you never wanted to work with me again; and you called me names. Or don't you remember?' There was the tiniest of pauses, with crackling on the line.

'Of course I remember, and I have lived every day since with the deepest regret about our last conversation. I am sure that you realise that on my part I never meant those things I said – it was frustration and despair, Leon. I am hoping very much that you have forgiven me.'

Leon Deshpande, the consummate professional, the heroic figure, had a fatal flaw: arrogance exuded from every pore. Many a senior officer, commissioner, civil servant, politician and assorted do-gooder had had his nose put out of joint by remarks from Mr

Deshpande, often disparaging and contemptuous, made over the volatile decade of his diplomatic career. And so often, just to make matters worse, time proved Leon to have been right.

Now Deshpande worked freelance, a specialist adviser, an inter-mediary in some of the difficult trouble spots of the world, his authority derived from extensive military and security experience. And for this he received generous rewards, offered equally by gov-ernment departments, state organisations of various persuasions and private corporations that needed an insider's viewpoint that was both pertinent and discreet. It had been a move that Leon more than ever did not regret, escaping as he had done in one piece from the intimidating atmosphere that pervaded the corridors of Whitehall, before all of his ambition was utterly drained away. Leon had his three-million-pound mews house in Marylebone, private and convenient. He had the flash car in the garage, the celebrity beauty on his arm, two little accessory children, the inter-national standing and freedom to travel almost anywhere – what more could a self-reliant egotistical alpha male want? London was his playground for relaxing, for holidays, now that he no longer worked there. His main residence shared with Ramona was in Switzerland, with its wealthy environment, its cleanliness and order, its proximity to the best ski resorts in Europe, all of which suited his new growing family well, a good place to bring up children with confidence. He also kept a smart mansion in Constantia, Cape Town, where, incidentally, he was born. And where his father still lived. Leon had no need to return to London for work.

'I'm in Nairobi tomorrow, then flying back with the family on Friday to Geneva; then I'm planning on attending the Summit in Tehran next week, for the Non-Aligned Movement for Developing Nations. And Ramona's due our third in three or four weeks, so I can't be getting too involved in any of your typical London mess-ups, Hubert.'

'Unless the money was right?' Hubert ventured with care.

'Well, for the right contract, Hue, I could make an exception, especially for you, dear boy.'

'The PM is desperate, he will agree to anything. You could ask practically what you want, actually.'

That was the sort of thing Leon loved to hear, a politician almost begging. 'Well, I could give Tehran a miss, I suppose, although there were going to be some pretty interesting networking opportunities there. We will need to talk fees, so you better have clearance – it'll need to be up front.'

'I need you back within days, Leon,' Hubert continued. 'I have to report daily to my committee, so the sooner the better. I'd really appreciate it. I could meet with you in the Mews, say Sunday morning? I'll bring round all the information and background we have.'

Leon screwed up his eyes against the light, watching a tanker move slowly across the horizon a long way off. The roller had gone. They talked for a few moments more, coming to an understanding. Leon would gather up his little flock to fly back on Friday via Nairobi again – God that place was awful – into Geneva, home to Montreux, settle them in and then London early Sunday morning. Doable. He would have to make his excuses to the lovely Ms Gloriana Rattanda of the UN committee for the Tehran conference. It was possible, just needed Ramona's say-so.

An early-morning taxi from Heathrow Airport brought Leon through the slumbering Sunday morning city to Devonshire Mews South. An overweight tabby cat, disturbed from its warm patch of rare sunshine, scampered across the cobblestones out of the way, squeezing between a gap in some railings. Leon hopped out, paid the driver and tugged his suitcase from the side door. Inside the house, he pushed aside a pile of post and newspapers and disabled the alarm.

Upstairs, the air was stuffy. Nobody had been around for a week, and so he moved from room to room opening windows to let in some fresh summer breeze. On his mobile he called to order milk, croissants and bacon from the local deli along in Portland Place. He threw his case into the bedroom, taking out a few things, leaving the unpacking till later. He showered quickly and dried off, spraying himself with liberal amounts of deodorant and dabbing his face with aftershave as he eyed the mirror. His tanned and stubbled face made him look rugged and adventurous. He dressed in a light grey suit, open shirt, soft brown brogues.

Back in the kitchen, part of a large first-floor living space with French windows onto a balcony, he set the coffee machine to work and selected music on the Bose player. Excerpts from La Traviata filled the room and the mews, and there was no one around to complain. He fired up his laptop, obtained an internet connection and logged into the news channels. The provisions arrived, delivered by a young lad on a bicycle, whom he chatted to for a few moments and then carried the box upstairs. He made bacon and cheese croissants, heated in the microwave, and was ready with fresh coffee by the time the bell sounded at exactly eleven o'clock.

Sir Hubert Lansbury was dropped off in the narrow mews by his driver in a standard-issue silver bulletproof Range Rover to the sound of Verdi from Leon's upstairs windows. Hubert smiled at the familiar habits of his lifelong friend. Even on a Sunday, he was as always perfectly turned out in a Prince of Wales check beige single-breasted suit, with pink tie chosen with precision by Roger, and soft desert boots that moved silently over the cobblestones. He carried a heavy-looking brown leather briefcase.

Leon opened the door to him and they greeted each other with smiles and a hug, a habit that Hubert had always found awkward. They mounted the stairs, coming closer to the source of the music and the smell of coffee and cheese. 'You look remarkably well, Leon, I must say. All this international stuff must be doing your health a power of good.' The contrast between Hubert's gentle tan and Leon's deep brown was striking.

'To say nothing of my wealth, eh, Hue,' Leon smirked.

They sat at a long wooden table in the open space, close to the windows, where full-length net curtains were fluttering in the breeze. Hubert felt comfortable, enjoying the easy ambience and hospitality. He was sipping fresh orange juice and biting with relish into soft crumbly croissants, leaving greasy smears on his fingers. They chatted about Africa, Ramona's forthcoming delivery, Leon's return to London this morning and life at the top. Hubert was happy that they were the best of friends again. As for the wealth, he knew Leon was loaded, obvious to the casual eye scanning the house. Happy to be rich and for people to know it, that was always Leon. Tended to be just a touch showy for Hubert's liking.

'Leon, I am so grateful to you giving us some of your time like this.' Leon slowly tapered the music volume down with his remote until distant traffic and the occasional siren could be heard as they prepared themselves for the work ahead. A terrible sense of failure tugged at Hubert's insides, but discipline and his natural work ethic were powerful motivators to press on positively with the matter at hand. 'The PM is deeply thankful too. He has invested in me a sort of *carte blanche*, a do-whatever-it-takes remit, to get this incident sorted and closed. The bald facts are in here,' and he dropped a heavy hand onto his briefcase on the table, 'but the real details are pitifully sparse and uncorroborated, I'm afraid. Not through lack of trying. Whoever did this has been bloody clever.' Hubert seldom swore, but he particularly stressed the 'bloody'. He reached into the briefcase, brought out a thin Japanese silvery laptop, sprang it open and fired it up. 'I suppose we admired Bin Laden for the cleverness of his plot in attacking the Twin Towers, though of course we were not allowed to say so. But this, this man . . .'

'Man?' asked Leon. 'You know it was a man?'

'No, not for certain, but there was a dead steward with his larynx crushed that would have required brutal strength, so I suppose we feel it probably was a man.'

'Still, there is no need to admire this . . . man,' Leon said with a hint of scorn, while starting to look at photographs Hubert had taken from his case and was now placing in a row along the table in front of him.

'OK. Shall we make a start?'

Hubert assumed the role of chairman. 'This incident took place at around ten minutes after eleven on Sunday night, August 12th, two weeks ago, towards the end of the closing ceremony of London 2012: spectacular, noisy, lots of movement happening in the arena, dancing, celebrities, loud pop music, fireworks all around the edge of the stadium roof with a pitch-black sky as background. The Spice Girls,' and a look of complete incomprehension came over Hubert's normally conservative expression, 'were performing centre stage and were riding round the arena in black taxi-cabs, the crowds were cheering and clapping wildly, everybody taken in by the spectacle, watching down at ground level or up at the fireworks. No one could have seen any figure clambering around on the roof. If the killer had worn black, blackened his face, he could have been jumping up and down on the roof there for ages and nobody inside the stadium would have seen him behind the bright lights and the fireworks.'

'Right, I've got that, Hue,' said Leon, raising his hands in surrender. 'What about somebody outside the stadium looking up? Or from the helium balloon, the camera in the sky? Nothing there I suppose?'

'No. We have had the footage sifted over repeatedly this last week, hours of it, wonderfully presented by the BBC, but the cameras on the zeppelin were all remote controlled and focused at that time on the events inside the stadium.'

Leon held up some pictures of the stadium showing the roof in detail, one with the floating silver-coloured balloon eerily lit up in the sky. 'So the gunman would have been on one of these cross runways, would he?'

'Companionways, yes, there are fourteen of them, connecting the outer rim with the inner rim and equally spaced around the roof, and they allow for passage of service, maintenance and lighting people,' Hubert explained.

'He would have had to lie face down along the line of the companionway, I suppose.'

'Or crouched in one of these lighting huts,' Hubert explained. 'There are a few of them along the sides on the inner rim.'

'So which one do you think he was in or on? Or do you think there was more than one gunman?' Leon sounded increasingly interested.

'The victims were all in the corporate or VIP blocks down here, along the west side,' said Hubert, pointing. 'We'll go over the details in a minute, but all the shots must have come from either this companionway or that one.' On one of the photographs he indicated the front edge of two adjacent companionways on the roof opposite the strike areas.

'What is thoroughly amazing,' waxed Leon, 'is the massive size of this stadium.'

'The dead security man was found at the foot of the ladder leading to this one, number 4. The stadium was searched twice, every inch – it took over two full days and forty officers on their hands and knees with dogs, metal detectors, you name it. Nothing.' Hubert paused and sipped his coffee while Leon concentrated on the pictures in front of him. 'I suppose there could have been more than one shooter,' he then mused. 'Two identical rifles, 8.59mm calibre, one on each of those two companionways, perhaps. It is

239

difficult to reproduce the exact trajectories, but either of these would work. The shooting seemed to be in sequence, rather than together. The ballistics favours one rifle. But we have found no signs, nothing was left behind – no casings, no signs of cordite powder, no smudged footprint, no fingerprints, no left-over chewing-gum papers . . . we are guessing.'

'Were you at the ceremony, Hue?'

'No. I was invited by the PM, but I don't do these things. Five was represented though – we got the royal handshake.'

Leon paused, deep in thought. 'How would this gunman have got into the stadium with a rifle, may I ask?' He filled their cups with more coffee from the pot. He snatched a big mouthful of croissant, and then wiped his fingers on a tea towel.

Sir Hubert Lansbury shook his well-groomed head, the immaculate central parting remaining undisturbed. He was smooth faced and shaven to perfection, his strong aftershave mixing uncertainly with the coffee aroma. His once-blond hair had started to grey at the temples, giving him an attractive mid-forties distinction and gravitas typically favoured by the Civil Service. 'That's a big mystery. He probably didn't bring it in on the night – everyone coming through the gates was searched and screened. If it was someone who worked at the stadium or in the Olympic Park, then it could have been at some time long before the Games began maybe; but if it was someone from outside, then an insider must have hidden the gun beforehand and the shooter came in under instruction, knew where to find it. All staff had individual ID badges that they had to use at every entrance, every door, even into the changing and toilet areas, and some doors had a security code. The door to the roof access area, number 4, just required a swipe of the card. The dead steward was on duty at that door all evening. All vehicles coming onto the site were searched, from way back, end of last year, when the site became operational.'

Hubert looked tired and a doubtful expression appeared across his wide mouth. Leon noticed hints of darkness under Hubert's eyes that he had been unable to disguise that morning. 'We just don't know, Leon.'

Both men remained thoughtful for a moment. They continued looking at the photos strewn over the table. Hubert was opening up all available reports on the incident on his laptop. 'So, these are all the initial reports, showing what has been done and what has been found so far. I shouldn't be showing you these, but . . . also I have hard copies of all the up-to-date reports, which I can leave you with,' and he pointed to the pile of papers now on the table. 'This is a summary report of the events as they happened on the night – including a list of casualties, in chronological order, or our best guess at the order in which things happened – as well as a report on assumptions made, motivation and possible connections, and finally, a list of possible suspects. The police trawled through countless criminal groups and known terrorists all over London, bringing them in under Home Office emergency rules, hundreds of them. Nothing concrete. Do you know, there were over two hundred and fifty real threats to the Olympic security in the four weeks leading up to the start of the Games, and that isn't counting the threat to the Israeli team from the Iranians, all of them properly investigated, committing hundreds of police officers at any one time. But I repeat, I'm afraid we have no hard evidence pointing towards anyone in particular, no one is under arrest, although some remain as possible suspects.'

Leon looked undaunted by the pile of papers that had accrued on his dining table and leafed through a few of them as if gauging the time it might take to read through them all. He stood up and slipped his jacket off, hanging it over the next chair. 'The security recruits for the Games, and I know there were thousands of them – were they vetted in any way? Did they have to have experience, come with references? How did they get their jobs? Or did they just walk in?'

'Strict recruitment methods, high specifications to begin with,' Hubert explained, 'but I think there was a lot of desperation nearer the start of the Games, many more were needed than at first predicted, and so the process was rushed through; they could not get the numbers, so more or less anybody able-bodied who remotely looked the part got a job. They were all allocated security tags and numbers, but I gather from the Head of Personnel at the Park, it was a bit shambolic, with some getting no security tags, some numbers repeated and other mix-ups. Then of course the Army was brought in.'

Sleeves rolled up, Leon stretched and then strolled over to the open French doors, stepping through the nets and standing on the balcony edge, breathing in the London air. He had to decide whether he wanted to be involved in this investigation and work for Hubert's committee. At the moment he saw it as a fascinating challenge. From inside the main room, Hubert was talking, a little louder. 'We really need someone to give it an outsiders' look, a new perspective, Leon. We need some new angles, something we haven't thought about, something we can get our teeth into. That's why I need you.' At which point, unable to resist any longer, he reached for a cigarette.

Hubert had laid out two A4-sized documents – the forensic reports from the post-mortem examinations of the victims, and a list of all people interviewed, cross-referenced to the digital file. Putting aside the coffee pot and plates, and collecting up the photos into a loose pile, he laid out side by side along one edge of the table in front of Leon a new set of glossy colour pictures of faces, pale, lifeless, dead faces, close-up, scrubbed, eyes closed, photographed with their names printed in strips along the bottom of each.

Leon returned to the room and sat down. 'We will need to visit the stadium together, Hue, as soon as.' And he began to scan the pictures of the dead, one photo at a time.

'Absolutely, I've laid on a visit tomorrow, Bank Holiday, early morning, before the Paralympics get going on Wednesday. The main sites of the shootings are protected, but we should be able to look at what we want without getting in the way of the other things. Together with Inspectors McIntosh and Broderick, and the Olympics site manager, a London Olympics Organiser, and somebody from the Home Office forensics team, plus Professor Donald Spottiswode from the Colindale Laboratories - they will be able to take you over the events as they see them.'

As always Hubert was super-organised and prepared. A good man to have at the top of any organisation, even if intellect might not have been his strongest point. Leon murmured his approval and wanted to share first impressions at this point, trying to sound as certain as possible. 'All right, this is your killer – male, a professional marksman, trained in unarmed combat, probably ex-Army; super-fit, late twenties, early thirties; probably working alone, but with support; hired and paid, probably a lot of money; an insider, working in security. He will be known to other Stratford Park staff, and on the employment lists.'

Hubert found the document on staff employment at London 2012 and held it up for Leon. It was over one inch thick. 'So this is a complete list of all staff employed at Stratford Park, from the managers down to the cleaners; including porters, handlers, removals men, canteen staff, caterers, workmen, gardeners, plumbers and electricians, security officers and guards, stewards, advertising people, company reps, the medical teams, ambulance, fire protection, business teams, secretaries and clerks, accountants, laundry, stores, social workers, the chaplaincy, psychiatrists and motivation psychologists, et cetera et cetera. You name them, we have them: over twenty-six thousand names. About sixteen thousand are men. Not including the tens of thousands of volunteers, of course.'

'Christ!'

'This list is the best possible data record, but as I said, with the recruitment issues, it may not be as accurate as it should be.'

Leon turned away, realising the enormity of the task, and started to closely study the portrait photos lined up along the table. 'These are the victims? Let's go over them, shall we, one by one?'

Hubert reached for the bulky first report and turned to one of the inside pages, folding it back. It contained a printed table, with headings across the top, names down the left-hand column. Next to each name in the columns were gender, age, who they were, how they died or were injured, approximate time of death and any comments. 'This table was constructed by the Met, showing the victims, listed in chronological order of events as understood, after multiple witness questioning, and you can see, it's dated August 22nd, that was last Wednesday, the up-to-date picture, as we saw it then.'

Hubert sounded apologetic, as if he knew Leon would find it somewhat scanty in terms of detail. 'And on this aerial photo, coloured dots mark the places in the stadium where each victim was hit.' Hubert placed an enlarged colour print showing the stadium in sunshine, taken long before the Games began, with its now-familiar 'Polo mint' canvas roof and pink running track, the bright green rectangle of perfect grass in the middle and rows and rows of concentric empty black and white seats around the periphery. There were some round spots in different colours stuck in places in the mid-tier along the west side, the segregated VIP areas, where the seats were purple, orange and turquoise. Leon studied these pictures for a while and then leant over to read the title at the top of the Met report listing the victims. 'So who is on this committee, Hue?'

Hubert had a separate typed list that he handed across the table. From the Prime Minister down to the Home Secretary's under-secretary, the Metropolitan Chief, heads of MI5 and MI6,

PRIME MINISTER'S OFFICE — DOWNING STREET
CABINET OFFICE BRIEFING ROOM
THE STRATFORD INCIDENT (AUGUST 12, 2012)

The shooting at Stratford Park Olympic Stadium, London, on the night of August 12, 2012

The following casualties were sustained, with details and outcomes (in proposed chronological order of events):

Anthony Butt, male 26, Security Personnel, attacked, respiratory failure/ asphyxiation, approx time of death between 9 and 11.30 p.m.
Abu Masoud Zadeh, male 48, Iraqi Olympic official, shot in head (11.08 p.m.), instant death
Gerry Morley, male 58, ex-British PM, shot in head (11.09 p.m.), instant death (exit bullet into upper arm of man behind):
John Faulkner, male 55, civil servant, shot in arm: exit bullet from previous (11.09 p.m.), lodged, severe wound, recovering
Amanda Morley, female 57, wife of British ex-PM, shot in chest (11.09 p.m.), death within 2 minutes (approx 11.11 p.m.) (exit bullet into groin of man behind):
Peter Cheshire, male 46, civil servant, shot in groin: exit bullet from previous (11.09 p.m.), lodged, severe wound, recovering
Pietro Cavalli, male 38, Italian Olympic official, shot in head (11.10 p.m.), instant death (exit bullet through neck of woman behind):
Pamela Collingwood, female 31, public relations, shot in neck: exit bullet from previous (11.10 p.m.), lodged, severe wound, carotid artery damage, dead on arrival at the Royal London Hospital (approx time of death 11.21 p.m.).

[August 22, 2012]

the Armed Forces Chief, the Cabinet Office Secretary and assorted high-profile ministers, Leon knew them all. 'Yes, I get the picture; all bristling with gongs and indignation, worrying about their own positions and manoeuvring themselves accordingly.'

Leon had summed up the scene perfectly, and he did not envy Hubert one bit. 'So, first up on this list is Anthony Butt. What was he doing there?' Leon looked at his photograph, young face, open and innocent, somebody's unfortunate son, with bruising and distortion at the front of his neck clearly visible.

'It would appear that Anthony Butt was on security duty on the door to roof access number 4 all evening. There are nine of these access areas, ladders leading onto the roof, behind a metal cage effectively, meshed; no public access. He was unarmed. His body was found under the ladder at around 12 a.m. Post-mortem says there was severe bruising to the front of the throat, with a crushed larynx. Also bruising to the side of the head, fractured skull and bruising to the outer genitalia. So they think he was kicked in the goolies and the head, punched in the throat and then stood on with a boot, crushing his voice box. His radio was next to him, unused.'

Hubert could refer to the text of the report, but had no need to. Leon grimaced while he listened. 'And there were no other guards on the roof? No eye witnesses to this?'

'Apparently not. These ladders were only used by maintenance staff and engineers and a few lighting technicians for the spots during the ceremony. Low-level security point.' Leon nodded. 'Moving on,' continued Hubert, who found a certain pleasure in presenting the evidence and facing the ritual cross-examination, 'the first shot fired is believed to have killed the Iraqi, Abu Masoud Zadeh. At approximately 11.08 p.m.'

'So did anyone hear the noise of a shot, a rifle? Or see the flash on the roof? Was anyone asked about that?'

'The report says nobody interviewed heard a shot or saw a flash,' said Hubert. He had finished one cigarette and it was all he could do not to reach for another. 'The first security man to get to Abu Masoud was a police officer, who a couple of Arab gentlemen called over from one of the rear exits; this was in block M13 at the back, row 35. By the time he got there, this was PC Peter Fleming, who is quoted as saying (and here Hubert leant over the open report to read the quote), "There was panic among some spectators, who thought they were under attack; some were crouching behind the seats, screaming, trying to hide, some were clambering over the back seats and were pushing towards the exits, there was a lot of pushing and shoving, and shouting." I think,' Hubert continued, 'that by the time Fleming arrived on the scene it was at least two minutes after the first shot, by which time all the other shots had been fired, all the victims hit, and either dead or wounded, and our killer had probably withdrawn from his position, and was on his way back down the ladder and out, whichever route he took.'

Hubert lit another cigarette, having offered the packet to Leon, who shook his head with a look of mock disapproval and self-satisfaction. 'A ricochet bullet chipped the glass in the wall behind and was found on the concrete floor twenty-five feet away, and didn't harm anyone else. This was an 8.59mm bullet, unique to a British Army rifle, the sniper's L115A3.' Hubert found a colour photograph of the sophisticated rifle they thought had been used, and showed it to Leon. 'The bullets are heavier than in other systems, supposed to travel with less deviation to cover longer distances, even up to a mile, apparently. They produce a neat entry hole, but a bigger exit, a bit messy.'

'And all the other bullets match, the same rifle?' Leon was holding on to the picture.

'According to ballistics, yes,' said Hubert, pointing to the report on the table that he had referred to earlier, 'they all match, they think they were all fired from the same rifle; it's likely there was only one shooter.'

'It's just that Army snipers, and maybe police marksmen, use spotters,' said Leon. 'They operate together as a pair, stay together sometimes for days or weeks on end. So perhaps we have one shooter, with his own spotter?'

'Yes, it's possible.'

Leon held up the photo of the sniper's rifle with his left hand; in his right, he had a photo of the dead Arab, full-frontal face view, lying on a mortuary slab, ceramic white skin contrasting starkly with trimmed black beard and hair. A small blackened hole with neat edges perfectly placed in the middle of the forehead stared back like a sinister third eye. 'That was one hell of a shot, from what distance, a hundred and fifty yards?'

'Forensics reckon one hundred and seventy-five yards.'

'Wow. One silent shot from the dark, perfect hit from a distance, the victim sitting among a sea of a thousand faces – how did he pick him out? Did he know him well, so his face was so familiar that he could recognise him in the dark from that distance?' Leon sounded almost disbelieving.

Hubert looked up into Leon's face and recognised the improbability. 'He was bloody clever.'

'So you have said, Hue, and I am getting the same message. He must have used night vision with magnification. So who was this man, Abu Masoud Zadeh?'

Hubert took a deep breath in. 'Again, there is a long, detailed description in here,' resting his hand on the open report, 'but basically a man in his forties working for the Coalition Baghdad government, a Sunni Moslem with family and connections there. He was in London with the Iraqi Olympics team, security organisation et cetera. But he was a bit of a terror in his youth, heading various breakaway jihad groups, came out fighting after Sadam was toppled. Violent, trained insurgent. But he changed sides as it were, to save himself, I guess.'

'There must be a connection between him and our killer somehow,' mused Leon, deep in thought.

'But is it possible,' Hue asked tentatively, 'that this Abu Masoud was a random face in the crowd, chosen, why? As a warning, a lesson? Just for the shooter to show the world how good he is?'

'As a preliminary to the rest of the proceedings, you mean?' Leon frowned. 'Seems weird, doesn't it? There is a magnification system on this rifle, latest Army issue, you say. Where did he get it from, I wonder? But that's another line of enquiry. He sees his targets through, what, ten times, twenty times life size? So, more likely in fact that our killer knew this Abu Masoud, recognised him and executed him, for all to see.' Leon paused and then stated with clarity: 'There is a connection – our killer was either hired by someone who wanted Abu killed, for past events unknown, or something actually happened between these two, and our killer was taking revenge on his own account.' Leon was thinking, resting a tanned wrist on the thick wodge of paper that comprised the employer's list, that somewhere in there was the man they wanted. 'British troops were stationed in Iraq from 2003 to 2009. I am presuming something happened during that time that involved Abu and a British soldier. We need to dig into this man's history. If necessary, send a team out to Iraq.'

'Yes, I agree.' Hubert wrote notes, while admiring his friend's clarity of thought. He was unaccountably impressed by the dark tufts of hair that grouped on the back of Leon's fingers and by the generous covering over his thick forearms.

'And we need to find out how he could have got hold of this sophisticated rifle – on the open market? Black-market import, Eastern Europe, in the back streets? Was it stolen, or is this another inside job? We need some leads here. And where is it now? Did he walk out with it, has he dumped it somewhere? Is it still on the roof of the stadium?' Leon's thought processes kept throwing out more questions, and Hubert made sure that none of them, familiar as they all were, were missed. 'All I can say at the moment,' mumbled Hubert, scribbling, 'is that it has not been found.'

The dining table was covered with papers and photos, but Hubert was sorting them into orderly piles at one end. Leon replaced the two photos he had been holding back into the sequence on the table from where they had come, looking as if he was about to play a game of patience, which in a way was precisely what was required.

'Next is Gerry Morley himself,' said Hubert with resolve, 'which is painful for me, because I had got to know him quite well during his time in office. Quite liked him, as a matter of fact. We played tennis at Chequers once,' and he laughed at the memory. 'And I helped him with a barbecue on the back lawn one summer afternoon. And then next, Amanda as well. I still cannot believe it actually. What madman would want to do this?'

The question was rhetorical. While Leon was sympathetic for his friend, he did not quite view his dilemma in the same way, in understanding the motive behind the shootings. The ex-British Prime Minister had surely done quite enough to upset a whole crowd of people who would have been delighted to see him bumped off and not have thought twice about paying for someone else to do the job. Leon could think of a number of them, if pressed. He spoke with a matter-of-factness that he thought was appropriate, without letting any personal bias colour his comments. 'This killer was either paid to assassinate Morley or took it upon himself to do so while engaged in the killing of the Iraqi, Abu Masoud. The Iraq war is a connection. But why Amanda too? That is difficult to explain. Was he sort of tidying up, thinking that she was just as culpable as he was in many people's eyes for a whole host of misdemeanours, so why not take them both out, sorting out the whole problem in one go? Maybe he thought her to be as evil as Morley was. I mean, as he thought he was. I don't know, he might have been paid to do both, but somehow, I feel some personal decision was brought into play here.' Hubert remained quiet.

Looking at the stadium photo with its coloured dots, Leon continued, 'Let's look at the shooting of Gerry Morley. The bullet penetrated his skull on the right side, around the temple. He must have turned towards her, she was sitting on his left. Another perfect shot. Seconds later, she is hit in the upper chest. You think all this happened a few seconds after the first shot at Abu Masoud, from what people have said?'

'Yes, but the people around Abu were slow to react, they clearly didn't notice straight away or raise the alarm, there was some delay. So it's difficult to be sure which occurred first. The TV controllers instinctively redirected the cameras away from the crowd scenes, when we could have benefited from some images to help us piece together the run of events, but they were protecting the sensitivities of the watching audience. There was some TV footage from inside the stadium that had just scanned the crowd along that block, panning a view from right to left, and it seems to catch the movement of spectators reacting around the Morleys, suddenly standing, turning round, panicking, scrambling away and so on, before such movement can be seen up at the back around the Arab group, but they are far apart, and it's not certain.'

Leon looked thoughtful. 'So Morley died instantly but Amanda was seriously injured and died from blood loss about two minutes later. Why did the killer not shoot both in the head, why Amanda in the chest? Was this some sort of gender deference, being kinder to the woman, not disfiguring her face? Or was that just a slight miss of his target? I mean, this man shoots his targets at will, doesn't he, with supreme skill.'

Hubert looked puzzled. 'I don't know. She obviously suffered more than he did in the end, she was exsanguinating on the floor between rows of seats. Their two personal bodyguards, who had been sitting at the end of the row behind (so about five people away to their left) scrambled across, pushing their way through, and spent time warning people to get down and back away; they didn't really know what to do. They eventually carried her out with help, and then Morley. Both covered in blankets, so you couldn't see who it was they were carrying, and it was five minutes or more before they got them downstairs in the lift to the medical centre. They were both dead by then, so it's difficult to know how long she had lived. There was less panic among the spectators than you might have expected – they must have thought these were sudden illnesses, heart attacks or something.'

Hubert helped himself to more coffee, his mouth unusually dry with all the talking. 'The police were calming people down, persuading them to stay put and sit down. The TV commentary didn't know who had been hurt, but speculated by where the gaps in the crowd were and by which areas were affected. The security personnel wanted everyone out, everyone important. The royal party was ushered out quickly and left at great speed with the usual police escort. And a stream of others followed, the politicians, the heads of state; the PM and his wife, most of our ministers. It was too risky to hang about, obviously, in case there was more to follow. It was not until 11.23 that the Armed Response Unit was alerted through a call from a senior security officer, but it was chaos by then and no one was able to take command of the situation, not properly. There was debate about lockdown, but the decision never came – fear of public panic I suppose. I'm sure the killer was out of the stadium within five minutes, probably just walked out with everyone else, cool as anything.' There was anger in Hubert's tone, anger and frustration that the smooth and efficient security services of the UK could have been made to look so foolish, in their own backyard, in front of the world.

Hubert was showing the strain of the last two weeks in the

worry lines around his eyes that had become more obvious while he had been speaking, and Leon studied him with a sympathetic smile. 'Of course, the first reaction in the Morleys' seating area was from these two guys sitting behind – John Faulkner and Peter Cheshire, the two unfortunate civil servants. They both shouted out. The people in the rows behind were spattered, and so there was instant alarm there. Faulkner was clutching his arm and moaning with the pain, there was a lot of blood apparently, and he seemed paralysed. Cheshire was clutching his stomach and slumped to one side. So the attention was on them at first before the Morleys were noticed, you know, many seconds later.'

'By touching them and moving them, of course, all the forensics were contaminated,' Leon observed.

'Yes, quite. But people wanted to help the victims, security wanted them moved to safety or to medical help. And, of course, to spare the crowds and the cameras from the sight of it all. There was virtually nothing picked up on TV cameras that is recognisable as a gun attack, which is remarkable.'

'Oh, quite understandable, I'm not really criticising.'

'You must see the TV footage for yourself, it might help just in setting the scene, bring it all alive to some extent, if you see what I mean?' Appalled by his own unintentional pun, Hubert was caught between wanting to apologise for his irreverence and feeling a strong desire to swear rudely for the unpremeditated, undeserving turn of events that quite clearly had upended his comfortable world. He sat back instead, resting with eyes closed for a moment, and thought about Roger, wondering how much longer *that* could possibly go on, given his restlessness that had particularly come to light first thing this morning.

'Have you got any private pictures or video that the public took? Amateur photos sometimes pick up things that the professionals miss.'

'We are trying to get as much as we can, there have been appeals to the public – but so far nothing particularly helpful, just out-of-focus images from mobiles taken well after the event,' Hubert replied.

'So both Faulkner and Cheshire have survived?' Leon resumed after a further moment of reflection.

'Both needed operations to remove lodged bullets, both had severe blood loss and it is a great testament to the emergency services and the surgical teams that they did survive – the speed that they were taken to the medical room and then to the Royal London Hospital was remarkable. They are both recovering, discharged from hospital now, I understand. Cheshire needed a second operation, so was in longer. Still with armed protection, in case they might be targets of a lone gunman; the news about them has been low key. The Prime Minister visited them last week actually, without any fuss. The day before the Morley funerals. They were last Wednesday in Westminster.'

'Yes, I saw the news and the pictures in the papers.' Leon got up suddenly. 'Listen, Hue, I just need to email my daughter, won't take a minute. I should be meeting her this week. Shall I order some lunch from Luigi's while I'm up – beer and some French bread, chicken, salad and so on? Suit you, Huby?'

Leon reverted to the familiar name he had for his friend which Hubert naturally detested. But he said nothing, just smiled at the memories it brought back of their time at Cambridge, where together they discovered some of life's wonders. There was the theatre, the local politics, all that play-acting; and the rowing, of course. They had climbed walls to get into the back of colleges, punted girls up and down the Cam at weekends and made love to them afterwards in the fields in all weathers. All in those irresponsible glory days before he realised he was not too bothered with girls and then disappeared into the Civil Service for an age while Leon went on to officer class in the Royal Dragoon Guards, before joining the Special Forces of the Parachute Regiment for a while. He had always been a bit more serious than Leon, who never seemed to stop playing pranks at university, but then Hubert was a bit older and from a less well set up family.

'How are we doing for time?' Leon asked on his return a few minutes later, knowing that Hubert would have a pretty busy diary in front of him even on a Sunday and conscious that already a number of text messages had come through for him. He looked at his watch; it was after 12.30 p.m. 'Crack on?'

'It would be useful to get through the rest of the victims,' said Hubert.

'So, to the last two: Pietro Cavalli and Pamela Collingwood. What do we know about Mr Cavalli, anything?'

Hubert picked up some papers and resumed. 'He was with the Italian delegation, used to be an Olympic cyclist, apparently. Thirty-eight, unmarried, had been in London for the last two years, working for a sports company. Not sure what connection if anything he had with the others. Ms Collingwood was working for the firm that did most of the PR for the Olympics, marketing stuff, and had corporate seats on that basis. But had no apparent connection with any of the other victims. Cavalli seems to be random and Collingwood collateral.'

Leon shook his head distractedly. 'There has to be some reasoning, some link. I do not get the feeling that this was just a gunman gone mad. That would have involved lots of shots at lots of people, random, whatever – this sniper was picking out a few designated people from the enormous crowd, that is what snipers do; look at the distances between the victims. The key lies with this Iraqi gentleman, Abu Masoud Zadeh. We need to know exactly who he was, what he was doing at the Games, and what he had done in the past. This gunman would only perform such an atrocious risky act in the full glare of the world's TV cameras and surrounded by the general public for a pretty rich reward. But I also think something personal came into it. One can imagine any number of organisations queuing up to have a go at Morley, and for revenge, a terrorist group might well hire someone to do the job for them. But why in public? That's like a public execution. The gunman wanted to make a show of it, the publicity, the humiliation – but then why have we not had any public statement? No group has stepped up to claim responsibility, has it? Hubert shook his head. 'So this is a more personal revenge, not a terrorist; someone hires a hit man, an expert, who then uses the opportunity provided by the situation to take out the ex-PM's wife as well. The Arab might be a random choice in the crowd, to obfuscate. Or the Arab is a specific target as well. And then what about Pietro Cavalli? Abu and Pietro Cavalli. Is there a connection between these two, an Iraqi war connection? Was Cavalli ever in Iraq, between 2003 and 2009? What role did the Italians play there?'

Hubert was writing more notes. Leon was moving the pictures about the table, putting the faces in a row side by side, or in pairs, trying different combinations. 'We have assumed that Faulkner and Cheshire and Collingwood were innocent casualties, have we not?' He had Pamela Collingwood's picture, her face washed clean, pale and flat, half covered by Cavalli's picture, thin face, pinched, deathly white. He moved aside Cavalli's picture and looked at Pamela Collingwood's image behind it. 'Or was Collingwood a prime target and Cavalli just got in the way?' he asked almost innocently, bringing Cavalli back in front of Collingwood. 'So what else do we know about Pamela Collingwood?'

'Well,' Hubert began, his eyes widening, flicking through a report that gave him some details to read from, 'this is where it might get a little more interesting.' And just as he was about to launch into the only area of the whole investigation that had seemed to be leading somewhere, the details of which he had held back so far in order for

Leon to cover the rest of the ground first, the front-door bell rang, like a school bell announcing the end of lessons for the morning.

Leon dashed downstairs to let in Luigi himself, who explained with passion that he had brought fresh bread, cheese, meats and a bottle of Chianti, with the compliments of the house, to Mr Leon and friend. Leon brought up the box, and Luigi helped with the unloading and the uncorking of the bottle, while flexing his droopy moustache. He proudly poured two glasses of the ruby-coloured wine from Casa Sola and shook hands with the two gentlemen, pleased to be of service. Seeing that they were deeply involved in work, Luigi slipped away without fuss, leaving the bill discreetly folded on the edge of the kitchen table. 'Enjoy, please. Cin cin,' and he bumbled himself out.

They moved into the kitchen to fix themselves a well-earned picnic, eating voraciously and drinking sparingly, before settling down once again over the various papers and reports at the dining table. Hubert lit another cigarette to have with his coffee, with relief and guilt in equal measure.

'Pamela Collingwood.' Leon was holding up her photo again. 'It's interesting again that the woman is shot in the neck,' resumed Leon with determination, 'rather than the head. Cavalli was shot in the head, instant death, and she's just unfortunate being behind him – but unlike Faulkner and Cheshire, who were collateral but survived, she died.'

'Your point, Leon?'

'I'm not sure I am making one – yet.'

Hubert picked up the trail. 'There is not much to add actually. Pamela Collingwood worked in the Merriweather & Dunn offices in Victoria. Her immediate boss, Caroline Quigley, said she was a busy worker, always stuck to her task, used her own initiative often to get what she wanted, was well liked by the clients and other staff. She started low down in the pecking order and had been making good progress recently, expected to achieve further promotion soon. No particular rivals at the firm, the usual level of competitiveness. The London Olympics were an obvious opportunity for her and the whole company. Quigley was completely shocked by the events, of course, said she could see no connection between Cavalli and Collingwood, although Collingwood had worked with a number of the foreign delegations over the build-up months, including the Italian contingent. Quigley had never heard of Cavalli specifically. Pamela was married, but Quigley had never met Mr Collingwood – it seems Pamela never spoke of him. She had no children apparently. The couple lived somewhere in Islington. She drove a Nissan, tried to wear expensive designer clothes, but seemed to struggle a bit with the finances. Would party late and hard. Occasionally drank too much.' Hubert paused from his brief. 'I'm really running out of anything else to say about her.'

'Bank account, insurance, was there a will? You know of anybody gaining from her death?'

'Well, only if it was an accident; I can't see any insurance company paying out after this. Anyway, nothing special, there was no will, as far as I know. But of course attention then focused on her husband, and the police and Five have both had a good go at him. Jarvis Collingwood. Thirty years old, a British Army Paratrooper, an expert sniper, served in Iraq, came back in 2009 quite a hero for his exploits. Good service record. Now works for his brother's security firm, SecureLife, which won a number of Olympic Games contracts, including the stadium throughout the three-week period. He was head of a security guard team all three weeks, including the morning of August 12. He was off duty for the closing ceremony, but he attended with a legitimate ticket and claims to have sat up in the audience on the south-east side, block 230 all through, saw nothing, went home and was staggered to learn of the death of his wife later that night.'

'One hell of a coincidence here, isn't it?' Leon was sitting up, alerted, feeling a prickly sensation under his scalp. 'Pamela Collingwood, who is a nobody, happens to be married to an ex-Army sniper, working in security at the Olympic Stadium; and is shot dead on the night in question, in the Olympic Stadium, probably by an insider, an ex-Army serviceman with obvious shooting skills . . .' Leon's eyebrows had been rising steadily up his forehead in synchrony with the rise in pitch of his incredulous voice, and he almost shouted, '. . . by accident?'

'But why would he kill his wife? And in such a manner?' Hubert was smiling at his friend's animated performance of incredulity.

'I can think of lots of reasons why a husband might kill his wife,' Leon shouted with sarcastic laughter in his voice, 'although thank goodness most jealous husbands don't choose to do it quite like this in public, even when they are a bit upset.'

'If Cavalli was one of his intended targets, could he have made a genuine mistake, not seeing her sitting behind?'

'No, no, this was deliberate, Hue. The Cavalli shooting was merely to make us think he was the target when in fact all along,' Leon was thinking aloud, 'the ricochet shot that ripped his wife's carotid artery was the prime instrument of death – Cavalli just happened to be the unfortunate person sitting in front of *her*. Jarvis Collingwood? You have grilled this man?'

'Yes, several times, police and MI5. He seems the perfect fit, but there is absolutely nothing on him, no witnesses, no forensics, no weapon, and nothing in his working or social connections. He comes over as genuine.' Hubert's brows had also risen, but he looked blank. 'It's all in the reports, interviews, house search et cetera. There was even a psychiatric assessment. Nothing.'

'I need to meet this man, he does sound interesting. A strong possibility in my book. There are just too many coincidences here.'

'A multi-assassination for a number of grievances? I don't know

. . .' Hubert seemed unconvinced.

'Those must have been some big grievances – this was a public execution, Hubert – I repeat, a punishment. This was a man who had the expertise, who worked at Stratford Park, and who had one or two or three specific targets. Presumably from his position on the roof, he could have taken out anybody, couldn't he?' Leon's expression was one of amazement.

Whereas Hubert's face portrayed sombre reality. 'Yes, the Prince, the Duchess of Cambridge, other royals, the current British Prime Minister and his wife, the US Secretary of State, a couple of heads of state from around the world, the London Mayor, the head of the Olympics movement and many more, the list goes on.'

'My God, it could have been nuclear! The guy could have wiped out a significant number of our political leaders if he had cared to. And I suspect that is precisely what he wants us all to realise. The power that was his. Amazing.' Leon stretched backwards, his arms behind his head and his fingers intertwined, tilting his chair. His heart was racing with the incredulity of it all. 'Hubert, we need to go through every name on the employment list, again. Our killer will be there. He will have been paid a large sum of money. We need to run traces, go back some months. We need to check the backgrounds again of Abu and Cavalli. Is there another possible reason why anyone would want Pamela Collingwood dead? Was she actually working for anyone special, or was this something entirely personal? Was she two-timing Jarvis, with the Italian, perhaps? It's as if this killer was dealing with a number of unrelated vengeances, as you said. Maybe this was a demonstration of his power, look what I can do. In which case, there should be a note, an announcement in a paper, on the internet, Facebook, Twitter, something – this killer will want everyone to know, the great power of the man, what a feat of skill; he will be a selfish narcissistic egomaniac.'

Leon suddenly got up, his eyes bright. 'But he will slip up and reveal who he is – we just have to find a snippet of something – GCHQ? Need to direct them onto more domestic traffic. This is not terrorism, Hue.'

'Then that cuts out Five. This becomes a matter solely for the Metropolitan Police.'

'Oh God, Hue, you can't leave it to them.'

For another hour Leon and Hubert, shirt sleeves rolled up, with more coffee on the go, continued to pore over the details, trying to tie up loose ends. Leon took no notes, whereas Hubert wrote a few words in lists on his notepaper every now and then, reminders of things to do.

'Thanks, Leon. This has been so helpful, and therapeutic for me. I can face the team in better spirits on Wednesday. Fantastic. You'll stick with us? Perhaps I could prevail on you to attend with me, meet the others on the committee? In Whitehall.'

'Yes, maybe. Hubert, you are all right with this, aren't you? I mean, you are dealing with this situation with your usual brilliant calm and authority? No one has the edge on you for this sort of thing, Hubert.'

'There is a great deal of pressure from all sides.' Hubert looked robust, if nothing else. 'At the first meeting at Number 10, the room stuffed full of top brass, standing room only, I was appointed by the Prime Minister to coordinate all investigations and report back daily to him personally. I could seek and expect help from anyone and everyone, all resources were at my disposal. "A swift conclusion, Sir Hubert, please" was Mr Cameron's end comment. So I am just saying, Leon, I need some material progress that I can feed to this beast or they'll think I'm not up to the job, whatever *you* think, dear boy. This *has* been really useful.'

Hubert went to relieve himself and returned to gather all his papers. Leon was stretching and looking up at the ceiling. 'This was the most protected and highly secured public event ever held in the UK,' he stated. 'There were more members of the Armed Forces standing by than are deployed in Afghanistan. MI5 had the most sophisticated devices, able to scan up to a hundred and fifty-four thousand people per day.'

Hubert ran his hands through his silky hair and adjusted his cufflinks. He piled the hard-copy reports on the table, together with all the photos, for Leon to read later. He phoned his driver for his transport back to Whitehall.

'Yet one man gets through this barrier,' Leon continued. 'We don't know how he gets a sophisticated sniper's rifle into Stratford Park. And we don't know whether he took it out again, or has left it hidden somewhere in the stadium.'

'All spectators on the last day, as they were every day, were scanned with their bags on entry with a ticket,' said Hubert. 'These were all online pre-bookings, so we have email addresses and credit details. No one was allowed into the stadium without a ticket.' He shut down the laptop. 'But on leaving, no one was scanned, the gates were opened to let eighty thousand people get out effectively at the end of a day, without crushing. As for the rifle, he could have hidden it somewhere in the Park many weeks before the events started, retrieved it on the night, used it and left with it still in his possession, folded in a carrier bag.'

'All coroner's reports are in, are they? Magistrates have returned verdicts of misadventure?' Leon was asking. 'Have all the bodies been released?'

Hubert sat down again. It was after two o'clock and he needed to return to his office to complete a pile of paperwork and review telephone messages and emails that would have accumulated since Friday: better to have them out of the way before Monday morning began. 'Yes, I think so. Abu Masoud was flown back to Iraq last week. Pamela Collingwood's funeral is on Tuesday, I believe.'

Hubert readied himself to leave. 'To put this in perspective, the security network intercepted, or became aware of, over three hundred and fifty separate terrorist or security threats in London in the three months leading up to the opening ceremony – all had to be taken seriously and investigated. At GCHQ they were daily picking up underground chatter and background that was a thousand times more active in this period than it was normally. But nothing prepared them for what happened. I'm not finding excuses, but this has been a really testing time.'

For you especially, Hubert.

'So I'll pick you up tomorrow morning, Leon, after 10 a.m., and we'll travel to Stratford, then to the coroner's office.'

'OK Hubert, see you then. Get some rest, you look tired, you know.' The two old friends shook hands warmly, looking each other in the eyes. Hubert tripped into the mews, where the Range Rover was waiting. Leon watched the heavy machine purr away smoothly, bouncing over the cobbles, its red taillights disappearing round the corner into Weymouth Street.

The Monday morning spent usefully at Stratford Park served to emphasise the enormity of the task in front of them. The rain had been unpleasant again for a few days and the wind was howling through the vast open spaces of the empty stadium, which dwarfed the small band of grim-faced police and officials accompanying Sir Hubert Lansbury and Leon Deshpande along rows of folded-up seats, down flights of stairs, up lifts, along passageways and corridors, and out onto the concourses. Leon met the managing director of the stadium, the head of security for the Games, chief inspectors, and sundry other top officials, along with their assistants and deputies. There were dozens of other people, workers and technicians, dispersed all over the site making preparations for the Paralympic Games scheduled to begin later in the week, but still the place echoed with a sense of forlorn anti-climax. Behind white plastic sheeting that flapped frantically in the draught, they were shown the three shooting sites, the blood-stained concrete floors, stains on the plastic padded seats, the ricochet mark on the glass wall, even the blood trail along the route to the underground medical rooms. All the evidence was individually labelled with coloured tags and numbers, with police tape wound around the seating. This all needed to be cleared by Wednesday, the stains scrubbed clean. The forensics people were happy by now that they had gathered all possible material from the site.

Deshpande was keen to get up on the roof to get a sense of what the sniper had had to tackle and to see what sort of view he would have had. Conditions were not perfect, the air was damp, the sky overcast and there were countless rain puddles over all the surfaces, making them slippery. By the time he had climbed up all the steps to the top of the upper tier, imagining this was the route taken by the killer, Deshpande was puffing and welcomed a rest in the small roof-access area. Further tapes indicated where the young Anthony Butt had met his untimely death. Deshpande now climbed the ladder to the roof, following his guide, a junior police inspector, John Graham, and was immediately confronted with the wind blowing so hard into his face that, teetering on a precariously narrow metal gangway with a sheer drop to the concourse below, he had to cling firmly on to anything he could to steady himself. The vast height and the stunning views of the massive concrete jungle that formed this monster city were mind-boggling. He struggled to get his breath and to adjust his reeling senses.

With care Deshpande walked over the bridge companionway, recognising how narrow it was, and how in the dark with all the distractions on the night of the closing ceremony it would have been especially tricky to negotiate. A good pair of boots with rubber soles that gripped and a torch would have been needed. Graham led him over the canvas roofing towards the inner ring. The height was astonishing, and Deshpande felt dizzy. He could not bring himself to go too near the edge and had to look away over the distant skyline to feel stable again; he gripped the thin rail at his left hand. The silvery skyscrapers of Canary Wharf shimmered, One Canada Place looking like a giant phallus on a bend in the river, light glinting off its reflective peak. In the daylight he had a clear view of more than half of the inside of the stadium, the arena and the seating opposite; he imagined himself standing at three o'clock on a giant circular clock face, so his field of vision ran from about five o'clock all the way round to one o'clock.

He was looking for a hiding place, a cover, a box, anything where the shooter might have hidden a folded rifle. He inspected a lighting hut on the inner rim, and was assured by Graham that they had all been inspected thoroughly, with no evidence of tampering or abnormal usage.

In the darkness of that fateful evening, with all the distractions below, it would have taken a massive feat of concentration to find and focus on the faces the shooter was looking for. But with telescopic sights providing twenty-five-times magnification, once he had identified the relevant faces, they would have appeared larger than life. Deshpande recognised the skills that would have been required, for he had once possessed them himself. Such maverick bravery appealed to his own sometimes wayward instincts, and he found himself marvelling at it.

Once again he looked down towards the boxes one hundred and seventy-five yards away and far below. *Who were the real targets?* He could see all three of the white sheeted incident areas, and recognised how far apart they were from each other, one off to the left at the back in the middle tier (our Iraqi friend), one over to the right at the front of the upper tier (the mysterious Mrs Collingwood and the Italian), and then one just right of centre in the middle tier (Mr and Mrs Morley). Four clear shots, picking out specific people to assassinate, in cold blood. *So what is the link between them all? Were you just collateral, Mrs Pamela Collingwood? Was this your husband taking revenge? For something you did to him, some dreadful wrong?*

On finding his way back over the gangway against the wind, he noticed the black pipes running around the outer rim and lay down on the meshed metal on his stomach, reaching underneath, feeling the width of a dusty plastic pipe. He felt queasy again looking down through the holes in the mesh and over the outer edge of the stadium to the concourse below. He descended gratefully via the ladder and many concrete steps, and felt thoroughly relieved to regain solid ground.

They headed over to the forensics laboratory in Colindale, where they were met by Donald Spottiswode, late of the Charing Cross Hospital Academic Unit, who headed up the laboratory side. On the way, Sir Hubert had explained to Leon that this was now a private company to which the Metropolitan Police outsourced all their work after the recent controversial abolition of the Forensic Science Service. Although it was driven by the usual city business types and capital equity partners all looking for profit, Spottiswode was, Hubert had reassured him, 'a good bloke, very traditional and close to his roots'.

He turned out to be younger than Leon had expected, around the same age as him, and was a handsome Yorkshireman who wore Harris Tweeds and large brown leather shoes. He had a close-cropped designer beard, but it was his big hands that gave him an air of certainty, which Leon found comforting. He showed the visitors the retrieved bullets, laid out on a display table in a laboratory, each in a small sealed plastic bag. The one found at the rear on the concrete floor was distorted and shiny, squashed into a tiny silver box shape. The one from Faulkner's upper humerus and the one from Cheshire's femur, both of which had retained their perfect shape, were shiny silver and looked harmless enough, although Spottiswode described how difficult it had been to obtain them, embedded as they were in living human bone. And the last one, from Pamela Collingwood's neck, lodged in the fourth vertebral body and obtained after death, was distorted and discoloured. DNA traces on these items all confirmed identity of the victims from whom the bullets had been retrieved and the number of possible humans they passed through first. So Faulkner and Cheshire's bullets showed, respectively, DNA traces of Gerry and Amanda Morley, and Collingwood's had DNA traces from Cavalli.

Four bullets, seven people struck, five dead. All over in twenty seconds. All fired from a British Army L115. No other bullets, no misses. Highly professional.

The man earned every penny he was paid, was the thought uppermost in Leon's mind at that moment. *I swear I shall catch this bastard.*

2

It was mid-morning on a day in late August and it seemed like any other, except that, sixteen days since the shootings at London 2012 in the Olympic Park, Jarvis Collingwood, accompanied by members of his family, were gathering for the delayed burial of Pamela Collingwood, nee Beacham, at St Leonard's Church in Tooting Bec Gardens. Jonathan and his mother, together with Pamela's family, had made all the arrangements – the coffin, the transport, the flowers, the catering for a small reception, the guest list and the invitations. All Jarvis had to do was play the part of the shocked widower as calmly as he could, imitating the appropriate level of grief and bitter upset. He was staying at his brother's house in Dalston, which was thought best, rather than coming from his own lonely place where morbid feelings might have got the better of him, and they were all to travel together to the church. After the service, Jarvis had promised to return to his mother's house for a day or two, so that he would not be alone at such a crucial time, which was fine by him under the circumstances.

He was keen to resume a normal life, wanting to return to work as soon as possible. At the weekend he had contacted Danny, who said that the situation had changed quite a bit since he was last down at Beacon Forest. Lord Stonebridge had put most of the work on hold, cash-flow problems or something. Danny and a couple of the lads were doing odd jobs around the county, but things were looking quiet at the moment; if Jarvis liked, he could contact him in a few weeks, and he would be welcome to join the gang again if things picked up or some new work came along.

Jonathan had been round to visit a few times, once with Brenda, to help his brother overcome his grief and deal with certain formalities. He would keep Jarvis on his books and even keep some pay coming in while he remained on compassionate leave. None of Jarvis's mates had called. He had had no word from Ainsley or Jimmy, but then he had not been to his lock-up where his old mobile was. He had not spoken to Naomi for over two weeks.

He was waiting for the opportunity to have a closer talk with his mother, but she had been so shocked since she had heard the news from Jonathan that when Jarvis and Gwendolyn did meet three days after Pamela's death, it was brief, painful and almost without words. The persisting sense of catastrophe made Gwendolyn look frail. She had trouble talking coherently to anyone without needing a little handkerchief to dab at her eyes. Which she continued to do all through the short church service.

Outside in the cemetery grounds, groups were forming along family lines by the graveside, bunching together in their sombre clothes with sombre faces and mumbled replies as the priest intoned familiar words: 'Ashes to ashes . . .' The coffin was lowered into the ground, handfuls of earth were thrown on top, a rosebud, a colourful wreath. Gwendolyn put her arm through Jonathan's and leant heavily on him as they moved away. Pamela's sister Belinda and brother Alan were there with their mother, pale and passive; they shook hands with Jarvis, exchanged a few difficult words before wandering off together across the wet grass, promising to attend the reception for a short while. Jarvis was left alone for a few final moments, standing on wet wooden planking in his charcoal grey trenchcoat, polished boots, head bowed, otherwise tall, straight backed, looking every bit the soldier he used to be on military parade.

A little later, with bright sunshine glancing through tall pines across the front of the old stone building, Jarvis did well in his unfamiliar role, standing handsome on the side of the pot-holed path to shake hands or grip shoulders with the guests who were slowly trooping out onto the road. Jarvis thanked them, said his goodbyes, pressed cheeks where necessary, and all the time looked as solemn and suitably stunned as he could. Leon Deshpande watched from a distance, from under some trees, noting the people coming and going. He especially watched Collingwood.

Jarvis was trying to believe that Pamela had indeed been the victim of some deranged killer with a gun, a ghastly random slaying; doing so made it easier with all the police questioning. He was trying to enter into a state of denial, even though night time often brought a frightening mix of real memories and dreamlike images. He saw himself in camouflage kit, his hands in rubber gloves breaking into the skulls of people familiar to him, including a tearful Pamela who begged him to be home in time for her dinner party. He still had the images as he stood solemnly in the late-summer sunshine by the gates under the pealing church bells; he felt the presence of Pamela standing close to him, watching.

When he turned, he saw it was only Stella standing back in a tight-fitting black suit, hat and shoes to match, last in line, watching over Jarvis, with her feet together, clasping a small black silk bag with both hands at her lap. His petite sister-in-law stepped forward with sympathy on her lips and warmth in her fair eyes. Slipping a hand through his arm, she squashed a soft breast against him. Shafts of sunlight caught the fringe of fine hairs on her upper lip and made her squint. 'Jarvis, I am not staying, I have to get back, I have a new job. Sorry.' He nodded. They walked on a few paces. 'Remember when you comforted me,' she continued in her sweet voice, 'after Ed was killed. You remember you came out to the flat and told me what happened. I was so grateful for that. Don't forget, I'm still there, Jarvis, I would be more than happy to see you, whenever, if you need someone to talk to, or a shoulder – just ring me, you know my number.'

Stella flashed an easy smile at him, pulled herself round so they were face on and stood up on tiptoe, holding on to his arms; she stretched up to plant a tickly kiss on his cheek near to a corner of his mouth. A small splodge of carmine lipstick remained there until some moments later, as he watched her thread her way along the street between other smartly dressed mourners towards her parked car, he wiped it off with a casual fingertip, rubbing it clean with his thumb. Her figure was nicely shaped, pinched in at the waist, rounded over the rear with good legs, and he made a definite promise to himself that at some point soon he would pay her a visit in Romford.

Deshpande slipped away without introducing himself to anybody.

In Jonathan's Audi later with his mother, on the way to her house for the night, while they drove sedately in silence, Jarvis was thinking about how to meet up with Naomi again and befriend her, regain her trust, planning exactly what he was going to say to her.

Later in the day, Leon was soaking at home in the bath before going out for the evening. Music was playing loudly in the main room and the bathroom door was open so he could hear and sing along. He had been thinking intently about the Olympic shootings ever since Hubert had left the mews on Sunday, and had the image of the straight-backed, grief-stricken Jarvis Collingwood in his mind. He had been reading through many of the reports piled on his dining table and had made a start on the enormous list of employees. Earlier, a private courier had delivered a box containing a dozen CDs with TV footage of the evening of the shootings and surrounding events, all of them catalogued, and he had been studying some of them with care during the afternoon to the point of exhaustion, without gaining much more insight. They served to reinforce how supremely skilful the shooter had been, considering the huge number of faces, all constantly moving, in the crowd and the darkness, the noise and other distractions all around. He had watched a recording of last week's Westminster funerals of the Morleys, conducted with due sombreness and a little pomp, exactly as the watching British public had come to expect for an ex-British Prime Minister.

He had still not figured out the connections or the motives. He had convinced himself that the killings were not random, that the killer had specific targets, although they were each for different reasons, not necessarily connected. The killer was punishing some people for past misdemeanours; he was tidying up. Which was why Leon was increasingly convinced that Jarvis Collingwood was the most likely man. He had read the interview transcripts and reports from the three extensive sessions with him, two at Bow Road Station, one at Scotland Yard under caution with a solicitor present, Broderick leading, and nothing in them persuaded him otherwise. Nothing of any interest had been found in his house, or in the safe, or on his mobile, and his bank statements were positively boring. Although the Met must have been sorely tempted to arrest Collingwood, which at least would have shown the public and the politicians that they were making some progress, it would have been unproductive if they had had to release him forty-eight hours later with no charge through lack of any significant evidence against him. Which is what seemed to be the case at the moment.

A uniformed police officer had been on duty round the clock outside Collingwood's front door in Hoxton, another officer in an unmarked car remained in place down the street to observe and report his movements, and his family liaison officer reported in every day, accompanying Jarvis to his police interviews. Some media people had somehow heard the rumours and had started to camp outside his house and chase him up the street, firing questions at him, with photographers in pursuit too. But Jarvis Collingwood was free to leave the house whenever he wished, and he could lead them all a merry dance when he chose to, losing any tail at will. Leon persuaded Hubert to talk to the Met to get them to intensify their watching teams, put sensors in the house, watchers in a building opposite, twenty-four-hour foot patrols and unmarked cars at either end of the street. But the Met disagreed over the value of such concentrated surveillance and decided to make do with no electronic sensors, a single car, and two officers on eight-hour shifts, with a gap in between, reporting to Inspector Broderick at Bow, who then fed Sir Hubert with occasional reports. Surprise, surprise, no visitors or other events even remotely interesting had been reported. Leon knew that Jarvis would be all too aware of the watchers and quite capable of managing them however he wanted without giving anything away. *He's a professional, for Christ's sake.*

Hubert wanted Leon to attend the week's COBR meeting that morning, but Leon said he thought at the moment his presence at the Cabinet briefing would only antagonise some of the brass – better to wait till there was something juicy to tell them, maybe next week. As he dried himself off and a mandolin concerto came to an end, Leon was planning his forthcoming interview with Jarvis Collingwood, which would be at his mother's house in Lewisham the next day, and which would give him an opportunity to see them both, at least for starters.

He was selecting a Ben Sherman from the cupboard just as his mobile buzzed. 'Leon, that you? Can you talk?'

'I'm all ears, Hue.'

'Two breakthroughs today, quite a drama. First of all, a drainpipe cut open and sealed with tape, found on the roof at the stadium, gangway 4, near where we were. You were spot on there, Leon. Inside a bundle of used cling film and a small piece of towel with cordite stains – no bullet casings. A likely storage place for our man.'

'I knew it. You can reach the pipes if you lie flat on the gangway

273

– that's good. How did you find it?'

'Not me, Leon, a keen young policeman following your advice yesterday – they've been going over the place again, piece by piece, and this turns up, clearly missed the first time. So they are going over the area and the pipe with detail, DNA and so on, and cutting through the pipe lower down in its course. So we wait.' There was a note of excitement in Hue's voice. 'And secondly, wait for this, Leon: our Pamela was having a fling with an Italian man, it turns out, who knows Pietro Cavalli – sorry, knew Cavalli. A wealthy playboy, some years younger than her, Antonio Vitomilecia is his name, has a place in Mayfair, into clothes design, inherited money as far as I can make out. He and Pamela sometimes shared his bed apparently, and Cavalli was a friend of his.'

Leon sat down on the edge of his bed to steady himself, astonished, not at the news, but that it had come so soon after their discussion. This was a real breakthrough indeed. 'Now that *is* interesting, although not unexpected. This Antonio bloke, did he come forward on his own?'

'Yes, left an email message for Broderick – it was a help line. Evidently he feels unsafe, thinking that Pamela's husband is trying to warn him or will even kill him – seemed quite terrified actually. He came into the Yard and was interviewed this afternoon and I've just finished listening to the transcripts. You'll want to talk to him.'

'Do you believe him?'

'Yes, seems kosher all right. Pretty worried as well.'

'And he thinks Collingwood is the killer?'

'Well, he seemed convinced that Collingwood found out about him and Pamela, and shot Cavalli as a warning; if Antonio had been at the stadium that night, he thinks it would be him lying alongside Pamela Collingwood now.'

'Yes, I guess that works. Why was he not at the stadium that night?'

'He didn't have tickets; he wasn't part of the Olympics team, but had known Cavalli for a number of years. Said he had other business to attend to.' Hubert again sounded brighter.

'OK, Hue, well done. Can you give me Antonio's address? Call him and tell him I shall be over in an hour. I want to talk to him before I meet Collingwood.'

'You still going ahead with that interview? Could be dangerous, if Collingwood thinks he is being cornered.'

'His place has been searched, he has no weapons there. Anyway, I'm going to interview him at his mother's house, he's been staying there. I'll be fine, Hue, I need to befriend him. I watched him at the funeral today – went without a hitch.'

Leon quickly finished readying himself for the day's activities, with a small detour to Antonio's place thrown in.

Leon found number 48 on the fourth floor and pressed the little brass buzzer, no name attached. Everything about the Mount Street block of apartments was expensive, from the grey marble floors to the glass chandeliers on every floor and the solid oak doors and frames. A smart brushed aluminium and glass lift had brought him up almost silently from the basement car park, where he had been admitted on punching in a key code that Hue had given him.

The door was opened with a sucking noise. A small olive-skinned face with deep black gelled hair in a ponytail with sideboards poked around the edge. 'Si?' He looked late-twenties, smooth and fresh, plucked eyebrows and mascara, and wore tight grey shiny trousers pulled in viciously at the waist by a moleskin belt. He was in black silk shirt open at the neck that exposed a tiny seahorse tattoo. He had a look of fright and was obviously relieved to see Leon's ID badge indicating a man of authority, and at least temporary safety. Antonio fully opened the door and said 'Welcome' too many times. A diamond stud in his left earlobe matched a diamond-encrusted

Rolex poking out from his sleeve. He wore no rings on his fingers, a simple gold bracelet on the other wrist.

Leon stepped into tasteful luxury, with subtle smells of leather, of jasmine and lilies in full bloom. The ambience was neutral cool with flashes of colour, like the orange and turquoise cushion covers, the multi-coloured rugs and the paintings and prints on the walls. Leon enjoyed the feel of the place but refused the offer of coffee or a drink.

'I mustn't, although it sounds lovely. I don't want to keep you long. I'm sorry to disturb you, Mr Vitomilecia. I know you have made yourself known to Inspector Broderick, and that's how I heard about you. Thank you for coming forward. I would like to ask some questions, if I may.'

'Come, sit down, please, Mr Deshpande.' He was holding Deshpande's card, reading it. 'I feel still worried about this man Collingwoods, so I keeping in hiding. I want to return to Valpolicella, my home town, but you police said I should stay in London for a while.'

'I am not police, Mr Vitomilecia, …'

'Please, Antonio, Antonio, it is fine,' Antonio pleaded, a slight frown furrowing his brow.

Leon wandered slowly round the main lounge, with its heavy gilded furniture, brown marble surfaces, a centuries-old onyx clock and a few art deco sculptures. Through open French windows he could hear the distant throbbing of traffic, but the late-summer air drifting in was pleasant, ruffling the trailing lace curtains. There were bold azures, violets and greens in mixes on the cushions and carpets. An impressive long-haired white Afghan rug had a central place in front of an ornate marble fireplace.

Antonio sat on a leather sofa, Leon hovered by the open windows, from where he could make out Hyde Park at a distance. 'I understand that you and Pamela Collingwood were seeing each other, Antonio.'

'Yes, she was most beautiful woman, so mature and sophisticated. I knew she was married but she said that it was a sham, that it was notta working as one would like, and she was going to end it somehow.'

'How did you meet her, Antonio, and when?'

'Oh, three, four years ago, I forget. There was a party in London, shortly after they returned from Singapore, and we were a little over-excited and intoxicated, but everyone so happy, and it was wonderful, and you know, one thing lead to another, a very British phrase, I like.'

'Yes, it's a useful one. So you would meet regarding work, and she would come round here sometimes?'

'Yes, she was getting quite serious, actually. I am, you know, Mr Deshpande, I am loving her but there are other women I see as well and she is not only one. Do you think this Collingwoods has found out?'

'Have you ever met Jarvis Collingwood?'

'No!' Antonio interjected with a sudden look of horror. 'Heavens forbid! I do not know what he looks like. Is he big brute with muscles that will tear me apart? Or will he shoot me down in the street with one of his sniper rifles? I don't know. It's not good situation. Pamela was really lovely woman. Poor poor woman. And poor Cavalli.' He was wringing his hands in despair.

Leon produced a photograph of Jarvis taken by the police in Hackney, during one of his interviews. He showed it to Antonio.

'Oh, my goodness.' That wide-eyed look of shock again. 'He's big boy, he looks very strong. He looks pretty too, no?' And Leon managed a laugh at Antonio's camp humour.

'And Cavalli, how long had you known him?'

'Many years, since we were boys, poor poor man. He was an athlete, doing promotions; he loved London, often stayed with me.'

'And why would anyone want to kill Cavalli, do you suppose?'

'Oh, no, they would not. I explain, I think he knew about Pamela and me and this was warning shot. If I had been there he would have shot me!'

'And why would he kill his wife, or do you think that was just unlucky?'

Antonio looked genuinely sad when he said, 'It was because of me, he was jealous, because his wife is loving another man.' He got up with a wipe of his delicate hands across his face and minced over to a heavy sideboard. From a drawer he removed a mobile phone in a pink cover. 'Look, Mr Deshpande, I better give this to you. Is Pamela's mobile phone. It was in bag. When she was shot the bag was left under seat, and another friend of mine who was with Pietro at the Ceremony picked it up, gave it into police, but this he took out and later gave it to me. He thought it might protect her and did not want it falling into wrong hands. He thought he was doing the right thing. You better have it.' Antonio walked over to Deshpande and handed him the Samsung flip device. Leon dropped it into a pocket of his suit and thanked Antonio for his honesty.

'You've not tampered with it in any way?'

'No, no.' Antonio held his hands up in an expression of innocence.

'So why were you not at the closing ceremony with Pamela, Antonio?'

'I was at business meeting, important contract with Argentinian suppliers, exotic leathers, that sort of thing. I wanted to be there but business came first.'

'And how can you be so sure that Jarvis Collingwood had found out about you and Pamela? Had you heard something, or had Pamela said anything?'

'She said he had seen a text from me on her cell; she seemed worried.'

Leon Deshpande did not stay much longer after that; there was little else to ask Antonio, and Leon believed that he had told him all that he knew. He did take away a photograph of Antonio that the Italian had offered him when asked and that Leon said might prove useful.

3

After the funeral, Jarvis spent time at his mother's, pretending to be the innocent grieving widower, while in reality he was in a state of frustration. He wanted to share with her some of his inner thoughts and worries, and once came close to telling her of the success of his exploits, of how he had used his exceptional skills to the full in overcoming the obstacles and how his performance had been one of near perfection. She would have been so proud. His father would have been proud of him too. The police were completely baffled, he would have reassured her; he had left not a single trace, and they were clueless. He had punished the people he had promised to punish. And he had done it for her, for the memory of Ed and of his father.

But dear Gwendolyn had looked so distraught, at Pamela's funeral and later, and preferred to talk about anything except Pamela's death, anything irrelevant. She was drinking more than usual. She told him she did not want to know if he had been in any way involved with the tragic events at the Olympic Stadium. The less she knew the better. A police inspector had apparently been round to the house last week to ask her lots of questions about Jarvis, about his upbringing and his marriage and his professional life. He had been very polite and she had told him nothing.

In truth, Jarvis was actually most unlikely to converse with his mother about anything important, and he planned to return to his empty home soon, having gained little by his short stay with her. He should not unload any of his worries onto her – she would not be able to handle them. Wound up and enclosed, Jarvis needed physical work to help let off steam. He had been confined indoors for practically two and a half weeks, which did not suit him. He could not go out freely because of the watchers and the journalists at his place, in their plain cars. He had not risked a visit to the lock-up, which was disappointing, as he wanted to sort things out, get his alternative credit card for some money, and get out on the Vespa. He wanted to return to some sort of work and pressed his brother to get him something, and was promised a string of jobs to keep him busy once he was back home.

Nor had he dared visit Naomi, which he was itching to do, as he knew it could compromise him if he was followed. He needed to talk to someone, to steady his nerves; he wanted her for the support she would provide. He was missing her, he had to admit; her silly ways, her gangly walk and toothy giggle, her physical presence. Her crooked smile and quiet sense of fun, he liked that. And she liked him, of that he was sure.

And then someone from Broderick's office had phoned to say that another investigator was calling this morning at his mother's house wanting to interview him. While he was eating toast in the kitchen in baggy trousers and a white singlet vest, wanting to do some gym work later in the day, the doorbell rang, around nine thirty. At the front door, hunched in the drizzle, was a solid-looking man in a crumpled suit and no tie, who looked vaguely familiar. Tanned, freshly shaven face, bright eyes, gelled dark hair, he stood facing Jarvis, offering a hand once eye contact had been made.

'Jarvis Collingwood? Good morning.' A policeman in wet uniform stood a few paces away on the drive, looking distractedly about the street. 'I'm Leon Deshpande, I'm helping the Home Office with their investigation. The Stratford shootings?' Jarvis put out a hand, aware of the sticky butter on his fingers and the toasty bits in his mouth, and mumbled, 'Yes, morning, all right?'

Leon saw a good-looking athletic young man with well-built, impressive shoulders, hair a dirty blond, a touch unshaven and a touch uncertain. 'I gather Inspector Broderick told you I would be

281

paying you a call. I'm very sorry about your loss. An awful business.' Jarvis turned back into the entrance hall. Leon closed the door, then wiped his feet on the mat and his hands on a handkerchief. They moved into the lounge, tidy and fussy with a lifetime's collection of knick-knacks on every surface.

Leon tried to sound sympathetic without being patronising. 'I just wanted to ask you a few things to try to understand the circumstances better.' They were both standing in the middle of the room feeling uncomfortable, sizing each other up and wondering how much the other knew and how much they could believe each other.

This is the man who more than likely murdered five people in cold blood, Leon was thinking. *He looks amiable enough, but capable. Do not be fooled.*

'Er, sit down. Do you want anything?' Jarvis was abrupt.

'Cup of tea would be fantastic, actually. I won't stay long.' Leon had his friendly smile on and perched his firm bottom on the edge of an orange velour seat. As the younger man sauntered out to the kitchen, Leon called: 'I'm trying to piece together what happened on the night of August 12th and why, and see if that leads anywhere. Is that all right? Er, no milk, no sugar, thanks.'

Leon's eyes darted around the room and settled on a framed photograph on the sideboard, four men in army uniform, Gwendolyn's boys by the look of them, father and three strapping lads of various ages, Jarvis looking barely out of his teens. Handsome family, taken some years ago.

Jarvis returned with two white mugs. 'Who did you say you work for?' He was aware that he needed to humour this man. Although not sure exactly who he was, he could tell he was fairly senior, competent. Inside he was on the alert. *Appears pleasant enough, must be good at what he does – Mr Desh whatever, but be careful, give nothing away.*

'Sorry.' Leon held up his ID card in a wallet. 'The Home Office, in conjunction with Scotland Yard. The police are doing their best with the enquiry, but it's not going very well at the moment, and I'm simply there to provide some help.'

Jarvis plonked the mugs down on the coffee table in the middle of the room. He felt Deshpande's presence: the man looked professional and efficient, robust, more than capable of looking after himself. He was not fooled by his show of kindness; he could see in Deshpande's steely lips a ruthlessness that was not to be underestimated. Jarvis sipped at his too-hot mug of tea.

To Leon, Jarvis looked tired, jaded, without a lot of energy. He had been cooped up indoors most of the time, on his own probably, although he must have had some visitors. But he could also see how lithe Jarvis was, big boned, a determined jaw with strong hands, a straight back, a natural soldier.

They both settled down. Leon was staring into his tea, taking occasional sips, hoping that Jarvis might volunteer some information. It was quiet and they could both hear someone pottering around upstairs. 'My mother,' explained Jarvis, 'she'll be down in a minute.'

Leon needed the presence of the policeman outside the house to give him enough authenticity in Jarvis's eyes, showing that there was backup available if necessary. 'You were in the Army, that's right, isn't it? Paratrooper?' he asked, at which Jarvis turned to look at him, nodding once. 'I was in the Paras too,' Leon continued, 'a bit before you. Spent a lot of time in Northern Ireland, for my sins. "Ready For Anything", eh? Changes you, doesn't it? The Army. Makes you see life differently, differently from the way other people look at it, anyway. I always say it makes a man appreciate why we are here.' And Jarvis made a small smile of recognition, knitting his eyebrows.

'Gives your life a purpose, I always think. Did you find it difficult getting back to civilian life? Well, daft question, we all did, didn't we?'

Jarvis nodded again a few times, staring into his mug. 'Yeah, a bit. Getting jobs and that.'

'Done various things, have you?'

'Yeah.'

'None of them satisfying though, right? What, driver, hod-carrier, general dogsbody?' Leon looked amused.

There was the sudden sound of a downpour outside and both men glanced at the rain slashing against the glass of the front windows, feeling sorry for the poor bobby outside. Jarvis turned back towards Deshpande. 'Look, we going to reminisce all day, or what?' Jarvis was holding the face of his wristwatch, looking anxious.

'Sorry. You're right. Can we talk about Pamela?'

Jarvis stared angrily at the older man, noticing peeling skin along the tops of his ears.

'I was wondering whether you might have a photograph of her, so I could picture her better.'

Jarvis hesitated a moment, then walked over to the low bay window where he retrieved a wooden framed picture from among many others on the sill, thrusting it under Leon's nose. 'This is one my mother has, quite recent.' Jarvis hated seeing that picture every day in the house.

In the colour photograph Leon saw a pleasant young woman, comfortable, clear brown eyes and a warm smile directed at the camera, a studio shot which brought out the colour in her hair, copper, cropped short.

'Married long?'

'Since 2003.'

'But knew her for longer, right?'

'Since we were teenagers.'

'How old is she here – in this picture?'

'About twenty-eight.'

'Tell me about her, Jarvis. I want to understand the woman she was, what motivated her and so on.'

Jarvis winced as if in pain. 'Really?' He thought for a bit. 'She was normal, she did the washing and the cooking mostly, we shared the shopping and things. She went out to work every day and I went to work, we watched a bit of TV in the evenings, she loved *Desperate Housewives* did Pam, what else do you want to know? That's all there is to it.'

Hoping for something a little deeper, Leon allowed these trivial revelations to sink in. 'No children then?'

'Nah.' He shook his head dismissively a few times, drank from his mug.

'What about her job, how did she view that?'

'Loved it, worked hard, out all day.'

'Ambitious?'

'Yeah, she . . . wanted to do well.'

'Any problems at work?'

'No, not that I noticed.'

'Did she want children?'

'No, not especially. We talked about it.'

Jarvis was not stupid, Leon was certain of that, but he was giving a good imitation. Still looking at the picture, gripping its sides, admiring the strong features of the rounded face, Leon said quietly, taking his time, 'I want to know who would want to kill her. Who would want to kill her in public and humiliate her.' He took a glance at the ex-serviceman.

Jarvis had been expecting this and kept his face bland. 'I don't know. I ask myself that question every day and I can't find the answer.'

'But you must have some idea, Jarvis.' Leon was gently pleading for him to rack his brains, just for a moment. 'Someone whom she had upset in the past: a feud at work, someone whom she was promoted over? Had she got involved with some ne'er-do-wells?

Perhaps a jealous lover whom she had jilted?'

'I thought you were thinking it was an accident. You lot said it was the Italian bloke that was the target, and Pamela happened to be sitting behind him and took the bullet in the neck.' Jarvis sounded angry. 'It was not intentional, I thought that was what you were thinking.'

'Oh, really, so who has shared those thoughts with you?'

'That inspector fellow, Broderick. He's talked to me a few times about this and that was the conclusion.' Jarvis sounded more defensive now.

'But what if that is precisely what the killer wanted us to think: that Cavalli was the target and Pamela was just an unfortunate accident, nothing to do with it really?'

'I don't know.' Jarvis put his face in his hands and rubbed his eyes. 'Look, I don't know, do I? I've been through all this with you people and told you everything I know.'

'The Italian man is interesting though, isn't he?' Jarvis said nothing. 'There is a connection, you see,' Leon suggested quietly, still looking at Pamela's picture.

'Cavalli is connected, how?' asked Jarvis, through his fingers.

'No, not Cavalli, the other one, Antonio; Antonio Vitomilecia.' Leon enunciated the name for the first time with great precision, mouthing the syllables with relish, so as to pronounce it correctly with just the right amount of accent, making it sound as if he knew the man. Jarvis looked confused. 'He was a close friend of Cavalli,' Leon continued. 'And he knew Pamela – indeed, he was having a bit of a thing with her, wasn't he?' Leon leant forward now, looking directly at Jarvis. He could not see his eyes, although Leon detected a suppressed biting of his lower lip. 'In fact, if Antonio had been at the stadium that night, perhaps sitting alongside Pamela, enjoying the evening's entertainment with her, chatting and laughing together, it would have been Antonio with a bullet in his brain, and not his innocent friend, wouldn't it?' Leon studied the younger man's face for a reaction. 'Sweet revenge. What do you think of that, Jarvis? Can I call you Jarvis?'

The gaze from each man was equally cold.

'I don't know what you are talking about.' He tried to look baffled. *He's bluffing, he knows nothing.*

'It must be very difficult, I know, when you have just lost your wife, to then find out that she was actually having an affair with someone else.' Leon fished the 5 by 7 cm photograph out of the inside pocket of his suit, and handed it across to Jarvis. 'This is Antonio Vitomilecia. Ever seen him before, Jarvis?'

Jarvis stared at the picture of Antonio, who was just as he had imagined him to be, a slimy little toad that Pamela ran to so often, but he did not blink an eyelid. 'You obviously think I have, or you wouldn't be asking. Well, I have never seen him before. Pamela lived her own life as she saw fit.' Jarvis under pressure reverted to a bit more London street accent. 'She regularly went out with people from work, with clients and that, and with the Olympics she had been dealing with lots of people from abroad, Italians, the Spanish, Germans, everyone. I did not interfere. I let her get on with it, and she let me get on with my life, without interference. All right. That's the way we were.' He thrust the photo back towards Leon. 'I have never heard of this bloke.'

Neither man had heard the steps on the stairway, but they both ceased their staring at that moment as Gwendolyn arrived at the lounge door, apologising that she had been a long time coming and checking whether the inspector had everything he wanted.

'Yes, thank you, Mrs Collingwood, I am fine, I have tea,' and he slipped the single photo of Antonio back into his inside pocket, at the same time standing up and passing a small card across into Gwendolyn's brown spotted hands. 'I'm Leon Deshpande, from the Home Office. I'm not a police inspector, I'm afraid.' Gwendolyn, in conventional twin set with navy skirt, moved anxiously over to the settee Jarvis was sitting on, and settled at the opposite end on the edge, turned away from him with her knees together and arms folded, looking weary.

Leon continued, wanting to keep a certain momentum going. 'I am sorry to intrude. The Olympic shootings investigation. We need to find Pamela's killer, and I needed some more background information, first-hand, if that's all right. So talking to both of you is really helpful.'

Leon sat down again, perching the framed picture of Pamela on its stand on the coffee table for them all to see.

'Fine – so what can we answer for you, Mr Deshpande?'

'Well, we were talking about Pamela, Mrs Collingwood. I wanted to know what sort of person she was. Did she have friends? Did she have enemies? Why would anyone want to harm her, do you think?' Again Leon was trying to sound sympathetic.

Gwendolyn gave a little shake of her head, passed a hand over her thin greying hair, replacing some strays. 'She was a splendid person. A good daughter-in-law, very loyal. She worked hard, loved life, always tried to be cheerful. Had been very supportive of Jarvis, you know, when he was away in the Army, fighting, it was always a difficult time for the wives left behind, I know, I had had my fill of that with Jarvis's father many times. You know I lost a son in the Middle East, fighting for this country. It is always very hard for the women left at home. You never know . . .' She left the sentence unfinished, with a sad expression, her fingers toying with the line of pearls around her neck, remaining just in control of her emotions and dry-eyed.

'Yes, tough. Did Pamela ever stray away – from Jarvis, I mean – at those times, those long periods when she was alone? There were no children . . .'

'Absolutely not, Mr Deshpande. She was loyal, they had known each other for many years. My husband always said she came from good stock, she was a perfect match for Jarvis.'

'I am simply wondering where along her life she had gained sufficient hatred from someone for them to want to shoot her dead in cold blood.'

'Mr Deshpande, I am sure this was all an accident. You will upset Jarvis with this talk of killing, it was an accident.' She looked indignant.

'How can you be so sure?' Leon interrupted swiftly.

'Pamela was well liked by everyone who knew her. She was a lovely woman.' And Gwendolyn was blinking, reaching swiftly up a sleeve for a small white handkerchief to squeeze her nose with and press against her eyes. Jarvis had remained silent during this interchange, looking down at the pattern on the carpet, as if the subject matter did not concern him.

After some moments of reflection, realising he was not going to get any further with Gwendolyn, Leon asked: 'I wonder if I may talk with Jarvis alone, Mrs Collingwood, for a little longer?' And he moved across to the door to hold it open for her. He fixed his eyes on her with a determined expression that said this was important, no argument, please.

'Oh, yes, of course, Inspector, if you must. But don't bully him with all this talk of killing. Just give me a call if you want anything.'

'I will, thank you.' Gwendolyn's joints creaked as she straightened up and, passing in front of Jarvis, she was unable to resist an irritating little ruffle of his hair. 'Much prefer you without the beard, Jarvis dear; wouldn't you agree, Inspector, he looks better?' And she wandered out of the room. Embarrassed, Jarvis rolled his eyes towards heaven, which said it all.

'OK,' Leon said, once he had closed the door and settled down again, 'back to where we were, perhaps. Pamela. You obviously had a mature relationship, you two, an understanding. You turned a blind eye when her fancy wandered. Did that mean that *you* were able to carry on with other people as well? She didn't mind?'

'Look, I don't know. I mean, she was easy like that.'

'That sounds like one hell of a marriage arrangement. A lot of blokes would envy you. She was a very attractive woman, wasn't she?' Jarvis made no reply. 'So was there anybody, on your side, I mean?'

'No, there was not. I was loyal . . .'

'And did Pamela have other men, do you know?' Leon persisted.

'No,' Jarvis said emphatically.

'So you knew about Antonio?' Leon made a quick U-turn.

'No.' Emphatic again.

'But did you suspect? You must have suspected something, Jarvis, there must have been little signs. You were with her over ten years, you would notice something, surely? You know, wearing sexy underwear for work one day, extra perfume, late returns in the evening, unexpected calls, flowers, little gifts, staying over unexpectedly . . . no?'

'I really didn't care actually – as I say, we lived our lives pretty much as we wanted.' *But of course how right you are, Mr Desh-clever-dick.* There had been lots of little clues, if Jarvis cared to think about it, and he had been made to feel aggrieved many a time; but he had shrugged and carried on with his own liaisons that he presumed Pamela knew nothing about.

'You say you didn't know about Antonio. So how would you know if she was meeting other men? I mean, she was obviously rather good at hiding the evidence.'

'I don't know. I didn't particularly suspect her, of anyone special, she didn't show any signs, that's all I'm saying.'

'So you didn't get on with each other terribly well, did you? It sounds as if you were at odds most of the time, was that right?'

'Yeah, pretty much,' Jarvis replied, perhaps too quickly. 'Well, we had our good times and we had our differences, like any marriage, right?'

Leon let it go. 'I guess that's right.' Jarvis was quiet again. Leon glanced at his watch. Reverting to his casual best: 'Did you know Abu Masoud Zadeh?' Again he was careful to pronounce the foreign-sounding name correctly, using his lips and tongue to form the sounds with precision.

Jarvis looked at the other man with a vacant expression and knitted his brows together so that deep furrows formed. 'Who?'

'Abu was the Iraqi official, the first victim in the stadium, shot through the forehead, between the eyes. Like an assassination. An expert shot. Do you know who he was?'

'Well, I had never heard of him, till his name was in the papers, wasn't it?'

'Never met him, in Iraq, for instance?'

'No, like, why would I?'

Leon continued: 'And nobody offered you any money to assassinate this man?'

'Are you mad? I had never heard of him before. All right?'

'Jarvis, you must have looked at the details of what happened, with four people shot dead, including two well-known famous people. Including your wife.' Jarvis flopped back into the settee with arms in the air, head back, looking up at the ceiling in despair, but he listened all the same. 'We think only four shots were fired, from the roof of the stadium in the dark with many distractions going on all around, exploding fireworks, all the crowd noise and movement. Shots from one hundred and seventy yards, each one spot on target, perfect shots you might say.' Leon was speaking fast, but with precision. 'I mean, it must strike you that this could only have been done by a very small number of highly specialised skilled shooters. Marksmen, from the Army or the police. The rifle used we know was a specialised British Army issue, quite sophisticated, the L115A3. Are you familiar with such a weapon?'

Jarvis sat up. 'Well, we never had anything quite so good in Iraq. They were introduced later, 2010 or something, used a lot in Afghanistan.'

'Yes, a British Army sniper has just set a new record for distance. With this rifle. At just over a mile, hitting two Afghan insurgents in Helmand.'

'Yes, Jamie Ogden, I met him. He was good.'

Leon looked up with delight, seeing a way in. 'Oh, right. So was anybody else working at the stadium that you knew? Any ex-Army blokes, with these sort of shooting skills?'

'Yes, I guess there were one or two.'

'Jarvis, you probably know who did this. The way our thoughts have been going, only one or two people could possibly have done this. An Army, or ex-Army sniper with supreme shooting skills. And when your wife is involved, we naturally think of you as one of those people.' With firm deliberation, Leon was asking: 'Who would want to kill your wife, Jarvis, if not you?'

Jarvis stared with fury into Leon's green eyes for an instant before jumping up, smacking his palms on his thighs, almost stamping his foot, and turning away to look out of the window. 'I have told you all I know,' he shouted. 'I did not kill her. I miss her, and I . . . did not kill her'. He managed a whimper as he stood still for a while looking at the rain outside before coming back to sit down again slowly.

Leon sighed and smiled briefly. 'OK. Tell me, how would you get hold of a rifle like that? Where would you go?' Jarvis looked askance at Leon. 'I mean, what would you have to pay on the black market, I wonder?'

'Not a clue, mister. You would need contacts in the arms business, it's all black market outside the Army. Probably twenty thousand quid. Or steal from Army HQ, I don't know.'

'You been keeping up your shooting skills, Jarvis, over the last few years, since leaving the Army?'

'No.'

'No firearms practice?'

'No.'

'Do you have a firearms licence or a weapon of any sort, at home?'

Jarvis was shaking his head. 'No. No.'

'OK. What I want you to do for us is to go through our employee list, people working at the stadium, and see if you recognise any of the names and whether you think they might have been capable. OK? Will you do that for us? You just might know of some blokes with the sort of shooting skills we are talking about – see if they are on the list.'

Jarvis wiped his face in his hands, felt the dampness on his fingers. He looked tired. 'Yeah, I suppose so.' He composed himself. 'Am I under arrest?'

'I'm not a policeman, Jarvis. But as far as I know, there are no plans to arrest you, at the moment. There is a lot of evidence missing. But you still remain interesting to the police, so don't go far away. OK, Jarvis, we'll leave it for now.' Leon was getting up. 'I know it's difficult for you. Thanks for talking to me. We will need you to come in. We will get in touch, maybe tomorrow, so stay around.'

'I am going back home later today.'

'OK. We'll find you. I can see myself out. Thanks for the tea.'

With Jarvis bent forward over his knees unmoved, Deshpande left the room. He let himself out the front door. The rain had slowed down, leaving the drive covered in puddles. He nodded his appreciation at the damp officer on the gate and walked away to his car.

Jarvis sat still, reviewing the previous half an hour. *That man knows nothing. We did all right. It could have been worse, but we gave nothing away*. For a moment he thought of Naomi, wanting her to listen to his side, needing her good sense and good-naturedness and comfort. He needed her reassurance.

Leon had promised Zoe that he would pick Jamila up outside Kew Gardens in the afternoon, bring her over to the mews, and they would spend some time together, perhaps go out for a meal. It was late August, the last days of school holidays, so a trip across town to the South Bank, taking in some art somewhere along the way, would be good. At sixteen Jamila was an awkward teenager going on sophisticated young woman, who would be secretly thrilled to go to smart places with her handsome father, whom she seldom saw but obviously adored. She could stay the night and Leon would return her safe and sound the next morning to Richmond. Surely her mother could not object to that.

'Of course I don't object to that, as such,' Zoe had trilled in Leon's ear over the phone earlier in the week, while he was trying to finish his exercise routine before breakfast, 'it's just your blasé attitude, Leon, as if you can come and take my daughter away at will, and return her when you've finished with her. Like an accessory to your flash lifestyle. She seriously needs more of you, Leon. She's at the age where a father's influence . . .' But Leon had stopped listening; he had heard it all before.

'So what's Simple Simon doing in this modern arrangement of yours?' he retorted. 'He has responsibilities as well, taking on you and yours.' Simon was something in fine wines, Leon was never quite sure what exactly, and Zoe hated him taunting her second husband as if he were a sixth-former with pretensions.

'And yours too – she's not just my daughter, you know.'

'I know, dear, I'm paying for St Paul's and the rest.'

In the end Zoe had agreed and so, rather than talk to Hubert in person or attend the early-morning Downing Street COBR meeting, Leon was duty bound to entertain his sixteen-year-old, whom on affectionate occasions he was just as likely to refer to as Jam.

Jamila was currently labelled Gothic, as far as a girl who was still at school could be without causing a furore and being gated. Her thick black tresses were chopped into shards, spiking down to bare shoulders. Her clothes were shapeless greys and blacks, ripped flimsy tops and tight belts, tiny bottom-hugging black skirts, chunky studded Chelsea boots, no tights. Around her neck, a black leather dog collar with studs. An elongated face, with a small nose like Leon's, gave her a boyish look and made her appear older than she was. Today, around her emerald eyes was painted a purple and ox blood decoration that contrasted with her lily-white skin. Wine-stain lipstick, a silver ring piercing at one end of her right eyebrow and a new piercing of her lower lip completed the predictable image.

Leon almost regretted his arrangement when he first spotted her on the pavement, standing alone by the high brick wall, with fingerless gloves thumbing a mobile, but then realised as a product of his intellect and desires, this was his adorable little girl. And realised how vulnerable she was too, so that he wanted to whisk her away to safety. As she flopped into the front seat of the Carrera and proffered a cheek for him to place his kiss, his attention was drawn to her surprisingly ebullient cleavage that had not been there the last time he looked, which immediately set him wondering whether she was wearing a bra and if she was sleeping with anybody.

She pretended not to like the smell of the tan leather, the smooth quietness of the ride, and said nothing, just tilted back-wards into the soft luxury, showing yards of bare leg. In the mews house she slouched around the rooms looking at the books and the pictures, picking things up and putting them down somewhere else. A large black-and-white photo of Ramona on a far wall caught her attention, and she studied smaller colour pictures of her and the two baby girls taken in various sunny spots of the world that made her smile.

To Jamila, Leon was a giant of a man, physically imposing, intellectual and charismatic. She was never going to be able to match up to him, and was fearful that she disappointed him, although he was careful never to have even hinted as much. His power and his wealth were symbols of his success that she was proud of, and which she readily exploited in her social circle at school to impress, but they were also like heavy yokes around her neck, waiting to restrain her when her achievements failed to reach up to the high standards he had set. She could hardly bring herself to say anything to him, as she wanted to make him work for their friendship – after all, it was he who had left the family home five years ago, meaning her mother had introduced that soppy idiot Simon into their lives; as always, Jamila wanted Leon to pay.

'Jam, there are some nice things in the fridge, salads, some avocados, cheeses, and fruit in the bowl,' he told her. 'Why don't you stop prancing about and make yourself a little something? I've got some J2Os – so help yourself, just while I make this call. It's to the Home Office so I need some quiet here,' he added as he turned off Radio Galaxy at the hi-fi and muted the TV sound.

He took his mobile into his bedroom, where he lay full length with ankles crossed, admiring his brown brogues, and rang Hubert.

'Afternoon, Hue. Can you talk? I'm reporting in as promised.'

'Oh, hello, Leon. Just back in the office.' They chatted briefly but quickly got into business mode.

'Just wanted to bring you up to speed, Hue. I have started on the employment list at the stadium and in the Park. I gather the rotas had staff working in more than one site, so we have to look at all of the people. As you said, there are over sixteen thousand males on the list. Most of them had declared what their previous experience was. There are lots of previous Army, police, other security; their age, racial background, although I don't think that's relevant. So I took an age cut-off, we picked males, ex-Army, ex-police, twenty-five to forty. McIntosh's lot, they worked with LOCOG and they sent me a list of over six thousand. I have looked at it, and I have to say this is impossible. We would have to interview each and every one of them to find out who would have the Iraqi connections, which they might deny. Then to see whether they had other connections, for example to Pamela Collingwood.'

'It might be worth having Collingwood go through the lists with you. He's obviously not going to pick himself out, but if he's innocent, he will provide useful information – after all, he must know some of the Army people in the security business,' concluded Hubert.

'Yes, I agree, I've already told him that. Next, I saw Antonio yesterday, and obtained from him Pamela's mobile phone that one of his Italian friends at the stadium had picked out of her bag for safe-keeping. It was dead but I managed to recharge it with an old one and I've had a quick look at it myself, contacts and messages, and there's nothing special – her friendship with Antonio is obvious now that we know about it. There are no other clues in there – you might get Five to go through the memory store and see if there is anything else deep inside, but I doubt it – could you send a courier over for it?'

'Yes, I'll do that now. You've done well, Leon. I can get the Met to provide the legwork with the employee list, the interviews and so on. So long as they are clear about what they are looking for, and then they alert us to a smaller manageable number. It may produce results. Until we can get some proper forensic evidence, though, we are never going to be able to build a case – without a confession.'

'OK, thanks, Hue. I saw Collingwood and his mother today, but we'll catch up later – I mean, I didn't get a confession out of him or anything.'

He was up and ready to engage with Jamila, just as another call came through on the mobile, from Switzerland, and he spoke to Ramona. 'I miss you, girls,' Leon said in his soppy voice, imagining Ramona's large frame darkly draped over a settee looking out onto his most favourite view in the world, Lac Léman in the distance.

'I miss you too, soldier. I seem to be getting bigger every day.'

'Well you will be, but you've got another three weeks, right?'

'EDD is September 19th. Will you be getting over here for a weekend or something?'

'I'm really caught up on this Olympics investigation, honey pie, they are desperate for a result. They are paying me handsomely, my little angel, so we can have lots more nice trips away in due course. But I need to pack in the hours at the moment, there is so much stuff to get through. I'm starting interviews now, and that always takes longer than one thinks. Give me another week, and then maybe I'll find some free time to get over. I met my number one suspect today. He's going to be a hard nut to crack.'

'Oh, I didn't know you had a suspect already – that's good, right?'

'Oui, oui,' cooed Leon doubtfully; and so the phone call went on, with domestic conversation that pittered and pattered back and forth distractedly for some minutes more, while Leon nibbled on some nearby salad.

In the afternoon, at the Tate Modern roof restaurant overlooking central London, Leon and Jamila settled down to a late lunch at a window table, with impressive London views in every direction. It was bright and lively, with a high customer noise level. Leon had a large glass of Merlot. Jamila, undecided, was partly playing at being vegetarian, but eventually chose tuna in a risotto. 'I hope Mrs Davies is a forgiving soul, Jamila, when she sees you in her polished corridors next term – she's going to spot the piercing holes, you know.'

'I'll sort it.' Thick fringes of black hair flopped over her face. 'The girls are all at it, they can't expel all of us, or anything.' She was a dab hand at jaunty defiance.

'So what's behind it, Jamila, is it like a uniform, or some form of idolatry?' Jamila was slumped, round-shouldered, head down and eyes over her mobile, throughout the meal. 'What?'

'The Gothic look, the studs. I'm just asking. Have you got one in your tongue?' She stuck her tongue out at him, with a wiggle of her head, and it was clear and pink.

'Thank God for that. What about your tummy button?' Half in jest.

'Oh Dad, for God's sake,' she cried, standing up, scraping her chair back, bumping against the table and making the wine glass wobble, and tugging up the lower folds of her top to make a dramatic revelation in the middle of the restaurant.

'OK, OK, Jam, sit down, there's no need to . . . thank you,' catching a glimpse of a soft round belly and deep navel, with tiny silver stud. 'I didn't mean to pry. Sorry.' Leon was not at all embarrassed at the staring faces in the restaurant, actually was rather amused. He took a gulp of his wine and felt pleased that he had embarked on this precarious task, this day of responsible paternal bonding. He admired his blooming daughter for her attractiveness and courage. Despite all the war paint and quirky looks, she was Jamila, which meant beautiful. She had lovely skin and strong facial looks, Leon's determination and intelligence, and, as Leon had just discovered, a perfect body. One day she should make someone a perfect match.

They continued to munch slowly on their mains, Jamila thumbing her phone, still with her woollen gloves on. Leon thought about Collingwood for a moment; he was a shoo-in for the killings, surely, had to be. Leon had built up a mental picture of the man beforehand, and from his first impressions of him, he fitted rather well in reality.

They shared a piece of cheesecake, although Jamila hardly touched her half. Leon had noticed that she was eating sparingly, but was determined not to make a point of saying anything. 'Who are you texting, Jamila? Come on, give it a rest. Talk to me. We get so little time, or chance. Tell me what's happening in your life. Do you have a boyfriend or anything?'

'You wouldn't understand, Dad.' She carried on thumbing.

'Try me.' Nothing. 'So why do so many of you all dress and want to look like some celebrity nuthead, when you are so good looking and attractive in your own right?' She scowled at him. 'These people should have more of a sense of responsibility, they know that the young will want to idolise them, especially with the drugs and the drink.'

'Moralising doesn't suit you, Dad.'

'I mean, they have a moral responsibility to the young people who copy and idolise them, is all I'm saying.'

'Dad, celebrities have no moral responsibility whatsoever to those that copy them. Anyone who cannot find something better to do than idolise a celebrity pop star is a lost cause anyway.'

'It's a tragedy that so many young girls do idolise them.'

They left the restaurant together and wandered around the huge gallery below, eventually Jamila slipping her arm through his, which pleased him. Leon was still pressing Jamila about her work effort and what her aims were. He also acknowledged how well she had done earlier in the year with her exams. 'I always say, when you're tough on yourself, life will be easier on you. I want to see you stretch yourself this coming year, I think you could really make something of yourself. Yeah? Don't let it all go to waste.'

'Your money, you mean – your investment.'

'Yes, if you like, although I would rather think of you as my deserving daughter trying to make the best of her opportunities.'

They returned to the mews in Marylebone, via a gallery in Charlotte Street that Leon liked, and, exhausted, they relaxed with some snacks and the third Daniel Craig/James Bond movie, not yet released, that Leon had downloaded from an illegal website that morning. Jamila would stay over and return home in the morning to make her mother jealous with stories of Leon's exotic lifestyle and wealth.

Leon slept soundly that night, feeling satisfied that he had spent some valuable time with his daughter. She was hard work at the moment, that was for sure, but was capable, single-minded, had first-rate brains and looks, quite like her father, Leon decided. He liked her.

4

Late the next morning, Hubert contacted Leon again by phone, and Leon quickly summarised his interview with Jarvis. 'He denied everything, does not know who or why. As expected.'

'Actually, I wanted to bring you up to date, Leon, but I knew you were with your daughter, and I wasn't sure whether you would welcome an interruption.' *Ever the diplomat, Hubert.*

'That was yesterday. She returned to her mother this morning. But carry on, Hue, please do.'

'OK. Following the Iraqi connection, we have been working with a local news agency in Baghdad and with a contact at Al Jazeera looking for material for us on our friend Abu Masoud. They wired a report through this morning. It seems he was quite a maverick leader of a religious group, a breakaway in Baghdad in the early days, a mostly Sunni group called *Tawhid*, which means Oneness of God, which preached Jihad and was responsible for some horrendous murders, kidnappings and the rest. After the occupation, he was found working as a conciliator for the Mercari regime; he became respectable, worked for the Shia majority government, civil servant. He had been working with their Olympic team and advised on security in London, ironically. He came over with the small Iraqi contingent, was staying in central London. Always had bodyguards with him. He undoubtedly had lots of potential enemies in Iraq, both Sunni and Shia; there must be ex-servicemen who came across him. So any number of people might have wanted to kill him. He had been subject to death threats at home. No family, as far as we can make out – all a bit vague, but here comes the interesting bit. You may remember the David Chigwell kidnapping in September

2004, that resulted in his beheading – it was covered extensively on the news and Al Jazeera showed video clips on live feeds every night for a week, including the final show.' Hubert had been working in the Prime Minister's office at the time and remembered the angst and sense of misery among the staff at Number 10 when it all went wrong. 'David Chigwell was kidnapped along with some American engineers, and he was shown appealing live to Gerry Morley for his release, but it was not to be. Anyway, believe it or not, we think the man that beheaded him on camera was Abu Masoud Zadeh himself.'

Leon was alert and sitting up. 'How certain are you?'

'Well, our man in Qatar says he has seen the original video clips that were shown on TV – they have tapes stored on site. The beheading shows a tall, distinguished man, who removes his head-gear to get a better view of what he was doing, it would seem, and so his face is fully identifiable at the moment of strike. And he fits the description as far as one can tell – though this is eight years ago. We sent our photos of the dead Abu Masoud to Doha, and they have now confirmed a positive match using recognition technology.'

'Can you get all the material they've got couriered back over to us? I will need to see it all. What do we know of the Chigwells? They were living in Britain, do we know where? Who was in the family? Wife, children, parents? We need a briefing, and then we need to pay a visit to the head of family, as soon as.' Leon was energised, feeling that this was a real breakthrough.

'I'm working on this with the Met and MI5. Keep you posted.'

'Here we have a possible motive, Hue. Family of Chigwell seeking revenge. This is great. You're a genius.' Leon had leapt up and was pacing the floor at home. 'Anything to connect Collingwood with the Chigwells?'

'No, but Broderick is fully briefed and his team are starting on that. I'll keep you posted,' he repeated. 'I'll bring all the Iraqi material over tonight, shall I?'

Late on Thursday afternoon in Shoreditch, Leon was shown into a small corner office at SecureLife, just in time to catch his next port of call, Jonathan Collingwood, before he left for home. The company occupied the fourth floor of a building that was two hundred years old and originally used for storage and a trading warehouse, now converted internally with glass partitions and glass doors. Lots of activity could be seen throughout the various rooms, secretaries tapping away at computers, scuttling back and forth, people dropping papers into in-trays, taking papers out of out-trays, phones ringing. The firm's name was etched on the outer glass, and inside the receptionist was blond and cheerful.

'This used to be a tea house – East India Company owned it for export packaging and the like.' Jonathan spoke with an East London accent. 'Smart offices, IT and internet and retail companies in 'ere now. Mostly start-ups.' He had a deep tan. 'Yeah, just got back from a week in Thailand, with the wife and kids, very nice, bloomin' 'ot.'

His office had two windows, neither offering much of a view, just rooftops and dilapidated brick facades, faded and dirty, a few modern tower blocks of steel and glass further in the distance, and Old Street roundabout several hundred yards away to the west of them.

'We're doing all right for a small company. Business is picking up slowly, you know, there's more and more coming onto the books, and more of it is regular stuff, repeat contracts that keep us tickin' over. We took on a lot of staff for the Olympics, which will be cut back after the final Games have finished, but that was always short-term work. New contracts are comin' in all the time. Can't be bad.' Jonathan had a natural confidence and looked pleased with himself. Out the back in the yard, before he came up in the lift, Leon had

had a quick look at the many company vans coming and going, only a couple sitting idle. The man at the glass window on duty said there were more active security jobs on now than before the Games, so maybe Jonathan was telling it the way it was.

'So you had a good Olympics, would you say?'

'Well, yer know, we are still waiting for figures, but first quarter 2012-13 was our busiest, and we have seen enquiries increase four-fold over the last two months.'

'Even though you suffered the worst security breach in UK history?'

'Well, come on, I'm not sure that that can be laid solely at our door, there were many other security companies involved, and the police and the British Army. But we have not come to any harm, let's put it that way.' Jonathan still had a satisfied smile on his face.

'Good. I wanted to talk to you about your brother, Jarvis. As I said before, I'm helping with the enquiry into the stadium shootings, wanting to get a full background, and to understand the incident better. Now obviously your brother was directly involved in the security, especially within the stadium. How did that come about?'

'He worked for me much of the time. I got him involved, I needed the help and his skills.' Jonathan went on to tell Leon about his family, his relations with his brother, the death of Edward in Iraq, and the effect that that had had on their mother and the rest of the family. 'I don't think she has fully recovered. It was a year after Dad had died suddenly of a heart attack, and she took to drinking a bit after that.'

'These vans you have here,' continued Leon, jumping topics, 'Jarvis drive any of them?'

'Yes, he was often out in them, we use them on all our jobs. For the Olympics, we used the bigger transporter vans for the staff each day in and out of the Park, it was the routine.'

'Did Jarvis have access to this building, and to the vans?'

'Yes, he's a senior man here, he has keys and the security codes.'

'So he could come here at any time and select a van and use it for himself?'

'Yes, it would all be logged on the system, time out/time in.'

'And the alarm system?'

'Well, he knew the alarm, the locks to the compound and the automatic gates, so yes, I guess he could.'

'OK. Was Pamela part of the family? I mean, was she respected? Was she liked?' Leon sat in his grey suit in the middle of the room on a hard chair opposite Jonathan, who relaxed in a swivel executive chair behind an ultra-modern glass desk.

'Oh, yes, Mother got on pretty well with 'er, we all liked Pamela.'

'Was she loyal to Jarvis, do you think? Did she have any' – and Leon selected his words carefully from a range that had popped up into view in his mind – 'likes elsewhere, or flings with anybody else? As far as you know?'

At the mention of how everyone loved Pamela, Leon would have said a slight blush had become noticeable on Jonathan's cheeks, had he not been so tanned.

'Not that I knew of. Look, they worked well togevver – I mean, they weren't Brad Pitt and Angelina, but yer know, they was together, ten years or more.'

'No children, was that a problem?'

'I think Pam was good at her job, she wanted to do well in her career, and taking time off for babies would have been a bad idea for her, yer know, with 'er ambitions. I think Jarvis understood that, I don't think he was bleatin'.'

'Do you think there was a problem though, that he never confided in you, about not being able to have children, or anything like that?'

'No way, no way, Jarvis is a big man.'

'Did he have affairs with anyone else, do you know?'

'Not as far as I know, Mr Deshpande.' At first Jonathan was happy to answer questions, pleased to be of help, obviously enjoyed talking about himself and his business, but he was increasingly getting the impression that Deshpande was hostile, looking always for reasons to point the finger at Jarvis. The possibility that Jarvis was involved in the shootings had even started to niggle at the back of his own mind, although Jonathan was certainly not going to share that with this man. 'Now look, I think you ought to direct your questions to Jarvis, and not try to go behind his back.'

'Oh, I have already, don't you worry.' A rather conceited smile broke out across Leon's face. 'Ever heard of Antonio Vitomilecia?'

A frown creased Jonathan's otherwise smooth features. 'No, was he the Italian bloke . . . ?'

'No, he was Pamela's lover,' Leon replied straight-faced. 'Do you remember the David Chigwell incident, the Englishman kidnapped in Iraq in 2004 who was executed by beheading – shown on news videos every night at the time?'

'Yes, vaguely. What's that . . . ?'

'He was executed then by Abu Masoud, the Iraqi shot dead in the Olympic Stadium three weeks ago. Coincidence, do you think?'

'Blimey! This is all news to me.' Jonathan looked genuinely bemused.

'So, was there any reason that you can think of why Jarvis might have been involved in Masoud's execution or might have killed his wife?'

'This is ridiculous. Of course he didn't kill his wife . . .'

'So who did, Jonathan? Who would want to kill this bright, attractive, ambitious woman? In the middle of a public event, with the world watching? More like a punishment – Jonathan, that woman went through an agonising death.' Leon was only barely able to suppress a rising sense of anger in his voice. 'Who would want to do that, do you suppose?'

And Leon obtained the same repetitive answer he had had from everyone else he had asked: 'I don't know. It doesn't make sense. It was an accident.'

After Deshpande had departed, Jonathan was left wondering whether Jarvis had indeed found out about his little fling with Pamela. Poor Pamela. And whether Deshpande had found out too, somehow. Although he was desperate to believe in the innocence of his younger brother, the thought that Jarvis might have pulled off one of the most audacious and murderous attacks in the UK gnawed inside at Jonathan for the rest of the week.

5

Leon Deshpande and Sir Hubert Lansbury arrived in the Range Rover at the address in Wanstead, a small detached corner house overlooking the cricket club, before eight o'clock on Friday morning. They parked round the side in Draycot Road and the back-up squad car stayed on Overton Drive, pulling up fifty yards further on by the church, turning round to face west to watch from a distance and in comfort as the two senior men strolled together up the path to the front door. Weak sun was filtering through low-lying cloud, but neither could feel much warmth on their steadfast faces. Lansbury, clean-shaven and buffed to perfection, presented his usual impeccable appearance, in a matching pale blue shirt and silk tie under his light grey suit, although Deshpande, in regular crumpled light grey with brown brogues, no tie, and a still prominent tan, noticed that today there was no accompanying silk in the breast pocket.

It was Mrs Chigwell who came to the door, in nondescript green and a pair of yellow washing-up gloves, which she hurriedly started tugging off the moment she saw the two gentlemen visitors. She looked startled, became dithery, with some embarrassment in her voice.

Lansbury made their apologies for such an early intrusion, and also did the introductions, showing his ID card, while Deshpande waved his vaguely in her direction. She looked at them but failed to register either of them in her consciousness, so that when her youngest son later asked her who these two officials of the government were, she could tell him neither their correct names nor the exact department they claimed to work for. Only the word 'security' registered with her, and from that moment on she was terrified that something her husband or sons had done was coming home to roost. Such obviously senior figures visiting their humble home in person so early could only indicate the serious nature of the imagined offence.

She showed the two men into a cold reception off the hall that was sometimes used as a dining room, which overlooked an enclosed rim of grass and shrubs bordering the front of the house. When the two sat down on stiff-backed chairs, their view beyond the front garden was completely obscured by a thick laurel hedge, although Leon could still make out the church steeple down the road. There was a slight lingering smell of cooked breakfast, tomatoes and bacon.

They were offered coffee but declined politely. Leon fingered the mobile in his pocket. The emergency call was easy to make, a couple of touches and it was done, the men in the watching car knowing to respond immediately. They both cast their eyes around the room for a while, noting nothing of any interest, apart from a framed colour photograph on the mantel shelf showing a large family grouping of three generations of Chigwells, with two elderly folk sitting and the rest of the clan grouped around behind them, taken on a sunny day, probably in the back garden. Next to it an old Victorian clock ticked quietly.

Mrs Chigwell returned, leading her elderly-looking husband, who was slightly bent, holding a stick and wearing an old jacket, brown cords and carpet slippers, who shuffled in behind her.

Again Lansbury made the introductions, saying they were from the Home Office, and were making enquiries concerning the death of a foreign visitor in this country, thought to be Iraqi. 'I am well aware of your son's ordeal in the hands of kidnappers in Iraq eight years ago, Mr Chigwell, and I profoundly apologise for bringing back painful memories for you. But we are trying to trace someone we think might be able to help us with the enquiries into the

Olympic Stadium shootings.'

'Oh, yes, we were reading about those.' Mr Chigwell seemed to come somewhat to life at this, rather than moping about the tragic events of the past. 'There wasn't much on TV about it. Dreadful events, I'm sure.' And he flopped down into the only armchair in a corner of the room.

'You must be delighted, Mr Chigwell,' volunteered Deshpande with gentle sympathy and a broad smile, 'after all these years.'

'After all these years, delighted, why?' Chigwell asked gruffly. There was a short pause as the two visitors sat down at the table and fidgeted into comfortable positions as best they could.

'To know that the man who killed your son in Baghdad,' Deshpande continued with equal sympathy, 'has himself now been eliminated. After all these years.'

There was another pause, of at least a few seconds, while Chigwell lifted his heavy head and looked doubtfully at Deshpande. 'Really, can you be so sure?'

'Oh, yes, Mr Chigwell. He was one of the victims on that night. To be sure.'

'Do you know his name?' asked Lansbury.

'No, I never read it, I can never pronounce these Arab names.'

Mrs Chigwell had pulled up a wooden chair and sat upright against the wall next to her husband, apparently finding a great deal of interest in her hands, distracting her from the developing subject under discussion.

'It was Abu Masoud Zadeh, and we think he was responsible for David's execution. We have seen pictures and a video recording of the original event,' Lansbury explained. Mrs Chigwell brought a hand up to her open mouth and her shoulders started to shudder. With some embarrassment, Leon and Hubert both avoided looking her way.

'So you must be delighted – revenge at last,' Leon said again with a teasing tone. 'It's been so long, hasn't it, but all the more sweet for the waiting. Difficult to have to think about it all over again, we know,' Leon finished. There was no reply from either of the Chigwells; the old man sat still in a frozen frame, while his wife, thin and grief-stricken, wept silently, shedding no tears.

During a further pause, the faint ticking of the old clock on the mantel became discernible.

'Who do you think might have done such a thing, Mr Chigwell?' Lansbury asked.

'I, I don't know – what makes you think I should know?'

'It would have to be someone with supreme shooting skills, ex-Army perhaps?' explored Leon. 'What regiment was your other son in?'

'Paul? The Household.'

'He was a good shot, was he?'

'No, not particularly. What are you implying?'

Lansbury cut in straight away. 'Have you heard of Jarvis Collingwood?'

Arthur Chigwell suddenly moved his head and gazed sharply straight at Lansbury; his mouth opened to speak but he checked himself at the last second. 'Er, no, I don't think so.'

'You didn't hire this man, this ex-Army sniper, to assassinate Abu Masoud for revenge?'

'What nonsense! No, certainly not.'

'What would it have taken, I wonder? How much money would a job like that command, in your world, Mr Chigwell?'

'What are you implying?' the old man asked again, looking flustered. His crinkly cheeks were infusing with a slow flush, and the network of veins over his nose looked more prominent. His unkempt eyebrows gave his face an angry look. Leon fished out the black-and-white photo from his pocket, as he had done before with Antonio, and stood up to pass it across Chigwell's vision for his reaction. But Arthur Chigwell was good at this, and not a twinge of recognition when he saw the image of the young shooter he had hired so many months ago could be observed in his lined old face. 'I have never seen this man. Dorothy?' And he passed it across to his wife, twisting painfully in his chair and looking sternly at her. She stopped whimpering for a second or two and then, with a shake of her head, she handed it back.

The two men left the Chigwells soon after, having obtained the contact details for both of their sons, Paul and Ainsley, explaining that they would be interviewed as soon as possible so as to eliminate them from the enquiries. Deshpande was sure that Arthur Chigwell had recognised the name of Collingwood, even though he put on a convincing act when shown the photograph.

Jarvis Collingwood spent much of that Friday in the interview room at Bow Road Station, a room he had become boringly familiar with, looking through the thousands of names of men listed as employees of the London Olympic Organisation, in the presence of various junior detectives and minor officers from Broderick's office who were rotating around the clock, feeding him with tasteless sand-wiches from the canteen and equally tasteless tea and biscuits from their lockers. Broderick had called him first thing, before sending a car round to bring him across. The session ended at around four o'clock, by which time he had had enough, having offered up a list of about thirty names.

And the next day, the routine was much the same, finishing around midday, with a list of another twelve possibles. These were men under forty years of age with army or police experience whom Jarvis felt would probably have the necessary skills. On each day he pointed out repeatedly that singling them out like this was pure guesswork, as there was not enough detail about any of them and there were gaps in the data, some columns remaining blank. He was relying on his recognition of their names or his knowledge of their reputations, although he did know quite a few of them personally.

He became bored with it all very quickly, but went through the motions to give the impression that he was cooperating, and managed to give the police a few plausible names that would occupy them and distract them from further investigating him.

Leon interviewed each Chigwell brother separately on Saturday morning, with one of Broderick's team and a solicitor present each time. They arrived at Scotland Yard together and were directed to the fifth floor and a small waiting area on a landing, where a machine churned out some not unreasonable coffee. But they were called in to the interview room one at a time, and the routine was the same for both.

Background questions about the family and their own lifestyle were followed by more personal questions about David, their older brother, how much they remembered of him and the events surrounding his death. Paul, in a clean white shirt and black leather jacket, appeared restless and uncomfortable; he became upset at a discussion of the events in Baghdad that led up to his brother's beheading, and said he could not see any connection with the Olympic shootings. He had never heard of Jarvis Collingwood, except what he had picked up in the newspapers.

'So what would your father have paid to gain revenge, once he found out who was responsible?'

'That's out of the question,' Paul said firmly, and would not listen to any more questions about his father, who he said was not well, with chronic respiratory problems.

On the other hand, Ainsley, also in a white shirt, with a pair of jeans, showed no particular upset at the discussion of his older brother's death, which he said was a long time ago when he was quite young. 'I didn't know David well at all actually – to be honest, I can hardly remember him,' he said vaguely with a flick of his hair off his forehead and a sense of confidence that Deshpande found irritating.

Giving Ainsley a cursory glance, Deshpande calmly asked: 'When did your father recruit Jarvis Collingwood to do his revenge work for him?'

'What?' Ainsley had a huge grin on his young face, as if hearing a joke, waiting for the punchline. 'You are joking. My father is an unwell man, he has never recovered from the Iraq events. He would not have anything to do with anything like that.'

'How do you know? Could he have found and recruited Collingwood on his own, without you and Paul being involved?'

'Look, I don't think my father would ever consider such things, he is an honourable man, fought for his country in the South Atlantic. We have absolutely no connection with these events. This is ludicrous.' And he looked in a pleading way towards the other men in the interview room as if willing them to support what he was saying.

In the end Deshpande did not get anything particularly helpful from the two brothers. If they were involved in any way, they had rehearsed their lines well and had been able to keep any guilt out of their expressions. Although he did have their alibis for the night of the shooting checked out.

Meeting up at London Bridge Station on Sunday evening, Jarvis and Danny chatted over a couple of pints in The Oast House before Danny had to catch his train.

'I'm heading home, need to see the wife,' he told Jarvis. He looked tired and defeated, fiddling with the cap he had in his hand, although he tried to make out with a little show of bravado that he was still on top of things. 'Betty has been great, but she was getting proper fed up in that pub, not much reward, she wants more of a future. And I don't think I'm the one to give it 'er. She called her husband back, we had a bit of a carry on.'

'You didn't hit him, did you, Danny?' Jarvis had to suppress the desire to laugh as he visualised the scene.

'Nah, it were fine, but any road, decision was I was to leave, and now I've got to make it up at 'ome, so I'm off to face the music.' Danny managed a forlorn smile and a shrug of his big shoulders. 'Yes, 'tis pity about work at Beacon Forest. Lord Stonebridge has put it on hold for a few months, but likely as not he'll call us back when he's ready. So we might all get back together to finish job. The site's been left unattended at the moment, locked up like. But weeds'll be growin' about them caravans.' Danny said he was sorry to hear of Jarvis's loss. 'Such a tragedy, such a proper lady, that Pamela, and you workin' at stadium an' all.'

They parted in good spirits and promised to be in touch. Danny never once questioned Jarvis's story or thought for a minute that Jarvis had anything directly to do with the events.

A little later, in the darkness of late evening, Jarvis descended from the station at Bethnal Green. Kept warm by a thick zip-fronted hoody, he walked fast along Three Colts Lane, watching his back and taking some roundabout turnings. He saw nobody loitering or acting in a suspicious way; in fact there were few people about at all. He walked round to the main street to find a corner shop on Cambridge Heath Road, for a pasty, an apple and a fizzy drink.

His place was poorly lit. He ambled over, walked passed a few other arches and stood still in the shadows of the brick walls, motionless and watching for a while. A couple of oily mechanics were tinkering with an old banger in the road fifty yards away, leaning under the bonnet with torches. He turned back to his enclosed cul-de-sac and approached number 208, munching on his apple. He punched in the security code and the door opened inwards into darkness, chill and the musty smell of damp. Everything looked safe and like no one had been tampering with anything. He closed and locked the door and drew a heavy black curtain across so no light from inside would show around the edges.

He moved instinctively to the centre of the space and switched on the table lamp. The place was really cold. But he managed a smile, for the first time for three weeks. He was alone and among the things he treasured. He had access to his other identity and cash, if he wanted. His hidden weapons were in the cupboard next to the table. His old mobile phone was there, fully charged and available for use.

He sat drinking his cola, eating his pasty, savouring the moment. He felt less tired than he had for a while and he took that as an early sign of his recovery from all the emotional turmoil of the last three weeks. He started thinking lustfully about Naomi.

That Deshpande bloke had tried to be threatening, but really he knew nothing. He had no evidence, there were no forensics. Jarvis just had to keep quiet, stick it out a bit longer and they would soon get fed up and withdraw the surveillance on him – it must be costing them a whack. Deshpande was a bit of a dandy – he could outsmart him, outfight him too. *What kind of name was that, anyway?*

The noise of a train rumbling overhead lasted a full minute and the metal doors and shutters rattled, as flakes of dislodged dirt floated down from the ceiling. Jarvis surveyed the filthy brickwork high above him in the dark and into the shadowy corners at the back. His escape doorway was obscured by boxes and old tyres. He wiped his hands clean on a small towel. He was toying with the reserve mobile. Finally he switched it on, when the rumbling and rattling had all settled and the usual deathly quiet had returned, waiting for a series of bleeps. He selected 'menu' and, flicking through the list of messages, found a few from Ainsley:

25 July 2012 16:18. *Games starting soon – looking forward to events with excitement. Dad sends good luck!* Bloody cheek.

13 Aug 2012 08:14. *What a party last night. You want to talk?*

13 Aug 2012 18:45. *Where are you? Safe? Give me a call.*

14 Aug 2012 08:32. *Bloody hell. What have you done, mate? If you need any help, call me. Let me know where you are.*

15 Aug 2012 14:35. *Nothing from you – do you want me to call round at 208? Let me know.*

15 Aug 2012 18:32. *Still nothing. Have you scarpered? Job well done, by the way. Good luck.*

Jarvis paused. There was one more, a more recent one:

1 Sept 2012 19:02. *Need to talk. Interviewed by Mr Leon Deshpande today, awkward questions. Told him nothing. Need an action plan.*

He called Ainsley by hitting the 'reply' button, leaving a voice-mail message when he didn't pick up. The Chigwells were his weak link, so communicating with Ainsley remained risky, but while no one knew of his 'other' mobile he was confident it was not going to be traced. He finished his drink, slowly playing for time before ringing Naomi. Suddenly feeling nervous, he nipped outside cautiously in the dark to pee against a wall in a far shadowy corner. The two mechanics had gone.

Returning, he wiped off all of Ainsley's texts. There were dozens of texts from Naomi, some before August 12th, lots in the week after, but then they started drying up. There was one dated three days ago:

30 Aug 2012 17:05. *Josh, hi. Where r u? I have new phone (good I kept your number in purse) so maybe u have not had my txts. I have been worried so. Please txt me something. Please come round. I am thinking u have disappeared off the face – has it been so awful with me? Oh Josh,*

where are u? Hope u call soon. I will wait. Bye. xx

Two kisses. Poor Naomi. He continued to fiddle with the gadget, uncertain what to do. She must have been feeling desperate. He did not want to hear her voicemails or read her text messages. Instead he found her contact number at home. He waited, heard the ringing tone and then a click as the phone was picked up.

'Hello,' and she started to recite the number.

'Naomi, hi,' he interrupted.

She instantly recognised the voice, but could not speak for a moment. 'Josh? Is that . . . ?' Her voice was faint and crackly. 'Oh, heavens . . .' She found it difficult to pronounce his name.

'Yes, hi, Naomi. It's me. Sorry. You all right?'

'Yes, yes, where have you been? Are you OK?' She sounded weepy. 'I've been so worried.'

'I'm fine.'

'Where are you?

'I'm in London, home. I wanted to see you – I need to explain, I know, it's been three weeks.' Jarvis sounded so matter of fact, he needed to soften it, have more sympathy in his tone.

'So what have you been doing, where have you been, Josh, you can't just walk out and not say anything.' Naomi would move from tearful to angry if she was not careful.

'I know you're cross, you've every right, but I was doing something very important, a bit secretive, I couldn't tell you. I didn't want to endanger you. Let me explain, I can't say any more on the telephone, let's meet up.'

Josh sounded plausible and eager, and Naomi was wondering whether she had jumped to the wrong conclusions. 'Josh, it's late. Maureen is here. I'm working early tomorrow. It's late,' she repeated. Although she was desperate to see him again, her suppressed anger instinctively told her she needed him to wait and see her at her convenience. And he was not offering anything himself.

319

'By the time you got here, you know; come round tomorrow, can you, after work?'

'Yes, OK. All right.' Jarvis was relieved that Naomi had suggested tomorrow – he felt he needed another day to prepare himself. 'I'll meet you at the hairdresser's. Around four o'clock. Tomorrow, yes?'

'Yes, OK. You sure you're all right?'

'Yes, really. I miss you.'

'Bye then.'

'Naomi, I'll tell you everything tomorrow.'

When Naomi heard her flat phone ring, she was thinking about going to bed. She was already in pyjamas, her glasses sliding down her nose, curled up in an old armchair with a magazine and an American TV soap on that Maureen and Mickey were watching. She thought about not answering, she couldn't be bothered. But flashing up in her mind came Josh's image, with his big blond head and prickly beard, and she could never explain why, but she knew it was going to be him. During his three weeks' absence, after he had just vanished from her life without warning, she had felt like a bereaved wife, lost in a vacuum of nothing. She had no useful thoughts, no desire to do anything, no ability to concentrate on anything, finding nothing around her of interest. What thoughts she had were more about the awful things she must have done to send him away. She felt pathetic and useless, and sometimes angry, having a few rows with Maureen.

When she heard his voice, she squeaked with delight, surprise and fear at the same time. She held the phone with a shaking hand. Afterwards she realised how relieved she was. He was safe and he was alive and he sounded plausibly sorry. She really thought he had just had enough of her and walked away. But it was the last day of the Olympics when they had last seen each other, and there had been all that fuss over the shootings in the stadium.

For days the papers had been full of it, and at the shop so many people talked about it, everyone with different opinions as to how it was done and who it might be. She noted that nobody had been arrested and then started reading some of the headlines on the dailies that were delivered to the shop. She knew that the former British Prime Minister and his wife had been among those murdered, which was horrifying. She read in one paper a full list of the victims' names and the outcomes of their injuries, but they meant nothing to her. She fairly dismissed the incident from her mind, and continued to think either that Josh was being pressurised to stay with his wife, who must have found out about Naomi, or that Josh had just suddenly got fed up with her and had ended the whole thing the only way he knew. Lacking the courage to face her directly, he had just walked out, presumably unable to give her a proper reason. Either way, she was stunned and, for days, tearfully miserable.

But maybe Josh was connected in some way to the shooting. Naomi knew that he had been on duty as a security guard that morning, and that all of the security staff were under such pressure and had been, for a concentrated three weeks during the events, seemingly on high alert most of the time. He said on the phone he was doing something important, secretive he said – presumably to do with security in some way. Maybe they had all been kept at the stadium on duty ever since, not allowed out until they had solved the mystery and found the killer. No, that couldn't be right, he would have been able to call her at least.

For three dull anti-climactic weeks she had struggled to keep it together, working without enthusiasm, staying in alone in the evenings, ignoring her other friends, loafing around disconsolately over the weekends. Now she was all of a dither, not knowing whether to feel absolutely happy that her man had returned and wanted to see her or completely miserable for being treated so badly and being plunged back into a doomed relationship that was inherently destined to fail.

Tomorrow Josh was going to tell her everything to her face, one way or the other.

6

Jarvis had not slept at all well on his camp bed in the lock-up, for all sorts of reasons: he was uncomfortable, being too big for the narrow-framed structure, with its thin mattress; he was cold, with the oil heater turned off and only a single blanket to pull over himself; and the reverberating noises of trains that trundled overhead seemed to rock the whole structure. After each train had passed, millions of tiny flakes of soot floated down from the high brick ceiling and girders above, so he found himself covered in a dirt layer by the morning.

He had set the alarm for seven o'clock and tried to ready himself for the day ahead. He was cold and hungry. He lit the heater for a short while. There was nowhere to wash or shave, he pissed in the shrub area out the back, wore the same clothes. He snacked on apples and bread and milk left over from yesterday. He found yesterday's papers to read and played stupid games on an old Nintendo.

Ainsley arrived just after eight o'clock, knocking and rattling at the door. Jarvis went over with a heavy metal bar in his hand, before cautiously opening it.

'Well, Jarvis, what a hero you are – and nobody allowed to know!'

Ainsley slipped past Jarvis into the gloomy space, noting the iron jemmy he was holding, while Jarvis peeked cautiously out over the yard and along the road back under the railway bridges, satisfied that there was nothing there. He bolted the door, pulled the black curtain across, and put the heavy bar back down beside the door jamb, before turning on a light.

'You were safe, no one following?'

'Why would they?' Ainsley, looking spruce in tight pin-striped grey suit with waistcoat, white shirt and spotted tie, stood by the

323

central table surveying the warm lair and admiring the presence of his superhero, the specialist sniper.

'Sorry about the smell – it's the oil, but at least it's a bit warmer now. I can't offer you anything either,' Jarvis apologised, but Ainsley held up a plastic carrier bag that looked heavy; inside, two cans of lager. They sat opposite each other and ripped the pulls with a fizz. 'A bit early, I know, but . . . cheers. Congrats. Job well done. How you doin', eh? You're looking a bit thinner, mate. Still keeping the fuzz at bay?' Ainsley seemed worried, as though he begrudged his companion's success.

'So far. They have no evidence.'

'You are one hell of a cool bastard, do you know that?' laughed Ainsley with that characteristic flick of his fringe. 'Dad was impressed.'

Jarvis nodded, saying nothing.

'Why did you have to take out the others? It has made the whole thing a damn sight more complicated. Your wife? Why, Jarvis?' Ainsley looked bemused.

'Business I needed to complete. Your father paid up for the rest. Listen, Deshpande is a new dude on the investigation, keeps saying he is not police. He's an ex-soldier. Don't underestimate him. What he ask you about?' Jarvis was edgy now, his leg nervously bouncing under the table.

'Asked if I had ever heard of Jarvis Collingwood; told me that the Iraqi shot dead was Abu Masoud, who had beheaded my brother eight years ago. Did I see a connection with the shootings and was my father seeking revenge?'

'He will keep plugging away, be careful.'

'He and another civil service chap were at my parents' house on Friday morning. So they are moving fast. They demanded information about the business and the accounts, took some books away and other things were collected by the uniform.' Ainsley flicked the fringe off his face, as if to say sod them, they know nothing. 'Your money should be coming through in different lumps over the next few weeks, all right?'

'Yes, I had noticed.'

'Rich bastard, as well!' laughed Ainsley again.

Suddenly Jarvis realised he did not trust the Chigwells not to spill the beans if put under pressure. He made it clear to Ainsley that he would show the police any evidence he had that would implicate the Chigwells as being just as responsible for the shooting as he was, if he was caught. Ainsley said he understood, no need to worry, nothing to fear from his father. 'Apart from being a man of his word, he was rather good at playing the dead-pan know-nothing game – he had experience from the Cold War in East Germany in the 1980s,' Ainsley said with a triumphant flick of his hair, before downing the last of his beer.

Jarvis was more concerned that Arthur might send in a hit man to silence him.

'I'm going to move out of town for a few days; I want you to watch my back for me. Let me know if there are any new developments. Text me. Just don't let me down, Ainsley; and I won't let you down.'

'Where are you going?' Ainsley tried to sound unconcerned.

'Never you mind.'

He returned to the house at Baring Street later, slipping in over the back wall and through the kitchen door, although he reckoned the unmarked car that he regularly sneered at was gone. He saw no signs of it at either end of the street; maybe only temporarily gone. That did not make him immediately pleased, just more aware that the watchers had probably been moved back to a more distant point and were operating from inside a safe house or somewhere, with clever electronic and telescopic equipment.

A few hours later, his nervousness building up, he was preparing himself for his walk up to the hairdresser's to meet Naomi at around four o'clock when the roar of a car engine close by in the street, followed by the slamming of a door, drew his attention. A moment later, his own front-door bell buzzed, and when he saw Deshpande standing solidly at his threshold in his ruffled suit and with his apparently kindly face, Jarvis had to dig deep to maintain his control and nonchalant attitude.

He eyed him studiously, saying nothing, and Leon smiled back. 'Sorry. I know I'm barging in. But I was in the area and I wanted to ask you some more questions.'

Liar.

'Would you mind?'

'No, come in. I was about to go out, but, hey. Alone this time?' He saw no uniform standing sentry on the pavement.

'Yes, spur of the moment. I won't keep you long.'

They both walked into the front room, cluttered and airless, an ironing board on one side under a mound of clothing, used plates lying on surfaces, a few geraniums in pots looking tired, their curled leaves and red petals shed onto the carpet. The curtains were only half drawn, not much daylight coming in, and the room felt chilly with a sense of neglect.

'I know how difficult it is when the lady of the house leaves or there's an accident like this,' said Leon, with sympathy. 'It's hard to keep on top of things, keep up the routine.'

For appearances' sake, Jarvis had left pictures in place, and all of Pamela's things were still in the house, her clothes in the wardrobes and chests, her coats hanging in the hall, everything; he figured it was important that he left them where they were for the time being, though he was itching to dispose of them all. The place was a mess, but it gave the right impression under the circumstances. He pushed some clothes aside for Leon to sit down on one of the chairs. 'Sorry,

I must clear up sometime.'

Ignoring the chair, Leon wandered over to the window to look out over the quiet street. 'You were out all night last night, Jarvis, not at home – mind if I ask where you have been?'

Jarvis stood still in the centre of the room. 'Erm, I slept away, spent the night with a girl I know in town.' So Deshpande must have kept his watchers on duty somewhere nearby, in a car further back perhaps, or street walkers.

Deshpande turned with a quizzical look on his face. Then he quickly reverted to investigator mode. 'I went to see an old man called Arthur Chigwell last Friday. Now he's an interesting chap. I bet he could tell a story or two.' Leon was testing him, wondering whether Jarvis might have been contacted with an early warning, but he detected not a flicker in Jarvis's calm expression.

'Is this another of your ploys, Mr Deshpande. Arthur who?'

'I think he will talk. Arthur Chigwell, father of David Chigwell, innocent British engineer beheaded in Baghdad in 2004. You must be aware of the story, an Iraq veteran like you?'

'Not really.' He had a confused expression across his face and sat down, but remained alert in a sort of crouch, waiting for more revelations.

'If not Arthur himself, then one of his sons will, or even his wife. Have you met Arthur Chigwell? Did he offer you a chance to earn lots of money, perhaps? A chance for him to exact revenge for his son's murder eight years ago?'

'What are you blathering on about?' Jarvis almost shouted, unable to keep the anger out of his raised voice, its tremulousness giving him away. *Deshpande is fishing. All right, so they can name Abu Masoud and they know he executed David Chigwell. But they have no evidence to link me with that.*

'They only have to admit that they recognise you, that you came to the house, or met up with them somewhere. Even if we don't find the money.' Leon just wanted to stay long enough to put the seeds of worry into Jarvis's head. 'Ainsley your coordinator, organiser? He get you the rifle?' There was no reply. 'I'll leave you with those thoughts, Jarvis – if you remember anything about the Chigwells, you have my number. I'll leave my card here in case you have misplaced it.' He snapped a stiff white card onto a side table and moved out of the room, heading back to the front door. 'I'll see myself out,' he called. 'See you soon, Jarvis.'

Jarvis watched from the front window. And was not in the least surprised to see Deshpande drive himself away in a red Porsche.

He should have set out by now to meet Naomi as promised, but there was something worrying him about Deshpande. His supreme confidence and outward affability made Jarvis feel vulnerable. Did he know more than he was letting on? Had he set a trap? He was playing a game of hide-and-seek, planting thoughts in his head, observing his reaction, hoping to press Jarvis into panic. Jarvis might be feeling paranoid but he was convinced that Deshpande would have placed some watchers on his street, not uniform to alarm him, but ordinary-looking folk doing ordinary-looking things. He knew that Deshpande wanted him to become complacent, lazy. Then he might make a mistake. If he headed up to Naomi's place now he would run the risk of giving the whole thing away.

Instinctively he felt like leaving town tonight, like he told Ainsley, under cover of darkness. But then he had a security job that he was doing for Jonathan tomorrow. He would stay this night, since they knew he was here already, but tomorrow night after dark, he could climb the back wall, pick up the Astra a few streets away, with an overnight bag and some food, then he could spend a couple of nights at Witan Street and head south to Beacon Forest later, where he could sleep in one of the caravans, keeping himself away from danger for the time being.

Naomi spent the day in a whirl of nervous excitement and worry, unable to concentrate, not listening properly to what people said to her, missing comments, not paying enough attention to her customers, trembling at times when she thought of what she and Josh might say to each other. She repeatedly imagined him dismissing her and angrily sending her away. She had to shake her head physically to bring herself back to the present. As the time drew nearer she became a little more calm, telling herself how kind and sensitive Josh was. But as four o'clock came and passed, with no sign of Josh, she became more nervous and agitated.

The shop closed just before 5 p.m. as usual, with a quick clean up around the surfaces and the floor, a gathering up of all clothes and coats, and finally Johnnie bringing the shutters down, locking up behind them. There was no sign of Josh. Naomi called goodnight to her workmates. She wandered slowly along Upper Street trying not to get angry or end up weeping, ignoring the noise of the traffic and the people rushing past her or towards her on their way to destinations of their own. She envied their apparent purposeful activity. She slumped in a heap against a wall near the Angel aimlessly watching the faces passing by and tried desperately to think what to do. A dog came by sniffing around her ankles. An old woman with a deep brown leathery face and dressed in layers of tatty clothing with a supermarket trolley stood for ages staring and muttering at her, waiting for a donation. Naomi rang Josh's mobile number again, but there was no answer; the call was blocked, the phone switched off.

Maybe he had got held up, could not call and was on his way, she thought, and so rapidly retraced her steps back to the shop to see whether he might be waiting there. But there was no one. Anger bubbled up in her chest, for all the build-up and the hope, for her being taken in by Josh, the handsome rake. He probably had no intention of leaving his wife, probably had a string of other girls, how was she to know? Why had he picked her up in the first place? She was beginning to question so many of his actions, reading all sorts of obscure meanings into them as her imagination got the better of her. Tears were starting to sting her eyes, her chest heaving a few times. Blinking released the floodgates, warm drops trickling down her face, drawing little notice or sympathy from the busy passers-by.

Should she wait or give up and go home? She would go round to her girlfriend's flat later. Celia was sensible and would put a positive spin on it, that was what Naomi needed. She phoned her on her way home and Celia sounded pleased, confirming that she was in all evening and that they could spend some time together, get a Chinese maybe. By the time Naomi reached her flat, she was footsore and tired. Desperate, she went over and over in her mind her fragile connections with Josh, increasingly aware, as the interval since they were last together grew ever longer, that her role in this sorry tale had become painfully tenuous.

She washed, changed and tried to look her best in black leggings and leather jacket, putting on a new bright face before setting out for Celia's, a ten-minute walk away. They greeted each other with hugs and giggles. Celia, a little older than Naomi, worked at the big hospital in Highgate. She had cropped blond hair in stark contrast to her friend and was dressed in tight white jeans and a white lacy top, with a sleeveless denim waistcoat. With Taylor Swift playing in the background and small glasses of wine and crisps to hand, they settled down in the sitting room among beanbags and cushions, and Celia asked directly what was troubling her friend.

With an instant wet-eyed whimper and a tremble of her lip, Naomi confessed that she had not seen Josh for nearly four weeks now and she was distraught that he had probably abandoned her, and without a word of warning. She filled the story in with some more detail, between more shrugs and embarrassed wide-mouthed smiles, wiping mascara in smears across her cheeks. Celia fetched some more tissues and topped up their wines, before settling down on the floor again at Naomi's feet, resting her arm and head on Naomi's folded knees and looking directly into her friend's face.

Celia was a practical girl, kind and unselfish without any pretensions. She had always been able to avoid any deep involvement with men, apparently just having fun and being able to move on whenever. 'You poor thing. Men can be such bastards.' She made the first syllable sound short and venomous, like they did up north. 'They're all the same.'

'But he may be caught up somewhere,' Naomi was insisting. 'It must be to do with this shooting business at the Olympics. What if he is involved in chasing and following the killer and he has not been able to get away?'

Celia twisted her head round and cocked her eye, looking quizzically into Naomi's eyes. 'And not get a *single* message to you?'

'But he rang me yesterday.'

'And then did not turn up tonight. He's playing with you, Naims. I think you have to decide now whether this guy is right for you, and worth pursuing – in which case I will help you, of course I will – or like, is a complete bastard and you should give up on him and like, not reply to any more calls. And move on, Naims, that's the thing. You know, there are other fish out there.'

'But he's so nice, he's such a hunk, we have been so close. I thought he really wanted me.' Her sobbing breast heaved some more and Celia had her arms round her neck.

'Come on, darling, no more crying. There there. It's true, he is pretty hot, we girls have all said that, you were so lucky with him, we thought. But then so many other women think he's hot, and maybe he can't keep his hands off other women, and he's been lured away, not that like there are other women as super as you, Naims, but you know what men are like. Fresh bit of nooky tempts them, a bit of cleavage and they want to get their leg over, even when they have all the comforts that they need right in front of them at home. They just can't help it.'

Naomi had to admit that she still did not know where Josh lived with Pamela, that he had managed by a series of excuses to avoid revealing anything useful on the home front. 'I don't know where to look, around Hoxton somewhere, I mean I've thought about walking the streets.'

'Come to think of it,' said Celia brightly, 'is Pamela real? Have you seen her or a photograph of her? Suppose he was using this fictitious character to play you along?'

'I really don't want to think of any more gloomy possibilities. I just need to find him.'

'We don't know what effect his wife might be having, especially if she had discovered the two of you. Might she have tied him up, chained him to a four-poster, and thrown away the key? She pleasures him every night and won't let him go – maybe she suspected there was another woman and she has imprisoned him . . .'

'Celia, are you letting your imagination run away a little bit?'

'Sorry.' Celia gulped the rest of her wine down. Naomi sipped hers more delicately. Celia grabbed a handful of crisps and stuffed them into her open mouth from her palm. Naomi took one small piece from the packet and popped it onto the top of her tongue, before gently swallowing.

'I think we should either set off into darkest Hoxton,' said Celia, turning over their possible courses of action in her mind, 'to roughly where you think he is living, and find his car, the red Astra, yes? Then we look through all the windows nearby until we see him. And just knock on his door and confront him.' She paused, a wide-eyed expression on her face, with brows raised and hands splayed sideways in a mock quizzical pose. 'Or,' and she paused again while she thought of an or, 'we could go to the local police and report a missing person. They can be very good at finding missing persons.' Naomi looked sceptical. 'We don't have to tell them much, but at least they would be looking, and there may be a simple explanation.'

They both sank back against the settee and were lost in their personal thoughts for a while, contemplating Celia's two choices of action. 'Have you got a photograph?'

Sir Hubert Lansbury, in need of company and intelligent conversation, drove himself in his white Jaguar to the mews house in Marylebone to call on Leon, unannounced. Leon at the front door looked fresh and alive in the fading daylight.

'Hue, dear boy. What a nice surprise. Come on up. I was just thinking of you. Let me put some coffee on – you look as if you could do with some.'

By contrast, Hubert looked vaguely dishevelled, in an open-necked shirt and casual jacket. His hair was ruffled, the day's facial growth unattended. He seemed worn out and Leon frankly wondered whether he had been overdoing the drink.

They were in the long lounge, with music playing and subdued lighting. 'Sit yourself down, I won't be a minute,' said Leon.

Hubert as usual enjoyed sinking into soft leather and allowed the pleasant atmosphere of the place to envelop him. He closed his eyes for a moment and listened to the less-than-familiar operatic work that he was sure Leon would wax lyrical about in due course. 'Don't tell me, I'll guess,' he called out, but after some minutes he admitted that he was stumped, unable to name the powerful soprano or the composer.

Leon returned with two cups and the newly brewed coffee in a jug. 'No?' Leon was teasing him. 'Give up?' Hubert shrugged regretfully. 'Stabat Mater, Pergolesi, and it's Dorothea Röschmann singing. What a voice.'

'Absolutely.' Both men looked warily at the familiar pile of papers stacked at one end of the long table, where Leon had obviously been working. There was a half-empty wine glass nearby and a plate with crumbs on. They sipped at their coffee.

'Is there any news that we need to catch up on?'

Hubert put his gold-framed glasses on and was trying desperately not to reach for his cigarettes. Despite his appearance, when Leon might have expected Hubert to be rather slow and vague, he actually warmed to his task and showed his usual sharpness and firm grasp of his subject. 'The stadium pipe. The cut, almost certainly a power drill, jigsaw type, taped cleverly back in position, disguised. Probably used as a storage place for the killer's rifle, it's wide enough. No fingerprints, no evidence of DNA or anything else nearby. He had constructed a sort of grille with coat-hanger wire across the inside of the pipe to stop big objects from sliding through, but smaller things he could have pushed down the pipe. But nothing else found – certainly not the weapon. They had engineers examine that pipe all the way to the ground level.'

'Broderick still smarting that he didn't make the discovery earlier?'

'Oh yes.' A rare smile came over Hubert's face, although he seemed distant. 'The Chigwells are an interesting family, into all sorts of businesses, trying to be respectable, quite well-off, with connections in Europe. For example, they have an import-export business, car parts and engineering; they have offices at Tilbury Docks and Hamburg and Zeebrugge, all convenient ports for moving things around the UK and the Continent, if you don't want them to be seen. Well-known black-market-activity hotspots. They've influence around the East End, hire car, transport, some retailing. Mostly cash in hand, but it all looks reasonably kosher. The sons are in various businesses, gradually taking over from the ageing father, it would seem. Paul is in head office mostly, Ainsley seems to do logistics and transport.'

'We need to find a money trail. If they brought in the rifle and offered other support for Jarvis, or whoever, and then paid for the work, you're talking what? Fifty thousand, one hundred thousand? What's the going rate for assassination these days? Is it more for an ex-politician?'

'We're looking at their accounts, tax returns, and so on, but it can all be lost among everything else – I mean these are not your usual domestic shopping bills; the payments would have been split into small quantities, losable and mostly cash, I imagine.'

'Yeah. OK, I can report on my second Collingwood interview: nothing! I was planting the Chigwell story, saying I thought they might talk, asked him direct if he had met with any of them. He was his usual cool, denying he had heard of them. Hubert, I will admit to you, since the Met called off their men, I have put my own watchers in the area, although I'm not hopeful of anything; it's so difficult to do properly. I mean, you would need three or four cars and six watchers and walkers – and he would spot them, he is good.'

'How many?'

'It's all right, I have contacts, it's through the private agency and I'll be paying, but I'm hoping it will only be a week, two at the most. I have one old black Audi, two couples sharing, twelve-hour shifts. As I say, I'm not hopeful, but I felt we needed something there.'

'Yes, I agree with you, but McIntosh has some new leads supplied by Collingwood from the employee lists – a number of suspect characters who got through the vetting onto the security detail – quite how is astonishing, but there are some dodgy blokes on that list. They've already had three or four men interviewed, and some lines of enquiry are being pursued – we wait and see. But he is not convinced about Jarvis Collingwood as a suspect.'

'The man's a fool.'

'How reliable is Collingwood anyway, in terms of providing leads, given that as far as you and I are concerned, he remains our prime and only suspect?' Hubert asked.

'Oh, totally unreliable, Hue – nothing about him stands up to any reasonable examination. So, I did some cross-checking today with two other ex-servicemen that I was put in touch with. Both these guys are Iraq veterans, neither have had anything to do with the Olympics, one's a sports fitness trainer and the other is breeding dogs in the West Country or something. Both knew Jarvis Collingwood. They independently confirmed his role in Iraq and his service history, his reputation as a soldier and the fact that he's an excellent shot, loyal, hard-working, extremely fit; neither would entertain the idea that he might have been responsible for the shootings. However, they both confirmed that they thought he could do it from a skills point of view, but said that he just was not the sort of bloke, he was a normal tough soldier with a huge sense of loyalty to the men around him, his regiment and his country.'

They both nodded to each other, absorbing what was said. 'Leon, well done, good work. These statements need to be in the incident file.'

'They are'

'So all right, we still do not have any other favourites, then? These two Army boys, did they venture any other names?'

'No, to them, all ex-servicemen are heroes.'

'Yes, well that fits the usual picture.'

'I've also got an updated summary from Officer Fisher at Scotland Yard,' Leon continued. 'He's been helping me go through all the direct line messages, over five thousand of them – but there is nothing there really. A few photos and a few sightings, suspicious-looking people entering the Park, suspicious-looking people leaving the Park, but nothing concrete.'

They both sat silently cogitating and sipping their coffees. 'And that's it?' Hubert looked disappointed.

'What did we get from Jarvis's house search?' Leon asked.

'Nothing. No clothes, shoes or gloves to connect him. A small rucksack, nothing in it. There was nothing of value in the safe: deeds of the house, in Pamela's name, some solicitors' papers, jewellery and cash, not worth much.'

'I'm thinking in terms of mobiles, credit cards, keys; have we checked all keys, anything to suggest a hidden locker somewhere, a cupboard, another car maybe?'

Again Hubert had nothing to add. 'No, I'm afraid not. Only the one mobile, which we have examined, and there's nothing in it, except for a couple of old girlfriends' names – they've been checked out at their addresses and nothing, no hiding places as far as we could see. No unexplained keys either. Sorry.'

'I'm convinced he has a lock-up or something, a locker some-where to hide his stuff. I have asked Broderick to do a check of all lost-property offices, station lockers and archway lock-ups – these are either Network Rail or council, rented, for small businesses. There are records – we could see if there have been any new tenants recently, could be using a false name. I'm waiting on that. And how about Pamela's mobile? Anything on that?'

'No, just the usual. A few messages with Antonio, as you said, no odd connections or other links – she was an unfortunate victim.'

'Of Collingwood's jealousy and anger,' Leon muttered.

Hubert at last lighted a cigarette and was looking distracted. They remained sitting in silence, somewhat deflated, lost in their own thoughts. The light of the day was fading, the music playing quietly in the background, but they had stopped noticing it.

Leon turned to Hubert. 'Now, old friend, tell me about your problems.'

Hubert took a deep inhalation on his cigarette and started speaking with smoke pouring out of his nostrils and swilling about his face, making him blink rapidly to stop the irritation to his eyes. 'The COBR meeting last week was a touch acrimonious.

It's probably a good thing you were not there, Leon – red rag to a number of bulls. I was accused of poor management, no progress, incompetence really. I was up facing the Metropolitan chief – Max O'Connell – this morning: he was pointedly aggressive – security services getting in the way of the police investigation, using outside unauthorised personnel. The PM has been advised that this was not a terrorist attack, or part of one, that it was a civilian matter, a terrible crime, meaning that it reverts entirely to the responsibility of the Metropolitan Police, nothing I could do to keep Five involved.'

'And my role, does that still have the PM's approval?'

'The PM took some flak last week. But I told him that you were working closely with Scotland Yard and that there were still some loose ends that you wanted to pursue, that you were making some progress – I was trying to buy some time. I think the PM is wanting to close this whole thing down – it's an embarrassment that there is no result, so he wants it to go away from the public mind, which is all very well, but the coroner's hearings will be in a couple of weeks, so it will all hit the headlines again.'

'So for the moment I can carry on?'

'Yes, but it will be limited, Leon. This afternoon I had a call from Adrian to attend a meeting in his office up on the eighth floor – I spent a difficult hour with a couple of the executive directors and the long and the short is they want changes at the top, a whole new raft of sub-section directors. They will have to square it with the PM, and he would probably hang out for me, and put in a good word. But there are so many jealousies on that floor, they all want to take their chance at the top job. Difficult to know what's coming next.'

'This is precisely why I made my exit three years ago. You should think about it too, Hue – might open up a whole new area for you. Man of your experience, they are mad dumping on you.'

'Well, they haven't done it yet.' Hubert stubbed out his cigarette.

A look of pain crossed his lined face again. He hesitated, reluctant to talk about something so painful. 'And Roger has left. Walked out at the weekend.'

And suddenly Hubert's face, normally a calming canvas of symmetry and comfort, disintegrated into countless cracks and splinters, like the thin film of carwash water left on the windscreen, which turns opaque in the blink of an eye, rippling and crinkling on acceleration, before the wipers wash it all away. Leon had no wipers on this occasion, but just had to listen to Hubert telling him the story as best a man with such inner pride and desire for privacy was able.

'He says he was feeling used, that his position in my life had been downgraded; that I was taking him for granted. The truth is rather more prosaic, I'm afraid: he's found someone else to shag basically, a younger model actually.' Hubert was blowing his nose rather loudly, wiping his eyes. Having spoken the difficult words, articulated his personal angst in reasonably coherent sentences, Hubert felt better for it, and was already smiling and telling Leon not to worry about him, he would find someone else, there were other Rogers around.

'Yes, but he was a rather nice Roger, wasn't he? I thought so. Had a nice bum.' And Hubert spluttered with laughter, as if Leon had told a dirty joke.

7

Leon Deshpande visited Pamela's mother at her home in a narrow terrace off Streatham High Road nearly opposite the Odeon Cinema, where there was a post office on the corner. Sarah Beacham, in her late fifties, lived on her own in a cramped ground-floor flat, with its front bay window pressing outwards almost onto the pavement.

She introduced herself as she proudly showed him into her lonely abode that she kept tidy, saying Pamela was her first daughter, Belinda was her second and Alan was her only son. Her husband, who had survived service in Northern Ireland, had been an active postal worker until he had died almost six years ago following a blood clot in his leg.

It was the middle of the morning, so Mrs Beacham made coffee for them both, and tried her best to be helpful. Deshpande apologised again for his intrusion and said emphatically how sorry he was about the loss of her Pamela. He sat on a threadbare sofa in the front window aware of the traffic and other noises outside, while Mrs Beacham, in a navy blue woollen two-piece, perched with knees tight together on an upright wooden chair with her arms folded under her neat bust. A large colour photograph of a happy-looking young Pamela dominated the room, hanging as a centrepiece on one wall. A row of well-burnt white candles and a brass statue of Christ on the cross stood in a line along the mantelshelf beneath. Deshpande caught sight of the main bedroom beyond a sliding door, that she closed before sitting down.

She was shattered by the loss of Pamela, whom she had thought was such a success, what with her making good money and meeting all those celebrity people. A mother did not expect to outlive her own daughter. She could not understand how the events had happened. 'Such an appalling thing, in the Olympic Stadium, in front of all those people. I cannot believe anyone would want to do such a thing.'

'Do you think Jarvis had anything to do with it, Mrs Beacham?' Deshpande enquired innocently.

'I honestly don't know,' she replied earnestly. 'It seems so out of character, he was always so polite and thoughtful. He never was angry or lost his temper. They seemed to get on quite well although Pamela had not had any children and I kept telling her not to put it off for too long, because it can all turn out to be too late when you finally decide to go ahead. Why, why would he do it? It doesn't make any sense.'

'No, it doesn't, you're right.'

'Mind you, I didn't like his brother much.' Mrs Beacham seemed to be casting her mind back to some past event, waiting patiently for the details to float into her consciousness so she could share them with her visitor. 'Alan did some work for him, driving a van in London, this was ages ago, but Jonathan didn't half tear a strip off him when he did something wrong, delivered a parcel to the wrong address or something. He was quite horrid, actually.'

Deshpande watched as she recalled the events with pinched lips. 'We had words actually,' she added and flicked her head back and her eyebrows up to the ceiling, as if to say, there's no pleasing some people. 'I wondered whether Jonathan had had a thing for Pamela,' she continued, 'you know, whether he fancied her. It was when Jarvis was away in the Army, in the Middle East, I think, I saw them together on the Common one afternoon, I was coming back from the bingo and they were walking together holding hands, and she was leaning into him, all sort of lovey-dovey, you know.'

Deshpande listened with fascination.

'Was there anything else that made you suspect? Had you seen anything else, over the years?'

'Well it was a long time ago, and I think when Jarvis came back it stopped. But I was never sure, really.'

'Did Pamela ever have affairs with other men, as far as you knew?'

'I don't think so. No, she was a good girl. Well, she never would talk to me about it. And Linda wouldn't talk to me either, so I don't know, actually.' Mrs Beacham's mouth was working a little extra and she reached for a small white handkerchief from up her sleeve to wipe under her eyes, rather as Mrs Collingwood had done last week.

'So Jarvis and Pamela didn't have particularly bad fights or arguments? Got on all right, did they?'

'Yes, yes, I think so.'

'Money worries, do you think?'

'I really don't know, they both seemed to be earning quite well.'

'And the lack of children, do you think that was a point of argument?'

'Yes, maybe. Pamela loved her job, she would not have wanted to do anything that might have got in the way. Women do have such difficult decisions these days. They all want to work, don't they, and they want to have children – so difficult for them.'

And really Deshpande achieved nothing more with the interview, other than making Mrs Beacham feel a little better, knowing that there was such a nice man and an upright member of the Services doing his very best for everyone.

The Stratford Incident hotline had been open since the day after the Olympic Park shootings, for the public to call in freely with any information they might have relating to the incident in question. It was to encourage anybody who might have seen something, or who had taken some useful photographs, to report in. Clerical staff and police officers were assigned to listen to the messages, to log them, and sometimes calls were made in return to clarify or enquire further. There were also internet and text alternatives.

There was also a professional enquiry line, with a flyer sent to all police stations in London and the Home Counties and beyond, as well as to airports, station ticket offices, bus stations and ports; with a telephone number that went directly through to an answering service at Scotland Yard; these were logged and reported directly to Inspector Broderick's team.

On a drizzly night in early September, more than three weeks after the shootings, when most people seemed to have forgotten the events and all the behind-the-scenes police activity had yielded precious little, while the Paralympics were proceeding at the Park with evident success and praise, and when still there was no suspect under arrest and the surveillance teams had all been recalled, a message came through on the enquiry line at Scotland Yard that was logged by one of Broderick's subordinates, Detective Constable Bruce Fisher: *Wednesday September 5th 2012 at 19.15: two women reported at Canonbury Police Station a missing person – male, blond, Josh Cooper, 30 years old, 6 foot 1 inch tall, weighing 12 and a half stone, ex-Army, athletic, no health issues, worked in security in Stratford Park, last seen on afternoon of Stadium shootings (August 12) in Northchurch Road, Islington. Unknown home address, somewhere in Hoxton area. Photo supplied.*

After a morning of driving and delivering security parcels like a glorified postman for SecureLife, Jarvis spent the afternoon finding empty boxes he could use to pack up Pamela's clothes and things from the house. Later he went off to the gym for a hard session on the treadmill and bikes, after which he showered and changed and went home to get some food. Once the overcast sky of the day had turned rapidly to darkness, he crept out the back, climbed over the wall and along to the top to drop down into Wilton Square, before heading south with an overnight bag filled with a few belongings, junk food and juice. It was after nine o'clock and there was no moon to light his way, just the forlorn and sparse street lighting. He wove his complicated path on foot to his lock-up, his second home, turning down side streets, cutting through connector paths, doubling back on himself, and his final approach was from under the railway lines from the south. He was certain that nobody had ever followed him before, no watchers from the house, but on this occasion, on approaching his open area from a narrow side road, he became aware of a shadow out of place, an unfamiliar outline, and the hairs on the back of his neck prickled. Instinctively he turned aside, behind a parked van, and then silently slipped into a side cutting between buildings, from where he was able to look across in the gloomy light to his entry doors.

A stout, impatient figure was watching from behind a brick pillar along the viaduct, blending in poorly with his background, fiddling with his feet and pacing a few times along his patch of pavement, looking back along Three Colts Road or under the railway arch or across to number 208. He was stocky, early forties, with a close-shaved head of grey hair, wearing a dark overcoat. He was clearly bored with his job, waiting to catch Jarvis, and had probably been thereabouts all day, now with sore feet and a desire to get home to some warmth.

And Jarvis couldn't make up his mind what to do. Should he turn round and walk away? Surely the man would then go away until another time. Or should he draw the shadowy figure out, confront him in the street, although he would certainly be armed? Or he could make it look as if he hadn't noticed being watched and just walk apparently untroubled to his lock-up. And wait inside.

With the casual stride of the unconcerned, swinging his holdall in his grip, Jarvis had emerged from his watching place and moved easily along to the front of number 208, sure that his watcher had seen him, then punched in his security code number on the key pad and pushed the door inwards. It closed behind him with a reassuring clunk and he drew the bolts across. He dropped his bag and switched the table light on, pressing the lampshade down close to the surface to reduce the amount of light emitted, just enough for him to see by. He retreated to the back of his space, where he moved aside the boxes and rubber tyres to reveal the half-size rear door. Sliding two bolts clear, he pulled the door carefully inwards just a little, feeling a rush of cooler outside air. Then he retrieved his heavy iron jemmy and laid it down across one end of the table. Next to a pair of leather gloves. From the fridge he took out a carton of juice and sat calmly in the dark, sipping at the drink, eating from a bag of crisps. And waited.

It was about fifteen minutes before tentative knocking and rattling on the outside of the metal door alerted him. Jarvis stood up, gloves on, jemmy in hand. Switching the table lamp off, he moved silently over to the doors and stood by the old-fashioned metal switch box on the wall. He listened intently for any sound outside. Then he pressed the red button firmly and darted to the back to his escape door. With some creaking and a motorised whirring, the roller door stiffened and cranked up from the concrete floor, moving noisily with agonising slowness. A gap appeared along the bottom, gradually growing as the wide old metal slats heaved upwards. Standing to one side, a heavily built man with the flattened nose of a professional fighter was standing with his legs planted apart and a Luger in his hand. He had a slightly worried expression on his ugly face, surprised by the noisy opening of the garage door, expecting rather the side door to open to reveal an unarmed young blond man standing in the frame whom he was supposed to silently shoot down, bullet through the head.

While the mechanism was still whirring and cranking the roller door upwards, the gunman ducked underneath, impatient to see what was happening on the inside. Taking some purposeful strides into the middle of the space, gun pointing vaguely into the unknown, he found himself blinking rapidly in the near darkness and acutely aware of a dank mouldy smell. He was unable to pick out any detail within the enclosure and did not see his target standing nearby waiting to be executed. In fact the place seemed to be empty.

Then there was a slight footfall behind him, the merest hint of a sound, obscured by the final rattling of the door mechanism. Before he could whip round and confront it, a sharp pain, the like of which he had never experienced before in his long and distinguished career as a thug, crashed across his right forearm and his gun rattled onto the concrete floor. He looked in horror and sympathy at his stricken arm, and before he could let out the huge scream that was welling up inside him, he was kicked sharply in the lower back from behind, which sent him tumbling forwards painfully onto his knees, causing whiplash to his neck. Another sharp kick in the back sent him crashing forwards onto his good arm that tried to cushion the fall. And before he was able to emit a scream of even greater proportions than the one he had failed to emit last time, his adversary had jumped onto his back, crushing the broken arm under his own weight, pinioning him violently to the ground, his face grazed sideways against the cold concrete, knocking the very breath out of his solid frame.

Jarvis placed the thick metal jemmy across the thug's neck and applied pressure with his gloved hands on either end like a see-saw, using the full force of his body to crush down on the man's airway. Into the man's ear he whispered: 'Who the fuck are you? Who sent you?'

The heavy guy wanted to cry. Jarvis released the pressure, without moving position. He repeated: 'What is your name?'

'Bill,' Jarvis thought he tried to say.

'Bill, that's nice. How do you do, Bill? Who sent you, arsehole?'

The man was crying, 'Christ, my arm is broken, I can't breathe.'

Jarvis applied pressure on the jemmy: 'I will ask you once more, Bill. Who sent you?'

The man was choking, his face beginning to bloat and swell around his piggy eyes. Jarvis applied more pressure, digging deeply into the fleshy neck. Then he relented, bending closer towards the man's mouth and catching the sour smell of sweat and fear mixed with cheap aftershave. 'Once more, Bill. Don't disappoint me.'

His tears were flooding over his face as he whimpered a name. 'What, what was that? Again.'

'Mr Chigwell.'

'Chigwell. Would that be Arthur?'

'No,' he croaked, with a tiny shake of his head, 'the young one – Ainsley.'

'Is there anybody else here with you tonight, Bill?'

He gave a tiny shake of his head again. 'No, I'm alone.'

With a concerted period of intense pressure on either end of the metal bar, Jarvis, his teeth clenched and holding his breath, crushed the man's windpipe, and after a minute of tongue-protruding struggle and shaking, the big man died.

After a moment Jarvis stood up, sweating, and hit the 'close' button on the wall. The motorised slatted door started to come down again just as slowly as it had risen a few moments before. He darted to the back wall and closed the hidden door there too, bolting it, as the front door came to rest, fully closed on the concrete floor.

Jarvis was breathing fast. His pulse was racing uncontrollably, the adrenalin surging. His arms ached. He was thinking hard. He needed to dispose of the heavy body. And then he needed to dispose of that sodding Ainsley. He had seen him only that morning. The one man who could and probably would squeal everything to the police if he was under pressure; and he was obviously feeling the pressure.

In a pocket of the dead man's coat, Jarvis found an Oyster card and a mobile phone, switched off. With power on, he selected 'menu', then 'store', and a list of contacts came up in alphabetical order. 'Chigwell, Ainsley' appeared, and Jarvis pressed the green button.

His anger boiled over on hearing Ainsley's voice; he wanted to shout into his ear what a cheating bastard he was; he wanted to strangle him. 'Mission accomplished, boss,' he growled into the gadget and then pressed the red button, disconnecting the call. He thought Ainsley might be fooled for a while, perhaps not recognising his voice. But he was sure he would send another team, more experienced, more of them perhaps, when he found out Jarvis was still alive.

And Jarvis had no intention of hanging around to be a sitting target.

8

Jarvis spent two whole days at Beacon Forest, rewarding days in isolation, revelling in the space and freedom he had. The stolen keys let him through the gates into the compound, where he hid his car behind the large storage shed, away from prying eyes from the road. He was able to use the big caravan, where he slept in luxury on two mattresses on the biggest bunk, with an abundant supply of blankets. He had brought some bread and cheese, biscuits, a packet of German sausage and bottled water. There was no lighting or a working fridge, without setting up the generator, which would be noisy, but the oil radiator created a cosy fug inside.

He felt secure and his anxieties drained away. During daylight hours he meandered through the forest, along the old familiar paths that the gang of woodsmen had marked out and prepared, and along some new ones, previously unused and overgrown. Even in the middle of a bright day not much sound penetrated through the woods and not much light filtered down through the thick upper foliage, the ground under foot dull, soft and deathly quiet. Intoxicated by the extreme quiet and pungent aromas, he inhaled deeply as he lay still among the overgrown wild parsnip and garlic at the grassy edges, catching some sun on his face and studying the barbed leaves and cherubic yellow flowers of dandelion swaying in the breeze. Here in the twilight, armies of little brown rabbits came out to graze and play and he managed to shoot one with a direct hit from the pistol. It roasted deliciously on a spit over a fire that he created in a dry hidden dipped area in the middle of the woods.

In some of the clearings where sunbeams streamed through gaps in the leaves and branches, wild laurel and holly thrived, and he would watch sparrows and tits frolicking among the berries, and a regular red-breasted robin foraged unmolested around his feet. Of the life of the inner forest, Jarvis became ever more familiar, its twists and turns, its colours and smells, its birdsong,. And there were some other sounds to listen to: raindrops spattering across the leafy roof, dripping randomly onto the inert floor long after the rain had stopped; the occasional crack of old wood splitting or the thud of a branch falling to the ground; the winds rustling continuously through the high branches above, making their own distinctive music.

He had bundled the heavy body from his lock-up into the back of the Astra. First he had wrapped it in black plastic bags and taped it round thoroughly with insulating tape, sealing it, while it was still on his concrete floor. Then he fetched his car, reversed it into his space, still in pitch darkness, and hefted the awkward shape over the bottom edge of the boot, like manhandling a floppy rolled-up carpet. He placed the jemmy in the boot beside the body. He cleaned his floor with water and an old rag. He filled the rest of the boot with most of his other possessions, including his newly acquired Luger, with its six-round magazine. Jarvis was grateful for the darkness outside and the feeble street lighting. He was sure there was nobody about to see him drive away, after carefully locking up.

He had escaped to the anonymity of his beloved forest. During the hours of solitude since his arrival, he had reflected openly on the strange sequence of events and the direction his life had taken. Pamela occupied too many of his thoughts and there were some moments, especially at night, in his dark steamed-up caravan, when his being alone struck home more potently than usual, when he missed her cruelly, even calling out for her once when he took a short walk across the deserted compound in the heavy darkness. He gazed up at the black skies where thin clouds were scudding across a miserable moon. The chill air gripped him like a cold shower, as he stood in bare feet in a thin T-shirt wet with sweat. He confessed out loud, 'I do miss you, Pam, sod it!' *Why did you cheat on me? I am sorry. We could not have gone on the way we were.* Tears welled up in his eyes as she danced with teasing body movements beside him. Once his dream involved Pamela and Jonathan, wiping their hands clean on white tunics as they ducked away out of sight, laughing together. He would wake in the night, hearing her calling his name and begging for mercy. His mother's voice was there once, offering her life instead, standing between the gun and Pamela's head.

Naomi came into his thoughts as well, in a less brutal way. There was no burning desire, more a need to share some time with someone familiar. Jarvis had come to like talking to her, she was good like that, and he felt better for it. Her absence was a nuisance, like when something precious gets misplaced and cannot be found despite looking everywhere, but at the same time knowing it will turn up sooner or later. And when it does, nothing has been lost, except a little temper and a small chunk of time. But uncertainty came with Naomi, whether she could be trusted to be on his side when the chips were down. She was a nice girl but she would always resort to the truth, which might not be in his best interests.

On the second night he drove the Astra deeper into the forest, winding up along the new roadway and way out of sight of any random passers-by. He hauled the black plastic bundle out of the boot and dragged it into the overgrowth towards the darker parts, finally tipping it over a ledge into an overgrown recess, where it dropped and rolled to a stop out of sight. He jumped down through the thickets, pulling branches and kicking dead leaves over the black plastic shape until it was completely covered.

One day midweek, in more of a confident mood than he had been in for a while, Jarvis was waiting patiently in The Green Man with the phone at his ear. The mid-morning business there was quiet, only a couple of village regulars at the bar talking with Betty. An elderly couple in thick matching jumpers, their bright anoraks folded on a spare chair beside them, slowly ate the hot lunchtime special at a small window table, saying nothing. A log fire was roaring in the deep grate opposite. Bright sunlight streaked across the main lounge, where Jarvis had to bend his head forward to avoid the cross-beams in the ceiling. He was leaning inside the rounded plastic hood that shielded the telephone, staring aimlessly at the scribblings of other customers on the wall, names and numbers.

Jimmy came onto the line. 'Jarvis, lad, it's me. All right? How's you bin?'

'Jimmy, I'm fine. Good. Did you manage that address for me?'

'Yes – no problem. Sidney's boy, Damian, helped me out. The address is in Highgate, 43 Claremont Road.'

'You sure that is Ainsley's place, not Paul Chigwell's?'

'Yes, absolutely, I made sure he knew exactly who we were wanting. No problem, Jarvis. Now don't you go getting up to any more mischief, right,' he joked, and Jarvis imagined Jimmy's sneering smile as he went off to spend the rest of the afternoon romping in Rhoda's bed, his cap still pulled low on his head.

'Of course not. Thanks, Jimmy. Best be off.' Jarvis hung the receiver back in its cradle, already plotting an unannounced visit to Ainsley's place late one night soon, with mischief foremost on his mind.

Leon Deshpande worked tirelessly during this time, mostly at home, still studying some of the video footage that had been taken at the stadium on the fateful night, looking through the employee lists, re-reading the interview transcripts, trying to match any information about possible suspects with other names in the frame. But without the breakthrough he needed. And without any evidence, forensic or otherwise, Deshpande was only too aware of how difficult it was going to be to charge Jarvis Collingwood with anything.

On Thursday afternoon, he took a taxi over to Scotland Yard and Broderick's department, where all the evidence and data that had so far been collected resided. He wanted to hear how the other team had got on with its data search, and he also wanted to push the search for Collingwood's lock-up. Jarvis had identified at least three men with dodgy pasts all fitting the initial criteria and there were profiles from the forensic psychologists to work through. Broderick himself was away on compassionate leave, following the unexpected death of his father, and two juniors had been delegated to oversee his work, Leon managing to avoid them as he slipped into the adjacent incident room. Here the walls were covered with photographs and paper messages, string and coloured pins, all related to the Olympics Shooting Incident August 12, 2012, enlarged pictures of the Park and Stadium, blown-up maps of the area, pictures of the crowds, the final night of fireworks and celebration, the victims with their names attached, some official and some private, as well as TV material showing the sites where the violence had occurred. Around the shelves were boxes, files and thick reports; on the desks were computers and printers, telephones and fax machines; all around the room, in disorderly chaos, telephones were ringing, printers buzzing, voices calling, doors slamming.

Everyone around the office knew that Mr Deshpande was the senior man on the investigation and was the link to the PM's office, which made him more or less in charge of the enquiry. They generally showed him respect, even though at the same time they knew that it upset their boss. Three other people were working in the room at the same time, young officers detailed to routine trawling and data searches. They all nodded at Deshpande by way of acknowledging his presence and then he was left free to look at or access anything he wanted.

He was hunched over a pile of reports at a workstation, getting stiff around the back, a fresh cup of coffee and a doughnut from Peelers at his elbow, while reading about a name that Collingwood had identified, Martin Jones, that had cropped up more than once. A lot of resources had already been employed to track this man down to some rundown backstreet in Mansfield, and local police were alerted for an early arrest. Jones had been in the Army but had been demoted following some disciplinary incident at Catterick a few years ago. A brother had been killed in Iraq. Then he had got himself involved in some cranky religious group with Muslim tendencies in London, and this had been like a red rag for Broderick.

A portly officer in grey trousers and tight white blouse stood over Deshpande's desk, a sheaf of papers in her short, stubby hands. 'Mr Deshpande, when you have a minute?' She was quietly spoken, London accent.

'Umm.' Seeing that Deshpande had just closed one thick file and placed it with relief onto the 'done' pile, the diligent DC had stepped up.

'These are printouts for you, sir, of the Chigwell businesses, the ones Ainsley Chigwell identified to you. There are quite a few, as you can see.' She laid the papers in front of Deshpande on the desk. 'WPC Joan Summers', Deshpande read on her dangling label. She had boyish fair hair, severely short.

'For example, Chigwell Motors is a small repair car business in Mile End. They have Chigwell Cars, a hire-car and taxi service, in Bethnal Green.' She was pointing down the list. 'There is a small builder, nothing too grand. Mostly it's trading companies, import-export, with warehousing on the docks. They have a transport and logistics group. You asked about premises, storage, garages and lock-ups. Well, they own quite a few actually: warehousing, storage, parking lots et cetera. And garages. These are the London ones, mostly east and north. Network Rail put me in touch with a company they use, South Eastern Railways Holding Company, who own and rent out most of the arches out from Kings' Cross, St Pancras, Liverpool Street, Fenchurch Street. And the Chigwells or their associated businesses are listed tenants at about a dozen of them.'

'Good work, Summers.'

Deshpande was paying attention to the printed lists on the papers in front of him, trying to visualise where they all were. 'Show me a map of this part of London.' Deshpande then highlighted with his yellow marker pen those out of Liverpool Street, which were located roughly along a line through Spitalfields and Bethnal Green towards Bow. 'These are our top choices, as they are more reachable from Collingwood's address.' He had marked seven in the list. 'So we need warrants to search all these – together, one after the other. And while that is happening, I will bring Ainsley Chigwell with us to visit these places in turn, with a police escort. He should know who works there, who has access, who's in charge and so on. He won't have a chance to warn any of them. Can you set that up for me with your boss?'

'Yes, absolutely. When for?'

Deshpande was thinking beyond that, to how important it might be to put a watch on Ainsley Chigwell's house in Highgate.

'Soon. Very soon.'

DC Bruce Fisher ambled in a while later and placed a small bundle of papers on the table near Deshpande, a collection of messages received over the last few days, he said, from the public hotline. And he was repeatedly tapping the top paper. 'This one rather caught my eye, sir.' He remained standing.

'Do sit down – Fisher, isn't it?'

'Yes, sir, thank you, sir.' He sat on a chair at the end of the table. He was in his shirt sleeves, loose collar, young and careless with ginger hair and freckles. The afternoon session was closing rapidly and Fisher was concerned about getting away early, to attend a family dinner party with his girlfriend's parents. 'It's from Canonbury Police Station, came in Tuesday, missing person, Josh Cooper. I asked for any photos to be sent over, and I've just seen this one, it arrived today.'

Deshpande read the top message and lifted the page up, looking for the photo underneath. It was a colour print, of two young people in T-shirts looking directly into the camera, taken on a bright day. The young woman, whom Leon did not recognise, was smiling emphatically with a wide grin, showing large white teeth and a tiny beauty spot on her cheek as distinguishing features. The man was a square-jawed tough-looking bearded blond with bulging chest in a tight white T-shirt. The two were obviously friends, leaning into each other and holding hands. Deshpande almost stopped breathing for a minute, blinked and looked again. 'But this is . . .'

'I don't know who it is – Josh Cooper is the name reported, but he has gone missing apparently,' butted in Fisher, hoping to be able to leave Deshpande soon, so as to have time to tidy things up for the day. 'But it was the reference to him being a security guard at Stratford Park and ex-Army and the fact that he had disappeared on the day of the shootings that just caught my attention, sir. Maybe nothing in it.'

'Yes, Collingwood,' murmured Leon distractedly, having recognised the man in the photo as the all-too-familiar Jarvis Collingwood. 'I don't believe it. And he's been reported missing, by this woman? Where does she live and what's her name?'

'The names of the two women who reported it and their addresses are here, with telephone numbers. They are friends, apparently live near each other; they've been told that we may want to contact them.'

'Well done, Fisher. That's good, very good.' Fisher had not seemed to realise that the photo on the incident-room wall, taken of a clean-shaven Jarvis Collingwood four weeks ago in the police station over in Bow Road, a black-and-white full-face, showed the same person as the man in this colour picture, taken goodness knows when, who was purportedly a bearded Josh Cooper with an unknown girl. 'And this girl is?' asked Leon.

Fisher read the writing on the back of the photo. 'Well, it's Miss Naomi Lonsdale. If I could be excused, sir, I need to do a bit more sorting before I leave tonight,' he said, handing the photo back and itching to go.

'Yes, yes, of course, you run along, I'll deal with these.'

Leon was sweating under his arms; he took some deep breaths. He looked closely at the photograph, read the transcript that had come with it from Canonbury, looked at the photo again. At last, after such an intense two weeks since leaving Africa, he saw possibilities, something about to happen. A young woman declaring Josh Cooper had disappeared, but showing a picture of Jarvis Collingwood. And Leon knew that Collingwood had a home in Hoxton, although he had not been seen for a day or so. But he had not gone missing. Obviously the two women did not know him as Collingwood, but also they did not know where he lived. The address for Naomi was Northchurch Road, not that far from Baring Street, Leon noted. Collingwood had a double identity, as he suspected.

Leon needed to visit Naomi Lonsdale, as soon as possible, and he reached for his mobile.

It was after five o'clock when Naomi, on edge, opened the front door of her flat after just one ring of the doorbell. She had rushed home from work after Deshpande's call, and now, in tight jeans and pink shirt buttoned to the neck, her hair neatly brushed, she looked prepared for her visitor. On the doorstep, with a friendly smile, stood a stocky man with short black hair in a dark blue shirt, chinos and well-worn brown brogues. Naomi noticed the fading tan, the expensive-looking watch, the calm confidence that oozed from the man, and knew that this was someone's reassuringly solid and reliable father. She suddenly felt in need of arms around her, preferably solid and reliable, for support and comfort. The man was so self-assured. And she thought she detected a slight South African accent. Which, when he later admitted he had family connections in Cape Town, pleased her because she had always prided herself on being quite good at recognising where people came from.

'You must be Naomi, Naomi Lonsdale?' He had an easy manner. He held up his ID. 'I'm Leon Deshpande. We spoke on the phone earlier. I am working for the Home Office just now and I know Josh Cooper. May I come in?'

Deshpande had said on the phone that he had seen her message from Canonbury Police Station about the missing person and he had some information that would help her, if he could come round and discuss things with her. Naomi immediately was convinced that something serious had happened to Josh.

Without another word, Deshpande followed Naomi into her humble sitting room, aware that this neat, ordinary young girl in dark-rimmed glasses probably knew nothing of Jarvis Collingwood's real history and was likely to defend him were she to think that his freedom or reputation was at stake. He had seen infatuated lovers in the past defend each other even in the face of evidence of some pretty awful wrongdoing. If she gleaned that Deshpande and the Home Office were trying to find ways to prove that he murdered five people in cold blood, she might obstruct their enquiry and try to lead them away from her boyfriend. On the other hand, Leon saw a way of getting to Jarvis through Naomi.

Naomi was absolutely terrified of what Deshpande was about

to tell her, but he reassured her that although he was unable to say that nothing serious was going on, he thought Josh Cooper himself was well.

He noticed, while she was out preparing coffee, black for Mr Deshpande, a couple of photos in frames, and it was weird seeing pictures of Josh/Jarvis with beard in someone else's house. There was also a picture of Naomi's family, he presumed, an older man with his three children, Naomi and two boys. He was waiting patiently with hands in trouser pockets when Naomi returned with two mugs clasped in one hand and a small plate of biscuits in the other. 'Oh thanks, that's kind. Can I put it here, the mug?' he asked, so as not to make a hot ring on the bare wooden coffee table, and she dropped a magazine on the edge for him. He pulled up a small chair and sat with a Jammie Dodger in his hand. He started munching, awaiting her questions.

'So please, tell me Josh is all right.'

'Yes, he is, or at least he was fine when I saw him last week.'

'Thank God.' She sighed visibly. 'So that must mean he just does not want to see me.' Naomi's eyes flicked skywards and she smiled resignedly before her face collapsed into a soft spasm of hopelessness. Leon recognised the fragile look, the eyes close to crying, the red reaction along the borders of her lower lids. 'Which makes me unhappy.' And she certainly looked distressed.

'How long have you known Josh?'

'About six months.'

'How did you meet, if I may ask?'

'I'm a hairdresser and he was a regular customer, actually for some while before I noticed.' She giggled and gave him a poor version of her goofy smile. 'He asked me out about February time, and we clicked,' she said nervously, realising how feeble it sounded. Leon recognised the happy-looking girl's face from the photo.

'And are you in love with him?' Naomi was nodding thoughtfully.

'Did he actually move in here with you?' Naomi shook her head, wiped a few strands of stray hair away from her face, together with some lower-lid moisture.

'No, he had a house down in Hoxton, I believe. Well, that's what he told me, anyway.' She stopped.

'Where he lived with his wife, is that right?'

'Yes, apparently.'

'He told you that, did he?'

'Yes.'

'Or did he hide that from you and it was extracted by you, after some argument perhaps?'

'Something like that. What's he done?'

'Well, it's complicated, Naomi. Josh Cooper is really someone else. His real name is Jarvis Collingwood. He must have been doubling up as Josh Cooper, for some reason. The Home Office and the police have been interviewing Jarvis in association with the shootings at the Olympic Stadium on August 12th. He has not told us anything about you, he's not mentioned you at all.'

'Collingwood, Jarvis?' She sounded incredulous, uncertain, pronouncing his name with a sneer, questioning whether they had got it right. 'The Olympic shootings. You must be joking?' Deshpande retrieved the old photo again, the black-and-white police mug shot that he had kept in his inside jacket pocket, which he showed to Naomi, and she said yes, that's Josh without his beard.

'To us that is Jarvis Collingwood, 30, 6 foot 1, ex-Army, we've seen his passport. He was married to Pamela and they lived in Baring Street, actually not far from here.'

'Lived?' asked Naomi, with a frown of her usually straight beetle-black brows.

'She was one of the victims in the shootings at the stadium, took a bullet in the neck and died that night.'

Naomi had opened her mouth and eyes wide in horror, her

hands coming up to her face, where she smothered her lips and closed her mouth again. 'Oh my God. That's horrible.' Tears were welling up in her eyes as an uncontrollable sob wrenched through her chest. 'I remember the name now, when I read the names in the paper, I remember the woman was Pamela, just like Josh's wife, but I thought that was just coincidence. Poor Josh.' She was breathing in fits and starts. 'Or Jarvis.'

'The thing is, Naomi, as I understand it,' Leon continued before Naomi had time to think through what they had just said and ask the difficult question, 'he never told you where he lived, and you never saw or met Pamela. And you last saw him on the afternoon of the closing-ceremony day at the Olympics, that Sunday, August 12th. He has not been back here to your place since and you have not seen him since then?' Leon looked at Naomi for confirmation. 'Or heard from him, by phone, by mobile or text? Email?'

'No, no, that's right. No. He came over from being on duty at the stadium, in the afternoon, finished early and said he would be at home to watch the closing ceremony on television. I was going over to see my dad in Kilburn that evening, as he had to go into hospital for an operation Monday. I was expecting to see Josh after a day or two. I had lost my mobile that day, which I could not explain, so infuriating, and so could not contact him until I got a new one, but that was after a week. He wasn't answering his mobile. I didn't know where he lived. I never saw Pamela. And he contacted me at home for the first time since, only last Sunday evening. We were going to meet on Monday and he said he would tell me everything. But he never showed up, and Celia, my girlfriend and me, we decided that enough was enough, and we were worried that maybe he was in trouble or needed help, so we went to the local police station, last Wednesday.'

'And you did right, Naomi, you absolutely did right. You said he contacted you on Sunday, how? On your mobile?'

She was wiping her lower eyelids, smearing black mascara mixed with tears sideways out over her narrow cheekbones. Leon was reminded of his beautiful Jamila: when he dropped her off back home in Kew last week, still in the Porsche and parked in Zoe's drive, Jamila had genuinely squeezed his arm, kissed his cheek and said she had had fun and could they do it again more often, and that she missed him. With a sadness in her eyes, she wondered why he and Mum couldn't get together again. 'Jamila, darling, your mother has jumped in with Simon, they are married; and I have Ramona, so there is no way that we are going to be together again, ever. I'm sorry. Don't you like Simon?'

'Silly question, Dad. He's a ponce. I just get in his way. I bring out the worst in him, he says. His temper is something else.' Jamila was holding her mobile but not actually fingering it, which Leon took as a compliment, her attention fixed on this, their parting.

'Promise, I will be in touch soon.'

'Anyway you're going to be a daddy again,' she was singing, 'in a couple of weeks? I want to come out to Switzerland to see you all and the girls. Please, please.'

'We'll see – it would be lovely, wouldn't it. Maybe for your October half-term. OK?'

They embraced, awkwardly twisted in the front seats, arms intertwined round necks, faces pressed together. Her cheek had felt cold and he was wary of getting smeared with black or purple and wondered again about her social life. She was so soft and Leon recognised a wave of tenderness towards this young girl that he wanted to nurture. But he had to go, meetings to attend to, more data to sift through, people to interview. 'Wish Ramona my love and all the best,' was her parting call as she had hopped out of the car and slammed the door.

Leon took a handkerchief of his own and gestured at Naomi's face. She used it to wipe away tears and mascara marks from under both eyes, looking at the black smears on the cloth. 'Sorry,' she said before wiping again. She smiled. 'Sorry.'

'No, don't worry. Tell me, when you met, was it him making all the moves, or did any of it come from you? You know, who took the initiative really?'

'Well, he did at first. He bumped into me outside the shop, and he was the one wanting to meet again, but I was quite happy with that.' Some more sheepish smiles.

'So what attracted you to him, Naomi?'

'Oh, I dunno.' She giggled. 'He was nice, good-looking. He seemed interesting, you know, the army stories were sad mostly, powerful. He seemed lost in a way, and I thought I could help him find his way back to a normal life. He said he was unhappy with his wife, and wanted to leave her, but that she was hanging on; he wanted to gradually change her mind, not suddenly up sticks and leave, and anyway his money was in the house, he couldn't afford to leave just yet.' Naomi realised how unconvincing it all sounded and hung her head to one side, allowing her hair to cover her face this time, telling herself she was not going to cry but convinced she was.

Leon said some soothing words. Naomi settled back in her chair. Leon drank some more coffee and devoured in one mouthful another biscuit. 'How did Josh travel that Sunday, the last day you saw him?'

'Transport to the stadium and back was often by company coach or van. It went round pick-up points, collecting them.'

'Jarvis/Josh drives a car, doesn't he?'

'Yes, he has a red one, can't remember what it is, but he doesn't hardly use it, in London he walks mostly. Tube and the like sometimes.'

'What about a bike, a motorbike, or a scooter?'

'No, I never saw him with one, he never mentioned any.'

'Josh's mobile? You have the number?'

'As I said, I lost my mobile on that day. I've never found it. So I have a new one, and I had his number written down in my purse.' Naomi had opened her contact list and showed the small screen to Deshpande.

'OK, thanks. And you said he has not got in touch with you since August 12th?'

'Well, on the flat phone – last week to meet me, but he didn't show.' Leon nodded. 'And so you think that Josh had something to do with the shootings?'

That was the difficult question, Naomi; what do you think?

'Well, possibly; we have not been able to find any concrete evidence, but he remains a suspect.' Leon wanted to deflect her from those areas of the conversation. 'Did he keep any things here in your flat, any books, papers, a holdall, an overnight bag, a suitcase? Anything at all here that belongs to him?'

'Oh, not really. There are some clothes – sometimes I did washing and ironing shirts and so on; a pair of shoes, I think.'

'No mobile phone or computer, iPad, keys, cards, anything like that? Can I see what there is?'

Naomi went off into the next-door bedroom and then into the bathroom, and came back with a shirt, some underwear, socks, a pair of battered trainers, a beanie, a towel, a toothbrush. 'Not much, is there?'

Naomi seemed to have gone into a shell, hardly speaking now, lost in her worries, wondering what on earth Josh could have done to warrant this attention, not really wanting to hear any more. *Is Deshpande really saying he killed all those people?*

'Did he have anywhere where he might store things, a cupboard in the house, under the stairs, a shed in the garden, a locker at a station or maybe a lock-up somewhere, under a railway line?'

'No, don't think so. He never said. Nothing here.'

'You see, in his house we found no other keys, just for his house, his security-job office, and a locker there, his Olympic security tag in the name of Jarvis Collingwood and a key to a locker at the stadium. But there is nothing untoward in these places, nothing in the lockers, in his office, in his car. Nothing to suggest his second identity. Did he ever show you a passport?'

'No.'

'But we think he must be hiding some things – clothes, other keys, security.'

'Why must he? He didn't have much. No. I'm sorry, Mr Deshpande, really, I never saw him hide anything away or have other keys or something.'

Leon was sure the mobile number Naomi had for Josh was not for the mobile Jarvis had with him. Jarvis must have been using a second mobile, registered in another name to work with his second identity – or not registered at all most likely. *But where does he keep it?* Leon wondered if he could get a bigger surveillance team on Collingwood again, but presumably not from the Met; it would have to be supplied through himself, using the agency. He would have to at least double the size of the team.

'Naomi, you are very brave and you've done the right thing. I am worried about Josh/Jarvis. I don't want him to come to harm. But I do feel that he is not telling us everything, and we need him to fully explain to us what he did, and to explain his whereabouts. I think you could help us a lot, Naomi.'

'How do you mean?'

'Well, if you could persuade him to be honest with us? That it would be in his favour if he did?'

'So you think he killed those people?'

'I'm not sure, but if he came clean with us we could help him prove that he didn't if he is innocent. Perhaps he is shielding someone, I don't know.'

'So you want me to talk to him? Tell him I've seen you?'

'Well, I'm going to see him again, and after that I imagine he will be contacting *you*. You need to persuade him to meet me at his lock-up perhaps, or wherever his hiding place is, so that I can help him to prove that he isn't the killer. Because at the moment the evidence is mounting against him.'

9

Ramona looked radiant as she waited inside the arrivals gate at Montreux Airport. On the other hand, Leon looked tired and travel-weary, desperate for a few days' rest over the weekend. They had not seen each other since he had dashed back to London at Sir Hubert Lansbury's request two weeks ago, and since then he had been working non-stop on the Olympics shootings investigation. Her pregnancy had moved on dramatically and the impending arrival of their new baby was obviously looming. Leon loved Ramona and the way she waddled.

They had a two-storey villa on the rural outskirts close to pastures and farms in Vaud, set in the undulating land along the northeast shore of Lac Léman. It afforded them ideal views from their upstairs veranda, year-round snow-topped mountain shapes with see-saw patterns providing the backdrop to the glittering beauty of the vast waters of the lake. Where they were was constantly in the shadow of the great Alpine range and the feeling was always one of calm.

Once they were home there were further emotional welcomes, including from the little girls, and later Leon took advantage of the steamy indoor pool, which helped soak away his tiredness. He showered and then Ramona delighted in massaging his bear-like shoulders on a pool-side canvas bed, where he drifted off to sleep, his cares dropping away with each swoop of her hands across his back, the oil smelling of wood bark and mango. To his relief, Collingwood's image faded from his mind – at least until the next morning, when he woke with the dawn and sat on the slatted veranda of their bedroom watching the coloured patterns of the early sunrise playing along the far jagged white mountaintops and reflecting spectacularly over the calm waters, wondering how he could trap the bastard.

As he had suspected, Jarvis Collingwood had a second identity, passing as someone else at least to his girlfriend, Naomi Lonsdale. He had also managed to hide his previous life completely away from Miss Lonsdale, somehow keeping her at arm's length, even to the extent that she knew not where he had lived with Pamela. Leon felt sure he must have a hiding place where he kept his gear out of the way and where, once they located it, they would find the incriminating evidence. Call it obstinacy or his ego getting the better of his logic, but Deshpande cherished the idea of catching Collingwood by being the one to make that final discovery and then rubbing his handsome nose in it, the final denouement. As an ironic gesture to his former colleagues and masters, those very people Leon Deshpande had fallen foul of, what better way to remind them of their loss, than having him return from abroad to solve the London mystery?

Ramona was not far off her expected date and, as she was planning a home delivery, she was especially worried that Leon would not be able to be with her, that he would be stuck in London with his wretched police investigations. 'I would like you here, Leon – this will be your first boy,' she pleaded with girlish excitement. 'As far as I know!' she added, teasingly.

'Too right, sweetheart, I'll be here,' he promised, ignoring her little innuendo. 'Promise. It's not for two weeks, right? I hope to have the London shooting job done and dusted by then. Then,' he paused and took Ramona round her big waist with a hug from behind, 'I want to take you down to the Cape, with the girls and the newborn. Dad sounded very excited when I spoke to him last night.'

'How is he?' Last time they had seen Leon's father he had a bad back and had been laid up for a while.

'Much better, he says. The arthritis restricts him a bit, but he's driving again, and went on a winery trip in Stellenbosch with a couple of his old mates recently, so he must be better. The warm weather would have done him good.'

'And the wine, no doubt.'

Ramona, her tight belly protuberant and swollen breasts weighing her down, waddled away from him. His bare arms stretched around her from behind, Leon felt some movements within. 'That was a kick, I felt that.'

Ramona laughed, and four-year-old Jesabelle wanted to feel as well. Leon held her hand up to Ramona's tummy and pressed it carefully on one side. 'Let's try here, shall we?'

'I need to sit down.'

'You OK, Ramona?' asked Françoise, bringing her over to a soft armchair.

'Yes, thanks, I'm fine. I just feel ready to have this baby.'

Later, when they were alone again, she said to him once more, 'You'll be here, won't you, Leon?'

'Of course. I'm in London from Monday for a week, but I'll be back next Friday, I've booked a ticket. And you are not due until the week after.'

Leon swam twice a day in the pool and once took his two girls down to the lake, with Françoise helping, leaving Ramona to snooze during the afternoon.

After more time enjoying the solitude of his own company, calmly coming to terms with what he had done, Jarvis Collingwood started forming a longer-term plan. New adventures were possible, there were new avenues to explore. He rang his shy sister-in-law before she left for work one morning and his spirits were lifted when Stella sounded enthusiastic, inviting him round to her place that evening. Stella had always had a crush on him, big handsome Jarvis, ever since they had first met, at his mother's house before his first tour of Iraq, when Ed had turned up there with her, a petite fake blonde whom he had been secretly dating for six months without telling anyone. The two married within a matter of weeks and Gwendolyn was ecstatic. They had always seemed happy enough, through the downs of separation when Ed went off to war and the ups of reunion when they were together after a period of sheer hell worrying whether he would return with all his limbs in place, his faculties in working order, or would return at all. Jarvis had shown no particular interest in her though, finding her, frankly, plain looking and rather too serious for him. But she was lonely, being deprived of close companionship and was probably still attracted to him, he convinced himself with a smile.

He was worrying that the police might decide to arrest him simply out of frustration and the need to be seen to be arresting someone. His imagination kept flooding with images of armed uniforms pounding on his front door in the early hours, with snipers on the roofs covering the back of the house. Deshpande had discovered the Chigwell connection; the Chigwells had spilled the beans and shopped him. That slimy bastard Ainsley was confessing all even now.

He wanted to check that all his money had been paid, although the last time he checked at an ATM in the wall at the Co-op at Bethnal Green, he had over one hundred thousand pounds in his secret account. But Ainsley Chigwell, either alone or with the others' agreement, had decided that Jarvis alive was a risk to them all and they obviously wanted to cut him off before the police got to him. He would not be able to return to his hideaway for some time, not until he had dealt with Ainsley.

He still had the Josh Cooper option – disappear and hide out with Naomi in her flat, later leaving the country with her, travelling through Europe for a while, settling in the Mediterranean somewhere.

Jarvis returned to his home in London on Friday at midday, and the place was pleasantly quiet. He saw no watchers outside his door. Press and reporters no longer took an interest. Although he felt a tremendous affinity with the environment and atmosphere of Beacon Forest, he had been rather kicking his heels there, increasingly frustrated, and had returned to London with renewed energy, determined that the time was right to start clearing the house, chucking Pamela's things out or giving them away to charity shops. A new start, a clean broom. He would clean the house from top to bottom, get a new set of DVDs, buy some CDs.

After a few busy hours of activity sorting things, making piles and filling boxes, he lay on his back, an arm flung behind his head, on a settee in the front room, listening to the subdued noise of traffic outside as the evening began to close in, thinking that perhaps he should confide in his brother. He and Jon had had their differences but he did not particularly hold a grudge against him for the Pamela affair, he was inclined to blame her. Essentially they were loyal to each other, as brothers are, having had similar life experiences. Jon had shown him sympathy and had given him good work in his company – Jarvis had good reason to be grateful to him. Although Jon would not have believed what Jarvis had done or condone it, he would probably understand his motivation and the thrill of its execution. He would want to do his best to keep his brother safe and out of prison.

And what about Gwendolyn? She must be in agony, knowing her youngest, favoured son was in deep trouble, suspecting him of some awful misdemeanour that was too terrible to even think about, and aware of the possibility that he was responsible, Heaven forbid, for a grotesque act of violence. But she would not entertain the possibility of Jarvis shooting his wife, it had to be a mistake. The loss of Pamela was a severe blow to her, she had been fond of her, and missed those regular little chats they had; more importantly, Pamela had been Gwendolyn's source of information about Jarvis and her route to her son's mind. Pamela had been right for him, she insisted, and had been generally a good influence, helping to stabilise him and keep him fixed on the important things in life.

Jarvis was alone in his sombre house, dusty and disordered and no Pamela to disturb the peace. He needed to connect with humanity, he must not allow himself to be isolated. He called Stella to say he was back in town and would be on his way over soon, if she still wanted him. She sounded tense and excitable.

Stella rushed around her flat frantically trying to get everything tidy, including herself, anticipating his visit, unsure of what would happen, where it might lead. Free agents both, a close encounter, having had that early crush, might be irresistible. She showered, washed, shaved her legs and underarms with care, applied body creams and sprays all over and a touch of perfume behind each earlobe. She blow-dried her hair, disappointingly mousy and thin, but her eyes were sparkly, although a little grey. She chose her tiniest lacy knickers, pulled on tight black leggings and a long white cotton shirt, with a sleeveless pink cashmere over, trusting her little puppies would perk themselves up as and when. Around her throat a collection of gold chains and charms settled comfortably within the V-neck and gave a rich rattle when she moved.

When he arrived at her front door, she was in bare feet and had already nervously sunk a glass of Pinot. 'What a lovely surprise.' She smiled a genuine smile of welcome and waited tentatively for Jarvis to approach her. He appeared tough, bristly but clean, with a look of tired nonchalance on his chiselled face. She flung her arms up around his neck, having to stretch fully on tiptoe, and they hugged cheek to cheek.

'Hi, sister, how are you?'

'I'm good.'

'Sorry for the late arrival.'

She let him go. 'That's fine. You're here. You found it all right? Parking?' She whittled on nervously. 'Come in. We don't meet up enough, none of us. I mean, I hadn't seen you or Jonathan or Brenda since your mother's birthday party – until the funeral, of course. How are you? That was such a sad service. You were so brave, my love. I was over with your mother last week in fact, but I don't think she was with it actually, she kept on talking about Pamela as if she was still here.'

Stella was typically straightforward. Once over the immediate sadness and tears of losing Edward, remaining reluctant to talk about the time she shared with him, she quickly returned to the practical aspects of her life, without outward complaint. She was usually direct and plain-speaking. They stood in a brightly lit kitchen, with everything tidily in place and put away, clean empty sink, surfaces wiped down and free of clutter, the way she liked it. A fresh bunch of lemon yellow chrysanthemums stood in a vase by the window. Jarvis was reminded of a show home.

They moved to the lounge, Jarvis with a beer, Stella with another glass of wine. Curtains drawn, dimmed lighting, it was cosy in warm colours, an abundance of cushions and soft surfaces. They relaxed easily and spoke of their common sadnesses, sharing how they had each managed alone. Stella remembered many things about Edward that she missed, like the way he always had breakfast ready for her in the mornings, neatly lined up on the kitchen table, porridge and tea, eggs on toast at weekends, in a way that reflected his army training. Like the way he always whistled under his breath when he was preparing anything in the kitchen.

'Ed always showered and shaved before coming to bed each night, religiously, whatever the time was. He smelt musky in bed, I so miss that smell. He always called me his little star.'

Stella asked Jarvis how he had coped with all the attention since the shooting. 'It has stopped a bit now,' he said, 'although earlier with the newspapers and the police I felt trapped. The police thought I had been responsible and I've been waiting for them to come and arrest me – but they haven't got any evidence.'

Stella hesitated for a second. 'You mean you did have something to do with it? But you weren't there – we all thought you were off duty that night. We knew Pam was there – in fact she texted me at the start of the closing ceremony, she was so excited.'

'No. I was there in the stands, but I didn't see nothing, I left with Jimmy before midnight, and didn't see nothing till I watched the telly news at home. They arrested me for a night, lots of interrogation and that but they had nothing.' Jarvis had to fabricate. 'There's another bloke at it now from MI5 I think, he's onto the case, but I should be in the clear.'

Stella sat upright with a quizzical look on her face, her chest thrust forward, not completely certain that she had understood him correctly. Jarvis drank his beer from the bottle. He was feeling more carefree, watching Stella's pouty lips, he imagined kissing them. She stretched out a hand and pressed his forearm. 'That's all right – for a moment I thought you meant you were implicated there.'

Jarvis looked up into her face, catching her eyes, feeling her soft fingers on his bare skin. The chains round her neck clinked and he watched them disappearing into the shadows of her chest. Then he confessed, out of the blue: 'I have had a new girlfriend.'

'Oh, Jarvis.' Stella, truly shocked, felt her heartbeat stumble with a heavy sense of foreboding, and commented, 'that's good,' trying to sound pleased, 'isn't it?' Stella's soft spot for Jarvis, the handsome playboy brother-in-law, was now feeling a little squashed. Like a teenager on her first serious date, she had been frightened of putting him off and had dreaded outright rejection. Now she was beginning to feel disappointed and foolish.

'No, I mean I had a girlfriend before Pamela died. I was seeing this girl, and she was fun, and now that Pam's not here any more, I could be seeing this other girl a lot, but I feel sort of like frozen, I don't want to do anything.'

Jarvis managed to look hopeless and vulnerable. He had admitted to having had an affair when Pamela was alive. Stella was touched that he had confided in her. He dug further into the dark places of his dead marriage, from which escape had been hard. Pamela was a lovely woman, he admitted, but selfish and hot headed; they fought each other and they did not trust each other. Jarvis was sure that she had been carrying on with a smooth Italian man, Antonio. 'Had you ever heard about that, Stella?'

'No, Jarvis, Pamela never confided in me; we were not that close.'

'This Antonio, he was a bit soft like, all silk and mincing, tight drainpipes and jewellery.' Stella saw that Jarvis was jealous, but said nothing. 'Anyway, I met Naomi and we were beginning to get serious. I didn't know what to do.'

Jarvis was seeking Stella's sympathy with some embellishment, but without revealing too much. 'I loved Ed, you know,' he continued in his low rumbling voice, 'we used to share many things. He would tell me how he felt. He was over the moon with you. On that last tour, he kept this little framed picture of you on his chain, with his ID, so it rattled under his shirt. Only I could hear it, no one else recognised the sound.' Jarvis smiled at the pleasant recollection.

'I had no idea,' Stella admitted. She was perched on the couch next to him, her head resting on her hands, elbows on her knees. He fished a small gold oval frame out of his jacket pocket, hardly bigger than a 50p piece, an empty hole at the top, no chain, a little twisted. Stella edged nearer to him to take a close look. 'I've never seen this,' she marvelled. She took it in both hands and peered at the tiny frame, recognising the face of the young woman with a flashy smile and a ponytail as herself. 'Oh my gosh, it's such an old picture.'

Stella snivelled at the memories. She curled up on the settee, leaning against Jarvis's shoulder. He put an arm around her and they sat for a while, enjoying the closeness of each other.

He fetched repeat drinks from the kitchen. Stella was lying on her side, foetal position, her knees drawn up, hands together in a sort of prayer, still holding the frame. He wiped the tears from her cheeks with a finger and sat in front of her on the carpet, his face level with hers, and asked, 'More wine?'

He held out the glass. She took his wrist and together they guided the glass to her lips. She sipped and looked direct into his cool eyes. Some drops spilled and her tongue emerged to run smoothly across her lips to mop up. She smiled and reached out a hand to his neck, drawing him in. Their kiss was long and sloppy with wine drops. He passed his tongue over the jagged ridges of her teeth. She sucked on him, and then unexpectedly reached for his crotch. She rolled onto her back, rummaging inside his jeans with wriggling cold fingers, just as he was sliding a large hand inside her loose blouse and stroked the soft and silky bare flesh of her flattened breasts.

Her nipples hardened against his palms, just as he enlarged at her squeezing. His marauding fingers slid up the inside of her warm thighs, cupping the spongy swelling of her mound outlined so easily through the tights. Untouched for so long, she swooned at the thrill of it and allowed him to strip the leggings and lace panties off her. She discarded her woolly and shirt over her head and lay back for his eyes to feast on her, vulnerable and naked. Strands of her once-perfect hair were straying over her face, her cheeks glowing with a gentle blush, while the rest of her white skin made her look so fragile. She purred like a lioness, her head tilted to one side, her eyes narrowed, lips pouting. She writhed under his gaze, her pelvis tilting and twisting in a dance, her sex offered up in invitation. The sight of neglected and abundant bush hair sitting like a welcome mat at the entrance to her secret passage, moisture gathering within, drove Jarvis in a surge of desire. He thrust himself at her, immersing himself easily and deeply. She gasped and gripped his rock-like buttocks with both hands, digging her fingers sharply into his flesh, pulling him in. And like a gymnast, his gliding pelvis descended and ascended with controlled precision and increasing rapidity, his weight over her balanced carefully between his elbows and knees to minimise the risk of crushing her beneath. She took him fully and with gusto, and after a few frantic moments, he gushed inside her, grunting loudly. She panted and laughed and tried to hug him, but he fell pole-axed onto the carpet, breathing heavily, his beautiful body tense and shining, spread out beneath her, shrinking gracefully.

'Oh, that was good, that was so good.' And Stella moved herself to lie next to him on the carpet, resting her head on his belly, inhaling the beauty of his heated form at close range and reflecting on all that had gone before.

Deprived of such intercourse for so long, Stella felt relieved and satisfied for the moment; which made her smile, as she dreamt of more to come. She wanted him to stay the night with her. She rose up, careful not to disturb him, and slipped on his big shirt, which covered her effectively, without buttoning it up. She tiptoed out of the room, folding back the long cuffs. She found a spare duvet to cover him with and then returned to the kitchen, where she sat for a while with her daydreams and the remains of her wine.

Half an hour later, Jarvis walked naked into the bright kitchen, catching her at the sink from behind. He turned her round and lifted her up onto the sideboard, where she perched on her bare bottom, while he peeled aside the shirt to feast his eyes again on her nakedness, her high pointy breasts like cherry-topped cupcakes, the folding undulation of her tummy and splayed thighs, her tangle of auburn hair tucked into a tiny triangle. While he pushed her knees apart, she slid towards him over the marble top and hooked her legs around his waist, digging her heels into his hard buttocks. Rising to the occasion once again, easily penetrating her without resistance, he snatched her off to the bedroom, where they sank into a frenzied encore with noisy relish. They both grunted with delight at the moment of climax and lay out of breath, perspiring. They soon fell into an exhausted sleep in each other's arms until the quiet hours of Saturday morning, when they stirred stiffly, feeling the cold. He mumbled about returning home, but she soothed him with words and sweeping soft movements of her hands over his rigid torso. They settled back again, dozing comfortably until daylight sprinkling through the uncovered windows stirred them, with the early morning birdsong.

To avoid embarrassment she went to the bathroom first, showered and creamed all her newly sore places, dressed and retreated to the kitchen to produce breakfast. When Jarvis emerged a little later, dressed this time, he apologised to her for the previous night, while drinking coffee. But Stella was quickly by his side putting a soft hand round his neck, kissing his cheek and saying don't be silly, it was lovely. 'I would rather like to do it again sometime, if you wanted.'

Jarvis stalked the address on Claremont Road he had been given for Ainsley Chigwell. His first walk past on Saturday morning revealed a nice Edwardian terrace east off the Archway Road, and his was a narrow town house in the middle, nearly opposite the junction with Northwood Road. There were no passages around the sides, it was either the front or the back. The front was quite open, little cover. Unusually it had a garage with a steep short drive down into the basement and a set of remotely operated gates. There was a short path up to the front door at the top of several stone steps. The door was heavy with solid brass fittings which looked new, and on either side set in stone were original features, black iron boot scrapers with a tray to collect the mud. There was a security light but no CCTV, not that Jarvis could see.

Hopefully the back of the house would be more promising. It had a walled garden along a row with all the others, so he would have to climb up to the top of the walls from the end of the street and scramble along until he was opposite the right house, which might prove to be difficult to know in the dark, as they all looked the same, straight plain brickwork over three storeys, with tall wood-framed sash windows, some of which had ornate wrought-iron balustrades around small jutting sills. During this crawl along the narrow top in the dark he would be exposed, as there was little tree cover, and so the whole thing was risky.

All the properties here looked well secured, with alarms and electric gates. What concerned Jarvis more was a lone VW van parked up on the opposite side of the road, just past the junction, and about thirty yards from Ainsley's front door. It was placed in front of a rubbish skip in the gutter, outside a house that did look genuinely under repair, with some scaffolding up, ladders, mixers, shovels, piles of rubble and sand, and bags of cement lying about, and workmen coming and going. The white van, with a builder's name painted on the sides, never moved all day. It was still there late Saturday after everyone else had gone home. What gave the watchers away were their clean overalls, their sitting for hours in the front facing Ainsley's house without moving, with their packed lunches and thermos flasks, and a camera with a long-focus lens in one of their laps.

On first arriving early that morning, he had stood quietly behind the trunk and lower foliage of an old plane tree at the Stanhope

Gardens end, to observe the activity in the street. Then he took a wide berth casually around to the other end at Stanhope Road, where he had similarly taken stock for an hour. In a plane hoody he sauntered passed the white van on his second take and saw all he needed to be sure that Ainsley was being observed, and he guessed it was the work of Deshpande.

After midnight, creeping around the streets in the darkest of shadows, Jarvis returned, and just where Claremont Road turned a corner into Stanhope Gardens and out of view of the watching van, he climbed a low wall, made his way along to the high part and then crawled along the top of the garden walls at the back of the terrace, that included Ainsley Chigwell's. It was about eighty yards atop the narrow wall to the back of the sixth house along, where he carefully balanced and jumped down into Ainsley's garden, in complete darkness, using a bench to break his landing. A small wooden shed, its door open, stood in the corner, and inside Jarvis felt for a long-handled broom.

He had seen Ainsley go out alone by car earlier in the day, the automatic gates opening and closing behind him, and return some hours later with a woman companion in tow and lots of shopping bags, dashing from the car through the drizzly rain up the front steps and into the house. Jarvis, protected from the wet by a light-weight cagoule, assumed that by now Ainsley would be inextricably conjoined with his friend and sleeping partner, soundly unaware of the danger he was in. He moved silently across some paving, down several stone steps, and approached the back of the house, where more steps led down to a basement with its full-height glass door.

An outside security light partly obscured by climbing clematis over the back wall of the house suddenly flashed on, flaring in his face. He turned away to avert his eyes and darted forwards, to stand directly under the lamp, where he pushed himself flat into the soft foliage. After a moment or two the light went out and he was plunged into darkness once again. He waited, aching and expectant. He could hear no sounds from inside the house, nothing to indicate that anybody had been alerted. He reached up with the broom to the lamp that was fixed to the brickwork on an adjustable bracket about four feet above his head and pushed hard on the underside, tilting it upwards, and then pushed sideways, turning the whole assemblage into the wall, so that both lamp and sensor faced up and into the house, away from the path below. He moved with confidence over to the ground-floor windows and peered in through the glass. A series of LED lights twinkled from a row of shiny equipment at the far wall providing feeble light in a wide kitchen and living area, with a marble central island and high stainless steel stools at a breakfast bar.

He tried the handle of the kitchen door, knowing nothing would move. He nipped down the stairs to the basement door, again peering inside, although he could not make out anything within. The door handle yielded nothing. Suddenly a beam of light from a torch was thrown down open-tread stairs at the back of the room from above and a pair of bare male legs appeared at the top. They belonged to someone in a floppy dressing gown, who cautiously descended to the basement, flashing the torchlight over the room, that looked to be kitted out like a gym. The torch bearer also carried what looked like a fire poker, and from the shape and outline, Jarvis recognised Ainsley Chigwell.

Jarvis knew that if Ainsley saw him through the glass, or even suspected someone was outside prowling around on his property, he would call the police, not open the back door and venture out unprotected in his dressing gown holding a feeble poker. Jarvis would surely strike him down if he did. But that was not going to happen, not tonight at any rate; he needed to beat a retreat while he could. Back up the steps, across the garden to the back wall, up onto the top, along the slippery bricks at a crouch in the pitch black to reach the side wall on Stanhope Gardens, he dropped down onto the pavement and crawled away, his tail not exactly between his legs. He would have to return another time with another plan.

Deshpande caught his Sunday-evening London flight after the usual rush and panic, having reassured Ramona that he would be back next Friday evening and would be staying at home until the baby was born, and for some days beyond. He had some loose ends to tie up with the investigation and had some other London business to see to. With his next big contract with the Tanzanian government to be negotiated, Lucy-Ann had set up some meetings at the end of the week for him. However, deep down he recognised that he was being optimistic.

As the jet arced away from Geneva airport, leaving the lake behind reflecting twinkling lights along its shore, and headed south-west over France through a feathering of low cloud, the evening sun sank across the distant horizon, leaving fiery streaks of orange and red light glancing into the cabin momentarily, before blanking out like a light switch. Some passengers were pulling their window blinds down and settling in for a short sleep, but Deshpande was looking forward to his dinner with a bottle of Beaujolais and music on the headphones.

After the wine he started to nod off, his languorous mind filling with happy dreams of Ramona delivering his baby boy at home with the midwife. The tasks that remained to be sorted in the Stratford shootings investigation flashed up, like adverts on television. Jarvis Collingwood's chunky features loomed in front of him, dead-pan expression but with the occasional sneer at Deshpande behind his back. But come the day, Leon would be pointing at Collingwood and sniggering with all his friends about how he had trapped the Killer of Stratford.

Deshpande would dearly love to bag this man, for Hubert's sake, and to deliver his head on a platter to 10 Downing Street, preferably in the middle of a private COBR meeting.

10

Deshpande decided he would confront Collingwood once again. He wanted to shock him into doing something hasty and unplanned, he wanted to show him how close he was.

Early Monday morning, before most sensible people had even thought about leaving for the rush-hour journey to work, when the streets were still quiet and damp from overnight drizzle that reflected depressing splodges of inadequate light off the uneven pavements, and the first buses had barely started rumbling along their convoluted routes, a black Audi parked at one end of Baring Street just as Deshpande was parking at the other. The overnight report from his watchers said Jarvis had spent last night at home but had not been seen the previous four nights, and only once on Friday morning, confirming to Deshpande that either he was at some secret bed-and-breakfast or in a lock-up garage somewhere, or else he was dossing down with sympathetic supporters. Or lovers.

After a short wait in their respective positions, Deshpande approached on foot the familiar purple door, the number 15 displayed in brass on the central strip between glass panels. Looking back at the Audi eighty yards away, a watcher on his team in a raincoat climbed out of the car and made her way slowly along the street on the other side, looking like any typical housewife, up early. Some way short of Jarvis's front door, she stopped and perched herself on a low wall. The driver of the Audi remained watching from inside the car at his end of the street. Deshpande pressed the buzzer twice and waited more than thirty seconds before pressing again.

After another short pause, Collingwood, in vest and jeans, opened the door, and first looked surprised at Deshpande's unannounced appearance, and then a little annoyed. 'Oh, look, is this really necessary? It's not even half six. I have a job today. I was just . . .'

'Sorry, Jarvis, I knew you were an early riser. I wanted to catch you. There have been some—,' He paused and scratched his nose, '—important developments. Need to talk.' Deshpande noticed the brown holdall on the floor near the front door, looking stuffed full and zipped up. There were packing boxes piled along the hall.

'I don't have to answer your questions. Do I?'

'No. No you don't. But if you don't I will get a warrant for your arrest through Broderick and you will be banged up in the nearest police station.' Deshpande had his mobile out and looked poised. 'You would be entitled to a solicitor of course. But . . .'

'Look, I've nothing to hide, but you are beginning to bug me.'

'Won't take long, Jarvis, there's a good fellow.' A big smile from Deshpande, his shoulders shrugging in a friendly way. 'I need your help.' The two men stared at each other.

Jarvis was incensed by Deshpande's patronising tone and barely restrained himself from grabbing him by his collar and shaking him. Somewhat reluctantly, he allowed the door to open fully to allow the man of authority to enter. Deshpande muttered, 'Thanks, thanks for your time.' They shuffled into the front room, aware of the vague smell of toast, and Deshpande dropped his raincoat on a chair as he began to pace the room.

'Do you want a drink or something?'

'No thanks, Jarvis. I want you to talk to me,' and Deshpande characteristically stopped in front of Jarvis, looking him straight in the eyes, 'about Naomi Lonsdale.' He pronounced the girl's name as she did, with three separate syllables, and Jarvis flinched at the shared intimacy.

With his bare shoulders bulging, his tattoos exposed, and his silver neck chain and left earring on show, Jarvis was intimidating in his own way, but Deshpande was tough and well-shaped, and although a little shorter than Jarvis, he felt in no way inferior. In his usual grey floppy suit, this time he had also taken the precaution before coming out of tucking a Browning 9mm loaded with a twelve-round magazine under his left armpit, where it now sat comfortably in its holster. Their abdomens almost knocked against each other.

'Come and tell me about your girlfriend, Jarvis,' he repeated, standing firm.

Jarvis felt suddenly deflated, a sinking feeling that wrenched through his body. Hanging his head, he turned away quickly into the centre of the room, a short step away from panic. He spoke inwardly to himself. *Brace and fight your corner, this man has nothing on you.* And he managed to remain straight-backed and firm in his voice. He looked steadily back at Deshpande, who was inclined to pace the room. 'I know a few women, Mr Deshpande, sometimes I visit them, Naomi was just another one that I knew. She has absolutely nothing to do with this. I used to visit her place, and I was seeing a lot of her before . . . She knew I was married; thought I was getting a divorce from Pamela.' Jarvis tried to dismiss the whole affair with a wave of his hand.

'Has absolutely nothing to do with what?' Deshpande stiffened.

'With my life with Pamela and her death . . .' Jarvis tried to recover his composure, thinking he might have given something away.

'And were you and Pamela planning a divorce?'

'We hadn't actually talked about it. I had thought about it, several times. How did you find Naomi?'

'Why did you not tell me about Naomi, when I asked before?'

Jarvis shrugged, screwing up his eyes.

'Naomi was light relief from your quarrelsome marriage to Pamela, was she? Is that how you would describe your relationship?'

'Yes, if you like.'

'And did Pamela know about Naomi?'

'No, don't think so. Look, it's not a crime, I had a lover, several lovers – all right?'

'But you said you were loyal to your marriage. What else have you not been loyal about?' Deshpande stood four-square in front of Jarvis, hands loose by his sides. There was no answer. 'You stopped seeing her the day of the shootings, why was that?'

Jarvis looked down at Deshpande's face. 'You haven't told me how you found her.'

'Well, Jarvis, we have been busy.' He spoke with force and determination. 'Like we know about Josh Cooper. Your friend, your second identity, yes? Tell me how that works.'

'Oh, blimey, you guys think you are so good. I told Naomi a false name just because it was more exciting, it kinda protected myself. It allowed me to be someone else when I was with her.' Jarvis was pleased with his own performance. 'I'm a romantic, Mr Deshpande, it was part of the excitement.' Handsome and confident, Jarvis seemed unashamed by his admissions. Although these police discoveries came as a shock at first, he was able to take them in his stride and provide neat answers.

Leon Deshpande had to admit to himself later, when he went over the conversation again in his head, that Jarvis sounded convincing. 'When we looked at your mobile, there was nothing on it about Naomi, no messages or calls to her mobile. The mobile number she has for you is not your mobile, not the one you said was yours. The conclusion is that you have another mobile that you use for her, one that you have not told us about. That presumably will tell us all sorts of other things about your contacts. You are hiding this, I presume.'

Again Jarvis seemed to be sure of himself. He shook his head slowly. 'Honestly. I decided to drop Naomi a few weeks ago and I deleted her from my mobile; all numbers and messages. I don't have another mobile.'

'But you phoned her at home last week to see her again and tell her everything. Why, if you had broken it off with her?'

'With Pamela gone, unexpectedly like, I was feeling lonely and I wanted some warmth in my bed, if you must know.' Jarvis looked sheepish and his mouth puckered.

'So why did you drop her on the day of the closing ceremony?'

'That was a very busy time and we were all stressed out, and it all reached a head at that time, we had an argument, otherwise it was just coincidence.'

'So the number she has for you?'

'Is wrong. It must be. I used to phone her on the landline, hardly ever used my mobile. I called round at her shop, or I went over to her place. She never phoned me, because either I was here and Pamela would find out or I was working on some security job somewhere; so I always contacted her, she never phoned me.'

'On her contact list, under "C", she has "Josh" and a mobile phone number that is not the number of your mobile,' Deshpande persisted, and then turned away for a moment, not wanting to show his annoyance that Jarvis had got away with his answers so far. Jarvis was good, he knew that, but as he sat opposite him now, he looked a touch impatient, perhaps uncomfortable. 'You have no answer for that, right?'

'I just told you, she's got my number wrong. You've been round to her flat, have you?'

'Yup, we know where she lives.'

Now it was Jarvis who looked away, muttering to himself inaudibly. *Stay with it, he's fishing.*

'OK, Jarvis, for now. But we are watching you; you've been away for four nights this week. Where?'

'Various places, friends, Jimmy's place in the Mile End Road.'

'I don't want you disappearing again.' Deshpande wandered out to the corridor. 'I'll see myself out,' he called.

Deshpande felt that he must have implanted enough worries into Jarvis's mind by now, letting him know of their discovery of his second identity and the girlfriend, and the fact that he had been round to her flat. He desperately hoped his watching team were alert, as he was convinced Jarvis would make a run soon, tonight maybe. He knew he would be wanting to talk to Naomi as soon as he had left. He would ring her on his hidden mobile, with his Josh Cooper persona, he would not use the landline, he was convinced of that. He was sure the mobile was not here in this house – he had hidden it away, in a lock-up somewhere, and that's where he would be headed later tonight. Although trying to follow him would be almost impossible without Jarvis spotting them, in which case he would not lead them anywhere but up the garden path. Nevertheless, they had to keep trying.

During the rest of that working Monday, Jarvis was occupied with a job Jonathan's team had arranged, delivering secure high-value packages around the City from an armoured truck in his green uniform and protective helmet. On returning home in the early evening, he changed for a run, trainers and black Lycra gear, with no coloured markings, and a runner's rucksack with weights around his waist. He left openly by the front door, deliberately taking his time with repeated stretching and bending exercises outside on the pavement and using the low wall, all the time aware that the occupants of the black Audi at the end of the street had their beady eyes on him. He started to jog away out of Baring Street, noticing the slight figure emerging from the Audi. He set off slow enough for the first mile or so up Southgate Road, planning a four-mile circuit that would take him back via the canals. His tail was a woman in black tights, blonde ponytail swinging from side to side, thirty yards behind.

The woman was Evelina, a Swedish fitness fanatic and boxer in her thirties. She knew that however fit she may be, she could not possibly keep up with Jarvis if he was running at full training speed. But if he was meeting anyone or heading to some secret hideaway, Deshpande would want to know about it. With mobile tucked into a band on her upper arm, she would link with the driver, Sheldon, a funny black guy she had only met once before this job, who would drive slowly, following in the direction of both runners a hundred yards behind them.

Jarvis kept his pace in check, so as not to lose her. Soon he was jogging along Balls Pond Road leading into Essex Road, alongside the heavy traffic that squelched through the wet gutters, as lights were going on, reflecting and dazzling. He nipped along the quieter back streets through Islington, slowing down as he headed for the canal tow path from Noel Road, where he stopped, waiting long enough for Evelina to see him. He jogged down the sloping path from the street and ran past the lock towards home now in an eastwards direction to complete his circuit. In the darkening atmosphere, where the poorly lit path ran alongside the canal, there were few runners and cyclists about. A lone punt meandered on the water, fairy lights twinkling, breaking the surface and sending tiny waves to caress up against the stone sides with lapping sounds.

Jarvis knew these narrow canal pathways well. The waterways were constructed hundreds of years ago to allow business to be conducted along them, providing transport access across the city. Nowadays mostly unused, in places the canal was only twenty feet wide, its surface caked in layers of oily green algae, giving it a dull motionless appearance. The towpaths, well below street level, were originally designed for a horse to pull a barge along the adjacent water. Low road bridges crossed over at intervals every forty or fifty yards and the paths underneath were narrower, dark and wet, with no barriers at the edge, the water a couple of feet below. For anyone using them, it meant stepping aside for a runner or cyclist to avoid a clash and having to duck down at the same time because of reduced headroom, cyclists often dismounting.

For anyone using the towpath, the view ahead along any stretch of it only went as far as the next bridge, because of the narrowness and low position, and the path ahead only came into sight again on emerging from the bridge. A nightmare scenario for anyone on foot trying to follow a subject at a reasonable distance without being noticed.

Jarvis negotiated his way with confidence, the canal to his right peaceful, as he ducked under bridges and avoided and side-stepped a few runners and walkers along the way. He jogged comfortably under the next bridge at a crouch, and on emerging on the lighter far side, out of sight of Evelina, he twisted sharply off the path to his left and flattened himself against dry brickwork, where there was a stairway running up to the road above. He crouched, bent low next to some metal fencing. Aware of his heartbeat pounding through his chest, he pressed himself against the cold bricks and tried to hold his breath, waiting.

Evelina's footfalls and breath sounds became increasingly audible as she approached, slowing at the entrance under the bridge. She had had to push herself to keep Jarvis within sight on this run and was feeling winded. Along the towpath it had not been at all easy and she was uncertain where this was all leading. She was longing for it to end. Following at thirty to forty paces behind Jarvis, she ducked her head under the 'low headroom' sign, careful with the slippery surface underfoot, aware of unpleasant smells of urine. She straightened up from her semi-crouch as she emerged the other side into better light but had no idea where Jarvis had gone; she could not make him out along the next stretch of towpath. Too late she realised he must have taken a side turning, up the bridge steps perhaps. Without warning, she felt a painful kick on the back of a leg and a heavy man barging into her from the side. Much later, when trying to explain to an unsympathetic Leon Deshpande what exactly had happened, shivering with cold and wet and trying to remember the finer details, she could not be certain that the figure that had knocked her over, almost throwing her off the canal path, had been Jarvis Collingwood at all.

There was nothing she could do to prevent herself tumbling off the edge of the path, breaking the surface of the canal water with a splash. The sudden cold was shocking. She gave a half yell, but gulped mouthfuls of turgid water as she went under with her phone still on her arm, unable to breathe, and then seemed to stay underwater for an awfully long time.

No one saw exactly what happened, although one rider and a pair of runners turned at the sound of the splash. By this time Jarvis had taken the stairs beside the bridge three at a time up onto Bridport Place, and was carefully scanning the street with its poor yellow lighting to see if the Audi had kept up, and of course it was nowhere to be seen. He dashed across the junction at a sprinter's pace back to Baring Street, where he slowed to a casual jog, hands on hips, breathing heavily. His breath restored, inside the house he pulled on a loose tracksuit jacket, grabbed his prepared overnight bag and car keys. He was out the front door, carefully locking up, and back to a jogging pace within a few minutes. He found his car carefully parked behind a van, a few streets away at the end of Arlington Avenue, and he drove away towards Northchurch Road and Naomi's house without Deshpande's costly watchers having a clue where he was.

Parking in an adjacent street, he climbed onto a party wall that ran between two rows of houses, scampered along the top – reminding him of his failed escapade the night before at Ainsley's place, which still rankled – and dropped off the wall into Naomi's back yard. He knocked gently on the glass of the French windows. It was after eight o'clock, beginning to get dark outside. Naomi cautiously opened the door inwards a small amount and called out, 'Is that you, Josh?'

'Naomi, yes, it's me. Sorry it's so late.'

'Oh my God, you scared me, Josh.' She opened the door wide and stood still with both hands held up at her face, her eyes wide behind the black-rimmed glasses. 'Are you all right? You've been running.'

Naomi, in jeans and white shirt, backed away into the lighted room and Jarvis stepped inside. 'Come in. What's happening, Josh? Where have you been? A policeman came to see me earlier, I've been so worried.' She stood still, her hands clasped either side of her face, still looking worried, wanting to look happy.

'I know. That was Mr Deshpande, I expect.' Jarvis closed the outside door and drew the long curtains together. The room felt warm and homely, and Naomi backed away into the centre.

'He's not a policeman, strictly, but he's powerful,' continued Jarvis.

'So what's going on? He said you are not Josh, you're someone else.' Naomi was near hysterical, her voice squeaking ever higher.

Jarvis interrupted, with his hands held up in front of him in mock surrender. 'Slow down, girl, how can I answer your questions if you don't give me a chance? Now, calm, please.' He reached out for her hands.

'I've been so worried,' she said again, plaintively. 'I thought you were coming over last week, after you phoned.'

'Yes, I was about to, then I had to deal with the police, I'll explain.'

Naomi started bustling around the flat, picking things up, tidying around, clearing the seats, and went to boil the kettle. 'It's all such a mess, sorry.' She made some tea. She nipped to the bathroom. She was feeling suddenly nervous, her tummy was twitching and rumbling, and she was scared to get down to the real questions, wasting time with other things. Jarvis was satisfied he had got rid of his watchers, but was quietly fuming with frustration that it was Naomi, whom he had lured into his life in the first place for his protection, who had now put his freedom at risk. He felt that the police were only a short distance from ordering his arrest, and he needed to plot the next move ahead of Deshpande, which meant tonight. He would need to use Naomi.

Jarvis followed her into the kitchen. 'Naomi, stand still, let's sit down, please.' Naomi moved close to him with a regretful smile and reached up with both hands over Josh's collar, as she had done many times before; leaning forward, her lips touched his bristly cheek and he responded with a quick kiss on her lips.

'Yes, I've missed you too,' he said quietly and put his arms round her waist. They settled into a couple of wooden chairs and spoke softly, with only the light from next door to guide them, as if they needed to share secrets. Jarvis was flushed from his exertions and pulled his top off over his head, exposing in the semi-darkness bulbous shoulders bared and shiny with perspiration. He reached for a glass of water. Acutely Naomi felt his attraction, those pale languid eyes and that grumbling voice, so much part of his magnetic charm and she began to relax in the shadowy recesses of her little kitchen.

'So how come I get a visit from Mr Deshpande today asking me about you?' he asked.

Naomi hesitated for a few seconds, recognising with a jolt the slight antagonism in his voice. She sat up straight, her legs together, squeezing her pressed palms between her knees. She turned towards him with her goofy smile and open expression and Jarvis felt more disappointed than angry.

'I was like, so worried after you had not turned up, I saw Celia for moral support and advice and we both felt that we should like, ask the local police what to do. So they took some details and said they would put out an alert for you and make some enquiries. I didn't know what to do – you have never told me where you live, Josh. Then this big policeman came round and said you had another name, Collingwood, and that Pamela had been shot at the stadium. My head was in whirl, hang on, like, where had all this come from?' She was trembling.

'Okay, okay, let's slow down again. Let me tell you a few things.'

Naomi brought two mugs of tea to the table while Jarvis started to quietly go through the events. 'When I first saw you, in the hairdresser's, I was down, at a low, and Pamela and me were not getting on, right; I needed someone I could talk to and feel happy with. And you were so nice, you know, you listened and you didn't have any hang-ups, and you had no, like, obligations, so we could just be natural. And I used another name, I don't know, just because I wanted to be different with you. I had been so disgusted at myself and was beginning to hate my very name; I wanted to start anew, and having another name seemed like a transformation. I'm sorry, I didn't mean to deceive you.'

'No, I understand, Josh, or is it Jarvis? Gosh, that sounds funny.' She squeezed his hands and massaged them and so far was taking everything in. He was pleased with his ability to spin a tale and be sympathetic and pathetic at the same time. He realised that girls only really wanted someone they could mother, someone who needed their special help. And while Naomi felt like that, he was safe with her.

'At the stadium that night, I didn't know what was going on, but I got caught up in the police investigation. When they looked at all the lists of people working there, they came up with my name because of the Army past, my shooting record.'

'But you had nothing to do with it, did you, right?'

'No, I'm just trying to get them off my back. I've given them a list of possible characters – you know, some of the people employed in security there, it would make your hair curl, really, some were a load of thugs, with criminal records and all sorts; some Army people with the shooting skills they were looking for. There was this other bloke, Martin Jones, that they need to look at, he was a dodgy character, injured in Iraq and mixed with some odd types. When I found out that Pamela had been killed that night, I was gobsmacked, Naomi, I couldn't believe it. It was a complete accident, the guy was hitting another man in front of her and the ricochet hit Pam in the neck.'

Jarvis looked concerned, deep lines appeared between his eyes, his brows knitted tightly. His handsome face creased either side of his mouth, and he used a large hand to wipe his face, holding his fingers over his nose and mouth for a second. His eyes met hers full on.

'I had to identify her in the morgue in Bow Road Station that morning, they came and woke me up at five o'clock – it was cold as a fridge, and there were three bodies on trolleys under plastic sheets. She was under one, so white and lifeless, Naomi, I was upset. I'm not saying I was in love with her or anything, all that had passed, we both knew that. But like, when you see someone you know well like that, it was a shock.' Jarvis was obviously struggling with his emotions, his chest heaving.

'Poor Josh.' Naomi was reaching round his neck and pressing her face against his damp cheek. She wiped his eyes with her fingers and then through smeared tears they kissed, wet noses smudging. A stirring of passion that surprised him started to arise and he felt he wanted to swallow her up. His mouth opened over hers and he pressed her tight, his tongue pushing against her big front teeth. She nipped him with her sharp-edged incisors and he smothered her face with more kisses, while images of Stella flashed through his mind. He stopped, out of breath; her make-up was smeared.

'Heavens,' she mumbled, swooning backwards, 'I had forgotten how good that was.'

She cuddled up to him, awkwardly and he wrapped his big arms around her slim figure. She lay her face across his chest and she could feel his warmth and the distant pounding of his heart against her cheek.

'Because it was Pamela shot in that way, the police and this Mr Deshpande bloke, they think that it was me. I need to get him off my back, somehow. I need to disappear for a few days.'

Naomi looked up. 'Again?' she asked with a sarcasm unusual for her.

'I need to show him a few things, to prove it to him.' Jarvis was distant, speaking in a way that suggested he was really talking to himself, in riddles. 'I just want to gather my last resources, show him what I've been involved in, that I had nothing to do with the shootings on the roof. My security checks came though, they have no evidence.'

Naomi was feeling in need of some reassurance herself, with a niggling urge for him in her loins rousing her. 'Come on, Josh, let's go next door, I want you to . . . and then stay with me all through the night, like before.' She was tugging at him now to bring him back to life.

'I can't stay, Naomi. Deshpande will be watching now he knows where you live.' He pushed her away, reluctantly. 'I'm going down to Beacon Forest again, it's the only place I'm safe, where nobody knows where I am. I can hide there for a while, like before, I have food and heating, and a bed set up in one of the caravans.'

'I could come down and stay with you there.' Naomi sounded enthusiastic.

'No, not a good idea, not now. Give it a day or two. Someone might follow you. It could be difficult.' Jarvis did not want to appear dismissive, as if he did not really want her around him, but he knew he had to be kind to her. A few moments later he got up to leave, after a prolonged kiss on Naomi's soft mouth. Standing by the curtained French windows, she was left clutching herself forlornly and holding back her feelings, watching Jarvis disappear from her grasp once again, as he slipped out through the back garden, climbed the back wall and scampered along the top out of sight between the houses at the back.

He dropped down off the wall into the adjacent road and reached his car unnoticed. He drove away carefully and, in a circuitous way, headed through the City, over the river and down towards the A2 and Beacon Forest.

Sitting alone at the wheel of the black Audi at the front of the house on Northchurch Road, Sheldon noticed nothing and could only report back to Deshpande that after the towpath run he had lost contact with Evelina and there had been no sign of Jarvis at Naomi's place all evening.

11

Leon Deshpande and his police escort were up early again next morning, the weather suitably overcast and chilly. They were outside the address in Highgate with the relevant warrants before seven o'clock. Ainsley Chigwell lived in his smart town house off the Archway Road, which was probably more Crouch End than Highgate, but Ainsley liked the sound of Highgate better, it was posher, and it was where he told everybody he lived.

He looked childishly shocked when Deshpande, to whom he had taken an instant dislike when they had met for a short while a couple of days ago, insisted on coming into his house and searching the place. He had answered all questions in a straightforward and helpful way last week, arousing no suspicions, showing willingness any time to be of further assistance, giving his telephone numbers. He was thus not expecting an unannounced house visit, with uniformed officers at his front door and crunching noisily over his wooden floors from attic to basement, knocking against doors, turning things upside down in every room, wanting to know who else lived there, and then insisting on removing his laptop, tablet and mobile, to check whether he was hiding terrorists or weapons of mass destruction or something.

Finally Deshpande marched into his front room, where he had been detained for an hour, and said they were all going on a ride across to the Bethnal Green area to look at some garage lock-ups.

'You lied to me last time, Mr Chigwell – you said you did not own any lock-ups in town. Tut tut, we've got a list here of at least *twelve*.' Deshpande sounded angry.

'No, I said we don't own them directly, they're leased through an agency and I didn't know of anyone in our lock-ups that should not be there or that we had rented any to a stranger recently, or ever at all,' Ainsley whined with several flicks of his fringe, still dressed in a T-shirt and jeans that he had quickly thrown on when the front-door bell had started ringing so early.

Ainsley was bundled into the back of a big Volvo after he had dressed properly and then driven at an uncomfortable speed through the busy London streets with a couple of unmarked vans in convoy, until they reached Commercial Street. Chaos then ensued as the driver was uncertain exactly where to go, directions were shouted, mobiles used, maps consulted, hands raised and fingers pointed, with much swearing, as the car lurched up one side street after another, followed by some five-point turns and even more juicy swearing, all at a loud, breakneck pace. Which served to make Ainsley feel so sick on his empty stomach that he was oddly thankful he had missed his usual cooked breakfast that morning. Officers jumped out and started knocking on doors, rousing the occupants of the businesses and offices that were lined up mainly along Cheshire Street underneath the old brickwork of the Liverpool Street railway viaducts. Ainsley remained in the car, not wanting to attract attention or risk recognition, while groups of heavy-handed police in their bulky uniforms and yellow jackets moved from one entrance to another, checking with the occupants before pouring into the enclosures and then all pouring out again some ten or fifteen minutes later. Sniffer dogs and Alsatians pulled keenly on their leashes, their uniformed handlers leather-gloved. There was Chigwell Cars, which occupied two adjacent units, Chigwell Hire Service and two further unmarked garages, with smart black limousines closely parked on the forecourt in front. One was a storage space for a retail outlet, spare parts for cars and motorcycles. The searchers spent half an hour in one garage, looking into every space and hidden corner. Passenger trains passed frequently either way above them, while other officers and hangers-on stood around in groups waiting for results. From the back of a big white van a female officer had fetched some coffees from somewhere, and dispensed them lukewarm and sweet in paper cups, which was decent of her even if they did not much taste of coffee.

Ainsley sat nervously jiggling his legs in the cold, nursing his cup, smoking a cigarette and worrying about the jobs he should have been doing today and how the hell he would explain this to the secretaries in the office when he got to work – and hoping he was not going to shit himself when they dragged him along to Witan Street and asked him to explain the findings in number 208. Although he had not heard the name Witan Street mentioned, he dared not try to read the list Deshpande kept waving about to his officers in case he saw the name on it and turned white. He prayed that they would miss it, for some reason, any reason.

A good two hours into the process, having moved haltingly along the railway arches to another street, Deshpande called, 'Two to go, Mr Chigwell, according to our list.' He was standing outside one of the vans in the middle of Dunbridge Road in his brown overcoat and usual crumpled grey suit and heavy brogues. 'Witan Street, numbers 206 and 208.'

Shit. 'We have others further out towards Plaistow you know, and some down Limehouse way,' replied Ainsley from inside, unconvincingly trying to deflect their searches elsewhere.

'Yes, I had those on the list, but they're too far out; what we want is to find young Collingwood's secret little hideaway, and that will be nearer to home.' He had bent down and turned his gaze on Ainsley, looking at him through the open back doors with a determined grin on his still-tanned face.

'I don't know where Jarvis lives, maybe he's out that way,' said Ainsley with the characteristic flick of his hair. Deshpande detected a tone of familiarity in Ainsley calling Jarvis by his Christian name, that he thought was a giveaway. 'Jarvis Collingwood? You still searching for that man?' Ainsley added quickly, realising his slip.

'Oh, yes. Actually, you may know the little bugger under a different name: Josh Cooper mean anything to you?' And once again Deshpande was staring intently through the shadows in the van into Ainsley's flustered face.

'Look here, we have had nothing to do with this. I don't know what you are talking about.'

Deshpande connected with Ainsley's shifty narrowed eyes. 'Actually, Chigwell, I don't believe you. So let's go look at the last two lock-ups, shall we?'

And the cars and vans rapidly filled up again with bulky sweaty figures, with Ainsley and Deshpande squashed this time in the middle seats of a large transporter, which then moved the short distance to the end of Dunbridge Road, passing the station with the railway lines above them on their right, winding into Three Colts Lane, where the road turned under one railway bridge and then split, with one branch continuing on under a second bridge, and the other bending left, northwards, where it turned on itself in a sort of circle that connected apparently with nowhere in particular. It was a complicated little corner of small streets, some hard to name, but tucked out of the way and not apparently overlooked by anything else were numbers 206 and 208, in a sort of cul-de-sac, either side of a tunnel that ran under the railway (where number 207 once had been, Deshpande thought, but was now a narrow road passing through). The police vans parked up side by side on the open forecourts. While his officers looked over 206, Deshpande jumped out and was inspecting the area in front of 208, which was protected on three sides by brick pillars and walls and wire fencing. Through the adjacent tunnel, which was narrow and dark, under dripping steel girders with little natural light, and out the other side, he came upon a triangular bit of waste ground, head high with weeds and thistles, behind a high wire-mesh fence with sharp-looking spikes along the top, strewn with rubbish, boxes and palettes. It appeared to be immediately behind 208. Deshpande could smell dog shit and urine.

Number 206 was small and unoccupied. The police locksmith had the single door opened within half a minute and three police officers entered with torches and dogs. There was nothing interesting inside, apparently, just a small metal workshop, used by a sole worker who repaired boilers. Deshpande stood waiting in the chill air, hands in pockets, beside Ainsley, who fidgeted and reached for his cigarettes, his hands shaking. The crowd of officers soon came out, locked 206 and moved over the road to stand expectantly in front of the two doors of 208, the dogs pulling hard at their collars.

'So who occupies this one, Mr Chigwell? 208.'

There were no business signs on the outside, just the numbers painted large in white on the brick next to the side door. The slatted roll-up garage door, firmly closed tight to the concrete, looked a bit rusty and battered. The toughened metal door to its right, showing no keyhole, had a shiny numbered security lock and handle on the outside which looked quite new, and the locksmith studied the system for some time, mumbling to himself. 'The code would be useful, sir.'

There were piles of rubber tyres and black bags around the enclosed outside space, with its oily concrete driveway. Another overgrown waste patch next to them was walled off by a fence, with 'KEEP OUT DANGER OVERHEAD LINES' on a number of worn and rusty signs, their colour mostly faded with age. While waiting for an answer Deshpande noted the position of this particular lock-up and the potential convenience and privacy afforded it by the surrounding walls and pillars.

'Well, Chigwell?' demanded Deshpande.

'As far as I know this arch remains unoccupied. One of our older workers moved out some months ago, retired, I think.'

'The security lock – no key required, just a PIN. That's unusual isn't it? The only one like that we have seen today. Know the number by any chance?' Deshpande's heart was racing, he could feel he was getting somewhere. Ainsley's heart was racing too, he could feel himself going somewhere he did not wish to go.

'No, heavens no, I wouldn't keep that sort of information,' Ainsley declared, his dry lips stuck together and firmly pinched as he flicked the fringe off his forehead with an aloof and exaggerated movement.

Following a brief period of deliberation between the experts, cutting equipment was brought forth from one of the support vehicles, and after a few frightful minutes of sparks and screeching that put the dogs' nerves on edge, the metal door was pushed inwards onto a dark, dank interior bigger than a squash court and just as tall. Deshpande pushed Ainsley forward and through the entrance, shuffling in behind him. A neon strip light was switched on to give them some feeble light which hardly dispersed the shadows around the peripheries. The gloved-up team were walking cautiously all around the bricked-in space, confirming their first impression that it was unoccupied. They were awaiting instructions from Mr Deshpande, who wriggled his spade-like hands into rubber gloves and pulled his coat closer around him, feeling colder inside than he had felt outside. Taking a big torch from one of his officers, he started to walk slowly around the enclosure flashing bright circles of light into all the corners and recesses, mentally noting every object and detail that was revealed.

Ainsley flashed his eyes rapidly around the space inside, adjusting to the darkness, heaving a sigh, as there seemed at first glance to be little of interest in number 208. Jarvis Collingwood was not sitting in a chair sipping a beer waiting for them, sniper's rifle cradled in his lap, thank the Lord. His sigh of relief was almost audible. He nearly burst into laughter as he watched intently Deshpande move around methodically with his torch.

Water was dripping down a wall at the back, where the shadows seemed to be hiding a million truths. A rectangle of dull carpet covered half the floor surface inside the door. Placed at the centre of the room was a wooden chair and a bare table with a solitary biro on it, and at one end a landline telephone that, on picking up the receiver, proved to be still connected. Underneath, empty cardboard boxes that Deshpande kicked. To one side, a wooden cupboard containing piles of tools, hammers, spanners and wrenches and numerous old car repair manuals. Oily cloths and cans of motor oil and white spirit stood next to a battery-charged power drill, with several bits in a plastic holder and a set of screwdrivers in a moulded case. In a drawer under the table were some plastic knives and forks, some unused paper, a pencil, clips, matches, cheap sunglasses and a small key, black rubber bow with its own ring, unlabelled, which Deshpande picked out and held in his palm for the time being. A half-size fridge stood on the floor behind, plugged into a new wall socket, and the light came on when the door was opened, revealing a nearly empty plastic bottle of milk inside, a half-used carton of margarine on a shelf. A dirty oil heater stood next to it, cold to the touch, empty. A plastic wastepaper basket next to the table contained an empty can of lager, crushed, and a scrumpled cellophane sandwich packet, cheese and tomato, Raji Stores Ltd., £2.40, use by Sept. 4, year not revealed. He also noted the folded camp bed against one wall, with a crumpled pillow and some folded blankets perched on it. And on the wall above, a single empty metal coat hanger on a nail.

At the back of the space, in the dark shadowy recesses, Deshpande approached a scaled-down wooden doorway, less than a man's normal height, and which, from the fresh-cut edges at the wood joints and the new-looking pointing in the surrounding brickwork, compared with the aged look of the rest of the walls, appeared to have been fitted recently – which again he noted as an unusual feature, since he had not seen such a door in any of the other units they had examined. Deshpande unbolted it and pulled it forcibly open, to discover beyond it the area of waste ground he had seen earlier from the road, overrun with unpleasant weeds and prickly thistles, enclosed by walls and a fence. There were patches of grass and weed that had been trodden down, by human feet he presumed, and that vaguely led over towards the fencing in a corner, but there seemed nowhere to go, there were no paths out of the area.

Smeared marks in the dust on the concrete floor around the edge of the carpet suggested that it had been moved, tugged over a few feet nearer the doors. On a hunch, Deshpande bent down at one end, folded the edge of the carpet inwards and rolled it, kicking the roll across to expose the floor underneath. Even in the poor lighting, everyone could identify that there was a patch that was slightly darker than the surrounding area, and that appeared to have been wiped with a wet cloth perhaps, leaving dried stains in characteristic sweeping arcs.

Like the elephant in the room that nobody chooses to notice, only one significant item was now left for Deshpande to look at.

Positioned inside the closed slatted garage door, standing alone to one side under a grey plastic cover which Deshpande was carefully removing, was a Vespa scooter. It was a few years old, nine hundred miles on the little white clock on the front console, Deshpande observed, worn tyres and no registration required. In his gloved hand he held up the black rubber key (with Vespa initialled across it) he had found earlier, which perfectly fitted the ignition. The same key unlocked the seat storage box. Inside, a modern rider's helmet, black plastic with darkened visor.

Deshpande spoke with clear enunciation, pointing to various items as he moved around and resumed control. 'This needs to be dusted and taken away, with the plastic sheet,' pointing at the scooter. 'Helmet. Key. Sunglasses. Coat hanger. Power drill, bits. Screwdrivers. Pencil. All bagged, itemised and dusted.' With each item called, a couple of officers produced plastic bags from their pockets, placing and sealing each object inside. 'Telephone – we need to know if there is a storage system, if there are any numbers in it. Folded camp bed. The contents of the fridge and the waste bin, all bagged. The patch on the floor, samples please. That does not leave much else.'

He spun around, flashing his torch high up onto the walls and across the ceiling and around the floor again, and then he stopped in front of Ainsley, who was looking more relieved than anything else, pretty sure that Jarvis had cleverly left nothing incriminating behind.

Deshpande shone the light deliberately into Ainsley's pathetic face and hardly bothered to hide his pleasure. 'I think we have found Collingwood's secret hiding place, don't you?' And with that Deshpande led the way out, feeling more than halfway triumphant.

Back in his mews house, while relaxing over an early supper and coffee, pleased with the day's work and hoping for a quick forensic report so he could instruct Broderick to make a swoop on Collingwood, Leon took a call from Hubert Lansbury, who was sounding somewhat distraught.

'We're out, Leon, it's blown up.' He was almost shouting. 'I was given a choice of redeployment into the British High Commission in Buenos Aires or Burkina Faso. Adrian Manning is taking over at MI5 and all the sub-section chiefs are being moved out or sideways.'

'Hue, I'm sorry to hear this. I think you need to look at other opportunities though. Now is not a time to be trumpeting Britain's reputation around the world. But your experience is priceless, and if you sell yourself to the right people, then a whole host of alternative avenues will open up for you.'

'The investigation,' Hubert continued as if Leon had not said anything, 'remains wholly in the hands of the Metropolitan Police and Max O'Connell. McIntosh is promoted to Commissioner at Scotland Yard; he's been instructed to recruit two or three young guns from outside London ranks to shake up the investigation and get an answer in the next two weeks. Ha! What a nerve! And McIntosh has been the hardest one to deal with, obstructive and barely supportive.'

'So where do you want me to be exactly, Hue?'

'Well, you will continue to pick up your contractual agreement, paid up front. If you have any new stuff or new leads, then McIntosh will want you to share those with him – he may call you over in the next day or so to debrief. But otherwise he is expecting you to disappear as quietly as I will, I should think. Leon, I am sorry it's ending this way. I thought we would get to the bottom of this and at least have had the satisfaction of solving this together and presenting the success to the PM – but it looks now as if that will not be the case.'

Hubert moaned on a bit longer about this and that; he did not mention Roger, though, and Leon was not inclined to raise his name either. Nor did Leon see any point in revealing the discovery of Collingwood's second identity or the presence of a girlfriend, or the fact that they had found his lock-up today, even though he was dying to give Hubert the news of his progress. He did not want Hubert compromising his next moves and felt he needed better evidence to present; it would only take another day. Then it would be in the bag, and he and Hubert could report to the PM themselves. Leon thought low-key was the best policy just now, otherwise Hubert would send in the cavalry as a last act of defiance and frighten Jarvis off, whereas he knew that he needed to catch Jarvis with his guard exposed and then he could lure him, with Naomi's help, into a trap. Anyway, Hubert had a lot on his plate, fighting for his career at this moment. They rang off, with an agreement to meet up later in the week.

Ainsley was under no illusions. The police were close and Jarvis was going to be nailed. Forensics would find something to confirm his presence in number 208 and Ainsley would be implicated. He needed to get rid of Jarvis and soon, before he confessed everything. Anger mounted from deep within when he thought about the failure of the last attempt. No dead Jarvis had been discovered in the interval. No dead Bill had been discovered either, but if Jarvis had won that battle, he would have been ruthless in his efficiency at getting rid of the body. It was not Bill's voice on the mobile message left on his voicemail, he was certain of that.

Ainsley needed a more effective method of disposing of Jarvis. He had obviously cleared out of the lock-up and he could well guess where he was, imagining him in his forest sanctuary, in his element no doubt, stalking the place, living wild, close to Earth and Mother Nature. It would be somewhere near the spot where Ainsley's driver had delivered the initial package to him way back in March, although he was unsure exactly where that was.

Ainsley's computer and mobiles had all been removed, which was an added worry, although he was pretty sure that no Collingwood connection would be discovered there. All their telephone conversations and messaging had been on cheap handsets and multiple throwaway sim cards, disposables that were impossible to trace, which was why Ainsley had insisted on using them.

He rang Dave Bushall, the driver and general dogsbody, requesting that they meet that evening to plan a trip down to Kent. They discussed arms requirements, rounds and other equipment. Ainsley explained that first thing tomorrow they would be going on a hunt.

Epilogue

Jarvis Collingwood was awake and prowling around as the first light of the day filtered through the filthy windows of the caravan and across the compound. The early birds singing made him restless. His nights were frequently disturbed by dreams, but now there was something else challenging his peace of mind.

He had cut himself a sturdy hiking stick with a tapered shaft, hewn from an old sycamore branch, and he had been working on a head carving. With chewing gum and bottled water, he stalked through the undergrowth, in army fatigues and brown Timberlands, taking imaginary potshots at the squirrels and birds. He was measuring distances along pathways, between sections of different wooded areas, calculating walking times between landmarks. With so much rain over recent months the countryside beyond was verdant and lush, hedgerows overgrown, and the undergrowth around the edge of the forest had become thick and impassable in places with wild brambles and blackberries. The faded smell of honeysuckle along some of the south-facing pathways lingered in the still air even this late in the summer. Many of the areas cleared by the gang earlier in the year had sadly become overgrown again with nettles and yellow ragwort, their neglected 'village' area invaded by dandelions and weeds, purple burdock and ugly thistles.

Further into many unexplored areas of the forest, where the mass of thick foliage high above only allowed a weak twinkly light to reach the shadowy dry floor, the smell was more musty and earthy. Jarvis inspected some of the work areas, with hewn trunks waiting for transport down to the store, chopped logs in stacks, piles of sawdust trampled into the surrounding undergrowth, cut ends everywhere, and the new road clearing nearly completed at the north end. The smells of the cut wood and sap were less obvious here, much of it having dried and hardened with time.

Sitting on a cut-down trunk, he took off his stalker hat that made him feel hot. Around his neck hung both his army dog-tags, cheap tin on a cheap metal chain. His beard was re-growing. He drank from a water-bottle, as he recalled his last evening with Naomi. She was such an awkward creature, and ungainly, but he found her attractive, especially since she seemed to have developed a loyalty towards him and listened to him. Not like Pamela. *Oh God, Pam, why didn't you ever listen?* He would phone Naomi later from the pub and work out how she could get away without being seen by any of Deshpande's watchers. He could meet her at Gravesend, pick her up at the station, they could have a couple of days together, making love in the caravan by night, walking the forests by day. But then what? What were his plans after that? He remained in two minds.

Jarvis was sorry he had had to leave the scooter behind when he cleared out of his archway retreat, but he had no choice, he could not have taken it with him. The combination security number there was known only to himself, and no one was aware of his use of the place.

Except Ainsley. He needed to turn the tables on Ainsley and silence him. He was planning another drive back up to London after dark sometime, to Highgate. He had identified the basement door as a possible weakness, but he would have to break the glass. He had visualised the layout and Ainsley's probable room, as long as he was quick in and quick out.

But until he could get Deshpande off his back, he really would not be able to rest properly. Jarvis was frustrated by uncertainty and in need of a woman.

Naomi was awake early. She had not slept well at all. Her neck felt stiff and her back ached. A mixture of ideas and wild thoughts had been spinning around inside her head on and off all night. She wanted to be with Josh (or should she call him Jarvis?), to hear his rumbling voice and touch his soft smile. The excitement of her handsome man appearing unannounced on her doorstep, after so many weeks of not knowing where he was, was buzzing in her mind as she texted Celia the news; her fingers were trembling. At her kitchen table she sat sipping lukewarm tea, hardly able to believe that he had been there at that very spot only last night. Hot from his exercise, his broad shoulders bare with his outer top stripped off, he had downed a full glass of water in one before telling her what was happening. His smell was manly and enticing. She had wiped the damp shiny skin over his thick arms, caressing his tattoos, shrugging and giggling at his every remark. She was stunned that he was actually there in solid person and that Deshpande had thought he was obviously guilty. She had to start calling him Jarvis, although he still insisted that Josh was better. Suddenly everything she wanted to ask him had vanished from her mind. His hair needed her attention and his square-jawed and unshaven face with those cool blue eyes fixed on her, well, they still made her melt inside. She had wanted him to stay and was disappointed that he had not slept with her, unusual for him to have missed such an opportunity; and an internal nagging ache of frustration was left simmering deep within her all through the night.

But he had convinced her of his devotion, and through all his meanderings about being watched and followed and needing to free himself from accusations, there was a theme about their future together, which she warmed to. He wanted to please her. He needed to keep a low profile, what with that persistent dog, Mr Deshpande, crawling around him with the police tagging along behind. And he needed to be off again into the night before more trouble arrived, to be away to his forest hideaway, alone but safe, as no one knew where that was.

Except Naomi. He had shown her his forest lair. She felt certain she would be going down there again sometime.

Almost without knowing, Naomi had come to accept both Josh's involvement and his innocence, or more his justification and there-fore absolution from blame for everything surrounding the tragic events in the stadium. Pamela's death was an unfortunate accident, wasn't it? And his powerful words of persuasion were shaping her thoughts into a more positive frame. As she automatically got ready for work on another overcast morning, she promised herself she would definitely have an early night tonight. On her way out of the flat, in a sloppy black cardigan, tights and shorts, she firmly decided that she wanted Josh, no matter what. She believed in him. She wanted to be with him, even if that meant leaving her present life behind. She was convinced that that was what he wanted too, to be with her, as unlikely as that had seemed just a day ago.

It was seven o'clock in the morning in Switzerland, the air crisp and the sun already dispersing the early dew, clearing the mist away from over the far side of the lake. Ramona could see the grey spire of St Vincent's Church towards the town centre. She felt nearly ready. She had been up twice in the night to pass water and felt the hard head of her baby pressing down on her bladder. Which was slightly uncomfortable. Last night before going to bed she had had a sudden pain in her lower abdomen, sharp twinges that ran though her lower pelvis between her legs and down her back passage, and it made her cry out. She had had to sit down and grip on to the arms of her chair.

It had passed and had not recurred. She had made her face up this morning to look respectable, and would carry on plodding around the villa. She chatted to the children, read aloud to them, held them, and felt so grateful to have Françoise helping her; she would never have been able to handle the two girls on her own as well as deal with this latest addition. Without hurry, Françoise brushed Ramona's thick hair, standing behind her using long, luxuriant sweeps that calmed her with their rhythm and gentleness. The soothing warmth of the sun on her face made her feel sleepy, her heavy eyelids drooping periodically, until a yell from one of the children jerked her awake. She was slumped in the soft chair, her legs apart for comfort, her body bloated, inertia taking over.

Yesterday, she had alerted Madame Letrieve, her midwife, that she had felt a few 'funny' lower abdominal twinges. Later in the evening she had texted Leon, warning him that she did not think she was able to hang on until Friday. She knew he would be frightfully busy, rushing round to get everything done in time, but it seemed only fair to let him know. After all, this was to be his first baby boy.

Leon Deshpande had a headache. It was early and he was not prepared for daylight to upset his muddled head, keeping all the curtains closed. He was drinking black coffee, avoiding a desperately wanted smoke and trying to interpret the recent events in a more positive light in his overactive mind. His watchers had had a disastrous few days, Evelina getting a soaking in the canal and Sheldon losing all visual on his subject, then having nothing to report for thirty-six hours, no sightings at either Jarvis's place or Naomi's. He laughed. What a cock-up. But he was not surprised; Jarvis was good, as Hubert had said at their first meeting, and as he himself had been repeating all along.

Should he get Broderick to put out a police search now for Jarvis Collingwood? He needed to wait for forensics to report from the lock-up; they had promised to work through the night, and Deshpande needed to be patient for their findings. Although anything they came up with would still remain circumstantial; there had been no sign of the firearm or weapons, evidence that might stick. Would Jarvis be ready to confess?

Or should he let the dust settle for a day or two and wait? He had watchers on Ainsley and he was trying to find Jarvis. He might visit Naomi again, find out whether Jarvis had indeed turned up at her flat last night and if so, what went on. Or perhaps she met him somewhere else? Deshpande was sure she would be honest with him and he might advance best by persuading her to work with him, to lure Jarvis out into the open, getting him to cough up the evidence he needed.

But Naomi was a loyal soul. She would only play along with Leon and talk to him if she trusted him and believed that in the end it was in Jarvis's best interests for her to do so – that that was the best way for her and Jarvis to be together again. And at the moment Naomi seemed as likely to side with Jarvis, trying to keep him as protected as she could, revealing to him exactly what Deshpande was up to. Leon knew that somehow he needed to make her feel that she was in a conspiracy with him, Deshpande, for Jarvis's own good.

Jarvis might do harm to Naomi, particularly if he thought that she had let him down, collaborated with the authorities. After all, no one would ever have found out about his second identity if Naomi and her friend had not gone wandering into their local police station. Leon needed to protect her; he needed her to believe that he meant Jarvis no harm, just wanted to get to the truth. Anyway, he reasoned, Jarvis was a project man, his strict routine and discipline owing much to his military training. His had been a once-in-a-lifetime achievement, and he was not going to harm anyone again. There should be no further danger to others.

Or perhaps, Deshpande mused, he could use Ainsley as bait, to lure Jarvis out of hiding: if he got it into his head that Ainsley could shop him, even though that would incriminate himself and the rest of the Chigwells, Jarvis might decide that the risks were best dealt with by putting Ainsley out of his misery once and for all.

Leon was stark naked, about to step into his shower that was now running at the perfect temperature, when his mobile on the bedside table buzzed urgently. On the line was Archie Lee, trusted servant of the agency, someone he had worked with many times over the years. In his oriental accent he purred his account of spotting through his bins a determined-looking Ainsley Chigwell loading the back of his BMW X6 parked in his drive at Claremont Road with equipment, looked like walking boots and a hiker's jacket, big binoculars in a leather case and recognisably two shotguns which he was trying to cover up with a blanket. Followed soon after by the arrival of ex-fighter Dave Bushall, who worked for the Chigwells, a notorious thug and shooter well known to the parish. The two of them had just departed the Highgate property together looking as if they were up to no good, and were at that very moment negotiating the North London congestion, moving in a southerly direction.

'Stay with them and keep me up to date, every five minutes.'

His reverie so suddenly wiped away and his mind sharply focused, he stepped into the deluge for a quick dowsing, where he reviewed the current situation, making a rapid inventory of his immediate tasks: Ramona was heavily pregnant and close to delivery; Hubert Lansbury was in trouble and probably out of the reckoning; he needed Jonathan Collingwood for information; he needed Naomi Lonsdale for leverage; and he needed Broderick for back-up. And he trusted Jarvis would be able to look after himself.

Out of the shower, dried and only half-dressed, he urgently made some calls. 'Jonathan, it's Leon Deshpande here, sorry for the early call. Can you talk to me for a moment? It's important.'

'Yes, okay. I'm just trying to get the children together. Wife's going for a check-up, and . . .' Deshpande imagined the burly tanned Jonathan in shirt sleeves with silver elastic clips crossly trying to get the wandering youngsters dressed while under pressure to be elsewhere.

'Listen, I need your help. You mentioned before that Jarvis was working for you quite often on security jobs and so on. He's disappeared from the scene at the moment and we need to find him. Do you think there are any sites around London where he might be hiding, or taking refuge? Any buildings or places he might have come across in the course of his work . . . disused or unoccupied . . . I don't know . . .' Deshpande trailed off in the hope that Jonathan would quickly get the drift and offer something useful.

'Disappeared?'

'Well, we cannot find him at any known address. He's obviously sleeping somewhere. Perhaps you've seen him recently? Do you know of some friend where he might be staying? His mother's, do you think?'

'I haven't seen him for a week, he said nothing about disappearing. He does work for Danny Darthwaite, his forestry gang, they've been down in Kent somewhere, although I thought it had packed up since the autumn.'

'Forestry work, where's that?' Deshpande was intrigued.

'Beacon Forest it's called, near Gravesend. He has been working there on and off for about a year. I thought you lot would have known about that.'

After getting a few more directions, Deshpande quickly rang off and contacted his team in Broderick's office for some help in finding Beacon Forest, emphasising the need for armed back-up, this message for Broderick himself. Then Archie Lee rang through to confirm that Ainsley's BMW was on course for the City.

Deshpande darted back to the wall safe in the bedroom, from where he retrieved his Browning and a twelve-round magazine.

With it comfortably holstered under his left armpit, he headed out to the Porsche, where he had automatic Bluetooth connection. The engine rumbled and the car clattered over the cobbles as it roared out of the mews, aiming for the Euston Road, disturbing the dozing tabby that jumped off its pillar and slunk out of site.

Just as Naomi was about to close her front door, her mobile chimed. It was Mr Deshpande, sounding excited against a background of traffic noise. He said he had just received a report that two armed men, who had reason to do harm to Jarvis, were setting out from North London, and he was sure they were up to no good. He told her he was desperate to know where Jarvis was. Did she have any idea? And where abouts was this Beacon Forest exactly?

'Mr Deshpande. Oh, dear. Erm,' and she returned inside the doorway, to stand in the dark corridor of her flat. 'It was down the motorway, the A2, and the turning was just before Gravesend – or was it just after? Gosh, I can't describe it properly. It was very twisty. But that is where he is, he told me he was going there for a few days. He has a caravan on site.'

'Naomi, have you been there yourself? Would you be able to find it again if I took you there?'

'Yes, I've been there once – I probably could show you, but I'm expected at work in half an hour.' Naomi was terrified. Should she be involved, or would Jarvis be angry with her?

'Listen, Naomi. This is a matter of life or death. We need to warn Jarvis. Better still, I want to go there, confront these men, and sort this out. Can you show me? If I come round to pick you up in about fifteen minutes, say?' Deshpande was negotiating the tight lanes in the Euston Road underpass, with tall office blocks looming above, intending to whizz past King's Cross station in a few moments and then up Pentonville Road, the Angel, into Upper Street; yes, he could be there in quarter of an hour, if it wasn't for all the bloody traffic.

Naomi was all flustered and worried. She retreated inside her flat and sat on the chair in the hall, feeling faint. 'I could try to phone Jarvis, to warn him, but he doesn't always answer that number. We could go there, it would take ages, a couple of hours, through London traffic, Dartford and so on.'

'Great, Naomi, okay, I'm sure that's the right thing to do – I'll pick you up soon, I'm in the car now. Be looking at some maps in the meantime, can you? See you in fifteen/twenty minutes.'

Before Deshpande arrived, Naomi had changed into loose denim jeans, a pair of boots and a shirt, with a jumper and a fashionable padded black jacket. She dithered over whether she needed a hat. She had texted Jarvis on the familiar number that she had on her phone for him, telling him she was coming down to the forest with Mr Deshpande to help him sort things out; that two other armed men were ahead of them also on their way by car, and they spelt trouble. *Please watch out. Xx.*

A few moments later, sitting expectantly on the hall chair with a worried frown across her face, her glasses perched uncertainly on her long nose, she heard Deshpande arrive outside with engine roaring and a thump of the car door. She was uncertain whether Jarvis would have his old phone with him, whether the phone would be charged, and whether he would read her message in time. And whether he would be able to protect himself. She brought her black hat with her, just in case, she could always leave it in the car.

In the car, after Leon and Naomi had discussed the traffic and the weather, and their route to Kent (using Commercial Road and the A13 through East London, and then the Dartford Crossing, onto the A2 heading east), Naomi wanted to know more about the men who were after Jarvis, and why. Deshpande prevaricated somewhat, while Naomi leafed through a road atlas she found in a pocket of the car, mumbling the names of some of the roads around the village of Longfield, hoping desperately she would remember the route that Jarvis had taken in his Astra with her a couple of weeks before the Games, which seemed such a long time ago now.

Leon found some music on the radio for them to listen to. He noticed that Naomi seemed more confident when she was with him. From what she said, it was clear that she believed in Jarvis and that they were planning to be together when all this kerfuffle, as she called it, was over. Leon tried to imagine all the definite promises Jarvis must have made to her, to sound convincing. When she admitted that Jarvis had been round to her place last night, while he listened intently to what she was saying, he found himself wondering what kind of lovers Jarvis and Naomi made, with the sharp differences in their respective sizes and physiques, their backgrounds and attitudes, all making for an unlikely pairing. He was convinced Jarvis was just using her for cover.

What was Jarvis planning to do?

With a false passport and credit card in the Josh Cooper name, perhaps he was even now preparing to leave the country? Before picking Naomi up, Leon had, from the car, given Fisher a briefing over the phone so that he could alert Broderick, giving him an overview of the situation and informing him of Jarvis's second identity, using the name Josh Cooper. Deshpande realised that Hubert would have been very useful to have had on board right now, if only he had not gone and upset the hierarchy; he could have had alerts put in place at airports and seaports, railway stations and the Channel Tunnel.

Thoughts of his delectable Ramona in her pregnant state brought images of the lake as seen from their upstairs veranda vividly to mind, making Leon even more determined to resolve this investigation. Ramona had texted him near midnight last night to

421

say calmly that she thought she would be starting her labour quite soon and could not wait, but not to worry, Madame Letrieve was on hand. Leon was sure it must be a false alarm – she was too damn early. His next flight out to Switzerland was booked for Friday, so he reassured her lovingly that he was thinking of her every waking minute of his day, and would be seeing her soon. Indeed, he emphasised in the most romantic terms he could muster over the phone that the fact she was about to deliver for him his first baby boy was the very inspiration that drove him ever onwards in his work.

Naomi was trying to hide the distress she felt. She asked whether Josh/Jarvis was in danger. Josh had told her he thought that another security guard called Jones might be responsible for the shootings and he had said that he had some evidence to show Deshpande that would help clear his suspicions about him.

'So why has he not shown me before?' asked Deshpande reasonably.

Naomi shook her head a little. 'Perhaps he has only just got hold of it, I don't know.' She shrugged, with a subdued grunt and a weak grin. She was feeling slightly sick, what with all her worries and the movements of the car, which was warm inside.

'What is his mother like?' Deshpande asked after a little while, as much to have something to talk about as out of any real interest.

'I have never met her – he's hardly spoken of her.'

'What about his older brother – ever met him, Jonathan? Or been to his place?'

'No.'

'You know, if we could just straighten these things out, he could return to a normal life with you.'

'Do you believe that someone else did these things?'

'Naomi, it is possible, but we will need to check out this other man. We have limited evidence, Jarvis knows that. So if he has something that points to someone else, or that shows he was not involved, then he must show it to us; it is in his best interests. You and Jarvis could be together, for always, there's no Pamela now.'

'I don't know. Josh will be furious if I betray him.'

'You are not betraying him, Naomi, you'll be doing what's best for him.'

'You promise?'

'Absolutely.'

On the way to Beacon Forest, and while he was driving excessively fast, Deshpande received two further crucial calls. One was from Archie, who came through sounding furious. He had lost track of the BMW through the City, although he was sure they had crossed the river at Tower Bridge. He had travelled down to the Old Kent Road, but had doubled back without seeing them and was now north of the river, heading east without any luck.

'Not to worry, Archie. You might do better returning to Highgate, in case we miss them and they return there, but I think I know where Ainsley's going. I'll be over the Dartford Bridge soon. Stay in touch.'

As Deshpande was descending the slip road onto the dual carriageway after coming off the bridge, the second call came through, this time from Forensics, Colindale. He listened while the rumbling voice of Professor Spottiswode sounded as loud down the phone as if he was sitting with them in the back seat. 'There was precious little in the lock-up, 208 Witan Street. Everything wiped. Nothing from the floor samples or the bin or fridge contents. But we have a hair and some skin debris from the inside of the biker's helmet. And, surprise, surprise, they both match: Jarvis Collingwood, no doubts.'

The phone was on speaker; on hearing Jarvis's name, Naomi twitched her head towards Deshpande with a look of surprise and enquiry on her face. Deshpande hit the accelerator with renewed vigour on hearing the news and the Porsche surged forward into the sparse traffic. *Yes, yes!* he called in his head.

'Thanks, Professor, very helpful. I'll be in touch later. Goodbye.'

Deshpande hit the touch screen and called Broderick again to tell him the strong suspicions he had about Jarvis Collingwood had been confirmed by the recent forensic result (the first they had managed to achieve so far). He mentioned that two armed men in a Beamer were ahead of them on the road, probably heading for Beacon Forest to surprise Collingwood. Broderick agreed about the need for armed police back-up and confirmed that he had identified the position of Beacon Forest and said that a group of six police officers headed by Commander Stronghead was gathering at Gravesend Police Station and would be moving out in the next few minutes. He was on his way down, too, with some of his own men. 'Good show, Deshpande' he added emphatically. 'Should get this affair sorted one way or the other soon.'

'Good show, indeed,' murmured Deshpande, touching the screen off.

'What is going on, Mr Deshpande?' Naomi sounded hysterical, and Deshpande caught sight of her wringing her hands as she turned towards him, with a quivering lower lip. 'All this talk of armed police, and what was that about Jarvis matching something? I don't like the sound of it at all.'

'We need to get there, Naomi, and I will explain what I think is happening. Right now, I want you to concentrate and study that map and make sure I take all the right turnings. Do you recognise this road?'

'Oh, yes, I think so.' Naomi nodded without much enthusiasm.

Ramona was sitting on the veranda enjoying the sunshine and a cup of tea, when she had the sudden urge to go to the toilet. A gush of wetness soaked through her pants and ran down her bare legs, leaving a spread of water on the wooden slats that dripped through the decking. With some nervous anticipation, she called her midwife with the news of her waters breaking and sat looking over terrace rooftops towards the calming flat waters of the lake, taking deep breaths while waiting for her arrival. She wanted Leon, dreading the growing certainty that he would not be present at this birth, just as he had missed the previous two. The children had been up for a while and were playing with Françoise in the garden with sand and a watering can. Françoise was planning to take them down to the play area on the Rue Albache later, leaving Ramona with some peace and space.

Dave Bushall was driving and just before the humpback railway bridge, he turned off Whitehill Road, which skirted along the northeast borders of the great forest, at the point where a small road sign said 'VISITOR PARKING   PUBLIC FOOTPATH', heading down a narrow side road that lost its tarmac and became more a gravel track with a central grass strip after about a hundred yards. Another hundred yards of bending trackway followed, and it seemed to be headed straight into the depths of the woods, rising and twisting away out of sight. But suddenly the parking area appeared to the left, just as he remembered from before, back in March when he had been instructed to deliver a case, which he knew contained a special sniper's rifle. He had not seen Jarvis Collingwood close up that day – the man had kept himself well hidden while Bushall had dropped the heavy case into the back of his hire car parked nearby, staying put until Bushall had turned his van round and retraced his route out down the narrow track. Then at the road junction, which was on a slight rise, he had used his binoculars to look back at a tall well-built blond figure in a grey hoody ambling down a path beside the trees towards the car park. He felt sure he would recognise the figure and the walk if he saw him again.

Bushall left the BMW in the same spot where he had parked the Transit before, identifying immediately the public footpath that led through the overgrown areas alongside the edge of the forest. There were wooden posts with painted arrow heads on the top pointing the way, and as there seemed no other route out of the area, he advised Ainsley that that would be the way to go. He imagined it would take them up across some of the rough ground they could see rising alongside the forest and then into the woods towards the area where Jarvis must be holed up. Would he still have use of that smart sniper's rifle? That was the crucial question? Surely he would have disposed of it by now. They needed surprise on their side.

Ainsley, whose anger at Jarvis had settled into persistent rumblings under the surface, was nevertheless still determined to catch him unawares. He hopped out of the car, not wholly convinced that they were in the best place, and went round to the back to don his boots and hunting jacket. Then he unzipped the two canvas bags containing the shotguns. He emptied the ammunition on the carpet, loading both his pockets with loose cartridges, and Bushall did the same. With the weapons opened and the barrels hanging over their left arms, like professional hunters out for a day's sport, they locked up and set off on the pathway marked with its little arrows, Bushall in front and Ainsley happy to fall in behind.

Not more than five minutes behind Bushall and Ainsley, Leon, under Naomi's guidance, drove his Porsche up the same narrow track to the car-park area and immediately noted the presence of the all black X6 with a mix of triumph and caution. There was nobody around and the car looked unoccupied as far as he could tell through its deeply tinted glass. He reversed up on the opposite side, his nose pointing back towards the exit, the whole area surrounded by waist-high grasses and brambles.

'Stay here a moment.' Deshpande opened his door as quietly as he could and did not shut it, sliding out and reaching inside his jacket at the same time with his right hand. Gun in hand, he tentatively circled around the ugly black beast and approached it from the far side. He peered inside as he walked all around, feeling the bonnet and the front tyres. Then he darted back to the Porsche, to regain his driver's seat. Naomi had brought some chewing gum with her, and offered Deshpande a piece.

'No thanks, Naomi. Now, look at me.' And Deshpande adopted his most convincing solid and supportive fatherly attitude and voice as he prepared to give himself two minutes maximum to explain the situation to her. 'One of the men in that car hired Jarvis to commit the shootings in the Olympic Stadium, or at least to kill Abu Masoud, who was an Iraqi terrorist who had slaughtered a brother of theirs. They now see Jarvis as a threat to their own freedom – they think he is going to be caught by the police and shop them. So they want to silence him. And they have not been here long – we are only a few minutes behind them.'

Naomi's face had gone white and her eyes had widened in horror. 'And did he kill Pamela as well?'

'We have proof now, DNA proof, that Jarvis was hiding in a lock-up in Bethnal Green that one of those men provided for him, and that he used a motor scooter to get about. It's not much, I know, but it brings us closer to a conclusion – it's not proof that Jarvis was responsible for anything, but we need to find him to interview him and to protect him.'

They sat silently watching through the windscreen as the wind blew the grasses and trees wildly, the clouds flitting frantically across the bright sky. A flock of starlings burst into the sky way up ahead of them, skirting along the edge of the forest and descending over the far valley. Otherwise all seemed calm and quiet. Naomi could not suppress the heavy beating of her heart and a hollow sickness that she felt in the middle of her stomach. A couple of slow tears descended on either cheek, but she wiped them away before Deshpande could spot them dropping into her lap.

Leon felt a burst of excitement, an early sense of triumph that at last he had Jarvis trapped. He just had to deal with Ainsley and his armed mate first, although that might prove a bit tricky. But he was confident – he always got his man in the end. With patience and persistence, superior intelligence and logical thinking, he never gave up. By befriending Naomi and making her believe that this was the best way for Jarvis, Leon had won the upper hand, and he was anticipating Naomi at last – and with a certain sad irony – leading him to Jarvis's lair. A place that Deshpande expected would reveal all of Jarvis's secrets, including evidence directly linking him to the five victims of the Olympic Stadium shootings.

The forest was absolutely quiet, apart from their breathing and scuffling along the stony path. There were no other sounds to disturb the peace that reigned among the massed ranks of ancient trees, monuments to the slow passage of time, protectors of a past age. The public path rose all the way from the parking area in the northern corner up alongside the huge oaks, cedars and plane trees of the forest on their right, with wide open rough terrain undulating away to their left. They rose higher with every step over stone and rocks, wooden planks and muddy patches, until they began to get a view of a village away to the south the other side of a single railway line that ran unobtrusively through the rolling countryside below them. Nothing else was moving, it seemed, at this time, or not that they could observe anyway – no rabbits or squirrels, and even the birds seemed to be resting in the autumnal warmth.

Naomi remembered the route and led the way, having walked this path before with Jarvis. Even though the light was bright and the sun peeked through the low white clouds from time to time, she was pleased she had chosen her black zipped padded jacket as there was initially a chill in the air. Her boots gave her some grip and protection, although they weren't proper walker's boots, as Jarvis would have been quick to point out, meaning she was ill prepared for her hike. She was wondering what they were going to say to each other when they met, now that she appeared to have led Deshpande to his secret hideout, and she was thinking more and more that he was guilty of those horrid shootings and that he had used her for his own desires. Although her exertions naturally warmed her up, her inner fear kept her feeling cold as she became increasingly aware that her initial eagerness to see Josh/Jarvis was waning with every step. And the tiny knot of anxiety about today's meeting that had begun to form while she was in Deshpande's lovely leather-smelling car was now gnawing away with growing intensity at the pit of her stomach.

Leon was wearing khaki trousers and a green flak jacket, and sturdy walking boots that he had retrieved from the boot. He was of the firm belief that Naomi understood that Jarvis was guilty and was a potentially dangerous man who needed help. And that she wanted to find Jarvis's secret hiding place, and to warn Jarvis about the two men who were up ahead. He was unsure how Jarvis would be prepared for his visitors. Deshpande's plan was to warn all the parties that armed police were on their way and that further resistance or running was useless. He had an absolute conviction in his own abilities and would never have entertained the possibility that he might have underestimated the skills of an opponent.

In his camouflage kit with a flat brown beret pulled down over his forehead to eyebrow level, Jarvis had been positioned on his grassy hidden platform since early morning, when he had received Naomi's text, enjoying the total peace and in a state of expectation.

He often came up here, by himself, to survey the countryside, to birdwatch, to feel close to nature. He loved the smell of the earth, the wild thyme and garlic. It made him feel in control. With a thick copse behind him, he lay face down camouflaged among the soft tall grasses, on the raised flat area of earth he had previously found for his shooting practice, well able to watch across the waste ground about a thousand metres away the public footpath that meandered along in front of the edge of the big forest. He was also able to see from his vantage point Whitehill Road running along the valley floor, alongside the railway line and past the junction to the car park in the north corner.

The car park itself was obscured behind woods and the rolling landscape. Naomi had messaged his old mobile to say two men were on their way down to the forest looking for him and they were trouble, and he had a sneaky suspicion as to who they were. And then the fact that Mr Deshpande was bringing Naomi down here as well seemed like a bonus, an opportunity to finally sort everything out once and for all.

If Naomi were here beside him, he would give her some encouragement and tell her to think positive and not to be so nervous. On his stomach, lying absolutely still in line behind Martyn, his long-range sniper's rifle, his head resting easily on the cool stock and chin support, he watched the scene ahead like a hawk, silent and unseen. The sights, with their powerful magnification, gave him a perfect view of the pathway in vivid detail. At around half eleven, a black BMW arrived at the junction and took the siding to the car park, slowly bumping along until it was out of sight. And five minutes later, the red Porsche that he was expecting appeared and turned down the same track as well.

Now all he had to do was wait patiently, something he was extremely good at. It was a fifteen minute walk from the car park, uphill over a few rocks and down some dips. The pathway ran across his line of vision rising slowly from right to left, with occasional fence posts as markers. Sure enough, Jarvis soon picked out two trudging figures carrying shotguns. In the lead was a heavy man who Jarvis thought he recognised as the delivery man in the Ford Transit who had brought the loaded case down to the park last March. Some ten yards behind him was a lighter-weight male figure, with brown hair flowing in the breeze. Every now and again bright sunlight daubed the top of his head and he flicked the hair off his face in an ever-familiar fashion. He stopped as though to get his breath and turned away from the dense forest to take in the open terrain that undulated up and away from him to his left, where sunlight twinkled on a thin line of water cascading into a deeper dyke below.

Experiencing his own sense of elation and anticipation, aware of the thumping of arterial blood through his temples, Jarvis followed the hesitant progress of the two figures as they moved in and out of the sunlight that played across their path. He felt detached from any compassion, just as he had felt four weeks ago on the stadium roof at Stratford, and suddenly all the memories of that dramatic event flooded back as real as ever. A sense of overwhelming power throbbed through his frame; the lives of these people rested solely with him. The right to survival had to be earned, in the dog-eat-dog world of theirs. He focused his right eye through the monocular sights on the trailing figure and found himself staring straight into the face of his one-time associate. *Well, if it isn't my old friend Ainsley, you sly bastard.*

The rifle butt nestled neatly into his right shoulder, his grip solid, the barrel an extension of his own body firm on its bipod. He remained still and perfectly balanced, prone on his elbows, his body tense, legs slightly parted, the toes of his boots solidly dug into the ground. He took a slow extended breath in, watching the commensurate fall of the tip of the long barrel ahead of him, and then he slowly exhaled, the front sight ascending into position as he applied firm even pressure on the trigger with his right forefinger. With an 8.59mm bullet in the chamber, the thousand-metre distance between Jarvis and the two men would be covered in about one second, without wavering, and, with the suppressor attached, without a sound or a flash. And Jarvis would remain unseen.

Ramona lay on her left side, panting violently between contractions, trying to rest but exhausted after two hours of effort. Her right leg, bent up in the air, hung heavily across Madame Letrieve's shoulder, the midwife herself in gown and gloves crouching forward on her knees on the edge of the bed, her face poking between Ramona's legs, staring at the swollen labia she herself had earlier so neatly shaved. The dark wet hair of the baby's head was just visible when she parted the soggy flaps with her fingers, and on the next wave she reckoned Ramona would deliver her baby in time for her to move on to her next charge, on the other side of Blanche, a forty-five-minute drive away. Madame Letrieve expertly swept her fingers around the slimy head, feeling for any umbilical cord that might be wrapped around or caught in the canal, and was satisfied that all was as it should be.

Unsure how far ahead of them the other two men were, Deshpande and Naomi trudged on along the same footpath that rose steadily uphill alongside the great forest, not having had any sight of them. They were stepping over stones and along wooden planks and through muddy patches and making steady progress. They had covered about half a mile, having rounded the eastern flank of the forest and were now continuing along the exposed ridge with open ground curving up and away from them, when Deshpande saw the two men. Not standing across their path waiting for them or walking away from them in the distance as he might have expected.

But lying on the ground, strewn across the damp verge adjacent to the path, wrenched at awkward angles, their heads thrown back. Two discarded shotguns lay close to the bodies.

Deshpande saw them first, even though Naomi was closer.

'Naomi, stop.' She was but ten yards from Ainsley's twisted form thrown onto its back against a collection of rocks beside the path, and she gasped and stood perfectly still when she noticed it. The face looked straight up with open eyes, a neat hole punched in to the side of the temple, while thick liquid dripped onto a dark patch of soaked earth.

'Oh, my God.' Her voice was pitched high.

Instinctively Deshpande stepped aside and within a few firm strides was scrambling up into the shadows of the trees. He screamed at Naomi to step up into the thicker woodland to give herself cover. He felt vulnerable on the open path, exposed across the scrubland, probably being watched at that moment by Collingwood. For a moment Naomi was rigid, staring at the back of Ainsley's dishevelled hair. Then suddenly she broke free, darting away with leaping strides up the earthy embankment into the darker reaches among the trees. She came to rest against a thick sycamore, whimpering, and then moved further away from the daylight, jogging from tree to tree. Deshpande came over to her. They found a leafy dry patch between trees, and crouched in the shadows.

Deshpande had his phone out and was trying to connect through to Broderick's office, but either the network was feeble or nobody was answering. 'They can't be far away, surely.' Deshpande swore desperately under his breath.

'We're not going on?'

'Naomi, that was Collingwood. No one else shoots with such . . . ruthlessness. And we heard nothing. We should wait, we'll be safe here and the police will come and then we can decide where we go.' Deshpande reached for his Browning, which for the first time felt pathetic against the sniper rifle he presumed Collingwood was still using. He decided to risk creeping back to the path to grab one of Ainsley's shotguns. Ammunition would be in their pockets; at least it would give him more firepower. He moved back to the edge of the woods and Naomi watched him, terrified, his dark body silhouetted against the distant bright daylight in the open. He slithered down the bank on his side and she lost sight of him. Moments later his head appeared again and he was scrambling up the soft verge on his hands and knees, running over towards her, panting and laughing a bit.

He had a shotgun with a short barrel in his hands and had stuffed his pockets with ammunition, fat red cartridges with brass-coloured flat ends, which he dropped onto an earthy patch to count. Breaking the barrel, he found it was already loaded with two cartridges.

'Good, this will help.'

'Will it?' asked Naomi sceptically with her eyebrows raised. Deshpande handed her his Browning from its holster – its short-nosed shape would fit easily in her hand – and she took it reluctantly; it was heavier than she expected. He showed her the safety catch to push forward when she wanted to use it. 'You've got six bullets there, accurate at short range, if necessary, okay?'

She stuffed her right hand, holding the gun, into her jacket pocket. 'Jarvis is lethal and he's a bastard, isn't he?'

'Yes, I'm afraid he is.'

Jarvis had not long to wait for his next targets to come into view. Just a few minutes after felling Ainsley and his mate, he spotted the gangly Naomi striding out in front, stocky Deshpande some paces behind. When they stopped near the bodies and then darted into the woods, out of the line of fire, he muttered to himself.

OK, we will play a stalking game.

He retreated cautiously from his raised position, keeping low, and slipped unobtrusively into the dense cooler surroundings of the copse. He headed northwards towards the central ridge of the forest carrying his rifle comfortably at arm's length in an athletic crouch. He was in his element and he knew the terrain well. He would cover the distance through the forest in less than ten minutes at this pace and lie in ambush ahead of Deshpande.

He moved soundlessly with long, loping strides along familiar dry and darkened pathways, keeping low and stopping every fifty yards or so to watch and listen. He had no reason to rethink his task. In fact, everything was going extremely well as far as he was concerned. He came over the ridge, running low along a narrow twisted path covered in thick and soft dusty debris, and was soon descending towards the eastern edge and the public footpath that he had been watching.

He stopped again and listened, crouched behind an old sycamore that was twice his width. Then he moved again stealthily, making sure his footfall was silent. In the still air, he could just make out distant voices coming from further down. He peered out cautiously through more leafy growth. Although in places some sunlight filtered through the upper canopy, it was pretty dark down on the forest floor. He sank down to all fours, slithering from behind one tree to the next. The voices were a little clearer, Naomi's high-pitched trill easily recognisable against the deeper reverberations of Deshpande's baritone. He wriggled forward into a thick leafy patch at the foot of a plane tree to set up position. He could make out the movement of a stocky figure with a shotgun hung limply at his side and holding a mobile phone to his ear; and further away, he spotted Naomi, tall in jeans and black jacket, her hands in the pockets. Both looked anxious but unaware.

As Jarvis focused efficiently on the bulky figure of Leon Deshpande in the distance, in his head his mother's voice delivered cold and clear-sighted logic: together they would find the solution and Jarvis would find his freedom.

Naomi appeared frightened; she kept whining to Mr Deshpande about the surrounding darkness and their being lost with nobody to find them. Deshpande was leaning forward against a tree trunk, looking out from one side, and he reassured her that he would get her out safely. Jarvis fixed him in his sights and was able to look straight into his familiar face.

Only sixty yards separated them. Unseen and unheard, flat on a ridge of earthy loam, Jarvis Collingwood, the professional sniper, the patient hunter, camouflaged and blended with the background, relaxed like a wildcat waiting for its prey. His sights were on Deshpande as he moved through his usual preparation sequence, applying trigger pressure on slow exhalation. The kickback into his right shoulder recalled his old bruise from Stratford. The bullet flew at one thousand metres per second past Deshpande's head, hitting a tree trunk with a thud, wood and bark splitting twenty yards behind him. Although there was no gunshot to hear, the swishing noise made Naomi look up suddenly. Deshpande felt the movement past his ear and ducked dramatically flat into the earth and leaves at the foot of his tree. He indicated with a frantic hand signal for Naomi to do the same, and she tensed and twisted this way and that, panicked and lost her footing, slipping out of sight with an involuntary scream into a deep dip in the terrain, sliding into thick leaves and debris at a level below Deshpande, whom she could no longer see. What was Josh thinking of, she fumed, if it was Josh? Or was there some other weird conflict going on out there?

Deshpande gripped the shotgun in both hands, closing the barrel. He realised how desperate their situation was. Collingwood had the advantage and was not going to let them go. He slid himself awkwardly sideways, trying to get behind some thicker growth at the base of a plane tree so he could peep out. Maybe he could catch

Collingwood with the shotgun if he was on the move, but he could not make out exactly where he was; he must be at least fifty yards away up the slope, higher than they were, and he must have found a line of fire between the trees. He needed to gain the upper hand, move back and away from his present place, and then skirt around deeper through the woods so he could climb safely to a level that allowed him to view Jarvis from the side. He needed to be at close range with his shotgun to be sure. But he was also sure Jarvis would be able to see him.

No one moved. Naomi was hardly breathing, confused, not able to work things out at all. Jarvis waited some more, unmoved, annoyed that he had missed, but with his sights reset for this closer range. He knew precisely where Deshpande was, imagining him lying uncomfortably and aching, longing to stretch his crunched limbs. Naomi had slipped down behind him out of sight.

Five minutes passed without a sound or movement. Naomi was thirsty, trying to create some moisture along her dry lips with her tongue, but there wasn't any. Deshpande was tempted to shout out to Collingwood, to negotiate something of a settlement, tell him the police were on their way, he should give himself up. But that would only reveal the weakness of his own position. His legs were cramped awkwardly under him, the blood not circulating properly, and he wanted to stretch. Naomi was scared and had decided she would not move until the two men had sorted things out. Deshpande was praying for the sound of plodding police feet in the undergrowth and a whistle or at least a distant siren.

When another five minutes passed, still with nothing happening, nobody making a sound, Deshpande impatiently decided to make a move. He found in the undergrowth nearby a thick, short length of broken branch that he gripped in his left hand. Bracing himself against the effort, he hurled it powerfully over his back and upwards, aiming for it to land noisily some way away to Jarvis's right, attracting his attention and gaining Deshpande some distance; meanwhile, he dug the toes of his boots in, trying to find some firm ground, like a sprinter in starting blocks. With the shotgun in his hands, he pushed and rose in a crouch from his flat position behind the broad sycamore and fired off both barrels in succession aimlessly, planning to dash over towards a thick clump of trees some fifteen feet away in the opposite direction, to Jarvis's left. But a foot slipped and slid away from him, and his upper body, unable to move forward, was left horribly exposed above the protective line of ground. With his body not moving forwards, Deshpande's head was half turned towards Jarvis, magnified and clear in his sights, and Jarvis had the shot he had been waiting for.

'Oh, God, here we go. Leon!' Ramona screamed, clasping the plastic face mask delivering gas and air. 'Why are you not here? Damn it. Ah!' And with a Herculean effort, urged along by Madame Letrieve, her delicate hands gripping the outside of her thighs, fingers digging sharply into her own soft flesh, she pulled her chin down towards her knees and pushed down into her bottom with the next rising contraction. The pain was unbelievable; even to an old hand, the shock of it penetrating into her very core with such jagged intensity was indescribable. Ramona sweated, her face damp and dripping, her whole naked body swathed in a wet cover of concentrated pain, searing through her vagina and out into her pelvis. She had once likened the process to passing the biggest turd of her life, and with that crude analogy, and a further scream in homage to the absent Leon, she forced her male foetus into the outside world. It flopped with a gush through the midwife's hands onto the paper spread over the bed. Madame Letrieve gathered up the slimy creature, confirming the presence of its tiny penis. Checking for normality and waiting for the cries of the newborn to begin, she then affectionately laid the warm greasy boy in a towel face down on his mother's bare chest.

Ramona lay on her back exhausted, excited and elated, one arm over her new offspring, and wept. 'Leon, Leon,' in vain she cried.

Responding with perfection to the trigger pressure, the sniper's rifle steady and firm in its owner's professional grip, the bullet flew with deadly accuracy this time. Deshpande's head and body were wrenched dramatically backwards in mid-movement, twisting over a couple of times and slumping in an untidy heap on a bed of leaves on the edge of the dip where Naomi was hiding. She heard the thump as his body hit the ground, saw his dark head flung back at an obtuse angle lolling over the edge just above her, an arm thrown out in despair. Naomi screwed her eyes up, wanting to shut everything out and to scream, but no sound emerged. She tried to sink her body deeper into the leaves and bury her face in the dry dusty debris. She heard a slow drip onto the dry leaves next to her face and for an absurd moment thought it was starting to rain. She was trembling; she wanted to cry, but was too terrified.

Counting the ever-lengthening intervals between each drip, she opened one eye and was startled to see a pool of thick dark red liquid collecting on the fragile brown leaves in front of her, directly under the gaping wound in the back of Deshpande's skull. She jerked her head away, gave a silent giggle and finally looked up when a splash hit her nose, to see the shotgun still suspended in Deshpande's open hand, just out of her reach. She felt the heavy pistol in her own hand and dug her fists further into the thick covering of leaves. She refused to look up at Deshpande's head. 'Oh my good God, I am sorry, Mr Deshpande, this is all my fault.'

Although it actually wasn't.

She was crouching transfixed, and she knew, seeing poor Mr Deshpande lying like that, looking up at the sky with wide-open unblinking eyes and with that unnatural twist of his head, that not only was he dead but that her Josh, her Jarvis, had fired the deadly bullet. In that instant she realised that Jarvis had tricked her, tricked her from the start. In a spasm of hopeless anger, she recognised that he had fooled her, had never fancied her other than as a decoy and protector of his grand plan. And that there was nothing she could do to change that.

Suddenly, directly above her, Jarvis's face appeared looking down at her, still with his beret on. Naomi shrieked, 'Oh, gosh, you scared me, Josh.' He was standing triumphantly over Deshpande's lifeless body, with his rifle held at arm's length, savouring his victory and now contemplating what to do with her.

'What are you doing down there? There's no need to hide. Do you want some help up?' And he knelt down, offering her his strong arm and open hand. Naomi told herself that if she ever got out of this alive, it was the sound of the cracking of Josh's knees when he bent down to reach for her that she would always remember. His left hand loomed over her, in his right hand the ugly rifle, its bipod folded forward. Naomi was snivelling, her eyes filming over, and it was not with joy at being alone with Josh at last, but through fear of what Jarvis might do next. She looked straight into his steel blue eyes and saw a coldness, a disconnection from reality that she had not understood before. He seemed able to kill another with such calmness. There was no sense of remorse in his attitude, his self-satisfied smirk spoke of cold emotionless superiority. He was a dangerous man, she realised. She saw now with clarity his responsibility for the shootings; knew that he had gunned down Pamela. If she, Naomi, was to be his next victim, surely she could do nothing to talk him out of it.

She wanted to plead with him, but her chest was shuddering as she tried to suppress her crying. 'Please, Jarvis, please, I didn't do anything. I won't tell anybody . . . please, I won't hurt you . . .'

'Shh, shh, Naomi; what are you talking about? Come here, grab my hand, come on.' Jarvis was sounding friendly, but Naomi detected deceit in the voice. The disguised wolf in the forest, with such big teeth. She had been used and humiliated, she could not trust him; she did not want to see him any more. His large hand with those strong fingers was hanging just above her head, waiting for her to grab it finally.

Jarvis was pulling her up by her left hand from her leafy hole and she was gripping on the sides with her boots, like a rock climber at the final pull. As though he was trying to sound cheery through her crying and fear, he heaved with an exaggerated gesture, her light body not really testing his strength. 'Heave ho,' he called. And with a final effort she sprang up, the momentum propelling her forwards into his arms. Her right hand emerged free from the leaf pile by her side, shielded from his view. And the cold fingers were gripping the steel butt of Deshpande's pistol, like it was a safe handle to hang on to, her forefinger hooked into the protected guard space. As he caught her round the shoulders, she stubbed the short barrel into his stomach, above his belt, and the gun cocked and fired once. She shut her eyes, she could not bear to look at Josh's face as the ear-splitting crack exploded between them. The rifle clattered to the ground. Overhead a collection of surprised birds took flight, flapping frantically. He tried to grip her round her neck and had a look of complete calm on his unshaven face. Her hand was shaking, her fingers vibrating, the gun feeling so heavy she could hardly hold it up. She grabbed it with both hands and pushed the barrel deeper into his body and the trigger fired again, almost involuntarily, the sound a little more muffled this time. She watched his pale eyelashes blinking, as his nostrils flared. He growled like a bear, gripped her even harder for a second, pulling her down to the ground with him, her legs buckling with his weight. His face suddenly contorted into pain, his eyes screwed up and he spluttered a mouthful of warm blood into the air, into the side of her face. All his tight tension disappeared and, sinking to the ground, he released her. He doubled up onto his side, knees drawn up, both hands holding his abdomen that was gushing forth like a drain overflowing, and his growls became groans, quieter and quieter, until they faded from his reverberating blood-stained lips and there was nothing.

There was no movement, there was no noise, the blood flow ceased. There was no more Jarvis Collingwood.

The forest was echoing with the dying sounds of gunshots. Naomi stepped away, dropped the heavy pistol to the ground, deafened and shocked. She flopped like a rag doll onto her knees. Behind her, the bodies of the two adversaries, incarnate warriors of the modern age, both bloodied and twisted, lay still in the gloom and near silence.

Naomi hung her head in despair and longing.

Naomi, naïve and well-meaning; Naomi, innocent and kindly; Naomi, alone on the quiet forest floor, uncertain and afraid, ears buzzing, shivering from the cold, her frame convulsing with sobs, letting her tears freely wash away the stains and the sadness.